Andrew Lang

Life, Letters, and Diaries of Sir Stafford Northcote, First Earl of Iddesleigh

Vol. II

Andrew Lang

Life, Letters, and Diaries of Sir Stafford Northcote, First Earl of Iddesleigh
Vol. II

ISBN/EAN: 9783337108670

Printed in Europe, USA, Canada, Australia, Japan

Cover: Foto ©Raphael Reischuk / pixelio.de

More available books at **www.hansebooks.com**

LIFE OF THE

EARL OF IDDESLEIGH

LIFE, LETTERS, AND DIARIES

OF

SIR STAFFORD NORTHCOTE
FIRST EARL OF IDDESLEIGH

BY

ANDREW LANG

IN TWO VOLUMES
VOL. II.

WILLIAM BLACKWOOD AND SONS
EDINBURGH AND LONDON
MDCCCXC

CONTENTS OF THE SECOND VOLUME.

CHAPTER XII.

THE ALABAMA CLAIMS AND THE TREATY OF WASHINGTON.

CHAPTER XIII.

CHANCELLOR OF THE EXCHEQUER.

332044

ILLUSTRATIONS IN SECOND VOLUME.

LIFE OF THE EARL OF IDDESLEIGH.

CHAPTER XII.

THE ALABAMA CLAIMS AND THE TREATY OF WASHINGTON.

ASKED TO JOIN THE COMMISSION IN WASHINGTON——PURPOSE OF COMMISSION——AMERICAN POLITICAL MOTIVES CONJECTURED—— SIR STAFFORD TO MR DISRAELI——EARLY MEETINGS OF COM- MISSION — THE INDIRECT CLAIMS — MISUNDERSTANDING—— SPEECH AT EXETER — LETTERS TO LORD DERBY AND MR FISH——DIARY OF THE COMMISSION——INTERFERENCE BY HOME GOVERNMENT——THE TREATY SIGNED——LETTER TO MR DISRAELI ——SOCIAL AMUSEMENTS, AND TRIPS NEAR WASHINGTON—— POEM TO A LADY — RETURN HOME — FRIENDLY SOCIETIES COMMISSION——OBJECTIONS TO THE BILL——APPRECIATION OF IT BY MEMBERS OF SOCIETIES.

ON Monday, 13th February 1871, Lord John Manners met Sir Stafford as he was leaving the House of Commons, and told him that he was being looked for in the lobby by Lord Granville. Sir Stafford went back, and was asked whether he would join the Commission which had already set sail for America to arrange the Treaty of Washington. In five days Sir Stafford, with his sons Henry and John, was on board the Russia—a Cunard steamer. On March 1 they reached New York, and were greeted by the usual imaginative emissary of the 'New York Herald.' They went straight on to Washington, where Sir Stafford joined the other British Commissioners—Lord de Grey, Lord Tenterden, Sir E. Thornton our Ambassador, Mr Montague Bernard of All Souls, and the Canadian Commissioner, Sir John A. Macdonald.

The purpose of the Commission was to settle terms of agreement about the Alabama and similar claims, about the Canadian fisheries, about San Juan, and other matters —terms which might be referred to a court of arbitration. As to the whole subject of arbitration in national disputes, Judge Hoar, one of the American Commissioners, told a story which illustrates the general opinion. "A man came into court and called the judge a d——d fool. The judge threatened to commit him for contempt of court. The man begged to refer the question to the arbitrament of the jury. The judge consented; whereon the jury decided that his referring to them proved he *was* a d——d fool, and gave their award accordingly." The Geneva arbitrators also gave their award accordingly when the time came. This being a foregone conclusion, it may be asked how Englishmen could be induced to sit on such a Commission? The answer is, I fear, that necessity knows no law. England is a country which practically cannot fight on points of honour and delicacy. In regard to America, especially, she would have to fight a most powerful people which is at home, while *she* is at an immense distance from her base. She has to fight with a vast undefended and indefensible flank—the whole frontier of Canada. She has to fight the country by whose corn her own huge and agriculturally unproductive population is nourished. Though she might do the States a good deal of harm, she could not cripple them nor dream of subduing them. " We shall have to give you a beating," said an Englishman once to an American. " What! again ? " said the other. The question was an answer. With starvation and probable rebellion at home, with certain loss abroad, is it likely that England will fight America if she can possibly evade the war ? It is needless to add reflections on the horror of such a strife between peoples of the same language, proud of the same literature, and united by a thousand private ties of friendship and kindliness.

As to there being no alternative at that moment but war on one hand or apology and arbitration on the other, Sir Stafford wrote to Mr Disraeli (January 24, 1873): " Our work has not been made more palatable by persons who have spoken as though the alternative had been war. *There was no such alternative;* and if it had been present to the Government, they ought to have taken a totally different tone, and doubtless would." The real alternative was an eternal hostility of feeling.

Judging by Sir Stafford's letters and diary, the Presidential election was the mainspring of the whole machine of the Commission.   Was General Grant to be re-elected ?   Much appeared to depend on the successful American conduct of the Commission.   I gather (these are private inferences) that the American Government wanted as considerable a triumph as possible, as conspicuous a defeat of England, without the disturbance and discomfort of actual hostilities.   Mr Charles Sumner, who had just been removed from the American Committee of Foreign Relations, was regarded as the great anti-Englishman.   It is only fair to say that, during the sitting of the Commission, his attitude was friendly and genial.   Foibles he had, caused or increased by the long excitement of the war against slavery ; and, it may be, by the cowardly assault on him several years before, by a Southern planter and politician. Despite these foibles, his relations with the Commissioners were distinctly friendly.

Before entering on the social and diplomatic adventures at Washington, it may be well to note what intentions and ideas Sir Stafford, for his part, had in his mind.   He conceived, as he wrote to Lord Beaconsfield, that here was a chance for neutral, maritime, and commercial nations to come to an understanding as to the rights and duties of neutrals.   England and America might give the effect of an international agreement to those parts of their municipal law which were common to both countries.   They might agree on a definition of contraband of war, and

might sketch a tribunal to settle disputed points. Other
Powers might accede to the treaty, and be represented on
the tribunal. A mode of settling the claims and counter-
claims arising out of the late war might be devised " without admitting any inconvenient pretensions."   " These
ideas," he adds, " are rough-hewn."

The Commissioners of either side, at Washington, had
some private intercourse, and euchre, before business regu-
larly began. At this semi-official euchre they seem to
have played " for love." On March 8, Mr Fish, for the
Americans, opened the Alabama claims, proposing that
they should try to agree to certain principles of international law, to be applied by themselves, or by the
arbitrators.   On March 9, the English produced their
counter-proposals; " another long wrangle, and —— ex-
hibits great powers of twaddling." It may be said that
this Commissioner was not of our party. On the former
day (March 8) the Protocol XXXVI. sets forth, in the
words of the American Commissioners, how, owing to
the Alabama and other ships, " extensive *direct* losses had
arisen in the capture and destruction of a large number
of vessels with their cargoes, and in the heavy national
expenditure in pursuit of the cruisers; and *indirect* injury "
(the italics are mine) in a transfer of a large part of the
American commercial marine to the British flag, in the
enhanced payment of insurances, in the prolongation of
the war, and in the addition of a large sum to the cost of
the war, and the suppression of the rebellion. And they

also showed that Great Britain, "by reason of failure in the proper observance of her duties as a neutral, had become justly liable for the acts of these cruisers and of their tenders; that the claims for the loss and destruction of private property which·had thus far been presented amounted to about fourteen millions of dollars, without interest, which amount was liable to be greatly increased by claims which had not been presented; that the cost to which the Government had been put in pursuit of cruisers could be easily ascertained by certificates of Government accounting officers; *that in the hope of an amicable settlement, no estimate was made of the indirect losses, without prejudice, however, to the right to indemnification on their account, in the case of no such settlement being made.*" [1]

All this passage is particularly important to the history of Sir Stafford's own conduct in the mission. Without entering into the long international controversy which followed—a matter for legists—one may say that a person of ordinary wits could understand the text quoted in only one way. In the hope of an amicable settlement, the *indirect* claims were not estimated, nor, of course, presented to the arbitrators, though the right to present them, failing an amicable settlement, was reserved. An "amicable settlement" *was* made, as I understand (compare, however, Sir Stafford's letter to Mr Fish, p. 10), and yet the Americans revived the indirect claims.

---

[1] The italics are mine throughout.

However, it is no part of our duty to discuss the rights or wrongs of all this, nor to revive an ancient dispute. As may be seen, all turned on an " understanding " differently understood, and doubtless blamelessly, by the persons engaged. What we have to note is the conduct of Sir Stafford Northcote in the matter. On May 19, 1872, he delivered a speech at Exeter, in which he touched on the question of the "indirect claims." "Two questions have been raised," he said: "one the personal question as to what was the understanding between the Commissioners at all events, and perhaps between the two Governments, at the time the treaty was concluded; the other, as to the general merits of the question which has been raised with regard to what are called consequential damages, or the indirect claims. *Now, with regard to the personal question I will only say this—that we, the Commissioners, were distinctly responsible for having represented to the Government that we understood a promise to be given that these claims were not to be put forward, and were not to be submitted to arbitration. That being so, we are, of course, brought into painful relations with, and painful questions arise between ourselves and our American colleagues upon that Commission.* It would have been most unjustifiable if, while the matter was under discussion, we had allowed any desire to make out our own case in this matter to interfere with a great international settlement going on. Whether the time will ever come for speaking fully upon the matter I do not know, and I comparatively little care." Though these events are distant, it seems needless to add to Sir Stafford's statement.

In consequence of these remarks, made in a public speech, one of the American Commissioners, Mr Fish, complained that Sir Stafford was "seeking *aliunde* outside of the treaty or of the protocol to establish a meaning, or to explain its terms," and that this had the anticipated effect of raising "a personal question." Mr Fish then denied that "such a promise as Sir Stafford stated that the British Commissioners represented to their Government as having been understood by them to have been made by the American Commissioners was in fact ever made."[1]

Sir Stafford explained himself thus in a letter to Lord Derby :—

"86 HARLEY STREET, W., *June* 5, 1872.

"DEAR LORD DERBY,—I observe that, in your speech in the House of Lords last night, you referred to a recent statement of mine with regard to the negotiations at Washington in a manner which shows me that you, as well as many other persons, have misunderstood my meaning.

"It has been supposed, and you seem to have supposed, that I said that an understanding existed between the British and the American negotiators that the claims for indirect losses should not be brought forward ; and it has

---

[1] 'The American Commissioners,' &c. Washington Government Printing Office. 1872. P. 11.

been inferred from this that we, relying upon that understanding, were less careful in framing the treaty than we
should otherwise have been.

"This is incorrect.   What I said was, that we had
represented to our Government that we understood a
promise to have been given that no claims for indirect
losses should be brought forward. *In so saying, I referred
to the statement voluntarily and formally made by the
American Commissioners at the opening of the conference
of the 8th of March,* which I, for one, understood to amount
to an engagement that the claims in question should not
be put forward in the event of a treaty being agreed on.

"I will not enter into a discussion of the grounds
upon which I came to that conclusion, but *will simply
say that we never for a moment thought of relying upon it,
or upon any other matter outside of the treaty itself.* We
thought, as I still think, that the language of the treaty
was sufficient, according to the ordinary rules of inter-
pretation, to exclude the claims for indirect losses. At
all events, we certainly meant to make it so.—I remain,
yours very faithfully,   STAFFORD H. NORTHCOTE.

"The Earl of Derby.

"Perhaps you will kindly read this in the House of
Lords to-morrow."

The conclusion of the matter then, is, that neither Lord
de Grey nor the other Commissioners had the faintest

intention of using language which admitted the indirect claims.[1] But what Sir Stafford meant, in his Exeter speech, by saying " whether the time will ever come for speaking fully upon the matter, I. do not know," is a question which may still puzzle us.   His letter refers

[1] This letter to Mr Fish explains Sir Stafford's position :—

"MY DEAR MR FISH,—I had hoped that it would be unnecessary for me to refer again to the vexed question of the understanding upon which the Treaty of Washington was negotiated ; but the correspondence on the subject of my 'statement' before the Exeter Chamber of Commerce last May, which has just been published by the United States Government, appears to call for some notice on my part.   I write now, as I spoke then, solely on my own responsibility, and without communication with my Government or my late colleagues on the Commission.

"When I said that we, the British Commissioners, were responsible for having represented to our Government that we understood a promise to have been given that what are called the indirect claims were not to be put forward by the United States, I meant to convey to my audience that I thought that our Government must have inferred from our communications with them that we understood such a promise to have been made by the American Commissioners.   I did not think it right at that time to go further into particulars ; but subsequently, in my letter to Lord Derby of the 5th June, which is included in your correspondence, I explained that the occasion to which I referred, as that on which I supposed the promise to have been made, was the conference of the 8th March 1871.

"You say, and all our American colleagues on the late Commission say with you, that no such promise was made on that occasion.   I of course unhesitatingly accept your assurance that it was not your intention to make one, and that you did not consider that you had made one.   I cannot, however, admit that there was anything unreasonable in the precisely opposite inference which I, at all events, drew from what passed on that day, confirmed as that inference was by our proceedings on several subsequent days.

"You will remember that it had been arranged that on the 8th March the American Commissioners should state their case with respect to the Alabama and the other vessels.   This you did in a written paper, which you read out to us, but which you did not hand in as part of the proceedings.   It was to the effect that, besides the direct losses occasioned by the

to the protocol only — to what did his speech refer? Apparently to some more "personal question," which neither his diary nor his correspondence elucidates. He says in a letter from Washington to Mr Disraeli, "I wish I had some of your power of reading character

cruisers, and the cost incurred in their pursuit and capture, it was believed by the United States Government that they had also a good and equitable claim for indirect or constructive losses. These latter, however, you did not prefer ; and you stated that your not doing so must be regarded as a great concession. You then proceeded, still reading from the paper, to propose that the Commissioners should endeavour to agree upon a gross sum, to be paid by Great Britain in discharge of the claims of the United States ; and you went on to say, still reading from the same paper, that, should the Commissioners be unable to arrive at an understanding for such a payment, the American Commissioners would be willing to refer the liability of Great Britain to some competent tribunal which should be empowered to assess damages. You added, however, that they would at the same time expect that certain principles of international law should be laid down, to be applied to the decision of the claims of the United States, whether those claims were considered by the Commission or by such a tribunal as had been mentioned ; and you propounded four articles containing the principles which you desired us to adopt. Of those four articles you gave us a copy, and we then retired for the purpose of considering your proposal in both its branches.

"Whether I was technically right in speaking of the declaration thus made as 'a promise' is a question which I will not discuss. I can only say that my impression at the time was, that you were proposing to us two alternative methods of settling the direct claims, coupling your proposal with the announcement that if either of the alternatives were adopted, the indirect claims would not be preferred. If this was not the meaning of the statement, I am at a loss to understand why the expression with regard to those claims was used at all. Of one thing I feel perfectly confident, that there was nothing in your proposal which could lead us to suppose that the indirect claims were to be waived in case of the adoption of one of your alternatives, and not in case of the adoption of the other. The proposal was made as a whole, without our interposing a word, and the four rules, which you handed to us, were stated by you to be rules which were to govern the decision equally, whichever mode of settlement just now." Perhaps in this case he read character or circumstances wrongly, though his power of seeing what was passing in people's minds was among his most useful qualities.

In an enterprise like that of the British Commissioners, political and social functions are so blended that it is difficult to keep their descriptions distinct. Dinner-parties, dances, receptions, and a queer kind of fox-hunt, with picnics and expeditions in the beautiful Virginia country, alternated with serious business and grave discussion. The Commissioners of either nation sat on opposite sides of a long table, and had each their private room, where they withdrew, on occasion, to deliberate among themselves. The English were fighting a triangular or even

was adopted. I do not think that it is correct to say that you first made one proposal, and that, when that had been rejected by us, you made another, to which the conditions of the first did not apply. Whether such an inference can be drawn from the terms of the protocol is a question upon which I will not enter; but I am quite sure that it would not be a correct account of what actually took place. Both the alternatives—the one which we rejected and the one which we in substance accepted—were laid before us at one and the same time, in one and the same proposal, originating entirely with the American side of the Commission. It is true that they were not discussed together. After we had taken them into consideration, we declined altogether, under the instructions of our Government, your proposal that a sum should be assessed by the Commissioners, and we urged you to agree to a simple arbitration, unaccompanied by any limitations. It was not till after the discussion had proceeded for a considerable time that the question of your second alternative was taken up and discussed in its turn. But I repeat that this alternative had formed part of the original proposal; and that neither was there anything in the statement you read to us which showed that the declaration with regard to the non-presentation of the indirect claims (whatever it meant) was confined to the case of the acceptance of the first alternative alone, quadrilateral duel.   They had to hold their own not merely with the Americans, but with the Home Government, and the representative of Canada.   Of Lord de Grey Sir Stafford wrote—

> " The U.S. Commissioners give him some trouble ;
>   He don't blame them for *that*—it's their duty, you know ;
>   And his Cabinet colleagues, they give almost double,—
>   *They* do it from love, and he likes it—so, so ! "

The Home Government kept putting in their oar, and once—for which much may by literary persons be forgiven them—they telegraphed that, in the treaty, they would *not* endure adverbs between " to " (the sign of the infinitive) and the verb.   The purity of the English language they nobly and courageously defended.

nor did you, after we had manifested our inclination to accept the second alternative, give us any intimation that the declaration in question did not apply to that case.

"I might go on to show, by reference to several portions of our subsequent conferences, that we acted throughout the negotiation on the assumption that the indirect claims were not to be presented, that we used arguments at certain stages of the discussion which rested entirely on that assumption, and that you never gave us a hint that the assumption was unfounded.   This, and much more, I might say if I were writing for the purpose of justifying the course of our British Commissioners in the negotiation.   But I think it better, now that the matter has been set at rest for practical purposes, to confine myself to the explanation I have given of my words at Exeter ; and I will conclude by expressing my earnest hope that the misunderstandings which have caused such painful controversies as those of this last spring may not be allowed to mar the good feeling which ought to subsist between our two nations, or to make us personally forgetful of the many acts of kindness and courtesy for which we had to be grateful to our American friends, and notably to yourself, during our sojourn at Washington."

"After having with much trouble brought the Americans to agree to some form of words, and sent it home by telegraph, we receive instructions that the Government prefer a different form of words, and have to begin our battle over again, often at a disadvantage. Still the Americans keep their temper very well," Sir Stafford wrote to Mr Disraeli. As to the rules which it was finally determined to concede,—while not admitting that they were part of the law of nations during the war,—he held that they "are substantially the principles embodied in our own Foreign Enlistment Act." As to the whole conclusion, with its King of Sweden, Emperor of Brazil, and all the other parade of arbitration, he says: "The world will probably laugh; but after all it will be a good thing if we can get these troublesome matters out of the way." Troublesome matters can usually be got out of the way, for the moment, by yielding. But is there any nation but England which would yield when arbitration went against her? Practically, arbitration is a farce; and *we* are like the French *bourgeois* in the play, who "always apologised." As to details, there was a week's wrangle over the choice of the word "constructed," or the phrase "specially prepared for war"; "upon which they must have seen that we did not mean to give way. We could not admit that a neutral nation was responsible for the 'construction' of a ship not possessing a distinctly war-like character, which is subsequently used as a ship of war." On the San Juan question, Sir Stafford would have

broken up the Conference.   Perhaps it is better not to
state the circumstances and arguments which led him to
this conclusion: they had less force with Lord de Grey.
As a general rule, however, he writes: "We are on the
best of terms with our colleagues, who are on their mettle,
and evidently anxious to do the work in a gentlemanly
way, and go straight to the point. . . . I see that our
friend the 'Times' is as usual trying to make mischief,
and swaggering in a most unnecessary way." On Good
Friday he was suffering from low spirits and telegrams
from the Home Government: "Our negotiations go on
slowly, and not quite in the line I like. We shall, I
suppose, come to a settlement, but I am not quite at ease
as to its nature; and Bancroft Davis has just been telling
Tenterden, by way of good news, that he thinks we may
get the thing done in six weeks from this time! I had
expected to be on the Atlantic by this time, when I left
England seven weeks ago. And as to having done in
another six (or sixteen) weeks, the only chance of it that
I can see lies in the possibility that the French cable also
may break some fine morning and leave us isolated. If
the other two cables get repaired before we go, Heaven
help us! We shall not be able to respond to the American Commission's question 'How do you do?' without
telegraphing home for instructions, and being informed
that her Majesty's Government prefer our saying 'Pretty
well' to our saying 'Not at all well.'   But, as old Sir
Stafford used to say, 'Don't you say I told you.'"

On the 10th of April the Americans accepted the "expression of regret" for the escape of the Alabama, and the rest of our misdeeds. On April 22, the Canadian Commissioner "seems to think that he has stood out long enough; certainly it has been longer than our idea of long enough." On May 2, we read : "Telegram from Home Government telling us to leave Washington as soon as possible after the treaty was signed. *Quam parvulâ sapientiâ!* And our bill for telegrams alone is £5000. Send strong remonstrance by telegram against insanity of Government. It would simply upset the treaty if we came away before the Senate met."

"*May* 3 (*Wednesday*).—This is a day big with fate. We have this day finally settled the treaty, and have sent it to be engrossed for our signature on Monday next. Our part is now nearly done. Nothing remains but to settle the protocols embodying in a presentable form the history of the negotiation. These will give some trouble, and their wording will be important as a commentary on the treaty itself; but the great work is completed. Is it destined to live ? or will the Senate smother it in its cradle ? Anyhow it is matter for thankfulness that we have brought it so far, and that we shall at least have the satisfaction of thinking that we have won our spurs as negotiators. De Grey deserves even more credit than he is likely to receive. None but those who have worked with him can appreciate his merits."

"*May* 6.—Held our last conference to-day. Confirmed

the protocol, and then made flattering speeches one to another. Read over the treaty, and saw the ribbons put in, ready for sealing on Monday. Five ribbons drawn through each copy (red and blue), so that one English and one American Commissioner may seal upon each ribbon. Something like the mode of assigning partners in the cotillion. We all carried off some of the ribbon as a memorial. Gave Mr Fish a copy of my Ode to the Fourth Article. Signed a number of copies of our photographs, the Americans signing theirs at the same time. A framed copy of each is to be presented to us."

"*May* 8.—A brilliant morning. Breakfasted at nine, and walked up to the State Department at ten. The American Commissioners had arrived, and we spent some time in talk, and in exchanging a prodigious number of autographs, while the seals were being affixed to the two copies of the treaty,—a slow process, as the unfortunate clerk who prepared them was both awkward and nervous, and Tenterden did not help to put him at his ease by dropping quantities of burning sealing-wax on his fingers. The poor man was so much excited that he burst into tears at the conclusion of the affair. Howard, who did the gratuity business for us, gave him forty dollars to buy a *souvenir* for his wife, which he accepted with some reluctance. The signing seemed to create great interest in the department, and all, or most, of the employees were present. A great quantity of flowers had been sent up by different ladies, and we were abundantly supplied with strawberries and iced cream, with which we relieved our feelings after shaking hands all round. And now the breaking-up begins."

May 21 saw "our last day at Washington, and quite a melancholy one. . . . It is curious to have made one's self so much at home there, and to have picked up so much interest in the small daily life of the place." They departed under a final sneer from the Russian Minister, "Blessed are the peacemakers." Query—"Blessed are the humbugs!" The settlement he considered, as he wrote to Mr Disraeli, "a fair and just one, giving no triumph to either party, containing nothing dishonourable to either, and having the merit of laying down principles which may be useful in the future. . . . But I am not a fair judge."

The rest of this letter (May 9) may be quoted as showing, if that were necessary, what in his opinion the treaty meant as to the "Indirect Claims":—

"I suppose the points which will be particularly criticised are, the insertion in the treaty of the expression of regret, the retrospective effect given to the three rules, and the Canadian arrangements. As regards the first point, I suppose we shall be told that such an expression in such an instrument is unprecedented. I believe it is, and I do not think the Government originally intended us to insert the words in the treaty itself. But we thought ourselves that it was well to do handsomely what was to be done at all; and we felt, too, that the insertion of the words in the place where they stand gave us a means of keeping out

Washington
May 8. 1871

My own C,

The first and only
use I make of this pen
after signing the Treaty
with it is to send you
a notification of the
fact.

Your devoted
Stafford H. Northcote

other words which the Americans were anxious to bring
in with a view to establish what they call their national
case.   You will doubtless observe that there is significance
in every line of the preamble to the first article.   'Incedit
per ignes,' &c.   The object is to remove and adjust 'all
complaints' as well as 'claims.'   The 'complaints' intended are those which bear on the 'animus' of Great
Britain, as evinced not only by her alleged negligence in
the matter of the vessels, but also by her alleged premature recognition of the belligerency of the South; and the
word covers all the allegations as to our having been
responsible for the prolongation of the war, &c.   The
same ideas are connected with the word 'differences' in
the first line.   You will remember that after the Claren-
don-Johnson Treaty was concluded, Mr Johnson told his
Government that the effect of the 'general terms' which
had been used would be to allow the question of premature recognition to be raised before the arbitrator.   On the
other hand, the Senate rejected that treaty, partly, at least,
on the ground that it took cognisance only of private
claims, and not of those put forward on the part of the
Government of the United States.   Our object was to let
in the claims of the Government without letting in all
those wild demands.   While therefore we refer to the
differences and complaints in general language, we submit
to arbitration only the claims 'growing out of the acts
committed' by certain vessels.   This limitation was not
obtained without much difficulty, and could not have

been obtained at all if we had not inserted the expression
of regret in its present place, and then pointed out to the
Americans that that expression in fact balanced, and
ought to be accepted as balancing, the complaints which
they had made on the score of national wrong, and that
they ought to be content with a provision which would
entitle them to bring forward claims founded on direct
losses (such as the sinking of the Hatteras) without
going further.　Of course it is possible that they may put
forward claims of greater extent, as, for instance, claims on
account of the cost of pursuing and capturing the vessels ;
but there is nothing in the article to give direct colour to
such claims, and our counsel will of course be instructed
to argue that they are inadmissible if they should be presented.

"As regards the three rules, and the retrospective character which has been given to them, one can only say
that it is of the essence of the arrangement.　The rules go
very little if at all beyond what we practically admitted
to be our duty by our Foreign Enlistment Act as it stood
in 1861-65, and what it may be said that foreign nations
cognisant of our municipal law had reasonable ground to
expect of us.　I think it can hardly be doubted that it is
for our interest to have these rules embodied in international law, while on the other hand it was not to be expected that the Americans should consent to be bound by
them for the future, if they were to derive no benefit from
them as regards the past.　I do not altogether like the

shape the arrangement has taken.   Personally I should have preferred to come frankly forward, and while denying any liability or conscious neglect of duty on the part of Great Britain, to tender a sum in order to enable the Government of the United States to make compensation for the losses sustained by American citizens, by the acts of vessels escaping from British ports, and then to have proceeded to argue upon rules for the future.   But no doubt there would have been difficulty in so wording an arrangement of this kind as to make it acceptable; and I am not on the whole dissatisfied with the treaty as it stands, though it exposes us to the risk of having it declared by the arbitrators that we had failed in our duty.

"As regards the Canadian arrangements, there is likely to be a complaint on the part of the fishermen, which may perhaps be taken up by some of the politicians; and we shall be told that we are sacrificing colonial to imperial interests.   The complaint is, I think, wholly unfounded. I doubt whether even individual fishermen will not gain more by the right of sending their fish into the American markets duty-free than they will lose by the competition of Americans in their waters.   I think that the general effect of Acts xviii. to xxxiii. is decidedly favourable to Canada, and that the only thing she loses (and that for a short term of years) is a whip which she liked to crack for the purpose of driving Americans into bargains, but which she would have been very foolish if she had attempted to use,—I mean the power of excluding American vessels from her canals. But beyond this, I am convinced that if it could truly be said that any local interests had been sacrificed for the sake of a general settlement of imperial questions, it could not be said that the interests sacrificed were those of Canada, and that the party for whose benefit the sacrifice was made was England; for I believe that no part of the empire has so direct and immediate an interest in the maintenance of friendly relations between us and the Americans as Canada herself. We remain here another ten days, principally because the American Government wish us to pay the Senate the compliment of awaiting their discussion of the treaty, and also because they think we may be able to influence particular senators, such as the Democrats and (still more) Sumner, over whom they have no party control. I had a long talk with Sumner yesterday, and De Grey is to see him to-day. He is very cautious, but I do not think him unfriendly. He is very anxious to stand well with England; but, on the other hand, he would dearly like to have a slap at Grant. We have paid him a great deal of attention since he has been deposed, and I think he is much pleased at being still recognised as a power. He certainly is one, for, though I think the Government could beat him in the Senate, he could stir up a great deal of bad feeling in the country, if he were so minded; while, on the other hand, if he declares himself satisfied, I believe every one but the Fenians and Catacazy (the Russian Minister) will be very much pleased with the settlement. Catacazy tries to make mischief, but I don't think his influence is very great now. De Grey has done his work extremely well, and has shown an amount of shrewdness, tact, and judgment, for which I was not prepared. The Cabinet have been terribly vexatious. We hope to sail on the 24th, and be in England by the 4th June."

Socially speaking, many members of the British mission "had a lovely time." "The goose hung high," as the young lady from Ohio is reported to have said. "Her language," like that of the Chicken when reproved by Mr Toots, "was coarse," but her meaning was not obscure. The Commissioners and their young men must have felt like the children in Grimm's fairy tale. If their hosts meant to end by devouring them, at least they fattened them first. It was proposed by a member of the Commission that they should take three blue pills proper by way of scutcheon. "I think I stand the feeding as well as any one," Sir Stafford wrote; but it is plain he began by having to eat more dinners than he quite cared for. Singular to say, he sent home no recipes for Transatlantic delicacies. He throws no light on the mysteries of Gumbo, nor terrapin-soup. A delicacy named "soft sawder" is alluded to Perhaps nobody pleased Sir Stafford more than General Sherman. This distinguished officer spoke in the most friendly manner about the success of the Abyssinian expedition, which he attributed in great part to the management of the Secretary for India. He thus found himself a prophet in the States, if not in his own country. The President, General Grant, seemed to him somewhat unfortunately shy in manner. The famous fox-hunt he describes thus in a letter to Lady Northcote :—

"WASHINGTON, *Ap.* 3, 1871.

"The enclosed extracts will amuse you, I hope. The reality would have amused you still more. I never suffered so much from suppressed laughter as on Saturday. The day began most gloomily with pouring rain, which, the experts told us, would last till evening. It lightened a little while we were at our early breakfast, and at about ten o'clock the carriage party started. We started well waterproofed, and got to Suitland about twelve, where we received the applause of the company for our spirit. We had to come in, dirty as we were, and were received by our host, his wife, and her father; Justice Miller and his wife; our colleague Williams and Mrs Williams; Judge Hoar, and a certain number of Marylanders and Virginians whom we did not know. A cold luncheon was set out, with lots of champagne, and two newspaper reporters had already succumbed to its influence before we arrived. There was a band and music, and some of the party began to play euchre. Presently the horses were brought round; we started for a wood about a quarter of a mile off—the ladies ascending to the observatory, or standing at the front of the house. The hounds were thrown in, and soon gave tongue.

I was in a horrid fright at finding myself galloping through a 'clearing' with a lot of burnt stumps everywhere; but our host presently called us out to the road, and we went back past the house, watching the 'dogs' running in full view about two fields off. I luckily judged their line better than most of the party, and found myself and Sir E. Thornton just crossing them. His horse ran away with him, but I pulled up to let them pass, and, as I did so, up came Mr ——. We rode after them together, when suddenly we found them quietly mouthing the fox. I jumped off and secured the brush, by which time others came up; and we returned in triumph to the house, where the band and the ladies received us, and I presented the brush to Mrs Williams. The odd thing is, that nobody ever saw the fox alive. After this grand triumph we set forth again, and made for some large woods three or four miles off, where we rode about for several hours looking vainly for sport, and going through some queer places, in one of which my horse came down with me, but without damage to either of us. Harry rode capitally, and elicited Mr ——'s approval by sticking to him to the last."

As to the injurious suggestion about the fox not being viewed in life, Sir Stafford confesses that "one ought not to suspect such gallant sportsmen of such practices." A practice much more fair and agreeable was that which permits young ladies to see their friends *en tête-à-tête*. They are said to have been "very nice young ladies," and were addressed in immortal verse by Sir Stafford. One Commissioner only was accompanied by his wife; "and having seen how married High Commissioners behave, she never means to let him go on a mission without herself." As an example of married "behaviour," perhaps a poem to a fair young lady of Washington may be quoted.

ADDRESSED TO MISS LORING ON BEING ASKED TO WRITE HER A POEM PERSONAL TO HERSELF.

I had not thought that you could ask,
    And I be guilty of denying;
I dreamed not you should set a task,
    And I should fail for want of trying.

Tell me to leap the hornèd moon,
    Or Andes from his base to sever;
I'd spoil a horn, or make a spoon,
    Succeed, or perish in th' endeavour.

But ah! that was a cruel jest,
    To bid me dub myself a poet;
What demon put it in your breast?
    How could you find the heart to do it?

Nor did you name a common theme,
    Such as might suit a dullard's rattle;—
A shepherd by a purling stream,
    A soldier's or a lady's battle.

I might have sung some maiden's wrongs,
    Some hopeless swain his fair adoring;
I cannot sing the song of songs—
    I cannot sing of Mary Loring.

> Yet how the tribute to refuse
>   To one so bright, so full of kindness?
> Between two sins I have to choose—
>   Ingratitude or stupid blindness.
>
> Divine despair my courage nerves,—
>   I'll quote yourself, fair dame, and brave it:
> The best of poems she deserves;
>   Deserves—and therefore cannot have it.

Washington was thought to possess the pearls of American girlhood. " They say that at Boston people ask about a young lady, *What does she know?* at New York, *What has she got?* at Philadelphia, *Who is she?* and at Washington, *Is she agreeable?*" A few extracts from diaries, containing descriptions of interesting American places and institutions, are added here:—

March 28.—Started about nine for the expedition to Mount Vernon. Reached Navy Yard and got on board the Tallapoosa about ten. Large party got up by Mr Robeson (Secretary of the Navy), including most of the Ministers, General Schenck and two of his daughters, the Chandlers, Edmunds, Williamses, Bancroft Davises, &c., &c. There must have been about fifty of us. The Admiral (Goldsborough), a very nice cheery old fellow, took charge of us. The Tallapoosa is a Government vessel, chiefly used for taking inspecting officers to visit the dockyards, run up the rivers, &c., &c.,—a sort of Admiralty yacht. We enjoyed our sail down the Potomac, though —— bored

me by making me come and play euchre in the cabin with
a filthy old pack of cards instead of looking at the view.
Reached Mount Vernon about twelve, and went on shore,
—Mrs —— being the lady assigned to me. The position is very pretty, and if the leaves had been out, the
view up and down the Potomac, which makes a bend at
this spot, would have been charming. We first reached
the mausoleum where Washington is buried, and looked
through the gratings at his coffin; then going further up
the hill reached the house. The place was bought some
years ago by a committee of ladies, who collect funds to
keep it in order. One of the regents, Mrs Emory or
Amory, was of our party, and did the honours. The
rooms have been recently painted and repapered, but in
almost every other respect the house is just what it was
in Washington's time, and many articles of old furniture
are preserved there. It is a quaint old place, with a com-
fortable home-like look. A great piazza in front of the
house, and the remarkable smallness of the windows,
make it dark. There is a fair entrance-hall, in one corner
of which photographs, &c., are sold; in another is a book
for autographs of visitors; the key of the Bastille (presented
to Washington by Lafayette) hangs near one of the doors.
There are several rooms on the ground-floor, in one of
which is a glass press in which some of the great man's
clothes are displayed,—not in the most elegant way. We
went over the bedrooms, and up to the lantern on top of
the house, then out at the back past the offices, negro
cabins, pigeon-house, &c., to the garden, where were some

fine old box hedges and the most glorious *Pyrus japonica* I ever saw. Bought a hickory-stick, and a pod from the coffee plant which Washington was planting (or sitting under?) when he caught the cold that caused his death. Returned to Tallapoosa, lunched on board, and reached Washington about five. Dined with the Catacazys.

March 29.—De Grey, Bernard, Tenterden, Howard, Cremer, and I, drove to the "Great Falls" of the Potomac, which it took us about three hours to reach. Some of the country was very pretty, and would have been more so had the leaves been out. The bursting maples, and a few Judas-trees which were just beginning to show colour, mixed well with the great masses of pine-wood. These pine-woods appear to be of natural growth, springing up on the old racked-out tobacco and corn lands, which have long since been abandoned as unprofitable. We stopped to bait at "Captain John's bridge," a great viaduct with an arch of enormous dimensions, carrying not only the road, but the aqueduct which supplies Washington with water, and on the top of which the road is made. The Great Falls are not falls at all, but very fine rapids rushing through the rocks. We spent an hour or two in scrambling about the rocks and looking at different points of view, and returned in time to dress for our dinner with Mr Cresswell, the Postmaster-General, where we had a large party, and varieties of ice in the shape of lions, unicorns, fish, flowers, &c., which reminded one of the stories of the fancy pastry in Queen Elizabeth's time. They were quite uneatable. Sat between Mrs Fish and Mrs B. Davis, both very agreeable, and had a good deal of talk with General Porter after dinner.

April 4.—No meeting to-day. Wrote letters to England. Went to Congress with Bernard, Tenterden, Goderich, and Cremer, to hear General Butler speak on the Ku-Klux bill. Our position in the diplomatic gallery being behind Butler, and his voice being by no means clear, it was difficult to hear him; but we had the advantage of seeing his speech, which had been printed in slips and lay on his desk. He seemed to skip portions of it as he read it, and at the close he delivered a few sentences without book, though apparently from memory. The speech, or address, was not a bad one, and was given with a good deal of energy. It occupied nearly the whole of the hour allotted to a speaker, and this without any interruptions. The way in which one member interrupts another, and the first yields to the second if he pleases, is very curious but not edifying to a Britisher. The total absence of applause or disapprobation is very striking. Went afterwards into the Senate, where a desultory discussion was going on between Senators Anthony, Morton, Casserly, and others, as to the time of closing their own Ku-Klux discussion, which they ultimately agreed to do at three o'clock to-morrow. Senator West from Louisiana then began to deliver a long harangue, to which nobody listened. Mr Sumner came and talked to us, commenting sarcastically on this practice of reading printed speeches for the sake of distributing them to constituents. The franking privilege enables a man, after having had his speech printed at the public expense, to have it sent free all over the country. We were much edified at his tirade, and took care not to ask him for a copy of his own San Domingo speech. One of the curious customs here is, that members of either branch of Congress have a right to go into the other, and sometimes seat themselves in a member's chair if it happens to be vacant. The other day —— came into the Senate while —— was speaking, took Senator ——'s chair and stared —— hard in the face when he spoke up for the South. —— asked him how he dared try to browbeat him, and a regular altercation ensued, in which —— twice called him a d——d scoundrel. Some senators interfered to prevent a fight, for which ——, however, would probably have had no stomach.

April 20.—Day of election of members for the territory. A territorial constitution has recently been granted to this (formerly) district, and this was the day for electing a representative to Congress and a body of delegates. General Chipman was the Republican, and Mr Merrick the Democratic, candidate for the representation. The voting took place for the representative and delegates simultaneously in each of the districts. The Republican ticket had the names of Chipman, and of A, B, or C, the candidate for the delegacy of that district; the Democratic ticket had the names of Merrick, and of X, Y, or Z. The Democratic ticket was white; the Republican striped. Agents of either party stood at the windows of the polling-offices and tendered their respective tickets to the voters as they came up. As many of the voters (especially the coloured men) could not read, they took the ticket of their party colour without examination. The agents therefore had tickets of their opponent's colour with their own men's names printed on them, and tried to pass these off, but apparently without much success, as the opposite agent was always alive to the trick. There was no attempt at secrecy, and the state of the poll was pretty well known all through the day. Chipman was elected by more than 4000 majority, and Republican delegates were returned in fifteen out of the twenty-two districts. The election was carried entirely by the coloured voters, of whom there were about 10,000, as against 17,000 whites. The blacks voted for Chipman almost to a man. The election was quite orderly; but from what we heard of other elections, it seems this is not always the case, especially in New York. Intimidation is said to be practised sometimes, and cases were mentioned of masters giving their workmen tickets with peculiar marks, and then attending the opening of the ballot to see whether they were all properly given in. Walked with De Grey, Bernard, and Cremer to the observatory. Dined at home.

April 30 (*Sunday*).—Went to early church, and after breakfast drove with Mr and Mrs Riggs, and Howard, to Greenhill, their country place about seven miles northeast of Washington. It was a lovely day, and the woods were in beauty with their various shades of green, and the masses of white dog-wood, azaleas, lupins, eyebright, wild heart's-ease (called " Johnny jump-up-and-kiss-me "), violets, May-apple (*Podophyllum*), Virginian thorn, peri-winkles, and a flower they called calceolaria, which seems more properly to be called Cypripedium or Venus's slipper. We saw also some magnolias, and a sweet-scented shrub—calacanthus. The banks were covered with dewberries and strawberries in flower. The Spiræa was in great masses in some of the gardens by the roadside, as were also the lilacs. In Mr Riggs's garden there was a beautiful tree called a fringe-tree; and a splendidly flowering crab-apple. I was much struck by the number of varieties of oaks. There were also plenty of maples, sycamores, tulip-trees, hickory, locust, red cedars, &c., and large masses of the common pitch-pine, which comes up of itself, and is good for nothing. The whole drive was a lovely one; but indeed one can hardly go wrong in the neighbourhood. Mr Riggs farms a good deal, and had some nice Alderney calves. I did not see the cows, as they were in a different direction from that of our walk, which was up a hill called Rowe's Hill. He showed me how the corn (maize) was planted. The field is cross-ploughed, and at each of the intersections (or "hills" as they are called) the sower drops in five grains,—

> "One for the cut-worm, one for the crow,
> One for the hill, and two to grow."

The "hills" are about three feet apart, and when the corn is about six inches high it is weeded, so as to leave but one stem on each hill. The success of the crop depends on constant cultivation, and it is regarded as the cleaning crop. It is sown in spring, and harvested in September or October, the heads being carefully garnered in houses with thorough ventilation. Corn is followed by wheat, and that by oats and clover. Turnips are little grown. The negro labourers are paid about $12 a-month, besides being housed and fed. They looked slovenly, even though it was Sunday. Mr. Riggs believes they do not lay by much money, but waste it in buying trash, particularly sweets. They take very little care of their children, and not nearly so many are raised as under slavery. This corresponds with what Census Kennedy tells us. Infanticide is now beginning. There is not much family affection among the negroes; but they have a strong attachment to places. Education may do something for them by - and - by; meantime they are generally well off, and now that they have the mastery in the Southern States, owing to the exclusion of most of the white owners of property from the right of voting (by the "iron-clad oath") they make the most of the opportunity, and lay on heavy taxes, which do not fall on themselves, but in the spending of which they have an interest. Mr Fish admitted to me the other day that the expenditure in the Southern States was enormously increased, and in great part for jobbing purposes, though he said part was for purposes of utility. Mr Thurman speaks very strongly on this point, and looks on the carpet-baggers as a regular set of swindlers. Mr Riggs said he thought the Southern States would pull through financially, though he was gloomy as to their political future. Cotton will best be cultivated by small holders, white or coloured, aided by Northern capital, advanced on condition of so many bales of cotton being delivered to the capitalist. He is working an estate in one of the Southern States on this principle. Drove back through Mr Corcoran's park, where no house has yet been built. Glad to hear that there is a possibility of his recovery. Saw at Greenhill an ingenious little machine for keeping off flies, wound up by clock-work. Walsingham dined with us. In the evening we went as usual to the Lorings—Mr and Miss Brooks, Miss Susie Lee, Miss Greenhow, John Davis, &c.

May 1.—A regular good May-day. A picnic to the Great Falls, under the auspices of Mrs Sprague, but really promoted (I believe) by Miss Mary Lee. The main body of the party started at 6.30 by the track-boat. They consisted of seven gentlemen and eight ladies,—Count Corti, Señor Valles, Goderich, Cremer, Harry, Pakenham, and Captain Ward; Mrs Sprague, Lady Macdonald, Misses Loring, Miss Greenhow, Miss Nellie Motley, Miss Portalis, and Miss M. Lee. De Grey, Bernard, and I drove over, starting about ten o'clock to meet them, and found they had been there some time when we arrived. We plunged into the woods and got to the rocks over the Great Falls, scattering a little. Masses of wild azaleas, lupins, pansies, and a variety of unknown flowers were gathered, and a grand crown woven for Mrs Sprague, which was passed on in succession to De Grey, Goderich, myself, and finally (so far as I know) Miss Loring. We had a splendid luncheon, and a good time by the lock-side afterwards, until it was time for us to drive home, as we had to dine with Governor Cooke. We brought away Lady Macdonald, who also was engaged to the Governor, leaving the rest of the party to return by moonlight if they liked. Dinner at Governor Cooke's; large party.

May 17.—Started at 6.30 with Bernard and Pattison for Richmond (Va.) By steamboat down the Potomac to Acquia Creek; thence by train through Fredericksburg to Richmond, which we reached at 2.30, or soon after. Dined at the *table d'hôte* (Exchange and Ballard's Hotel); took a carriage and drove round good part of the town, and to Hollywood Cemetery,—a beautiful piece of ground, and on this day crowded with people, as it was the day for decorating the graves—especially the graves of the Confederate soldiers. Nothing can be more striking than the difference in the tone of Richmond and of Washington. The memories of the war are fresh in both places; but while in Washington (whatever may be the undercurrent of private feeling, and it is strong) every public manifestation is of strictly Northern character, precisely the reverse is the case at Richmond. At Arlington the word "Rebel" is conspicuously carved upon the tombstone of every Confederate soldier, and the friends are forbidden to decorate any rebel's grave. At Hollywood, not only was every grave decorated, but a large cairn has been erected in the most conspicuous position, inscribed with "To the Confederate Dead," &c. Moreover, to-day a fine bust of Lee was displayed, wrapped in the Confederate colours, and profusely decorated with flowers. On it were suspended some spirited and outspoken verses to the Confederate dead. Two young ladies sat by it as guardians. The private graves in the other parts of the cemetery were also decorated, but to me the great interest was in the Confederate quarter. Perhaps as significant as anything was a little paragraph which caught my eye in a *Republican* paper, approving of the decoration of the Confederate graves, but timidly putting in a plea for a few flowers to two or three graves of Federals also. The whole town is still "Secesh" to the heart's core. Jeff. Davis was staying in the hotel where we dined and drank tea, and was at a table near us. The waiter said he was sure he would be glad to be introduced to us, but we thought it imprudent in our position to accept the offer. The town is very beautifully situated, and the view from the Capitol Hill is fine. The falls or rapids of the James river, though not equal to the Chaudiere at Ottawa, or even to the Great Falls of the Potomac, give great life to the scenery. The town, however, presents a painful spectacle,—so many large buildings, destroyed by the great fire at the time of its capture, still remain in ruins, and there is a melancholy air of sadness and poverty in the streets. Virginia is, however, better off in one main respect than such States as South Carolina. Though the ex-Confederates are excluded from taking part in Federal elections by the "iron-clad oath," they are not excluded from the State elections, and consequently the men of property keep their hold on the State Legislature, and

keep down the negroes and the carpet-baggers. In South
Carolina and some other States the ex-Confederates are
excluded from even the State Legislature, and the power
of taxation is consequently thrown into the hands of men
who have nothing themselves, and who can indulge themselves with a liberal public expenditure at the cost of their
richer neighbours. A gentleman whom we met in the
train gave us some not very agreeable accounts of negro
character, illustrated by some of their proceedings in the
time of the war, and some of their larcenies nowadays.
He was clearly of opinion that free labour was more
profitable than slave labour, and took us through an
elaborate calculation which we could not exactly follow,
but which went to show that, reckoning on one side the
interest on the value of a gang of slaves, and the cost of
keeping, raising, or replacing them, doctoring, clothing,
&c.—all which expenses had to be borne in respect of the
useless as well as the useful—and on the other side the
cost of wages and rations and lodging to the actual working men, leaving them to provide for their own families,
and to clothe themselves, the expenses of the slave system
were as $250, and those of the free-labour system, with
wages at $10 a-month, were as $120. Our friend was
certainly no nigger-worshipper; but he had an object in
making out the present system to be profitable, for he
wanted to induce English capitalists to come and buy his
land, of which he seemed to have a large amount, but to
be without the capital to farm it with. He told us white
labour was worth double the coloured labour, and that

they were gradually getting rid of the coloured men in
Virginia—the best going North for domestic service, and
the worst to the cotton States and rice-fields, where white
men cannot work.   Virginia should grow corn and fruit.
The country looked very desolate; a great deal of un-
cleared land all along the line, and what was farmed
seemed to be poorly managed.   Returned to Washington
by next boat.

At the close of all these sights and junketings they
"felt rather flat," now that it was "high time to come
home."   So the trip ended; the juleps were drunk, the
strawberries eaten.   Calypso consoled herself, or *ne pouvait
se consoler*, and Ulysses came home in the Cuba, carrying
the pen that signed the treaty, and reflecting—

> "We may proudly say,
> We too were there in that remembered May,
> And shared the work of Fish, the laurels of De Grey."

After the Washington adventures, official work at home
reads rather tamely.

On his return from the visit to the States, Sir Stafford was not allowed to be idle.   Mr Bruce (Lord Aber-
dare) invited him to preside over the Commission which
was to inquire into the working of Friendly Societies.   In
them he was naturally interested.   As he said at Stroud
ten years later, "They are admirable, because they spring
from the people themselves; the scheme originally struck
out by the people themselves, the difficulties faced by the

people themselves, . . . and they solve problems which are really problems of statesmen."

When the Commission began its journeyings, Friendly Societies were in this position: They were certified by registrars, and tables for granting annuities were certified by an actuary. This, it was found, did not prevent the societies from being, occasionally, either fraudulently or incompetently managed. Mr Tidd Pratt, indeed, believed that the proportion of incompetent or dishonest business was terribly great. The questions arose, Could legislation improve them? or, Should the Government certificates be dropped, as mere lures to ruin? To answer these questions, local inquiries in towns were needed, the Friendly Societies also were thought to require inspection.

In September, Sir Stafford, with his fellow-commissioners, left for Edinburgh. His domestic letters give a few particulars about his tour: "We are doing useful work," he writes from a most depressing hotel in Glasgow. "Our work is very interesting, and we rake up some queer disclosures," "discover no end of jobs." Bread and cheese were with difficulty procured on the voyage to Belfast. Dublin provided "the most luxurious hotel you can imagine." "There is a richer vein of rascality in Glasgow than one could discover at Belfast, though ' promoters had used the blessed name of St Patrick, Ireland's patron saint, to delude poor Catholics into joining a swindle.'" Is it safe to add that the Commissioners found the Liffey "a beastly ditch"? At Killarney the Commissioners learned that celebrity has its taxes to pay:—

" The distinction of being mounted, and accompanied not only by a gillie but by a bugler, drew upon us a tenfold share of attention, meaning solicitation, throughout the journey.   The favourite requests were, 1st, that we would take a drop of mountain-dew, a compound of milk and whisky; and 2d, that we would exchange a shilling for a lucky sixpence.   We accepted the mountain-dew twice—once to see what it was like, and once (by way of *doch-an-dorroch*) to 'make up' a young lady's 'marriage money.'   A very good-looking girl she was, and as merry as possible, not badly dressed, though of course without shoes or stockings, running laughing along by our side with a bottle of milk in one hand and of whisky in the other. 'Shure I only want seven shillings to my marriage money.   Shure ye'll take *doch-an-dorroch*.   Shure the last drop's the sweetest.'   I need not say we were softhearted.   Since we came in, I have been rather troubled by hearing a Canadian gentleman, who it seems is married to an Irish wife, give an account of his having bestowed a sixpence on the same Miss Bridget, and of her then falling back and conversing in Erse with her sister, not knowing that the lady understood them.   She expressed her opinion that her benefactor was a very soft gentleman— at least so his wife told him.   What she must have said of us, who gave a shilling each!   But perhaps the wife was jealous.

" We have decidedly met with more fun in the last three days than in the rest of our tour.   Some of the rules which the Friendly Societies at Cork 'condescended' to were delicious. Think of this: 'If any member is in the habit of striking and maltreating his wife (a most disgraceful and inexcusable practice, and one likely to lead to the worst consequences as regards the wife's health), he shall forfeit any benefit as respects the said wife.' In order to preserve peace and harmony, any member refusing to be silent when ordered, or any member challenging another to fight, is to be fined; and any member coming in with his face and hands dirty, or with a beard of extraordinary length, is to be excluded. 'If any member come in intoxicated, yet so as to be able to conduct himself in conformity with these rules, he shall be allowed to sit; but if otherwise, he shall be marked "troublesome," and if any member be three times called "troublesome" by the president and marked so by the secretary, he shall be'— I forget whether it is fined or excluded."

At Liverpool "we are taking evidence showing the rascality of a lot of scamps, but I have great doubts whether it will lead to much good." The journeyings ended safely, but a voyage from Pynes to town at the end of the year was marked by a railway accident, elsewhere described.

The results, the practical results of travelling much, and suffering many things of many witnesses, were expressed in the Friendly Societies Bill, which (to anticipate) Sir Stafford brought in, and withdrew in 1874, and which passed in 1875. A confidential minute of December 20, 1874, sets forth his ideas, his aims, means, and the possible objections to them: "The principal object of the bill may be said to be the maintenance and improvement of the Friendly Society system; that is to say, of a system which allows and encourages persons to form themselves into societies to provide themselves with pay in sickness, at death, or at other periods; which recognises such societies on their registering their rules with a Government officer, and gives them certain advantages, either in the courts of law or otherwise, which without some special legislation they would not possess."

One school said, the State had better leave the whole affair alone; the other school, that the State should make its interference more effectual.

His own bill went with neither school:—

"It aims in the main at these two objects:

"1. The giving of information, which may be of use to the founders and managers of societies, and may assist them in framing proper rules and tables; and,

"2. The requiring the managers of societies to give such information to the public as may enable intelligent persons to judge for themselves (and for those in whom they may feel an interest) what the real position of any particular society is, and whether it offers an eligible means of investment or not.

"In order to accomplish the first object, the bill provides for the preparation of good model tables of contributions and benefits, to be issued by the Government for the use of such societies as choose to adopt them.   It also proposes to give additional facilities for the audit of accounts and for the valuation of societies, by a proper attention to which managers may ascertain from time to time how their society stands, and whether any measures for strengthening it are required.

" In order to accomplish the second object, the bill provides for the registration of societies, not only at headquarters in London, but in the various counties in which they carry on their business, and for the registration, not only of their names, places of business, and rules, but also of the periodical valuations of their assets and liabilities, which are henceforth to be made compulsory, and which are to be made, or at all events abstracted, on a uniform principle. It is hoped that these may by-and-by be made so simple that any ordinary village schoolmaster or other fairly educated person will be able to understand them, and give useful advice to persons in humbler positions who may think of joining any particular society.

" Subject to these two conditions—the giving of sound advice, and the requiring of correct information for general use—it is the general intention of the bill to leave the managers of societies as free as possible to follow any course they please with regard to their constitution and management. There are, however, certain classes of societies for which some particular regulations appear to be needed. The principal of these are the great Burial Societies.

" These Burial Societies, composed, as they are, of the poorest and most ignorant part of the population, and to a large extent of mere infants, have for the most part a central managing body in some great town, which directs their operations all over the kingdom. The danger here lies, not so much in their adopting unsound tables of contributions and benefits, as in their spending too much on the management, and in their oppressing the distant or helpless members. The bill, therefore, contains some provisions for meeting the principal evils connected with this class of societies. These provisions will be found in the 30th clause of the amended bill of last session. They are, to a great extent, founded on those contained in a bill introduced by Lord Lichfield in 1868, which was defeated mainly by the opposition of the great Burial Societies.

" The bill also contains some restrictions upon the insurance of infant lives. This is a subject which is sure to evoke much popular interest on both sides of the question. On the side of the Burial Societies it will be urged that these restrictions will prevent parents from fulfilling their natural desire to make provision for the interment of their children. On the other side, it will be contended that they are necessary to prevent much culpable neglect, if not actual infanticide. It will be seen that this part of the bill has been much modified. In the first draft it was proposed absolutely to prohibit the insurance of children under three years of age. In the revised draft (sec. 27) the provisions are, that no child under three years of age shall be insured in more than one society, nor for a larger sum than 30s.; that none but the parent or his personal representative shall receive the payment; and that greater strictness shall be observed in the matter of certificates. These latter regulations apply to children under ten years of age. They are to be enforced by making the breach of them 'offences' under the Act, and as such they will subject the offenders to penalties of from £1 to £5.

"These, then, being the leading objects of the bill, we have next to consider the machinery by which it is proposed to attain them. This is partly old and partly new. In the main, however, it may be described as machinery constructed on the old lines, but strengthened and improved in some material points.

"In the first place, the bill proposes to consolidate and re-enact the bulk of the present Friendly Societies law; to continue a system of registration, though one which will differ in some particulars from that now in force; and to continue to registered societies the legal advantages which they now possess.[1] It proposes to make it easier for societies to register, and to place stricter limits on the arbitrary power of the registrar to refuse his certificate, which is now a cause of complaint.

"With these objects in view, it purposes to consolidate

[1] "These advantages are thus described in the Report of the Royal Commissioners :—

"They can hold property in the names of trustees :

"Can sue and be sued in representative names :

"Can proceed against their officers in case of any fraud or misconduct :

"Can recover property from their estates in certain cases :

"May make provision for the settlement of disputes among their members by arbitration :

"Can invest their funds with the Commissioners for the Reduction of National Debt :

"Are exempt, within certain limits, from stamp duties :

"And can be dissolved on cheap and easy terms when occasion arises."

the registries of the three kingdoms, which are now very inconveniently kept distinct, so that a society intending to carry on business in more than one kingdom may register for all alike at the central office. It proposes also to allow societies which carry on their operations within a single county, to register each with the clerk of the peace of its own county. It proposes to remove the restrictions which, according to the construction placed on the law by successive registrars, prevent the registration of the 'dividing' or 'sharing-out' clubs which abound in the rural parts of the country, and in some of the country towns, and in fact to admit to the privileges of the law almost any type of society. It proposes to give to the promoters of societies a right of appeal to a court of law, in case the registrar refuses them registration.

"But, in addition to these advantages, the bill proposes to call upon the registrar's office (which is to be strengthened for the purpose), to render other services to the societies. Tables of contributions and benefits, and model forms of accounts, balance-sheets, and valuations, are to be prepared there, and published for the use of societies, though their use is to be entirely optional on the part of the managers. These tables will afford a standard with which to compare the tables in use by different societies. The Institute of Actuaries are at the present moment kindly giving their attention to the number and classes of tables which should be prepared; and I hope to be in possession of their views before the meeting of Parliament."

It was proposed to render these periodical valuations compulsory upon all registered societies, and to record the results, and place them where they could be studied by hesitating investors.

He anticipated that many of the real objections would be "kept in the background." Many astute persons had a personal and pecuniary interest in "clipping the wings of the bill." Many would be jealous of all Government interference. Yet the moderation of the bill, on the other hand, would "render many ardent reformers indifferent to it. Its opponents would be bitter, its supporters lukewarm."

Indeed the 'Times' described the bill as modest, if not timid. "The measure was a compromise, and its provisions were mainly permissive." For, as it happened, the societies were *not* subjected to compulsory supervision. It had always been Sir Stafford's principle "to interfere as little as possible with the voluntary action of those who are managing Friendly Societies." "It is better that the societies should not be governed as well as they might be, than that Parliament should do anything in the way of governing them beyond what was absolutely necessary." What he thought they most wanted was "proper facilities for action, and, above all, they want proper information," which his bill gave them. The 'Times' justly remarked that "a storm of unpopularity" would have been the result of securing the members of Friendly Societies too effectually against their managers. And it is, or was then, a free country. *Nolenti non fit beneficium!*

The Liberal historian of the period,[1] with his love of intrepid enterprise, calls the bill "the mild and timid result of the long inquiry which the previous Government had carried on." At least one of the "inquirers" produced the bill. It was permissive, but the permission it gives has been acted on—which these sorts of permissions rarely are. Sir Stafford, indeed, was "told continually that the measure was inadequate and delusive." He believed it was "nothing of the sort. In those respects in which it was said to fall short, it was not from any weakness or timidity that it so fell short, but from a deliberate view that the only and true way of bringing about a development of the virtue of providence amongst the people was to make them work it out for themselves, and that our great desire ought to be to give fair play, and full play, to those institutions which have sprung from the people themselves; but not on that account do we mean to shirk our own duty in this matter."[2]

The Friendly Societies were true to their name when Lord Iddesleigh died. The Manchester Unity of Oddfellows sent a letter of condolence to Lady Iddesleigh, "expressing the sad and irreparable loss the Friendly Societies had suffered by the Earl's death." The London members of the Ancient Order of Foresters did the same. And the Manchester Grand Master spoke for upwards of 600,000 members, when he said "that England has lost one of the greatest supporters of voluntary thrift, as exemplified

[1] Mr Clayden, in 'England under Lord Beaconsfield.'
[2] Speech at Manchester, December 8, 1875.

in the working of Friendly Societies and of kindred institutions."[1]

The years 1872-73—years of comparative peace and rest at home and abroad—did not contain any events of much biographical note or interest. There were the usual flittings from Pynes to London and the House of Commons, and in 1872 Sir Stafford went on a yachting cruise with Lord Carnarvon among the Scilly Islands. A riding tour in Devonshire occupied in the same way the leisure of early autumn in 1873. The letters of this time are of merely domestic interest, and the work done was mainly on the Friendly Society Commission and at the Hudson Bay Company. We may pass over the times which, being happy, had no history of mark, and may reach the days of Mr Disraeli's Conservative success at the poll, and the appointment of Sir Stafford to the Chancellorship of the Exchequer. With the single exception of Mr Gladstone, there was no living statesman so fit for the tenure of that arduous and rather thankless office—the stewardship of English financial affairs.

[1] Mr Stoddrell's letter in the 'Times,' January 20, 1887.

CHAPTER XIII.

CHANCELLOR OF THE EXCHEQUER.

CHARGES OF "FRITTERING AWAY" MR GLADSTONE'S SURPLUS CONSIDERED—SIR STAFFORD'S FINANCIAL PRINCIPLES—HOW TO USE THE SURPLUS—LETTER TO MR DISRAELI—BUDGET SPEECH—SCHEME FOR REDUCING NATIONAL DEBT—MR GLADSTONE'S CRITICISMS—"PITCH-AND-TOSS" AND "NEEVIE-NICK-NACK"—SAVINGS BANKS—MR PLIMSOLL'S AFFAIR—THE PURCHASE OF SUEZ CANAL SHARES—LETTER TO MR DISRAELI—LATER BUDGETS—LEAN YEARS—FOREIGN TROUBLES—MR GLADSTONE'S CRITICISMS—THE DEFEAT OF 1880.

THE years of Sir Stafford's stewardship of English finance are full of "lessons." No lesson among them is more prominent than that of party criticism and its unkindness.[1] The charges brought against his administration of finance remind one of the stripes with which the Arcadians

[1] In a letter to a friend (May 3, 1876), I find Sir Stafford saying : " Case-hardened as I am myself, and accustomed to the injustices and the discouragements which a public man has to undergo, I can recall many occasions on which I have felt, as keenly perhaps as you now feel, the bitterness of official life. It has been hard to learn the lesson, *virtute mea me involvo.*" Perhaps the good-humour and self-restraint of public men is the most engaging feature in public life.

visited the statue of Pan, when he brought them no luck. They whipped Pan with nettles, for matters of which he was entirely guiltless. In the same way, Liberal critics denounced Sir Stafford for having " frittered away "—that was the consecrated expression—" a magnificent surplus," and for having, in a spirit of Conservative malignity, raised the expenditure, and lowered the income of England.

In opposition to this view, one may quote, from a letter (April 1875) to Mr Welby (now Sir Reginald Welby), Sir Stafford's principles of financial policy—the ideas to which he strove to be true. They are thus expressed :—

" 1. Prudent but not deliberately *under* estimates.

" 2. The habitual retention of a substantial surplus.

" 3. The retention of the income-tax at a low fixed rate, not to be disturbed for anything short of a national emergency.

" 4. The appropriation of a fixed annual sum to the charge for debt.

" 5. The avoidance of new taxes ; and,

" 6. As a corollary I must add, toleration of old ones.

" Parliament and the country ought really to make up their minds to deal frankly and courageously with these matters, to eschew sensationalism, and to act on steady principles."

The truth was, of course, that Sir Stafford's Chancellorship of the Exchequer fell in the lean years that followed the fat years, and he was no more responsible for their emaciation than was Pharaoh's chief butler or baker for the condition of the shadowy kine. When Mr Gladstone appealed to the country in 1874, our prosperity had been " advancing by leaps and bounds," and performing athletic feats which it has ever since declined to repeat. A Liberal Administration was not the cause of the good times, though, when the Conservatives came in, working men were heard to observe, " Now for bad times." The arrival of bad times was an affair of coincidence, not of causation; just as the lack of rain in South Africa was *not* due to the church-bell, the beard, nor the bag of salt of Dr Moffat the missionary, though these theories were broached by intelligent Basuto economists. What makes good times ? what makes hard times ? are questions which philosophers are unable to answer; but popular Liberal speakers and writers argued as if Mr Gladstone were a financial *Mascotte*, as if winged fortune were unwinged for his sake, and abode with him, $\tau\acute{\nu}\chi\eta\ \emph{ἄπτερος}$. On the other hand, the years after his return in 1880 have been years lean and plagued, yet rural patriarchs have already been known to observe, " When old Beaconsfield was gaffer, there were none of them bad times." However, Sir Stafford came into office with a noble surplus bequeathed by Mr Gladstone, a surplus reckoned at more than five millions. Ever since, ever since 1877, his opponents have been asking, *Ubi est ille surplus?* and their answer, as in the famous case of *ille sicarius*, has been *Non est inventus*. " Where is our magnificent surplus ? " they have cried, as if a surplus were usually put away in an old stocking; and Sir Stafford kept telling them where it was, and what he had done with it, but they marked him not.

" Don't talk to me," says your lecturer, " of Conservative finance. The Tories came into office with a surplus of six millions, bequeathed by Mr Gladstone, and they not only spent it all in their six years of office, but left a deficiency of six millions in its place." [1]

Sir Stafford remarks that " it is too much to expect that any one, who is not obliged to do it, should hunt up old Budget speeches." The task is irksome indeed, especially to " any poor child of Nature," as Mr Matthew Arnold described himself ; but a little research in old Budget speeches will show where the magnificent surplus went, and how little the Chancellor of the Exchequer was responsible for the " melancholy minus quantity."

Mr Gladstone not only left a surplus in 1874 : he had also proposed to get rid of the income-tax, if but the electors would restore him to power. Mr Chamberlain, according to Mr Clayden,[2] was not far from the mark when he described Mr Gladstone's address, containing these proposals, as " the meanest public document which has ever, in like circumstances, proceeded from a statesman of the first rank." Without adopting this rather rude estimate of Mr Gladstone's purposes, one may admit that it is not easy to see how he meant to do all that he intended to do. Sir Stafford, in his first Budget speech, wished to

[1] " Figures, Facts, and Fallacies." In ' National Review,' July 1883.
[2] England under Lord Beaconsfield, p. 17.

> "Call up him who left half told
> The story of Cambuscan bold,"

and make him reveal his mystery. But the secret will never be revealed, at least in practice. In his letters to Mr Disraeli we find Sir Stafford much perplexed by his bequest. How was he to employ his surplus of over five millions? Deputations came all day suggesting this or that method of giving themselves a slice. Even before the elections, even before he knew that the cutting of the cake would fall to himself, he wrote :—

"Take Gladstone's surplus, however, at five millions, and see what he has to do with it. He has, first, to relieve rateable property from a substantial amount of taxation ; secondly, to take off the income-tax ; and thirdly, I suppose, to remit the remainder of the sugar duties. The three operations together can hardly cost him less than seven millions, probably more ; so there must be at least two millions to be provided by fresh taxation. How is this to be got ? Not, I presume, by another match-tax. It must be by some kind of tax on realised property, and perhaps by licences on trades. You will remember what he said on this subject in 1853, when he pointed to the possibility of replacing the income-tax by a conjunction of three measures: one a tax upon land, houses, and visible property, of perhaps sixpence in the pound ; another, a system of licences on trade, made universal, and averaging something like seven pounds ; and the third, a change in the system of legacy duties. He then said that such a system would be, on the whole, more unequal and annoying than the income-tax, and that it would raise the difficult question of the taxation of the public funds in the most inconvenient form. I cannot help suspecting that if he were now to give us the details of his plan on the eve, instead of on the morrow, of a general election, he would find that a good many constituencies would say with poor Lord Derby, 'We prefer the gout.' What a funny view it is, after all, that Gladstone takes of the income-tax! It is, according to him, properly a temporary tax—a war-tax, admitted, however, into our financial system in time of peace for certain purposes of commercial legislation—requiring a temporary impost for their attainment, just as a war does. The purposes having been attained, one would expect him to say that the tax might be taken off, as it would have been at the end of a war. But no! 'It is *manifest* that we ought not to aid the rates and remove the income-tax without giving to the general consumer, and giving him simultaneously, some marked relief in the class of articles of popular consumption.' In other words, you find that the duties on articles of consumption are exceedingly high, and you believe that by reducing them largely, you can benefit the consumer without ultimately injuring the revenue, and if to cover the operation you lay a temporary tax upon property or income while the revenue is recovering itself, and if it ultimately does recover itself so that the temporary tax is no longer needed, still 'it is manifest' that you must not take off the temporary tax without still

further reducing or quite abolishing the duty on the article
of consumption.   What logic!   Logical or not, I am afraid
that it is true that the view is one which will so commend
itself to the masses as to make it impossible to extinguish
the income-tax without at the same time dealing with
some tax on articles of consumption.   The truth is, that
the income-tax has lost its temporary character, and has
become a fixed element in our financial system, which now
includes a much larger proportion of direct taxation than
it did in 1842.   So, then, whenever we reduce the income-
tax, we seem to be disturbing the balance between direct
and indirect taxation, and disturbing it in favour of the
wealthier classes, unless we reduce indirect taxes at the
same time.   To this, perhaps, we might resign ourselves;
but in the present case there seems an additional absurdity,
because it is not proposed simply to abolish the income-
tax, but to substitute for a portion of it some other impost
on property, while at the same time it is acknowledged
that the kinds of visible property which now bear local
taxation ought to be relieved of a portion of their burden.
In short, direct taxation is to be readjusted in order to
cure its inequalities, and to render it fairer.   This is a
difficult task in itself, and why we should go out of our
way to make it more difficult by imposing on ourselves
the voluntary obligation to reduce some taxes on consumption at the same time, I cannot (except with reference to electioneering necessities) conceive.   Upon the
whole, I think we have a strong case for warning the
country not to be misled or dazzled by the vague promises

of the address, and to distrust the great financial policy till they see what it is."

In this letter, by the way (January 25, 1874), Sir Stafford alludes to a paragraph in Mr Gladstone's address, "which appears darkly to encourage the Home Rulers."

To return to his troubles with the surplus. "Could we possibly expect to be allowed to retain such a surplus as that?" he asks, pathetically. "Supposing that you reduced the income-tax by one-half, and gave the £550,000 to local taxation, you would still have £1,000,000 surplus. Would not even this be too large, and should we not have an ugly rush at it?" Should they sweep away some of the Excise licences? Should they abandon the sugar duty?[1] The alternatives appeared to be abolishing the income-tax, or deciding against, or postponing, the abolition of the income-tax, reducing it to twopence, giving large grants in aid of local taxation, and repealing the sugar tax. But divers other schemes were selected and rejected. Sir Stafford maintained that "for any of these measures suggested, it is important that we should shake off that absurd maxim as to the simultaneous decrease of direct and indirect taxation." But he believed that, when *adding* taxation, "you ought not to place it upon the income-tax only; but you ought to accompany it with some call upon

---

[1] Sir Stafford was by no means of opinion that democratic taxation, relieving the less wealthy classes, would lead to a readiness to make war. "If there were to be a real war ferment at any time, I should be sorry to trust to such a sedative as the threat of doubling the sugar duties would be." The English democracy, at least, is by no means likely to be belligerent and pugnacious, as far as foreign countries go.

indirect taxation."[1] Through this period of incubating his first Budget, he "felt like a chess-player studying an important move, and seeing new combinations at every turn."

It is needless to fatigue the reader with all the combinations. The result was made public in the Budget speech of April 16, 1874. Sir Stafford congratulated the late Government very heartily on their economical and satisfactory management of the war in Ashantee. He defended Mr Gladstone against the charge, brought, of course, by the Tories, of having been too sanguine in his Estimates. "Instead of being too sanguine, he has been within the mark." The receipts from Customs and Excise had exceeded expectation. The public had been drinking enormously, for these were "good times." But he very strongly disliked this particular symptom of prosperity. If temperance and abstinence were only to increase, though the revenue from spirits would fall, " I venture to say that the amount of wealth such a change would bring to the nation would utterly throw into the shade the amount of revenue that is now derived from the spirit duty." Unhappily any fall in the tide of gin and whisky seems to be due to poverty rather than happier dispositions. Pleasant as it was to see the "consuming power" of the public increased, he had already been obliged to listen to prophecies of evil. The coming of the lean kine had already been predicted—the slackening of employment, the fall in consumption, had been foreseen. Expenditure must still be kept down. Still, there was the surplus of more than

---

[1] Budget speech, April 3, 1879.

five millions. Some might say that a country which had
a debt could never really have a surplus. He could not
agree with them, but the reduction of the debt was always
one of his main ideas. He proposed for this year to reduce it by terminable annuities with the £450,000 of
interest on advances at his disposal, using for this purpose
the balance of Post-office Savings Banks' money. As to
the whole surplus, apart from the £450,000 of interest, he
first touched on local taxation without approaching the
whole subject, as the Government was new in office. But,
having a surplus, he determined to relieve local taxation.
Lunatics were to receive a contribution from the Consolidated Fund—namely, four shillings a-week a-head to the
Unions for each lunatic in their asylums. Lunatics in
Ireland had already been selected by Mr Gladstone for
the receipt of benevolence out of the funds of the Irish
Church, so Mr Gladstone might be expected to approve
of this expenditure. To the police he assigned £600,000.
Then, advancing to the income-tax, he admitted, like one
of Shakespeare's clowns talking of his mistress, that " she
hath more faults than hairs," but also "more wealth than
faults." So he took one penny off the income-tax. More
than half the surplus was now " frittered away," exclusive
of what went to the reduction of the debt; and he next
proposed to abolish the sugar duties. As a source of
revenue they "do more harm than good upon the whole."
As to the competition in sugar refining with France and
other Powers, he could not rely on treaties, but " upon the
sense of its own interest which a foreign nation has in not

wasting its money upon subsidies to its refiners." But foreign nations do not understand "their own interest" as England does; England, it may be permitted to interpolate, has quite peculiar ideas of her own interest.

The sugar duties went for £2,000,000. I think it was on this occasion that a Liberal critic, in private talk, quoted about Sir Stafford what Steerforth said when financing a certain entertainment, "You're going it, young Copperfield." He "went it" still further, for he had still a surplus of £942,000. He would not touch malt, beer, nor railways, no, nor dogs, but he made a present to horses, a present of £480,000. And that was how he frittered away his surplus.

A Liberal critic remarks that this was "the Liberal Budget watered down to the standard of Conservative finance," and adds that Mr Gladstone's successor could only "muddle it away,"—the surplus, that is. He says, too, that Mr Gladstone "had proposed to abolish the income-tax as well as the sugar duties." But this very critic we have quoted as agreeing (more or less) with Mr Chamberlain and with the Opposition, that Mr Gladstone's proposal was a "huge bribe," his address "the meanest public document which has ever, in like circumstances, proceeded from a statesman of the first rank."[1]

He had agreed to the extent of saying that Mr Chamberlain's remarks were "a shrewd and on the whole a correct summary of the Address, but not entirely fair to Mr Gladstone." The unfairness appears to have lain in supposing

---

[1] Clayden's England under Lord Beaconsfield, pp. 17, 68, 69.

that the promises of Mr Gladstone were made for mere electioneering purposes.   That may answer the moral charges of Mr Gladstone's critics, but it leaves the practical question untouched.   *Could* Mr Gladstone have completed "the story of Cambuscan bold"?   And if not, what was the harm in Sir Stafford's less romantic performance?   Was the "opportunity" really there, the opportunity which was "muddled away"?   Even supposing that a heaven-born Minister could have escaped the Eastern troubles and the Zulu affair, could he have retained Fortune as his minion.   "Fortune is Pistol's foe," and the bad times, already looming, would have come, whoever was at the helm, and the income-tax could not have been slain except to rise again.

As to the frittering away of the magnificent surplus, Sir Stafford spoke at Liverpool (January 25, 1877).   He said the magnificent surplus was "got up to a certain extent by putting off a great many claims and charges which would ultimately have had to be met."   It was as if a man should decline to spend money on his estate in repairs, leaving them as Sir Pitt Crawley left his lodge-keeper's roof, windows, and walls.   The navy had been treated by the late Government as Sir Pitt treated Mrs Lock's cottage.   "They had not only put off a great many things which it was absolutely necessary to do—the repairing of ships, for instance, and many other matters of that kind; . . . but they had entered into large schemes and made large promises with reference to the army and educational reform, and other things which necessarily en-

tailed further expense upon their successors; and therefore, when we are asked, What have you done with the
enormous surplus of five millions? I say that you must
consider that a very considerable (*sic*) proportion of it
was necessary for the purpose of meeting the engagements
that you had undertaken for us."

But had the surplus ·been frittered away after all?
He answered, again and again, "You cannot eat your
cake and have it." Each person in Liverpool, where he
spoke, had actually received 1s. 3d. in remission of sugar
tax. But a vain people easily forgets a present of fifteen-
pence a - head. Owners of horses had been freed from
an "annoying" tax. Seventy-eight thousand pounds, in
Liverpool alone, had gone to lunatics and the police.
Meanwhile the Budget had, at least, not curried favour
with the friends of the Government.

The farmers, of course, were disgusted that no attempt
was made to reduce or repeal the malt-tax. But Mr Gladstone himself "expressed his general approval of a scheme
the main outlines of which were a faint reproduction of
his own."

So much for Sir Stafford's first Budget.

Continuing the history of his finance, we find him in
January of the following year saying to Mr Disraeli that
"the chance of getting through without any addition to
taxation appears very remote, though not *quite* visionary."
A good deal of money was wanted for the fleet, which
Mr Ward Hunt had found in a "phantom" estate—like
youth that grows "spectre-thin, and dies." Excise was

less profitable than common, because of the large and rich potato-harvest in Germany. German potato-spirit had "taken the place of British spirit, and paid us through the Customs instead of through Excise. This was a mere shifting of source of money; but there was that horrid navy excess of £160,000 in the background." The following lines from a letter (March 31, 1875) to Mr Disraeli, put in simple colloquial words the burden of his financial policy, permanence of arrangements, reduction of debt:—

"What I am now anxious for is the acceptance by the Cabinet of my proposal to grant the income-tax (at 2d.) for three years. There is no chance of our getting rid of it sooner, even if we wished to do so. But I don't wish to do so. I am anxious to keep the tax—keep it as it is, keep it low, and keep it unaltered and unalterable except in the case of a real emergency.

"This will give a character and consistency to our financial policy. We ought to show that we know what we are about. If we simply say, as we may be tempted to say, that we will let everything alone, we shall be taunted with having simply taken up Gladstone's surplus; spent it as he would have suggested, but without the finer strokes of his genius; been very lucky in just scraping through our first year, and being now content to drift. Then we shall be exposed to attacks of all kinds—some from those who will try to pledge us to get rid of the tax, others who will want us to alter it—and we may find ourselves driven into a corner, if we have not some fixed policy of our own.

" There is another matter on which I also wish to lay down a policy—the mode of dealing with the debt. I believe we can introduce more stability into this part of our system also, and lay down principles which will greatly reduce fluctuations in taxation. But I will not go into this matter now."

While occupied with his Budget, he had to consider and reject the proposal of a Government guarantee to a Euphrates Valley Railway, though Government " would gladly see the line constructed." His Budget speech (April 15, 1875) showed a surplus of £496,873 for the financial year just ended, which he thought would be " a disappointment—of course an agreeable disappointment " —to his Liberal critics. Had he not removed a penny from income-tax, his position would of course have been very much more pleasant. But he was the reverse of Horace's miser, with his

> " Me mihi plaudo
> Quum nummos contemplor in arca."

" I, on the other hand, console myself, whatever may be the hisses of a few instructors of public opinion, with the reflection that the money is not in my cash-box, but in the pockets of the people." He explained the spirituous consequences of Germany's great potato-harvest, which, after all, was mainly used here " for purposes of methylation " rather than of conviviality. Tea had produced £320,000 more than the year before; satisfactory, " as showing that tea, to some extent perhaps, is taking the place of spirits," and that the remission of the sugar duties had benefited English tea-drinkers. There was a diminution in stamps; the telegraph service was not yet remunerative. He again justly applauded his predecessors for their economical conduct of the Ashantee war. But he could not see any signs of a revival in trade, for the ill years were fairly begun—naturally, too, as the Liberals were out. Thus he could not treat the revenue as a thing necessarily bound to keep on increasing. As to the income-tax, he remarked: "We have been obliged to consider it; and whether it would be desirable to do that which it is quite possible to do—to make arrangements and readjustments by which we may dispense with it, or materially modify it." He admitted the objections to it, and to " the inequality of its incidence." These inequalities he considered inherent in the nature of the tax; inherent, too, is " its inquisitorial character." All these objections were gravest when the tax is high. He wished it to be " low, uniform, and, as far as possible, steady." He proposed to renew it at twopence in the pound. The most important part of this speech dealt with a scheme for the reduction of debt. Let us briefly state the matter in the words of the Liberal historian :—

Sir Stafford's great scheme, and that which distinguished the Budget of the year, was that for beginning the paying off of the National Debt. The interest on the debt for the year was reckoned at £27,215,000. Sir Stafford proposed to fix it in future at £28,000,000, and use the surplus in extinguishing the principal of the debt. This was to be done by three steps: £27,400,000 was to be charged for the current year; for the year 1876-77, it was to be £27,700,000 ; and for all succeeding years, £28,000,000. The scheme was severely criticised, but it was popular and passed. *It is clearly a prudent step, but it reduced* the surplus even of the current year by £185,000."[1]

Thus do measures which are prudent and popular "fritter away the surplus," and such was criticism, which regarded the surplus as a sacred thing, not to be reduced even by prudence.

In his remarks on this arrangement, Sir Stafford said that he was "no enthusiast" on the National Debt, "but I think we ought to make continuous and steady efforts for its reduction, and that our efforts ought not to be violent and spasmodic." Ever since the Finance Committee of 1828, it had been admitted as an axiom that " we can only redeem debt by the surplus of revenue over expenditure." The application of " casual surpluses" was insufficient. He stated the objections to terminable annuities. They might not be taken up, or not satisfactorily. You could invest savings banks' money in them, and so cancel your stock. But then any one might say that you were investing the public's savings " in what would be in the market an unprofitable security." . Again, terminable annuities "produce a kind of spasmodic action." When they fell in, the relief might be reckoned " a windfall," and treated as " windfalls " are usually treated. *Autant en emporte le vent.* He then proposed his own plan, which has already been given in a summary by a Liberal critic. If that plan were allowed to work by grace of " ordinary circumstances and the ordinary growth of the

---

[1] England under Lord Beaconsfield, pp. 144, 145.

revenue," by 1885 "you will have cancelled £21,000,000, and in thirty years from this time you will have cancelled £213,000,000." He foresaw and admitted the force of the criticism, " You will never be able to bind future Parliaments, and the very first time that a Chancellor of the Exchequer wants to raise an additional revenue without increasing taxation, he will put an end to your Sinking Fund." *Et puis après?*

" Under circumstances different from the present *I say that would be a very reasonable thing for a Chancellor of the Exchequer to do*. . . . But one thing is quite clear, that if we do not put it on, it will certainly come to nothing; and we shall be in the position of the gentleman who would not wind up his watch, because if he did not wind it up, it would never stop." He himself " thought the experiment worth making." He was *not* " binding future Parliaments." Nobody who wished to destroy his Sinking Fund (he did not use this illustration) would have to make his proposal, as in old Athens concerning the gold on the statue of Athene, with a rope round his neck.

In 1881, speaking at Edinburgh, he again described the scope and meaning of his measure: " Some years ago the practice of the Chancellor of the Exchequer was, in estimating for the expenditure of the coming year, to make provision, of course, for the payment of the interest of the National Debt for the coming twelvemonth; and as the National Debt was gradually diminished by the action of terminable annuities which had been created by Mr Gladstone and other Ministers, the amount that was so required

for the payment of the annual interest from time to time
somewhat diminished. The proposal which I made was,
that we should fix a certain sum—somewhat higher than
the amount that we were then paying for the interest of
the discharge of the debt, and that that amount should be
applied every year to the payment of the interest in the
first place, and with regard to the remainder, for the reduction of the principal. The object which I had in view
was this, to introduce something like steadiness into our
finance; and that we should not from time to time, because there happened to be a little reduction here in our
charges, or a little reduction there, apply a smaller sum
than we were doing to the reduction of the debt; and I
therefore called upon Parliament, and the House of Commons was good enough to agree, to raise the amount that we
were paying at that time—something like 27¼ millions—
to a fixed amount of £28,000,000 a-year, which £28,000,000
was to continue permanently, and so to cover not only the
interest but the reduction of the debt. You will easily
understand the operation of such a proposal as I made in
the event of additions not being made to the debt—that
is to say, if the £28,000,000 were enough in one year to
pay the whole interest of the debt, and to pay off besides
half a million or a million of the capital, the amount of the
interest to be paid in the next year would be less by the
amount of the interest on that half million or million; and
as this process was continued, the amount of charge for interest would every year become smaller, while the amount
applicable to the redemption of capital would every year

become larger.   When once these measures had been put into an Act of Parliament, the reduction of the debt would become a serious measure."   Such an Act of Parliament was his desire.

Mr Gladstone attacked the measure (May 7).

As to the scheme for reducing the National Debt, Mr Gladstone admitted that it had "the approbation of the most sagacious of all things inanimate—namely, the three per cents."   But, on the whole, he (like Sir Stafford's grandmother in an early page of this work) distrusted the splendours of his friend's imagination.   It had "taken a flight into the empyrean," and ranged down to 1905, beholding a surplus of £500,000 for every year in that vista of time.   Even this year the surplus (if I may quote Dr Johnson's remark about the ghost) was "something of a shadowy being."   As to appropriations to reduce the National Debt, "annual appropriations arbitrarily fixed by those who do not intend to find the money for them, but who think it laudable and creditable to lay it down that future Parliaments shall find that money, they have been tried and tested by experience"—Mr Gladstone gave instances—"and have failed again and again."   Mr Gladstone had remarked that there were three ways of reducing the debt,—the first, to maintain a surplus of revenue over expenditure; the second, a system of terminable annuities; and the third, by fixed appropriations.   In his reply, after defending the existence of a surplus, Sir Stafford maintained that there was really but one way.   The maintenance of revenue over expenditure could not be put in contradistinction to any other plan. But one legitimate way there was, the maintenance of revenue over expenditure. No puzzle with terminable annuities or anything else was of any avail, nor did Sir Stafford suppose that Mr Gladstone meant anything of the sort. As for binding the future, Mr Gladstone himself had left his successors "to provide for the terminable annuities which, at his suggestion, we have been paying for the express purpose of extinguishing debt, and it is just as fictitious and as unreal as any other system."[1] Mr Gladstone, "the most incredulous man I ever met," "keeps on shaking his head whenever I refer to him." Sir Stafford maintained that he had explained his scheme in ten minutes, while Mr Gladstone, in 1865, occupied half an hour, "gave every one a headache," and indeed divided the person of the Chancellor of the Exchequer into two —the Chancellor as finance Minister, and the Chancellor as banker. The difference between the two systems was the difference (illustrated in a novel of Scott's) of gambling away the half-crown at neevie-nick-nack instead of at pitch-and-toss. The Liberals had reduced debt with one hand while raising it with the other. Their right hand paid off debt by terminable annuities, their left borrowed for fortifications, and permitted the savings banks' deficiency, which he proposed to extinguish, to go on increasing. As to the terminable annuities, the Chancel-

---

[1] By way of a financial curiosity, one may remark that the idea of buying objects of art with surpluses, instead of diminishing the National Debt, had been suggested from South Kensington !

lor of the Exchequer, dividing the person, as one may say, making terms as banker with the Chancellor of the Exchequer as finance Minister, had been both buyer and seller of these annuities, and had fixed the price as he thought fit.

"If you attempt to rest any scheme for the reduction of debt on terminable annuities, . . . you will either make a bargain too favourable, and add to the debt, or you will make a bargain too unfavourable, and so rob those for whom you are trustees—the savings banks' depositors." He would retain terminable annuities to a certain extent by provisions in the bill; "but to say that it is the only really sound and sensible principle to act upon, and that the other which I propose is unsound and visionary, seems to me to be nothing but gross and sheer prejudice." He maintained, after alluding to Mr Gladstone's critical eye as worthy of "the Epidaurian serpent," that his plan was sound and stable, because it established a consistent policy of repaying debt, and yet could be set aside whenever the necessities of the country required that it should be put an end to.

Liberal critics have often alleged that Sir Stafford "could never stand up to Mr Gladstone," but in this little 'bout he does not seem to have been worsted by his old friend.

There was a return match on June 8. Mr Gladstone again objected to the real absence of a surplus. Sir Stafford remarked that, when in Opposition, it had been his business also to prove that there was no surplus, and "he knew, therefore, how far it was usual to go in that way," a queer commentary on this queer game of party government. The whole matter, he said, " had been thoroughly threshed out," and we may agree with Odysseus—

ἐχθρὸν δέ μοί ἔστιν

Αὖτις ἀριζήλως εἰρημένα μυθολογεύειν.

Hateful are twice-told tales.

In the long-run the Sinking Fund was carried by 189 votes against 122.

The subject of the savings banks' deficiency has already been alluded to. Sir Stafford, in the course of the session of 1875, introduced a bill dealing with the question, which, as he remarked (May 27), was "rather a complicated one." The bill was encountered with great hostility by the (for once) united Opposition. Sir Stafford explained that he did not, as Mr Fawcett seemed to think, propose to put the money of depositors in savings banks and friendly societies on security less stable than in the past. The depositors had the security of the Consolidated Fund. Tricks were not being played with the depositors' money. "This, at all events, is out of the question and impossible." I cannot give here the history of savings banks, the old and the new. To be brief, there was an increasing deficiency, which every one wished to stop in some way or another. There were proposals to lower the rate of interest, but Sir Stafford could not advocate this course. "You would make the present depositors in the savings banks pay for a deficiency which they had nothing to do with incurring "—that is, capitalists in the new banks would pay for a deficiency in the old banks. The dealings of former Chancellors, too, had contributed to the deficiency. The Post-office Savings Banks had made profits over and above the stipulated interest. These profits belonged to the State, and might be used to stop the leak in the old savings banks. Local securities were to be invested in. The depositors ran no risk. Local interests would be served. Mr Gladstone was "unable to travel with him a single step along the road on which he marches." He differed from his historical statement. The deficits were due "solely and simply to the fact that we have been banking on principles which no banker would have adopted." As a banker, to Mr Gladstone's thinking, Sir Stafford had no reserve. He was starting two kinds of banking, one not to pay, the other to pay, and to pay for the other too. Business, becoming a matter of sham banking and pseudo-benevolence, had made a sham vested interest. Sir Stafford was maintaining absurd and vexatious restrictions on the amount of deposits, which Mr Gladstone was almost ashamed to say that he had been compelled to introduce with the Post-office Savings Banks, so as to conciliate the old savings banks. In a reforming measure this "gross absurdity" was perpetuated. Mr Gladstone amusingly "took the case of an insane banker" to illustrate his criticisms. I wonder any of them are still in possession of their wits. The Imperial Government could not wisely become the creditor of small local authorities. Sir Stafford in his reply returned

to the deficiency. That was the question—How were you
to stop it? His plan was "just to all parties." In a
later debate, when Sir Stafford contended that the savings
banks were secured against "runs" by various methods
and resources, Mr Gladstone again complained of his
ardent " imagination." Mr Disraeli repeated Sir Stafford's remarks on the practical problem, the deficiency,
and how it was to be met. "How will you arrest the
course of compound interest, which has already produced
such terrible effects? The right hon. member for Green-
wich threw not the slightest light upon that point. We
must deal with the circumstances." They must carry their
proposal, or reduce the interest on the deposits in the old
savings banks.

The whole discussion is one on which only the opinion
of specialists is valuable. Mr Gladstone appears to have
been ideally right; perhaps his opponents were not practically wrong. Sir Stafford's position was that, "in dealing with the deficiency question, we ought to take care in
no way to prejudice the question of reform." His attempt
was a mere filling up of a leak, not a reconstruction of a
vessel. The bill was ultimately withdrawn.

Apart from finance, Sir Stafford played a difficult and
important part in Parliament at this time, and was becoming marked out as Mr Disraeli's successor in the
leadership of the House of Commons. The question of
the risks of seamen and of overloading vessels was before
the House, and excited much emotion in England. Then
came (July 22) the celebrated appearance of Mr Plimsoll

in the House of Commons as defender of the English seamen. The cause of Mr Plimsoll's indignation was the
proposed withdrawal of the Merchant Shipping Bill, which
was intended to give a very much needed security for
their lives to sailors. The affair is so vividly present to
most memories that it need not be described at length.
Let it suffice, by some letters of Sir Stafford's, to set forth
his position in the dispute :—

"*Private.*   11 DOWNING STREET, WHITEHALL,
                                         July 22, 1875.

"MY DEAR MR DISRAELI,—May I offer the following
suggestions as to the process of massacre ?

"1. Let the Attorney-General answer Dillwyn that the
Patents Bill will be given up for want of time, and let
him move then and there that the order be discharged.

"2. When the orders of the day are called, you might
rise and say that, after carefully considering the state of
public business, you had come to the conclusion that it
would be impossible to find time for a full discussion of
the Merchant Shipping Bill; that you thought it undesirable to attempt to pass a mere fragment of so important
a measure; and that you therefore moved to discharge the
order, promising, at the same time, that the bill should
have a first place among the measures of next session.
(This would be quite in order, but, of course, it might lead
to some debate both on merchant shipping in particular
and on the course of business in general; but I do not see
how you can avoid this under any circumstances.)

" You might take the opportunity of saying that you meant to proceed with Agricultural Holdings till it was through Committee, then to take Supply, and the Judicature and Land Transfer Bills; that with regard to other business it was premature to speak, but that you would be in communication with the Ministers in charge of the several bills; and that you hoped to be able to make such arrangements as would enable the House to rise by the 10th or 12th August, and possibly even at a somewhat earlier date."

On this very day, July 22, Mr Disraeli announced that he did not intend to go on with the bill which so justly and deeply interested Mr Plimsoll. Then came Mr Plimsoll's display of passionate resentment, followed by sympathetic public meetings under Mr Chamberlain and other philanthropists. Replying to Mr Sullivan on the same night, Sir Stafford said that, even if the Agricultural Holdings Bill had been out of the way, there was no time to discuss properly the Merchant Shipping Bill. The postponement of the bill " would forward the solution of the question rather than hinder it." Lord Hartington objected that this was " totally at variance with the statement which had been made by the Prime Minister," in announcing the withdrawal of the Merchant Shipping Bill.

On July 24, Sir Stafford wrote thus to Mr Disraeli :[1]—

---

[1] The conclusion of the letter is omitted, as bearing on personal matters other than those of Sir Stafford, and not desirable to discuss.

"I see that the newspapers take up what Hartington said the other night of a supposed divergence between what I said in answer to Sullivan, and what you had previously said in announcing the withdrawal of the Merchant Shipping Bill. I am not conscious of any such divergence, but, as it may be made a topic in some attack, I am anxious to tell you exactly what I had in my mind, and what I now think of our position with regard to that bill.

"The reason for my answering Sullivan was that several speakers in succession had charged us with indifference to the Merchant Shipping Bill, and with holding the Agricultural Bill as one of superior importance. I thought it would not do to let such charges go altogether unnoticed; and I therefore expressed again our great regret at having to withdraw the bill, and added that it was not from indifference, but from a sense of the impossibility of dealing satisfactorily with a measure of so much importance and difficulty at this period of the session, that we had done so. I said it would have been impossible to have dealt with it satisfactorily, even had there been no question of the Agricultural Holdings Bill. You had previously condemned the notion of passing a mutilated bill, and this is all that could have been done if we had gone on with it in a jaded House," and under other disadvantages which he describes.

"It would, I am persuaded, be most injurious to our character if we allowed it to be supposed that, having a fair choice between the two bills, we had deliberately preferred the Agricultural Holdings Bill. We may, or may not, have made miscalculations in the earlier part of the session as to the length of time which discussions on various measures would take; but that is a more venial matter. What really killed the Merchant Shipping Bill was the discussion which its first clauses underwent in Committee, disclosing the difficulties under which it would have to be fought. . . . Whether we could have got over these difficulties had there been less other business may be a question. But we were under imperative necessity as regarded the Judicature Bill, the Labour Laws Bill, and Supply; and we had not time to grapple effectually with Merchant Shipping as it had by that time revealed itself to us.

"And here let me call your attention to these points. We were proceeding with a bill drawn on the lines of the report of a Royal Commission. A Royal Commission does not encounter the various forces which make their appearance in a regular battle in a Committee of the whole House of Commons. Our bill was therefore undergoing a first sifting, and we were beginning for the first time to discover its faults and its deficiencies.

"But further, it was not a bill for applying a direct and simple remedy to an admitted evil. The direct and simple remedy of authorising the Board of Trade to stop unseaworthy ships had already been applied by the Act of 1873; and the other direct and simple remedy which Plimsoll desired, of instituting a Government survey of all seagoing ships, we were not prepared to adopt. The principle of our bill was to throw a more complete responsibility upon shipowners; and the working out of this principle involved very complicated procedure in order to attain the object without doing injustice to any one. Mistakes in legislation of this kind are easily made, and are apt to be very mischievous. To have attempted to hurry the bill through would have been a great error. What I hope is that next year we shall be able to bring in a much better bill, availing ourselves of the experience of this year, and of the popular feeling which will support us if we act vigorously."

" The Merchant Shipping Bill," he said to Mr Disraeli (July 25, 1875), " has caused me more annoyances throughout the session than all the other bills put together, and perhaps I forgot myself a little in speaking my own mind under the provocation of Mr Sullivan's attack. We have a far better chance," he added, " of passing a really creditable bill, than we had with the deceased one." He made to Mr Disraeli, at this moment, an offer most public-spirited and disinterested, of which it may be improper to give a fuller account. It is enough to say that he was ready to " take a lower place," and subordinate his personal ambitions to the needs of the Government. The offer was not accepted.

His own private views on the Merchant Shipping affair are contained in a letter to Mr Farrer (November 20). He wants to say to the shipowners, " We mean to do our part, and at the same time to insist on your doing your part to prevent preventible evils. . . . We must insist that you shall not evade your responsibilities under the specious plea of freedom of contract, which is, or may be, a good enough plea as between the contracting parties, but is one to be very jealously scrutinised when it affects the lives of other persons. I am anxious to develop some such view as this at the very outset of our legislation next session."

The great affair of the autumn of 1875, the purchase of the Khedive's shares in the Suez Canal for four millions, was necessarily a matter on which the Chancellor of the Exchequer had his opinions. The full truth about that very odd transaction may not be known at present, and it was by no means possible to see how it could "secure our water-way to the East." The best naval opinion does not seem to bear out the theory popular at the time of the purchase. Iron, not gold, is the metal for these ends. Our whole policy in Egypt has ever been pretty much what the French have always called it. Sir Stafford's public remarks on this matter exactly correspond with his private statements. He saw the affair with the eyes of a loyal gentleman. First, let us take his public speech at Manchester (7th December 1875.) The keynote of it is, that "England must do nothing mean. At home or abroad her policy must be noble and magnanimous." Now he distinctly and decidedly held that we had *not* been " magnanimous " in our dealings with France about the Canal. Here is an extract from his speech,—here he expresses his hopes and wishes as to our conduct in the future :—

" If we have become. the possessors of a considerable

interest in that important highway of maritime communication, and if we have become the possessors of that interest with a view to the maintenance of. our own communication with our Eastern empire, we have not done
so in a spirit of exclusive selfishness, but in the entirely
opposite spirit, of desiring to extend to all nations that
freedom of communication which we desire to secure for
ourselves. We honour and respect and admire the energy
and genius of those who planned, and who, against great
difficulties, carried through that great enterprise. We
desire in no degree to rob them of their fair share of
the honour, or in any way to mar the great work which
they contemplated. We fully believe that which they
always said, that they undertook that work not in the
interests of individuals, or in the interest of a single
nation, but in the spirit of those who wish to make a
name for themselves in the proud roll of the world's bene-
factors; and if we associate ourselves with that enterprise
now, we do so, not in order to thwart, but to forward that
enterprise: it is with the hope that the Canal, which will
always remain the monument of the energy and of the
perseverance of M. de Lesseps, and of the great nation
which has borne so large a part in the work, may be maintained as a highroad for nations, and not exclusively for
the benefit of any one. No.; the spirit of English foreign
policy must be the spirit of peace, not merely of an indolent or selfish peace, but of an active peace, and one
which will propagate its principles,—our peace must be of
a kind which is consistent with national honour. It must

be the peace of the strong man armed, and not of the timorous man who cries 'Peace' to keep the hands of others off him. It must be of a true, and not of a hollow character, and this pacific policy must be founded on a conviction of our duty and of our interests. England holds a high place amongst nations. We do not seek to compare ourselves with others. We are satisfied to know that our position is one which demands every exertion on our part to maintain and to justify. England must do nothing mean. At home or abroad her policy must be noble and magnanimous: we have a great opening, and if we are but true to ourselves, true to our fellow-citizens throughout the whole of the British Empire, and true in our dealings with foreign countries, I look never to see the time when England shall fall in the scale of nations."

So he spoke in public; and *this* was his language in private:[1]—

"Our policy, or our proceedings, with regard to the Canal, has not been such as to gain us much credit for magnanimity. We opposed it in its origin; we refused to help Lesseps in his difficulties; we have used it when it has succeeded; we have fought the battle of our shipowners very stiffly; and now we avail ourselves of our influence with Egypt to get a quiet slice of what promises to be a good thing.

"Suspicion will be excited that we mean quietly to buy ourselves into a preponderating position, and then turn the whole thing into an English property.

[1] Letter to Mr Disraeli, November 26, 1875.

"I don't like it."

He might well dislike it. Our dealings in Egypt have been a cruel and crying scandal. The blood cries out against us, from the blood of Hicks and of Gordon to the latest drop that has stained the desert or the Nile.

Sir Stafford frankly remarks to Mr Disraeli at this moment, "I know so little of the actual state of our foreign relations." Who did know about it? Lord Derby was at the Foreign Office. "What would best suit us," says Sir Stafford, "would be an international arrangement by which the Canal could be placed under the guardianship of all the Powers interested in maintaining the communication." In this letter he suggests the sending of Mr Cave to see how the land lay, as the Khedive was requesting the assistance of two English men of affairs in his finance. "I am more inclined to seek my leverage in the acceptance of this mortgage by the Société Générale than in any attempt to get it for ourselves, which I fear may set other countries against us. We ought boldly to avow our legitimate interest in the question, and make a frank proposal" (November 23). "We are in deep water. . . . I am much averse from holding the shares, and greatly desirous to bring about an International Commission"[1] (November 24). Exactly the same opinion recurs in a letter to Lord Derby of the same date. And writing to Lord Carnarvon (December 3), he says that he and others "are decidedly against purchasing." The purchase was made, however, and in the House Sir Stafford

[1] See his Speeches in 1876. Hansard and Annual Register.

had to defend Mr Disraeli's policy against the attacks of Mr Gladstone (February 21, 1876). "The question we have to determine is, whether the difficulties which my right hon. friend tells us are inevitable, would not have been quite as formidable, or even more formidable, had we not purchased these shares." He admitted that the whole transaction was "unprecedented," but so is "the Suez Canal itself." The Khedive had a purchaser for his shares, but gave the English Government the refusal. "The matter would not let itself alone." As usual, there was a choice of difficulties, and Sir Stafford defended, without undue emphasis, the conduct of the Government.

The spirit of these words animated his speech in the House of Commons (February 14, 1876) after the shares had been purchased. He admitted and regretted that England, in the first place, had "to some extent impeded the operations" of M. Lesseps in the first instance. "Incredulity has its dupes," and England had been among them. "The Canal has been made, has been opened, and has proved to be of great advantage to England, while as respects the political inconveniences that would result from it, they are at all events as yet undeveloped." They have developed well enough since the disastrous ditch was dug. However, "the Canal at all events is a fact;" and he paid a high compliment, and a deserved compliment, to M. de Lesseps. "I am most anxious to speak with full and entire admiration of that gentleman." As to the purchase of the shares, there was another bidder in the market. "There are cases in which, after all, you must trust to the judgment of somebody." Apparently enough it was not to Sir Stafford's judgment that the Government trusted. He went with his chief. They had been asked whether the purchase was made " with reference to a state of war or of peace." " I, in answer to that question, say that I look upon the transaction as one of great importance for preventing complications, and for preserving peace." We now combined the characters of shareholders and customers.

The Budget of 1875 had been made without provision for certain Supplementary Estimates, notably for the Irish Education Vote. He had relied on an excess of revenue over estimate, which was looked on as " rather a novel and adventurous course." But the results justified his action, and he maintained that in like circumstances he would act again in the same way. What with the Navy, Irish Education, the Prince of Wales's Indian tour, and so forth, the Supplementary Estimates reached the stately figure of a million and a half. His estimate of expenditure for the new year showed a considerable increase, which was exactly what critics expected from Conservative finance. There was more than a million for Army and Navy. This increase he did not discuss, admitting that, as Chancellor of the Exchequer, he " looked very jealously" on it. £1,756,000 had been added for Army and Navy since the Conservatives entered on office. As to the increased charges for the Civil Service, the growth of population, and such measures as the Merchant Shipping Bill, with its staff of inspectors and officials, had made the increase inevitable. Naturally, in a world that clamours to be inspected, inspectors must be paid. Between 1873-74 and 1876, there had been an increase in Civil Service expenditure amounting to over £2,000,000. Of this the Education Estimates amounted to nearly one million; the increase in grants in aid of local taxation over £1,400,000. He deprecated partisan charges of extravagance. The increase was due, not to extravagance, but to " the increase of the charge for education, which I believe everybody welcomes, and to local taxation, which both our friends and our enemies tell us is a mere bagatelle."

The estimated revenue for the financial year 1876 fell below his estimate of expenditure by £774,000. Was the deficit to be covered by extra taxation, or by tampering with his new method for reducing the National Debt? The latter course would at a blow destroy his system. As the consumption of spirits was falling off, he had to increase the income-tax, of course with reluctance. He added a penny to the tax, but he would carry further the exemption of small incomes. When he spoke, £100 a-year was the limit for total exemption. This limit he raised to £150. A deduction of £80 was allowed on incomes of £300. He extended this principle, and allowed a deduction of £120 on all incomes of £400 or less. Thus all incomes below £150 were totally exempt from tax; and incomes from £150 to £400 had £120 taken off. He estimated that the result would be a net receipt of £1,168,000; and, deducting the deficit of £800,000, the surplus would be £368,000.

This Budget, of course, was the Budget of a lean year. "The abounding surplus left by Mr Gladstone in 1874 had become a deficit," says the Liberal historian. What it would have become if Mr Gladstone had stayed in office and abolished the income-tax, doth not now appear. "Expenditure had begun to rise as soon as the Conservative Government came into power." *Why* it had risen has already been shown. The historian speaks of "decreasing trade," which affected the revenue of course. Is there any human being so credulous as to believe that, with the Liberals in office, trade would not have decreased? That, in the succeeding year, war expenses might not have been incurred if Mr Gladstone had been in office, and had managed Eastern affairs wisely, is a very different matter. That belongs to the science of hypothetics, and any one may sincerely believe that matters might have been kept quiet by a sagacious and well-informed policy. But our information came too late.

In 1877, Sir Stafford found his position fairly satisfactory; "not brilliant," but, considering the state of trade, not undeserving of thankfulness. The Supplementary Estimates were almost equalled (within £80,000) by the savings. "We may say that we have a Budget ready-made to our hands." Taxation could not be remitted, but need not be added to. The new Sinking Fund was working satisfactorily: £175,628 more than had been expected was applied to the reduction of the debt. He desired to keep down naval and military expenditure. There was a reduction in the estimates for the Army and Navy. The storms in the East soon called for more expenditure. It was natural for Liberal critics to impute the Eastern dangers to the Government; but foreign affairs, and Sir Stafford's opinions about them, must be reserved for another chapter.

In 1878 the Chancellor of the Exchequer, in his Budget speech, had to consider both the ordinary and the extraordinary expenditure. The vote of credit for £6,000,0000, passed when Russia was at the gates of Constantinople, affected the finance of the year that had gone, and of the year that was coming. The revenue had answered expectations. There was a surplus of £859,803 as regarded ordinary expenditure. The increase on expenditure was £778,268. And why was ordinary expenditure larger? The permanent charge of the debt was £300,000 more than in the preceding year; it had now reached the normal amount of £28,000,000. The Army charge was £186,000 more, the Civil Services were £648,000 more; but there was a reduction of £585,000 in the Navy, and of £170,000 in the Revenue Departments. As to extraordinary expenditure, of the £6,000,000, £3,500,000 had actually been expended. This, on the whole, left a deficit of £2,640,000. The Government had issued Exchequer bonds for £2,750,000, "a debt of a temporary character." The estimates of next year's expenditure and revenue showed a deficiency of £1,560,000. To meet all charges, the income-tax was raised to fivepence, fourpence a-pound was put on tobacco, and the dog-tax was raised from five shillings to seven and sixpence, sheep-dogs being now exempted. Puppies over two months were to have been, but were not included, to meet the case of persons " whose dogs are never more than six months old." " It is much easier to know a puppy under two months than under six."

All this was "a necessarily unpleasant statement." Mr Gladstone said it was "a painful Budget," and disliked the distinction taken between ordinary and extraordinary expenditure in this instance. Mr Parnell propounded a short way to Home Rule—namely, by the Irish boycotting whisky, and so making it not worth while to keep them. The Irish members have it always in their power to set the example of this temperate revolution.

In 1879, the Chancellor was more than commonly aided in his calculations by amateur advisers. He received eighty separate suggestions that cats, photographs, bicycles, and, one may hope, pianos should be taxed. He could not accept any of these suggestions. His estimate of the revenue in the past year had " turned out, on the whole, not far from correct." But no mortal could have foreseen the Zulu war, and the extraordinary expenses which made it impossible to pay off the Exchequer bills of the previous year. The expenditure had exceeded the estimate by nearly four millions and a half. According to the Liberal historian,[1] the expenses of the armament at the time when Russian armies were close to Constantinople, "were regarded as the last war charges the generation would have to endure." Optimists who thought this did not foresee Isandhlwana, nor Afghanistan, nor Majuba (a

---

[1] England under Lord Beaconsfield.

feather in the Liberal cap), nor Alexandria, nor the Soudan, nor a number of other war charges not usually shaded with laurels. But when a nation with a finger in all the wide world's concerns expects to get rid of war charges, the beatitude of "those who expect little" is not likely to be its portion. Plenty of war charges most countries have, and are likely to have, whoever is in office. The year was also one of the gloomiest and most poverty stricken of all lean years. There was a deficiency of £2,291,000 to be added to that of the previous year. Sir Stafford denied that "we are going on entirely by borrowing money, and not paying anything out of taxation." The original £6,000,000 for preparation against Russia would have been paid off in three years, as intended, but for the Zulu war. "In point of fact we have paid off one half, and have prospects of paying off the other half rapidly." As for the deficiencies which actually existed, they might be paid off in whole or part by taxation, or be added to the permanent debt; "or there is another process, we can throw upon another year a portion of the payment." Everything showed that times were hard, even among the well-to-do class, and that additional taxation would be distressing. To add to the permanent debt would be "mischievous and enervating." He preferred the *via media*, "to extend payment of that debt over one year more" (*A laugh*). He thought honourable gentlemen laughed because they at once escaped taxation and could "enjoy the delightful amusement of abusing the Chancellor of the Exchequer." He was not, at all events, putting the new debt out of sight in the bulk of the National Debt. It was kept before our eyes, till we had satisfied ourselves we could pay it.

The circumstances in which this Budget had to be prepared—the general distress and poverty of the country, and the unexpected need of money for an inglorious war—naturally offered Mr Gladstone an opportunity for criticism in the House and out of it. He spoke on April 28, attacking the policy which had led to the expenditure. " Errors of policy have led to a vast expenditure." The nature of these errors—and errors there had undoubtedly been—will be examined in a subsequent chapter. More to the present point is Mr Gladstone's argument, that it was an absolute and primary duty for the Government to meet the expenditure by adequate taxation. The Government had gone annexing about: "Thou hast multiplied the nation, but not increased its joy." The Chancellor of the Exchequer, however, was more concerned, not in wasting the millions, but in the mode and principles on which our finance was conducted. Mr Gladstone thought that, in the last forty years, no man had taken the office of Chancellor of the Exchequer " with as great a capacity for the discharge of its duties on the whole, from his general intelligence, his experience, knowledge, and assiduity combined," as Sir Stafford. But he, in Mr Gladstone's opinion, had wandered further than any " from the well-known traditional and salutary principles of English finance." Sir Stafford was informing the country, which does not read speeches but summaries, that there is a surplus of £1,904,000. Here one cannot but remark on the method of our Government. We are governed by "the country," and not more than one person in a thousand, according to Mr Gladstone, reads more than half-a-dozen lines of summary of speeches in the House. What a brilliant system of political rule! No exact estimate of the expense of the Zulu war could of course be framed, but "a large and a free estimate" should have been taken. Sir Stafford must be the "organ," not the "author" of the methods of the Government. Real financial control on such methods was becoming impossible. As to the distress of the country, where did Sir Stafford learn to regard *that* as a reason "why the public income shall not be made adequate to meet the charge"? As to the *via media*, Sir Stafford had once called it "a financial nostrum."

Sir Stafford defended himself as best he could. He had not shrunk from adding to the income-tax, nor from retaining that addition. His policy was to try to keep the income-tax steady. Very few other sources of taxation were left,—it was wiser to spread large and temporary expenditure over several years than to disturb taxation. As to "financial nostrums," that remark of his referred to another and very different condition of things. "I say, then, that it is perfectly legitimate and reasonable for us to take this course, instead of increasing the burdens of the people at this moment, and putting on them the weight of additional taxation. It would depress the commerce and trade of the country at the very moment when we seek to enliven it." Mr Gladstone himself had spread his expenditure for fortifications over twenty-five years, and had even postponed, in 1860, £1,000,000 of Exchequer bonds. The position of England must be kept up, expenditure or no expenditure, or must be frankly withdrawn from. "Let us close the chapter—as I think the glorious chapter—in the history of England; let us frankly say that we can no longer afford to maintain the attitude which we have hitherto endeavoured to maintain." Or let us pay for it! The attempt to find a *via media* in the Transvaal, for example, has not been a brilliant success.

I have tried to give as brief and lucid an account as possible of the main arguments on either side as to this Budget of 1879. It is not to be denied that it was far from an ideal arrangement, that Mr Gladstone had fair grounds for his criticism. But, on the other hand, the defence was not devoid of spirit and plausibility. The attack can always occupy the ground of the ideals of what might and should be, and so is always theoretically victorious. Mr Gladstone returned to the charge in the 'Nineteenth Century' (August 1879). With a complimentary reference to Mr Spurgeon, he remarked that "the stain of blood may be effaced from our coming, but not from our past, annals." Unluckily, our coming annals, under Mr Gladstone, were to be stained with blood, chiefly our own; and some persons with archaic instincts will add, still unavenged.

The Budget of 1880 was the last that Sir Stafford had to prepare in that period of Conservative rule. It was haunted by the influence of hard times. The estimate of

revenue was disappointed by more than £2,000,000. The
Zulu war had cost more than £5,000,000, a prodigious
sum to expend in a war with a wild people, armed with
stabbing assegais, and muskets with which they could
not shoot straight. The votes of credit had covered the
expenses, and left a balance of £177,000. This was a
grain of comfort. The savings had more than covered
the Supplementary Estimates. "The result, therefore, although it is bad enough, is not so bad as might at first
sight be thought." The Excise showed a huge deficiency
in the usual consumption of spirits and malt. There
was a floating debt of £8,000,000, £6,000,000 of which Sir
Stafford proposed to extinguish by the creation of a terminable annuity, to last till 1885. He was compelled to
appropriate his New Sinking Fund of about £600,000 to
this annuity, and to add to the usual £28,000,000, £800,000
for the next five years, applying that £800,000, with the
other £600,000, to the discharge of these annuities. In
five years the £6,000,000 would thus be paid off. When
the arrangement was complete, he left the Budget with
a surplus of £1,841,000, and he hoped for better times
(March 10, 1880). Mr Gladstone naturally did not repine
over the "immolation of the New Sinking Fund." On
March 15, Sir Stafford denied that he was about to immo-
late his New Sinking Fund—like a Carthaginian prince
sending his first-born through the fire to Moloch. He
only meant to use a portion of it for a particular purpose for a certain number of years. "The Sinking Fund
would go on all the while." He was satisfied that the

arrangement was one of the most reasonable that could be submitted, unless they increased taxation. He repeated that the increased expenditure of his administration was due in great part to the action of the preceding Government, as in the Education Act, and other costly "improvements."

The general election of 1880 ended, of course, Sir Stafford's tenure of office. His apologies failed to satisfy a suffering and ill-contented country, yearning for a change. It is common among early peoples in a similar strait, to kill the king, on a chance of better luck with a new monarch. We changed our Ministry. As for the heavily burdened Chancellor of the Exchequer, perhaps it may be admitted that he made as good a business as might be of an all but impossible task. How to make England stand where she did, without burdening a people which declines to be burdened, was the problem, a problem beyond human adroitness to achieve with complete success. The topic can scarcely be handled with good fortune, so embroiled it is in technical detail, and so lost in wildernesses of figures.

CHAPTER XIV.

THE TROUBLES IN THE EAST.

FOREIGN POLITICS—A NOTE OF SIR STAFFORD'S ON EASTERN AFFAIRS — THE MASSACRES IN BULGARIA — MR DISRAELI'S SPEECH — "WHAT IS THERE TO LAUGH AT?" — BESIKA BAY — CONVERSATION WITH MR BRIGHT — LORD DERBY'S RESIGNATION—SIR STAFFORD'S THEORY—RUSSIAN PROMISES —RUSSIA AT CONSTANTINOPLE—A BLUNDER IN A TELEGRAM —THE SECRET AGREEMENT—ENGLISH SENTIMENT—ANECDOTE OF PIGS AND TRUFFLES — SIR STAFFORD'S SPEECHES —BERLIN, RUSSIA, AND CABUL—SIR STAFFORD'S DEFENCE OF HIS CONSISTENCY—THE TRANSVAAL.

THE whole business of the Chancellor of the Exchequer had been thwarted by the course of foreign politics. Even more than most men the steward of English economy has need to pray for "peace in our time." But peace was not granted to us, and Sir Stafford's own views of the famous Eastern troubles of 1875-78, his own share in what was done and said, are matters of high importance in his biography. As it chances, he drew up "Some Notes on the Foreign Policy of the late Government," chiefly referring to the affairs of Turkey and Russia, shortly after leaving office in 1880.　Nothing can be more fair than to let him tell his own story, with such omissions, where others still living are concerned, and such notes as may be desirable or necessary.　It is unfortunate that the whole of the piece cannot be given to the world.　But every one knows how impossible it is to produce a version of oral discussions in which all persons concerned will agree; and this reason, not to mention the etiquette which protects, or should protect, Cabinet Councils, must reduce a most valuable document to fragments.

In this Note, which we are reluctantly compelled to mutilate, Sir Stafford writes:—

"I have no thought of making an elaborate exposition of the foreign policy of Lord Beaconsfield's Administration, but I wish to preserve a few things which were not generally known, or which may easily be forgotten or misrepresented.　Writing without the various memoranda before me, and after the lapse of three or four years, I may easily myself have forgotten some points; but I will try to put my recollections into shape.

"The troubles in the east of Europe began with the Herzegovinese insurrection in 1875.　Little notice was taken of this insurrection at the outset.　We were abroad for some weeks in the autumn, and the only reference to the matter which I can recall was in a paragraph in the 'Figaro,' in which the writer describes the Parisians as wondering whether *la Herzegovine* was the name of a new ballet-dancer or of a musical instrument invented by Herz.

"As the autumn advanced, and the inability of the Porte to suppress the disturbances became more and more apparent, our attention was naturally aroused. At length the Andrassy Note was drawn up, and our concurrence was requested."[1]

"We were unanimously in favour of adhering to the Note. Parliament subsequently approved our course, Lord Granville and Lord Hartington seeming a little jealous of our following the lead of Austria, and putting in a word on behalf of the 'independence of the Ottoman Empire,' Gladstone, on the other hand, cordially approving our acting with the other Powers, and expressing his hope that we were going seriously to press for Turkish reforms. I remember Disraeli's wondering what he meant by his rather curious speech, which at the moment seemed somewhat uncalled for; but it is worth looking back to as containing the germ of much that he has said since."[2]

"In the month of May the three Powers proceeded a

---

[1] In the Andrassy Note of Dec. 30, 1875, Austria, Germany, and Russia demanded that the Porte should grant promised reforms, hinted at further complications in Servia and Montenegro, and urged collective European action.

[2] Mr Gladstone, in his speech of Feb. 8, 1876, had said, "Europe, the Christian conscience, and the conscience of mankind, will expect some other sort of security for great and dreadful grievance than mere words can afford ; and however desirous we may be to maintain the integrity and independence of the Turkish Empire, that integrity and independence can never be maintained effectually unless it can be proved to the world, —and proved not by words but by acts,—that the Government of Turkey has the power to administer a fair measure of justice to all its subjects alike, whether Christians or Mohammedan."

step further, and drew up the celebrated Berlin Note, or, as it was afterwards called, the Berlin Memorandum. It was presented for acceptance to the Governments of England, France, and Italy, and an answer was requested by return of post. France and Italy agreed at once."

The Memorandum advocated a two months' armistice in Herzegovina, negotiations for peace, a mixed Commission to distribute aid, Christians and Turks to keep their arms, consuls and delegates of the Powers to watch over the promised reforms and the return of refugees to their homes.

Sir Stafford next states, at some length, the reasons which induced the Government not to adhere to the Berlin Memorandum :—

"It seemed to demand impossibilities, and was not in our judgment well qualified to attain its object. We therefore declined to make ourselves responsible for it; but we intimated that we should not offer any objection to the other Powers proceeding upon its lines without us. We have been much blamed for contenting ourselves with the rejection of the Note, without proposing any alternative course of action. I remember feeling at the time that we ought to make some alternative proposal."

Sir Stafford Northcote then describes his own scheme, and the assent and dissent which it provoked; but this is not matter for publication. He goes on :—

"But the revolution which soon after took place at Constantinople [1] seemed to change the whole face of things,

---

[1] It ended in the murder of the Sultan.

and we began to hope that all would go well. The action of England had produced a good effect abroad, and it seemed probable that our influence with the new Government of Turkey might lead to considerable improvements in her administration. The Berlin Memorandum was laid aside, and, if peace could be maintained, time might bring about a better state of things.

"The principal dangers to be guarded against were an attack upon Turkey by Russia alone, or by Russia and Austria conjointly, or a war between Turkey and Servia and Montenegro. There seemed no real ground for apprehending the former contingency, after the stand which England had shown her readiness to make. As to a war with Servia, it was pretty sure to end in her defeat, if she were not secretly supported by a stronger Power. The great object was, therefore, to bring the influence of the Powers to bear on Servia to induce her to keep the peace. And this it seemed probable that we should have effected, if it had not been for the lamentable 'Bulgarian atrocities,' and their *contre-coup* in the English agitation."

The Bulgarian atrocities were committed throughout May. The 'Daily News' published a letter on them from Constantinople, on June 23; Servia declared war on July 1.

"It was undoubtedly most unfortunate that . . . we were kept in almost entire ignorance until the public were startled by the horrible accounts given in the 'Daily News'; and we were at first disposed to believe that these accounts were monstrously exaggerated. The Prime

Minister, when questioned about them, meant to say nothing more than that he could not believe them; but very unfortunately the House caught up an expression which he rather carelessly made use of, and laughed as if he had said a good thing, thus giving the public an impression that he treated these horrors lightly. I was sitting next him at the time he spoke, and heard him say to himself rather angrily, 'What is there to laugh at?'"

The reference is probably to Mr Disraeli's reply on June 28, or to that of July 10: "Oriental people seldom resort to torture, but generally terminate their connection with culprits in a more expeditious way." The whole speech is at variance with the flippancy of this one unhappy expression, which, indeed, was tacitly apologised for by what followed.

"Gladstone was not in the House, I think, when the last discussion on this subject took place — on Evelyn Ashley's motion. It would have been better if he had been, and if he had made his attack where it could have been properly answered. He took the unfortunate course of a violent extra-parliamentary series of pamphlets and speeches, denouncing the conduct of the Government in the most outrageous and exaggerated manner. Answers were given; but they were of no avail, because they could not be given face to face, and it was easy to ignore them. The mischief done in England, indeed, was not very great. The public knew what this sort of party declaration was worth; and they were perfectly aware that the Conservatives and the Government were just as indignant with the Turkish Government as Mr Gladstone and the Radicals. They understood, too, that the action of the Government in sending the fleet to Besika Bay (June 1878) was not an indication of our intention to support the Turks in the commission of any barbarities, but was a step taken to prevent the possible 'ugly rush' which it was thought that Russia might make to Constantinople, and against which no other Power could be relied on to make a stand if England did not. But abroad a different effect was produced. The Russophil party believed, or professed to believe, that Mr Gladstone and the Liberals had made up their minds to join in, or to facilitate the overthrow of the Turk, and that they were on the point of carrying England with them, upsetting the Conservative Government, and giving the hand to the Russian emancipators of the oppressed Christians. The Turks, on the other hand, were undoubtedly led to believe that the Conservatives were their friends in the sense in which Mr Gladstone and his satellites declared them to be; and that, deny it as we might, lecture them as we pleased, it was certain that in the last resort we should be found ready to fight for them. Both parties, therefore, were for urging matters to extremity,—the Russophils hoping that, if a war broke out, the Conservative Government would be overthrown, and that England would come forward on the side of the insurgents; the Turkophils hoping that the Conservatives would carry the day, and that, if they did so, England would be found on the side of the Porte. Agents of the English Liberal press were actively employed, I believe, in stirring up the Servians, just as the Russian Slavophils were doing; and they succeeded but too well in precipitating the conflict, which the Cabinets of all the nations concerned were most anxious to avert.

"I remember a curious little conversation which I had this autumn with Mr Bright, whom I met in a railway carriage. He argued that we had no business to mix ourselves up in quarrels 3000 miles away, with which we had no concern. There would be horrors and sufferings, no doubt, if the struggle which we were endeavouring to avert took place, but we should do no good by interfering, and had better let the 'natural forces' work of themselves. I said, 'Yes; but what were we to call the "natural forces"? Was Austria, for instance, to be regarded as a "natural force"?' 'Certainly not,' he said; 'if we do not interfere ourselves, we must not let others interfere.' 'But how are we to prevent them?' said I. 'Oh!' said he, 'I suppose Russia is the greatest Power by land, and you are the greatest Power by sea; so if you came to an agreement with her, you could between you warn off everybody else.' 'And keep the ring?' I said. 'Yes,' said he. This was rather a foreshadowing of the 'hands off' policy.

"It cannot be denied that there were real though suppressed differences of opinion and feeling among the members of the Cabinet with regard to our Eastern policy. In private conversation Mr Disraeli gave a humorous account of the six parties in the Cabinet. 'The first party is that which is for immediate war with Russia;

the second party is for war to save Constantinople; the third party is the party of Peace at any Price; the fourth party would let the Russians take Constantinople, and would then turn them out; the fifth party desires to plant the cross on the dome of St Sophia; and then there are the Prime Minister and the Chancellor of the Exchequer, who desire to see something done, but don't exactly know what.'

"We could not stand by," Sir Stafford goes on, "and see Russia take possession of Constantinople. But how were we to prevent her? We could not join Turkey, for that would be to encourage her to persevere in her system of misgovernment, and we should be left saddled with the responsibility of either upholding what we most thoroughly condemned and abhorred, or of compelling the Porte to mend its ways, a task somewhat more than impossible for us to perform. We had also before our eyes the continual fear that Turkey might, after all, throw herself into the arms of Russia, perhaps invite Russian troops to Constantinople, and adopt an 'Unkiar Skelessi' policy."

Here Sir Stafford discusses the military position and strength of England, in case, for example, Gallipoli should be threatened. He expresses his regret that "Gladstone gave up Corfu, which would have been invaluable," and he hints at a pet plan of his own for buying an island dear to archæologists. Doubtless those desires led to the purpose of acquiring Cyprus.

He now turns to the famous incident of Lord Derby's resignation and revelations.

"It will be remembered that Lord Derby stated in the House of Lords that when he left the Government we had decided on a buccaneering expedition for the purpose of seizing some Turkish territory, and that Lord Salisbury very pointedly contradicted him on the authority not only of his own memory, but of the memories of several of his colleagues."

Lord Derby announced his resignation in the House of Lords, March 28, 1878. He "gave those with whom he had acted entire credit for desiring as much as he desired the maintenance of the peace of Europe, . . . but in the measures which they propose I have not been able to concur." On March 29, Sir Stafford, answering Lord Hartington, said that "when the resolution to call out the Reserves had been taken, Lord Derby dissented from it, and felt obliged to tender his resignation." On April 8, Lord Derby told the House of Lords that this calling out the Reserves "was not the sole, nor indeed the principal reason" for the difference between himself and his late colleagues. "What the other reasons are I cannot divulge, until the propositions of the Government, from which I dissented, are made known." On July 18, Lord Derby, in the House of Lords, said that he had quitted the Cabinet because "the island of Cyprus, together with a point on the Syrian coast, were to have been seized by a secret naval expedition sent out from England, with or without the consent of the Sultan."[1] Lord Salisbury denied that the account of this resolution

[1] Hansard, ccxli. 1793.

of the Cabinet was "true," as far as his own memory went, or "correct." Withdrawing the expression "true," he solemnly repeated, in the name of his colleagues, that Lord Derby's statement was not "correct," though, of course, it was only the accuracy of Lord Derby's memory, not his veracity, which Lord Salisbury impugned.

On this Sir Stafford writes: "Lord Salisbury was quite justified in his contradiction; but I have no doubt that Lord Derby gave correctly his own impression of what had passed. The Cabinet to which he referred was the last which he attended. It was at a moment of extreme anxiety, when the Russians appeared to be advancing on Constantinople, and when we had some reason to apprehend a still more inconvenient advance to the coast of Asia Minor, where they might seize points which would threaten the Suez Canal and the Euphrates Valley, and so intercept our communications with India."

Sir Stafford here gives his own version of what occurred at the Cabinet Council after which Lord Derby resigned. Certain proposals, concerning which his memory was rather indefinite, were made, he says, and "the matter was then laid aside." The question of calling out the Reserves was then mooted, as Lord Derby himself informed the House of Lords. In Sir Stafford's opinion, Lord Derby having made up his mind to resign, failed perfectly to distinguish between a *conversation* about certain undecided points, and a *decision* about another point, the Reserves. Perhaps this private and personal view of Sir Stafford's may fairly be given for what it is worth.

We now reach an explanation of his own conduct in
a matter where he incurred some blame, and where a
politician less transparently candid might have incurred
more.

"Salisbury had taken the Foreign Office, and his
'happy despatch,' as it was called, reviewing the situation of affairs as left by the Treaty of San Stefano, had
produced a great effect both at home and abroad. It
looked as though we might now hope to bring about a
fair and free conference without any more military demonstrations. The Easter recess was approaching, and it
was becoming necessary to fix the length of the holidays.
As Parliament had met on the 18th January, and Easter
did not fall until the 21st April, it was reasonable that
we should have a longer recess than usual, and it had
been long understood that it should be so; but there was
some uneasiness in the public mind, and many rumours
were afloat as to possible surprises, which caused some
of the Opposition to question me very closely as to its
being safe for the House to adjourn for so long a period.
I felt myself entitled to hold the most reassuring language," for which he assigns excellent reasons.[1]

"I gave my answer in the House in a tone which I
could not have adopted had I thought the Indian troops
were to be moved. Unfortunately, public arrangements
were being made for the immediate formation of a *corps
d'armée* for embarkation before the monsoon. These steps
were instantly telegraphed to England, and on the morn-

----

[1] Hansard, vol. ccxxxix. 1391, 1392.

ing after the adjournment they appeared in all our newspapers. The Duke of Richmond and I were in the train
together, I going to Osborne and he to Goodwood; we
bought the 'Times' at the station, and there, to the
amazement of us both, we read what was going on. It
was a great annoyance to me, for I felt that I should be
accused of disingenuousness; had the troops been sent
to any foreign country, which I daresay some would have
liked, I should have felt myself in a great difficulty." [1]

Sir Stafford now describes the internal difficulties and
dissensions of the Cabinet, which became sufficiently well
understood in the course of events. The position was
critical; Russia was almost at the gates of Constantinople. Her assurances about occupying Constantinople
only if absolutely necessary, and not for military honour,
were not exactly calculated to inspire confidence. In
war, as in love,

> "The strongest oaths are straw
> To the fire in the blood."

The nature of the terms of peace was not known, and
arrangements for armistice were delayed. As to the indemnity to be exacted by Russia, Sir Stafford has been
accused of "strange forgetfulness." On the 30th July
the Czar had told Colonel Wellesley to tell the British
Government that he would annex nothing but a portion of
Bessarabia, and another of Armenia, and the same promise had been made by the Russian Chancellor to our Min-

----

[1] See Hansard, ccxxxix. 1421.

ister at St Petersburg. Sir Stafford was aware of all this, and he is charged with "forgetfulness" because, on January 28, he had professed not to know what Russia's exactions of territorial indemnity might turn out to be. He is said to have "forgotten" these Russian promises. But, in such summary of the intended terms of peace as he had before him when he spoke, it was written, "Indemnity to Russia, in a pecuniary, territorial, or other form, *to be decided hereafter.*"[1] This was a clause which *donne furieusement à penser.* Could a statesman regard its vagueness as a guarantee that circumstances had not altered cases and old promises? At all events, the situation of affairs was most anxious, and it was desired to send the fleet to the Dardanelles. Then followed the wonderful confusion which Sir Stafford thus describes :—

"In the midst of these anxieties came the extraordinary telegram in which Layard announced that the terms or bases of peace had been agreed to, and that the last of them was that the question of the Straits should be settled between 'the Congress and the Emperor of Russia.' This fell amongst us like a bombshell. Our justification for sending up the fleet was, that we feared that a private arrangement would be made about the Straits between the Turks and the Russians, to the exclusion and the detriment of other Powers, and here were the Russian terms of peace, by which this question was to be reserved to be settled by a Congress! What could we say to justify

[1] Hansard, ccxxxvii. 540.

ourselves?   And how much would not the difficulty of
the situation be increased by the emphatic dissent and
resignation of Lord Derby?   After a little hasty consultation with those of our colleagues who were in the House
of Commons, I went up to Downing Street, taking Smith
with me.   We found Lord Beaconsfield in bed, but quite
able to talk the matter over with us.   The result was that
we agreed to stop Admiral Hornby before he entered the
Dardanelles, where he had been led to expect that he
might find orders.   Smith despatched an Admiralty telegram at once.   It was not in time to stop the fleet, but it
brought it back again to the entrance of the Strait.   Looking back, I think this was the greatest mistake we made
in the whole business: but at the moment we were all
agreed on it.   The next day came a correction of the telegram: it was not between the Emperor and the Congress
that question of the Straits was to be settled, but between the Emperor and the Sultan!   How we gnashed
our teeth!

"Lord Derby's first resignation was withdrawn, the
breach was patched up, but 'quod semel excidit'[1] does
not generally admit of being replaced, and there was no
very real cordiality during the remainder of Derby's administration.   The Russians kept up the anxiety which
had led us to call for the vote of credit, and we found
ourselves obliged to make more use of the money than
we had intended.   At length came the question of the
Reserves, and of the sending up the fleet to the Bosphorus,

___

[1] Quotation from Horace, Odes, iii. 5. 30.

and the movement of the Indian troops; and so Derby finally departed from us. Salisbury sprang into the saddle, and at once produced his celebrated despatch (April 2, 1878). Nothing could be more successful, and both at home and abroad it produced a marked impression.

"Nothing could exceed the immediate success of the new despatch, so far as applause went; but after a little while people began to ask what was to come of it. The object of all parties was to bring about a Congress which should establish a peace: the difficulty was to settle what questions were to be submitted to it. England was anxious that it should decide all matters that might be brought forward touching, or growing out of, the new arrangements that must be made for Turkey, excepting only such questions as were purely matter of concern for the two belligerents alone—such, for instance, as exchanges of prisoners and the like. Russia claimed the right of settling with Turkey alone all questions whatever, except such as she herself might allow to be of European concern. It was difficult to find a *mezzo termine* between these conflicting pretensions, and it still seemed doubtful whether a Congress could be brought about; while, if it should fail, the prospect of maintaining peace was very cloudy."

Sir Stafford now describes the reasons which made Lord Salisbury think it desirable to come to a separate and secret understanding with Count Schouvaloff. Without such understanding the Congress would never have taken place. "There was nothing discreditable in it; but there is no doubt that its disclosure, at the moment when that disclosure took place, was extremely embarrassing, the Prime Minister and Foreign Secretary having both left England."

The fragments which have been quoted may serve to explain Sir Stafford's own conduct and attitude on certain occasions. As to the whole phase of the Eastern question, which puzzled politicians and divided society in 1876-78, Sir Stafford's opinions were calm, just, and statesmanlike. Even the most excited friends of the oriental Christians could scarcely accuse *him* of "sympathising with the oppressors." Like any English statesman in office, he was compelled to see that the question was not simple, was not to be settled off-hand by kindly sympathy and sentiment. The Turks had behaved abominably; the Christians had been mercilessly treated—granted, but what was to be done? In the autumn of 1876 he had to speak on the subject in Edinburgh, and he uttered the daring truism (for in England a truism may be daring) that, as to foreign policy, "the people of this country, as a rule, do not understand it." They see a wrong done; they cry out to have it righted. How, by whom, and what next? These are questions too distant and refined. Our sympathies in a foreign war may be summed up shortly—some of us cry, "Go it, the little 'un"; some of us, like the landlord in 'Martin Chuzzlewit,' are on "the gentlemanly side"—the standard of "gentlemanliness" being eccentric; some of us, more generously, are partisans of the injured or the defeated. In his own words, Sir

Stafford told these truths to the people of Edinburgh, assuring them that the policy of the Government was the attainment of honourable peace. But at that hour most of the people who now (1890) cry out against co-ercing Ireland were crying out in favour of coercing Turkey. Sir Stafford declared that his party desired peace and the good government "of all nations." It was a question of means, not of ends, how these results were to be secured. At Nostell Priory (September 26) he tried to make his audience understand the outlines of the East-ern question, the complications. "You must study the question carefully, and you must not take short cuts to your ends, and think that by denouncing the Turks and the Turkish power you have done all that has to be done." At Bristol (13th November 1876), he denied that Ministers only exist to do the bidding of the noisiest agitators, in place of following the bidding of their consciences. "Let that doctrine creep in, and good-bye to our liberty." In his private correspondence he remarks, "We may escape war, and I am anti-jingo enough to go strongly for any-thing that will keep us out of it." "The Eastern ques-tion," he writes to a private correspondent, "is not to be solved by such simple phrases as *turning the Turks out of Europe.* How are you going to make them go?" Indeed, this sort goeth not out pleasantly. "Have you estimated the amount of human suffering that you must cause in the process? I say nothing as to the horrors of a general war, which may very easily be provoked by a false step; but looking to the position of the Christians in Turkey itself, do you think nothing of the calamities you may bring upon them, by arousing the fanaticism of the Moslem, and that, too, a fanaticism of despair?"

In another private letter to Sir Thomas Farrer (October 18, 1876), Sir Stafford remarks: "We are bound by every consideration of honour and policy to do what we can, whether it be little or much. Of the two courses between which, broadly speaking, the choice lies, one is easy enough—the promoting a general unsettlement and conflict of forces, in the hope of its resulting in some settlement of some kind. I mean that if we decided on this course, we should not have the smallest difficulty in bringing about the conflict; whether the settlement would come out of it is another question. The other course is far more embarrassing, how to get a settlement without a conflict, and it at once leads us to two divergent paths, one of which lies in the direction of European constitution - making for Turkey, and the other in that of calling on Turkey to make a better constitution for herself. I am greatly averse from the former alternative, believing that we shall simply make a messier mess than the present, and involve ourselves in great responsibilities without any adequate corresponding advantages. The latter seems to me more reasonable in itself. . . . We might criticise Turkey's proposals, and even offer suggestions, but we must leave the responsibility of making her constitution with herself. If everybody was disposed to give everybody fair play, this might answer. But our atrocitarians will denounce such proposals here, and the intriguers would do their best to make every constitution unworkable, so that fair play would be unattainable."

These selections from letters have been made to show the attitude of Sir Stafford at that unhappy crisis when England, as usual, was so divided. Many of us were in that old Puritan frame of mind, which could be satisfied with little less than the hewing piecemeal of the abominable Turk before the Lord. Not only had every humane feeling been hurt, but we felt a sense of national dishonour. But for England, Turkey would long ago, in all probability, have been free of pashas and Bashi-Bazouks. Mixed with this not unnatural nor unworthy sentiment appeared more party excitement than was creditable. In a letter from a lady to Sir Stafford I find her saying, " —— " (a versatile and prominent Liberal leader) "writes that he had no idea the Bulgarian atrocities would turn out such a clipper." *Turn out such a clipper!* is this a generous or a philanthropic sentiment ? We were hurried along then, by feelings good and bad, and many did not pause on such reflections as Sir Stafford suggests. If we had helped to " coerce " Turkey, and if Turkey, declining to be coerced, had preferred to go down with the Crescent flying, and to blow up the magazine ! little would philanthropy have gained by that, and the odds are long that, when Turkey sank, others would have been dragged down in the vortex. On the other hand, there was an unintelligent and braggadocio ferocity in the contemporary Turcophile, which disgusted a sober mind with our old ally and with his new partisans. It appears that Sir Stafford, who of all men could least be said to sympathise with atrocity, had no private wish, and aimed at no policy but that which would secure the maximum of reform with the minimum of disturbance and conflict. But conflict became inevitable. Whether a different policy on the part of England would or would not have evaded it, can only be called a problem in historical hypothetics. Russia was victorious, and with her victory came new dangers, not unforeseen. The present Sir Stafford Northcote tells us that a Russian gentleman of distinction once dined with Sir Stafford in the heat of the discussions about Constantinople. Whether he had drunk "in Scythian fashion" or not, he became very loud in abuse of England. Sir Stafford listened in silence till he said, "You English are like the pigs which hunt in dirt for truffles." "Say rather, monsieur," remarked Sir Stafford, "the dogs which drive the pigs away." The other filled his glass, put it down untasted, and said, "I have spoken too much."

What Sir Stafford thought and said elsewhere exactly corresponded to the line he took in Parliament. It is not possible, of course, to publish again all his remarks in the many debates of 1877-78. A very brief summary must suffice. He constantly resisted the attempt to saddle his party with a desire to make war for Turkey, or to encourage Turkey.[1] He reiterated that, from the beginning, the Government had asked Turkey to show energy, not in "stamping out" the insurrection, but by "manfully grappling with its real causes." He denounced the habit of

---

[1] February 8, 1877.   Hansard, ccxxxiii. 97.

"emphasising everything that can tell against your own country." The Government believed as thoroughly as Mr Gladstone himself in the necessity for reform in Turkish rule. They had used "the strongest pressure short of coercion." He put no faith at all in Turkish promises and paper constitutions. "Constitutions are the growth of centuries:" "it is ridiculous to suppose that the mere proclamation of a constitution, without guarantee that it will be properly administered, could produce any sensible results." As to "British interests," he spoke of them "in the broadest and highest sense," that of "honourable peace."

He denied that Lord Salisbury had pursued a private policy, apart from his instructions, at Constantinople. Again and again, later, he denied that the interests of England were opposed to the interests of humanity; that the Government preached "a gospel of selfishness." Government would go all lengths, short of threatening Turkey with war. They would not threaten, and then refuse to act. Such a policy would ruin any chance of what is called moral coercion, and true coercion "was not very far from meaning destruction."[1] His policy was strict neutrality. His conduct in the anxious weeks when Russian forces were almost within striking distance of Constantinople, has already been described. He maintained, with reference to our need of the vote for six millions, "that no one will be listened to unless he is strong."[2]

Reduced to its briefest and plainest expression, this is the sum of Sir Stafford's opinions and policy during a

---

[1] Hansard, ccxxxiii. 468.   [2] Hansard, ccxxxvii. 558.

bewildering and exciting series of events. Even his opponents could hardly reckon him among the amateurs of oppression ; and the charges of want of candour, in his answers in the House of Commons, which were brought against him, have been dealt with by himself.

There was very much more trouble and anxiety to follow. On the glorious advent of Peace with Honour from Berlin, it might have been hoped, it was hoped, that they would abide unwinged among us. But Russia had her revenge, and our Indian troops had scarcely gone back from Malta, when her Mission set forth and was received at Cabul. The whole tragedy of error that ensued cannot be unfolded here. We, too, must have our Mission at Cabul : its advance was resisted ; we forced our way by arms, and took the usual military steps towards making Afghanistan friendly and independent. Here we are only concerned with Sir Stafford Northcote's part in the unhappy business. He was well known as a believer in Lord Lawrence's policy, not a forward, but a backward style of defence. When he, then, remained a member of a Government whose style ,was emphatically forward, he might be charged, and was charged, with inconsistency.

On August 15, after questions as to the proposed Mission to Cabul had been asked by Sir Charles Dilke and others, Sir Stafford explained that the Ameer did not invite the Mission, but that a communication about it would be made to him by the Indian Government. He added that we did not ask for what we had never possessed, a European agent at Cabul. Parliament broke up ; negotiations and delays occurred on the Indian frontier ; Sir Neville Chamberlain, with a numerous armed Mission, set out from Peshawur on September 21, and Major Cavagnari was refused leave to pass the fort of Ali Musjid. The Mission returned to Peshawur. The rebuff of the barbarians excited many observers in India and at home. There were explanations, demands for apology, talk about a new scientific frontier, and India was reported to be in the state of Mr Mantalini's countess: "She has no outline, or if she has, it is a demmed outline." Afghanistan was invaded, and Parliament met on December 5.

From a letter of September 30, to an official colleague, it is clear that Sir Stafford, at that moment, had grave doubts as to the policy of Lord Lytton in India. The Ameer's conduct, he thought, "if not a breach of engagement" (in receiving the Russian embassy), "may be a virtual repudiation of the old state of our relations, and may justify and require a new departure on our part, and this I think it does. Only I think we should be well informed at the outset what the new policy is to be." In a later letter (October 2) he says: " The old policy used to be, to keep Afghanistan strong and independent, not to interfere with its internal affairs, not to annex or occupy any of its territories, but to cultivate friendly relations with its *ex officio* ruler, . . . and to obviate the danger of internal conflicts." As to the new policy, he says, " It may be right, or it may be inevitable, but we ought to know how far it is to be carried."

To a lay looker-on, it seems as if Russia had out-man-
œuvred us. If Cabul accepted a Mission from her, not
from us, where was our prestige? The word is unlucky,
but it does express that kind of influence of belief in her
by which England has governed India. Object as we may
to the word, or to what it implies, the fact is undeniable.
If, on the other hand, we bullied the Ameer, or put him
in such a position that he, too, must lose *his* prestige
among his own people, we were at once involved in all
that our enemies could desire for us. There may have
been a middle course; it may have been possible to turn
on our own side, and to our own profit, the oriental system
of delays. Experts may discuss this. As things fell out,
we took the second course, by affronting the Ameer, of
which we soon felt all the disadvantages and discredits.
The Liberal party, when Parliament met, maintained that
the Ameer had been misrepresented and ill treated, while
our old policy as to Afghanistan had been reversed. The
details are vast and complicated, and it is no part of our
business to defend or arraign either the Government or
Lord Lytton. Sir Stafford Northcote's own speech mainly
concerns us where it offers a defence of his own conduct
(December 13, 1878). He maintained that, after the incident of Ali Musjid, the Ameer had been given "ample
opportunity of recalling and apologising for his conduct,"
and that, as he did not apologise, the Government had no
alternative. "We could not have remained inactive." He
defended himself against the charge of "having turned
round," and after being known as an advocate of one

policy, embracing another. He rested his case on letters of Lord Lawrence, written to himself when he was Secretary for India. These letters gave Lord Lawrence's policy. He had agreed with it then, he agreed with it still, for Lord Lawrence had said it was "one thing to leave the Afghans to fight their own battles, and quite another to stand by in the same attitude while others are interfering." And Sir Stafford had, even then, recorded his opinion that if Shere Ali tampered with the Persians about Herat, we might give aid to his rival. Others were now interfering, by the Russian Mission, in Afghanistan. Circumstances had altered, and his mind had changed with them.

Again, Lord Lawrence thought we should await a Russian move on our own frontier. Yes; but in 1866 Russia had been far more remote from Afghanistan than she was in 1878. When a Russian Mission went to Cabul, avowedly because Russia and England were unfriendly, and Cabul was a vulnerable point, then, "the circumstances on which Lord Lawrence based his policy of not advancing were completely revolutionised." Thus there was, in his own conduct, "no inconsistency whatever." We defeated the Ameer, he died, we appointed Yakoob as Ameer, we got a new frontier, we were to be masters of Afghan foreign policy, we were to support the Ameer against foreign foes, and we were to have a British resident at Cabul. All this policy, Sir Stafford said, "was forced on us" (August 14, 1879). In three weeks the resident, Sir Louis Cavagnari, with the gallant Hamilton, had been massacred. Cabul was recaptured, the murderers were punished, but General Roberts was forced into the Sherpur cantonments, and Christmas came before he was relieved. In all this affair the unhappy Ameer deserved our regrets, the Russians, our disinterested congratulations; and as for the Government, it is easy to blame them, or commiserate with them, but hard to say what they should have done. It does seem as if, in these three troubles—the Bulgarian atrocities, the war with the Ameer, and the Zulu war—the Government was ill served abroad, and had its hand forced into directions not approved of by its judgment.

They were not more fortunate in that grave of men and of reputations, South Africa. In 1877 we had annexed the Transvaal, which "was drifting into anarchy, was bankrupt, and was about to be destroyed by native tribes."[1] According to Sir T. Shepstone, "most thinking men" were in favour of the annexation, but Sir Theophilus did not say that most Boers were. The annexation appears at least to have prevented Cetywayo from washing his spears, or trying to wash them, in the blood of Boers. It was in other blood that he performed this part of Zulu coronation ritual.[2] We annexed the Transvaal, its 40,000 white people, and its million of black people —unregarded dusky million—whom we took "for ever," and deserted in a few years. Cetywayo declared that he viewed the annexation with pleasure, though he re-

---

[1] Cetywayo and his White Neighbours. H. Rider Haggard, p. 117.
[2] *Op. cit.*, 119, 120.

gretted the neglect of that ceremony with the spears. Then came a difficulty about the Boer and Zulu marches. We took the side of the Boers. Sir Bartle Frere came on the scene, and bade Cetywayo disband his army. He refused. We invaded Zululand, and every one knows what followed.

As to all these disasters, when Lord Hartington asked who is to be held responsible, Sir Stafford replied, "Her Majesty's Government" (March 31, 1879). "We do not cast the responsibility upon our agents." They stood between Sir Bartle Frere and the sentence of Parliament. The Government itself censured Sir Bartle Frere, but did not withdraw its confidence. He denied that Sir Bartle had throughout, in his negotiations, been deliberately working for a Zulu war. He gave a history of all that led to the Zulu war, and really this history seems a very strong condemnation of Sir Bartle's conduct, especially of his extraordinary ultimatum to the Zulus. The history is of most interest as expressing Sir Stafford's theory of the Transvaal annexation, as a measure taken in the cause of peace, and "to stop any future wars with the Zulus, and other native tribes." If the Government censured and dismissed Sir Bartle, what then? What was their next step to be? Where was a Liberal policy, except Mr Courtney's policy, "Abandon confederation, and withdraw from the Transvaal"? That, Sir Stafford thought, would, or might, involve our withdrawing from South Africa as an Imperial Power. The wish of the Government now was to break up the Zulu military system, while leaving them the power of protecting themselves against native tribes. But, one fancies, the Amaboona (the Boers) were the only "tribe" from whom they needed protection.

In all this miserable business it is easy to criticise. Perhaps a really powerful nation would have simply enlisted the Zulus as its gladiators, and held South Africa with them. As it chances, we rescued the Boers from their assegais, only to "perish by the people we have made," only to ruin the finest natural soldiers in the world, and to give the world a typical proof of our inability to discharge imperial tasks. The Zulus were hardly overthrown before the Boers, now safe on that side, began to show their teeth. But the Boers were left to be dealt with by Mr Gladstone's Government.

CHAPTER XV.

SIR STAFFORD NORTHCOTE AS A PARLIAMENTARY LEADER.

ACCESSION TO LEADERSHIP—STATE OF POLITICS—HISTORY OF OBSTRUCTION—SIR STAFFORD AND THE *CLÔTURE*—MR BRADLAUGH'S AFFAIR—THE FOURTH PARTY—GENERAL CRITICISM OF SIR STAFFORD AS A LEADER.

THE two previous chapters, reviewing Sir Stafford's conduct as Chancellor of the Exchequer and in foreign affairs, do not deal with his other work as leader of his party in the House of Commons, both before and after the Liberal victory of 1880. To that topic we now address ourselves.

Sir Stafford Northcote entered upon his duties as leader of the House of Commons on the 8th February 1877, when the Parliament of 1874 met for its fourth session. On the 6th July 1885, he took his seat in the House of Lords as Earl of Iddesleigh and Viscount St Cyres. For eight sessions and a half he led the Conservative party continuously in the Lower House.

When Sir Stafford Northcote, at the end of the session of 1876, quietly succeeded Mr Disraeli, who had been created Earl of Beaconsfield immediately after the prorogation, he undertook in 1877 a task of much difficulty. A House of Commons elected in quiet times as a protest against over-legislation had been guided and amused for three years by a consummate master of tact and tactics. Lord Beaconsfield was depicted in 1852 by a contemporary poetaster as

> " Astute, sagacious, wary, stern,
>   Making the puzzled Commons fear
>   The measured passion of his scorn,
>   The icy glitter of his sneer."

But from 1874 to 1876 general good-humour prevailed in the political world, and Mr Disraeli had no occasion to be stern or icy.   He could afford to express sentimental regret for the infrequent attendance and sudden resignation of Mr Gladstone, to patronise the efforts of Lord Hartington, and to pour a flood of delicious banter over the luckless head of Dr Kenealy.   It was in the summer of 1876 that the first mutterings of the great storm from the East were heard; and when Parliament met in 1877, both sides of the House were swayed by the excitement of a keen and bitter agitation, which grew more intense during the next two years, and only ended, if end it ever did, with the general election of 1880.

The period of Sir Stafford Northcote's leadership may conveniently be divided into two parts.   From 1877 to 1880 he led the House; from 1880 to 1885 he led the Opposition.   During the first of these periods Sir Stafford Northcote's principal duties were to defend the foreign policy of the Government in the House of Commons, and to deal with the question of parliamentary obstruction. For these duties Sir Stafford was well qualified, possessing, as Lord Beaconsfield said to Mr Montagu Corry (Lord Rowton), "the largest parliamentary knowledge of any man he had met in his career."

The first of his duties was admirably discharged. During the whole of the Bulgarian agitation' the Conservative party under his leadership, in spite of tremendous pressure from multitudes of their constituents, held firmly together. They were constant in their support of the Government; the Irish party frequently lent their assistance, and the Treaty of Berlin was the final result. But questions of foreign policy have been already discussed, and we may turn at once to the question of parliamentary obstruction, with the beginnings of which it became Sir Stafford Northcote's lot to deal, and which is illustrated in the subsequent chapter of his diary.

Obstruction has indeed been traced to the dilatory proceedings of "the Colonels" on the bill for abolishing purchase in the army (1871), to Mr Gladstone's innumerable speeches on the Divorce Bill (1857), and to Sir Charles Wetherell's performances in opposition to the great Reform Bill. But organised obstruction in its true sense, which Mr Gladstone called "resistance to the will of the House otherwise than by argument," began with the South African Confederation Bill of 1877. It was initiated by Mr Parnell and Mr Biggar. The South African Bill, first introduced in the House of Lords, was merely a permissive bill.   It enabled the various communities of South Africa, British colonies and others, to confederate if they so pleased.   Lord Carnarvon brought it in, Lord Kimberley supported it, and there was no division in the Lords.   But before it came to be read a second time in the House of Commons, Sir Theophilus Shepstone had annexed the Transvaal.   The annexation was approvéd by the Crown, and did not require the sanction of Parliament.   It was on the whole a very popular move, and Mr Forster expressed the warmest approbation of it.   But a few Radicals strongly resented it, among whom Mr Henry Fawcett and Mr Leonard Courtney were prepared to go all legitimate lengths in resisting the bill, because it would allow the Transvaal to become part of the Federation.   Sir Stafford Northcote must have felt that the opinions of such men were not to be lightly disregarded.   Mr Fawcett's death was lamented almost as much by Conservatives as by Liberals; and Mr Courtney's conduct in the chair has been praised alike by his political opponents and his political friends.

But Mr Parnell and Mr Biggar were determined to "resist the will of the majority otherwise than by argument."   They had as coadjutors the late Mr Gray, Captain (now Colonel) Nolan, Mr O'Donnell, whose name is contained in the Special Commission Act, 1888, and Mr Kirk, who has dropped out of history.   On Wednesday, the 25th of July 1877, they prevented the House from making any progress with the bill, and in the course of the division, if so it can be called, Mr Parnell expressed his pleasure at having been able to thwart the intentions of the Government. There was nothing, as a Conservative member said at the time, particularly criminal in this remark, but Sir Stafford Northcote had been taunted with undue inactivity. His exemplary endurance gave way, and he moved that the words be taken down. There was the usual unedifying wrangle about what had been said and what had not been said, what must have been and what could not have been Mr Parnell's meaning; Mr Parnell was ordered to withdraw, and a motion of suspension was for the first time proposed. The debate was adjourned—it was never renewed—and the motion dropped. The phrase itself, or its equivalent, has often been used in the House without drawing a reprimand from the Chair. It would now be generally recognised as harmless in itself; but there was undoubted evidence of a conspiracy to stop the progress of public business, and everybody agreed that something must be done.

Sir Stafford Northcote was not eager to alter the rules of the House. He was extremely industrious, and did not mind sitting up. He was strongly of opinion that the assembly which managed the affairs of the nation should continue to manage its own, and that it should not be conducted as a school with the leader as schoolmaster. He knew that politics were a rough pursuit, and there was nothing effeminate in his character. Nevertheless, on the 27th of July he moved two resolutions. The first was to the effect that after a member had been twice called to order, the Speaker or Chairman might "name" him to the House or Committee as disregarding the authority of the Chair, and then, after he had been heard in his own defence, a motion for suspending him during the rest of the sitting should be put without further debate. This motion was carried by a majority of 250. It was only once enforced, but a similar, though far more drastic resolution, which is now in force, has been frequently used. The second resolution, which was carried by 243, is now a standing order. It restricts the right of making dilatory motions, but its precise terms are too technical to be of general interest.

The obstructive minority soon proved the bluntness of these weapons. The House again went into Committee on the South African Bill at a quarter-past five in the afternoon of Tuesday, the 31st July, and continued the operation till ten minutes past two on the afternoon of Wednesday, the 1st of August. This "record," as the saying is, has since been beaten, but it was then unprecedented. Yet nobody was suspended, and neither of the new resolutions was brought into play. Sir Stafford Northcote only left the House for a brief interval; Lord Beaconsfield looked down from the Peers' gallery with a sense of relief. Mr Forster was almost more ministerial than the Ministerialists; and Sir William Harcourt denounced the conduct of the Parnellites in exceedingly vigorous English. Mr Fawcett, however, protested against the determination of the Government to force the bill through, and Mr Courtney retired at four in the morning, feeling that legislation and deliberation had alike ceased. However, the bill passed, and the session came to an end.

During the session of 1878, a Select Committee on the procedure of the House was nominated, and took the evidence of Lord Hampden, then Speaker, as well as of Mr Raikes, then Chairman of Ways and Means.

In 1879, an unsuccessful attempt was made to act upon the recommendations of this Committee. The Army Annual Bill of that year, the Mutiny Bill, as it used to be called, was seriously obstructed by Mr Parnell and his friends. It must, however, be remembered that their object was the abolition of flogging in the army; that this object has been long since achieved; that the Government incurred the censure of their own supporters for not knowing their own mind; and that Mr Parnell was aided if not abetted by no less a personage than Mr Chamberlain.

On the 24th of February 1879, Sir Stafford Northcote carried, after a protracted debate, the now familiar rule, then only applied to Monday, that there should be no preliminary debate on Mondays and Thursdays upon going into Committee of Supply unless the Army, Navy, or Civil Service Estimates are first taken, and then only on some question connected with the votes to be proposed. No other resolution was passed in 1879. But on the 28th of February 1880, a few weeks before Parliament was dissolved, a very long and elaborate proviso was adopted, according to which a member could be suspended by the House, after being named from the chair, without being heard in his own defence. This rule was made a standing order, and still, in a shorter but more drastic form, survives.

An impartial critic of Sir Stafford Northcote's policy in leading the House would probably select as its weakest point his failure to apply the true, only, and sufficient remedy for obstruction. The *clôture*, or as Mr Gladstone prefers to call it, the closing power, is the one weapon with which the majority can at once terminate a factious and dilatory resistance. That the House of Commons continued to do without it from the days of Simon de Montfort to the days of Mr Parnell may be explained in a great variety of ways. Before 1832, the House had very little to do. Before 1867, it only represented the upper middle classes. Before 1874, it contained no members openly and avowedly hostile to the authority of the House as a whole. That a legislative or administrative assembly should have no right to stop debate and decide the matter under discussion forthwith is theoretically absurd. It becomes practically mischievous when the indirect influence of custom and opinion ceases, for whatever reason, to operate upon a particular class of legislators or administrators. In the year 1890, when Tories and Radicals, Unionists and Home Rulers, move, according as opportunity serves them, "that the question be now put," the old prejudice against the *clôture* is difficult to understand, and almost impossible to revive. But Sir Stafford Northcote detested it, and in moving one of his resolutions on procedure, he referred to it in the same tone of reluctance not unmingled with disgust, with which he would have spoken of the Russian knout or the Turkish bastinado. In the next Parliament, Mr Parnell had more than thirty supporters instead of less than ten, and the necessity for the *clôture* became urgent. But by that time Sir Stafford Northcote had ceased to be primarily responsible for the conduct of affairs in the House of Commons.

Sir Stafford Northcote led the Opposition in the House of Commons for five years. During the first year he acted as Lord Beaconsfield's lieutenant; but after the death of the latter in April 1881, the Conservatives were left under a dual leadership. It was determined to invest Lord Salisbury in the House of Lords and Sir Stafford Northcote in the House of Commons with independent authority, and this arrangement continued in force until the fall of Mr Gladstone's Ministry in 1885.

When the new Parliament assembled in the early summer of 1880, the Liberals were in a majority of more than a hundred, if the Irish Home Rulers were counted neutral. If they were added to the Liberal ranks, the majority became about 170. No one then thought of adding them to the Conservatives, though half of them— that is, the Parnellites—subsequently voted with the Conservatives in a vast number of divisions, and finally contributed to Mr Gladstone's downfall.

The most delicate and crucial incidents in Sir Stafford Northcote's career in Opposition were, perhaps, the case of Mr Bradlaugh, the debates on the *clôture*, and the rise of the Fourth party.

In dealing with Irish Obstruction otherwise than by the *clôture*, he gave a hearty support to the Government. In questions of foreign affairs he undoubtedly behaved as a good citizen rather than as a partisan, and declined to make unnecessary attacks upon the Ministry. His most serious attack, with which probably all members of the House in their hearts sympathised, was upon the Egyptian policy that led to the fall of Khartoum and the death of Gordon. Upon this occasion the small majority of fourteen was all that the Government could obtain.

An acute and well-informed critic has singled out Sir Stafford Northcote's treatment of the questions raised by Mr Bradlaugh as the best example of Sir Stafford Northcote's tact and adroitness. It was certainly successful. He defeated the Government in several divisions, owing to the discontent of the Whigs, and the scruples of the Nonconformists, while his adversaries exposed themselves to certain religious imputations, which probably did them more harm with the constituencies than anything else which happened during their term of office, except the fall of Khartoum. In the Parliament of 1885, the present Speaker refused to allow any interference with his taking the oath. In the Parliament of 1886, which is still sitting, Mr Bradlaugh has himself carried an Act which enables atheists to make an affirmation in Parliament, as elsewhere. But these subsequent triumphs, which have nothing to do with Sir Stafford Northcote, cannot blind a historian to the fact that Mr Bradlaugh never took his seat in the Parliament of 1880, except for a few weeks under statutory liability, when he incurred heavy penalties by law.

The story of Mr Bradlaugh's non-admission to the House in 1880 may be briefly sketched. Mr Bradlaugh made a claim to affirm instead of taking the oath in the ordinary manner. A doubt arose as to the propriety of this claim, and the question was referred to a Select Committee. The Committee reported against Mr Bradlaugh by a majority of one. Mr Bradlaugh, not being a Quaker, had no right to affirm in Parliament. He then demanded to be sworn, but before he could reach the table Sir Henry Wolff interposed. Mr Speaker Onslow, or Mr Speaker Lefevre, might have directed Sir Henry to resume his seat, and reminded him that there was no question before the House. Lord Hampden declined to exercise his authority, and left the matter to the judgment of the House. Again was a Select Committee appointed, and this time it reported that Mr Bradlaugh could not lawfully take the oath. The Committee, however, recommended that he should be permitted to make an affirmation at his peril; and after a special resolution enabling him to do so had been rejected, a general resolution enabling any one to do so was adopted. It would throw no light on Sir Stafford Northcote's leadership to follow the details of this tedious and protracted struggle. Mr Bradlaugh was once expelled for administering the oath to himself, and immediately re-elected at Northampton. Twice his seat was " vacated as though he were dead," and his constituents faithfully sent him back to Westminster as though he were alive. He was consigned to the Clock Tower on the motion of Sir Stafford Northcote; and on the motion of Sir Stafford Northcote he was released from that dungeon the following day. He lost actions, and won them. He was defeated in the Court of Appeal, and was victorious in the House of Lords. He was repeatedly placed at the bar, and at last told that he could be heard no more from that classic spot. Twice he administered the oath to himself. He sued the Deputy Serjeant-at-Arms for assault, and caused some excusable popular misconception by recovering damages from Mr Newdegate for " maintenance."   Meanwhile Sir Stafford Northcote continued his course, in which the legal tribunals supported him, by deciding, first, that an atheist could not make an affirmation in Parliament; secondly, that he could not take an oath anywhere; and thirdly, that the House of Commons was omnipotent over its own members within its own walls. Among the results of Sir Stafford Northcote's conduct was the defeat of the Government on the morning of the 4th of May 1883, when the second reading of the Affirmation Bill was rejected by a majority of three, although Mr Gladstone supported it in one of the finest speeches of his life. Nothing more readily proves the facility with which Sir Stafford H. Northcote was able to deal with unexpected difficulties than the manner in which he thus suddenly adopted the *rôle* of the House, and carried his point against a strong Government in their first session. So far as these issues can be settled by the Legislature, they have been settled in Mr

Bradlaugh's favour; and when an Affirmation Bill was no longer the battle-ground of party, it passed with ease. Sir Stafford's diaries, which follow, throw some light on his views upon this difficult subject. There is an interesting note in them to the effect that on the day of his final appearance in the House of Commons in 1885, the Speaker read a letter from Mr Bradlaugh, in which he threatened to insist on taking his seat as soon as the new Ministers were re-elected. Sir Stafford remarks in his journal that he ought in strictness to have renewed his motion for excluding Mr Bradlaugh from the precincts, but that he did not wish to conclude his thirty years of membership by proposing the exclusion of a brother member.

It is now generally, though tacitly, acknowledged that the Conservatives were wrong in resisting the *clôture*. On the other hand, few people would now contend that Mr Gladstone's form of the *clôture* was a satisfactory one. Both these statements may be tested by facts. Mr Gladstone's *clôture* Resolution was introduced on the 20th of February, and carried on the 11th of November 1882. It was debated for nineteen nights, and the House of Commons had to sit specially in the autumn for the purpose of passing it. It was only once enforced—two years and a half after it had become a standing order. Its origin, its grandeur, and its decadence are interesting and peculiar. On Monday, the 31st of January 1881, the House of Commons began a sitting which lasted for forty-one hours and a half. The occasion was the introduction of Mr Forster's Bill for the Better Protection of Person and Property in Ireland. At nine o'clock on the morning of Wednesday the 2d of February, the Speaker refused to call upon any more members, and peremptorily put the question. This was an extremely high-handed proceeding, which could only be excused by the tyrant's plea · of necessity, and which was totally unwarranted by precedent or practice. The Speaker was subsequently given power to frame in certain circumstances "rules of urgency," after thirty-six members had, on the 3d of February, been suspended for disorder. During the session of 1881, the House was content with the "rules of urgency." But at the commencement of the next session Mr Gladstone moved that the Speaker or Chairman might announce what appeared to him the evident sense of the House in favour of an immediate division, and thereupon put the question from the chair. Sir Stafford Northcote's speech against this resolution was a very mild one, but from the benches behind him the destruction of parliamentary freedom was copiously and repeatedly predicted. The debate was interrupted by the horrible tragedy of the Phœnix Park, and the coercive legislation consequent thereupon. But the acerbity of the resistance offered was much diminished by the Speaker's announcement that he should take the "evident sense of the House" from both sides of the chair. Lord Hampden, in point of fact, never applied the *clôture* at all. It was employed for the first time by the present Speaker on the 28th February 1885, when he came within an ace of receiving a most serious rebuff. The occasion was a motion giving precedence to Sir Stafford Northcote's Egyptian vote of censure over the ordinary business of a Tuesday evening. The rule provided that the *clôture* must be carried by more than 200 members, unless the minority was under 40. Some Conservatives, including even occupants of the front Opposition bench, voted with the Irish members, against whom the *clôture* had really been invoked, with the result that the Ayes were 207 and the Noes 46. The deduction of seven from the majority would have involved a severe reflection on Mr Speaker. Such was the net, and indeed the gross, result of a resolution which was under the cognisance of the House of Commons for the whole of an unusually protracted parliamentary year. In 1887, Mr Smith, as leader of the Conservative Ministerialists in the House of Commons, introduced a much more stringent, and a much more business-like form of the *clôture*, which is now in almost daily use.

. It would be undesirable to discuss the personal relations between Sir Stafford Northcote and the small group of highly talented men who were known in the Parliament of 1880 as the Fourth party, but it is easy to indicate their different principles of action.

. The Fourth party, as every one knows, consisted of Lord Randolph Churchill, Mr Arthur Balfour, Sir John Gorst, and Sir Henry Drummond Wolff. They apparently took the view that the duty of an Opposition was to attack the Government in season and out of season, and to pay no heed to the constant defeats to which it thus exposed itself. Sir Stafford Northcote, on the other hand, considered that it was bad policy for the minority to be frequently pitting itself against the majority. He held that such a course of proceeding involved great waste of public time, and that it placed the Opposition in a disadvantageous position before the eyes of the country. In his opinion it was best to give the Government full swing, and to adopt the tactics of Fabius rather than those of Minutius.

Events have rendered it impossible to decide as to whether Sir Stafford Northcote or the Fourth party were right. The partial defeat of the Liberals in 1885, and their utter rout in 1886, were not due to any Conservative policy. Mr Gladstone failed to secure an absolute majority in 1885, partly because of the indignation aroused by Gordon's death, and partly because the Irish, anxious to hold the balance in their own hands, desired to equalise as far as possible the numbers of the two great parties in the State, and so cast their votes for the Conservatives. In 1886, Mr Gladstone was defeated entirely in consequence of his adoption of Home Rule.

Mr Gladstone's Ministry was beaten in June 1885 on their Budget Bill, and at once resigned. It is probable that no event of a similar kind was ever less expected. It has been explained in a number of ways, but too little attention has generally been paid to the unpopularity of the Budget itself. It may be true that some Liberals, and even some Liberal Ministers, may have had reasons of their own for witnessing with complacency the resignation of the Government; but it is certain that the Budget, which proposed to put additional taxes on beer, spirits, and land, was open to severe condemnation. The revenue derived from beer was stationary, that from spirits was declining, while the condition of land seemed desperate; and the impolicy of imposing additional burdens upon them at such a time was strongly urged and widely recognised.

Such a Budget loudly challenged opposition, and Sir Michael Hicks-Beach brought forward an amendment to the Customs and Inland Revenue Bill on the 8th of June, which was carried by a majority of twelve. Sir Stafford Northcote wound up the debate on the Conservative side, and in doing so delivered his last speech of any importance in the House of Commons.

Sir Stafford Northcote had many qualifications for a leader of men. He was extremely quick of apprehension, he never missed the point of an argument, his courage and coolness never forsook him, his temper was almost perfect, he never gave personal offence to any one, and he always bore himself with simple dignity. He has been accused of timidity, but such an accusation is too ridiculous to notice. It has also been said that he lacked the sense of humour, but such a criticism is thoroughly superficial. Sir Stafford Northcote's sense of humour was often proved, and always showed itself to be of the keenest and most refined character. But he was chary of displaying it, and once remarked that the speakers who moved laughter were seldom respected.

Perhaps the two characteristics that were especially his own were his simplicity and his graciousness. A distinguished public servant wrote of him after his death, with perfect truth, that his graciousness concealed his greatness, and his simplicity tended to produce the same effect. For exaggeration of all kinds he entertained a profound contempt, and this habit of mind led him generally to make the least of things, and particularly of his own work. His simplicity also accounts for his utter indifference to authority for the sake of authority. To many minds it is a pleasure to issue commands, and to see those commands obeyed: it seems a satisfactory proof of power. But the exercise of authority gave Sir Stafford Northcote no pleasure at all. He loved to excel, and no doubt his political successes were sweet to him; but he regarded them much as he regarded the successes of his boyhood at Oxford. It was the victory itself, and not the fruits it might bring to him, that he loved.

It must be admitted that in some respects Sir Stafford Northcote's very virtues told against him in his character of party leader. He inspired much affection, but perhaps too little awe. He was certainly too candid and judicial to be a thorough-going partisan, or to be able to make all the sacrifices that the spirit of party demands; but perhaps his worst fault was a certain detachment of mind, which made him see things at the moment as other people would see them a week or a month afterwards. Sir Stafford Northcote was a man who knew himself, and he quite recognised that he was not by nature a party man.

He saw that this placed him at a certain disadvantage which could not be entirely recovered, however warmly he might throw himself into party business. No labour and no thought can ever quite supply the absence of natural instinct. If his conduct may at times have appeared undecided, and if he ever allowed himself to be over-persuaded by his adherents, the explanation is to be found in the fact of his extreme anxiety to render to party even more than its due in all cases when he could do so conscientiously. He was well aware that there were moments when advantages might have been snatched from the enemy by a more reckless and less scrupulous leader than himself; and to make up to the party for what they lost in this manner was an object so dear to his heart that it is possible that on some occasions he yielded to counsels that his own judgment opposed, careless as to the effect upon his own reputation.

But when everything has been said about Sir Stafford Northcote's merits and defects as a leader of the House of Commons, the fact remains that it was his misfortune to assume that office in immediate succession to Mr Gladstone and Mr Disraeli, one of whom may perhaps be described as the most powerful statesman, and the other as the most interesting political personage, that have appeared in England during the present century. Mr Disraeli, not long after the death of Lord Palmerston, once said to Sir Stafford Northcote that the coming struggle between himself and Mr Gladstone would rival the great conflict between Mr Pitt and Mr Fox, and it seems probable that his prediction will be fulfilled. Since the death of Mr Fox, no leader of the House of Commons has awakened an enthusiasm equal to that inspired by the two mighty party chieftains of the last twenty years, nor is it likely that we shall soon look upon " their like agen."

Sir Stafford Northcote once gracefully alluded to the ultimate judgment that he expected to be formed as to his career. In the spring of 1886, an extraordinary honour was paid him, and he was presented by members of both parties in the House of Commons with a testimonial in token of their affection and esteem. The testimonial took the form of plate, and on the various pieces were engraved the heads of some of the principal statesmen with whom Sir Stafford Northcote had been connected. Upon one of the candelabra was impressed his own likeness between those of Lord Beaconsfield and Mr Gladstone. In returning thanks for the presentation, Sir Stafford Northcote remarked upon this circumstance, and observed: "If I feel like the mortal horse who ran third in the chariot of Achilles with the two immortal steeds—if I feel that I am unworthy to be placed among such distinguished men, yet I cannot help being proud, when I remember that it was in such company that I played my part in the House of Commons to the best of my ability."

But let the verdict of posterity be what it may, Sir Stafford Northcote must have felt a sense of satisfaction that it is given to few men to enjoy when he could record in his diary that as he entered the House of Commons for the last time it was difficult to say on which side the cheering was more hearty or more general, and when he could remember that a generation of fierce political conflict left his simplicity and kindness of heart exactly where it found them.

CHAPTER XVI.

CAUSES OF CONSERVATIVE DEFEAT — THE NEW GOVERNMENT—
MR FORSTER — MR GLADSTONE AT THE ROYAL ACADEMY—
"HANGING TOGETHER"—ORGANISATION IN SCOTLAND—THE
BRADLAUGH QUESTION—MINISTERS EATING LEEKS—ORIEN-
TAL PROPHECIES — BRADLAUGH COMMITTEE — MR GLAD-
STONE'S "INCONSISTENCIES"—RABBITS AND HARES BILL—
MR BRADLAUGH'S CONDUCT — THE IRISH BILL — CONVERSA-
TIONS WITH LORD BEACONSFIELD AT HUGHENDEN — LORD
BEACONSFIELD ON HOMER — DEFEAT OF GENERAL BURROWS
—AFFAIRS OF GREECE—CONCERT OF EUROPE.

THE defeat of the Conservatives in 1880 left Sir Stafford leisure enough for the keeping of a diary, which, with some interruptions, he continued till his death. The story of the latest years of his life may be somewhat briefly condensed by the aid of these memoirs, but much that is most interesting is inevitably suppressed.

The diary was begun on April 20, 1880, at Elmley House, Wimbledon, lent to Sir Stafford by Lord Beauchamp. It records "our last council at Windsor," and, on April 12, "our last Cabinet."

DIARY.

Lord B. reckons the Whigs in the new House at 237, and the Conservatives at 240. There are, I think, 62 Home Rulers (of various shades), so there would remain 113 extreme or unclassed Radicals. Some disintegration may soon be expected in the majority, but we have first to see what the Ministry is like.

Our great defeat seems due to—

1. Want of suitable organisation, and some over-confidence and apathy.

2. The bad times, and a desire of change in hopes of better luck.

3. The effects of the unscrupulous assertions of our opponents.

4. The very large expenditure of money by them. Our chief losses were: A. Egerton, Lowther, Salt, Raikes, and some of our county members.

There has been some doubt whether we ought not to meet Parliament as a Ministry, and wait for a vote of want of confidence before resigning. There are other reasons, particularly in respect of Indian affairs, which make the continuance of a practically condemned Administration undesirable and even dangerous. It is not safe to leave it uncertain what policy is to be pursued in Afghanistan or in the Transvaal.

April 26.—The names of the new Government, so far as they are yet given, do not seem to give much satisfaction. The Radicals are much annoyed. Forster should do well in Ireland, though his manners are rough. The Irish remember his mission in the time of the great famine, when he came to distribute the contributions of the Society of Friends; and they will also take the appointment of so leading a politician to the Chief Secretaryship as a compliment. I think it is likely enough that a Conservative cave may be formed on the Liberal side, with perhaps Goschen as its centre, and that if we manage our opposition discreetly, we may often join hands with them, and perhaps ultimately bring some of them to take part in a Conservative Cabinet. At the present moment one thinks of such things only in the spirit in which the Roman purchaser bid for the fields occupied by the Carthaginian army. Still, it is necessary to lay our foundations properly.

Dined at the Merchant Taylors' Hall, where the freedom was given to Cranbrook and myself. We kept our spirits up pretty well, without committing ourselves to anything in particular. Our tactics ought to be as reserved as possible. Lord Egmont made a very good speech in returning thanks for the House of Lords. He may be worth looking after.

April 29.—Attended meeting of the House and election of Speaker. T. D. Acland proposed Brand, Sir Philip Egerton seconded him. Mr Brand having submitted himself to the pleasure of the House, O'Donnell got up before he could be inducted, and expressed "on behalf of the Irish party" his approval of the choice that had been made. This was meant simply to announce that the

"Irish party" intend to make themselves heard and attended to. Lord F. Cavendish and I then congratulated the Speaker, and the House adjourned. Symptoms of dissatisfaction are already beginning to show themselves in the Ministerial ranks.

May 1.—At the Royal Academy dinner to-night, Gladstone said that if he had any strength left for his great task, it was due to the kindness with which his distinguished friends (Granville and Hartington) had enabled him to enjoy comparative repose during the last five years; and now, having borne the burden and heat of the day, they had ceded to him the honour which they might justly have claimed for themselves! I wonder how they liked his partition of the oyster. Hartington, later in the evening, said to me, " I congratulate you on having less work before you; and I rather congratulate myself on getting out of the hardest part of my own." I presume he does not mean to take much part in the work of the House now. It is doubtful whether there is really much love lost between the " three great statesmen," notwithstanding the prayer of the Nonconformist minister that they might "all hang together." "Amen," said a voice in the congregation. "I mean," said the minister, "that they may hang together in accord and concord." "It doesn't matter what sort of a cord it is," replied the voice. The news of the day is, that a change has taken place in the proprietorship of the ' Pall Mall Gazette.'

I gave Smith a paper on the subject of the party organisation, and Barrington lent me some good remarks

on the defects of our party organisation in Scotland.
There is a great deal to be done. It is my notion that
we ought to have a small committee of parliamentary
leaders, who should keep themselves in constant communication with the managers of the Central Association.
Much might be done, and many mistakes avoided, if we
were better informed as to the feelings of the party
throughout the country. The writer of the paper points
out very well the mischief resulting from the want of
communication between the Conservative landowners in
Scotland and their general unacquaintance with the feelings of their tenantry. He also gives an interesting account of the ecclesiastical parties, and complains of the
mistakes made by us in passing the Church Patronage
Act. He attributes much of the recent Liberal success
to the efforts of Dr Rainy, Principal of the college
through which the Free Church clergy have passed for
now more than twenty-five years. The Episcopalian landowners stand apart from, and know little of the opinions
of, the ecclesiastical bodies. The Free Church will not
unite with Established, because they would lose the
buildings they have erected throughout the country,
which "would become the property of the proprietors
on whose lands they stand." (Is this so?) The U.P.,
who seceded in the last century, have always been
strongly political, and opposed to the connection of
Church and State. The leaders of the Free Church, in
1843, though seceding on the Veto and Patronage
questions, were not opposed to that connection; but their

successors (and notably Dr Rainy) have taken a more political line, and the majority became keen for union with the U.P. This has been resisted by the religious minority of the Free Church; and the minority have carried the day, because in case of a split they would have remained the representatives of the true Free Church, and would have retained all its buildings and property. The majority have, however, carried a plan constituting ministers of the two Churches (Free Kirk and U.P.) reciprocally eligible for charges in the two denominations; and the by far larger section of the Free Kirk are now in compact union with the Presbyterian Nonconformists of Scotland and England, from whom they had previously been separated by their refusal of Voluntaryism. On the other hand, the minority of the Free Kirk have not coalesced to the same degree with the Establishment, partly because of the question of retention of their special property, and partly from other reasons (such as the liability of feuars to contribute to the buildings of Established Churches); while the abolition of Patronage has rather alienated the Free Kirk, who used to gain by secessions of discontented minorities in individual cases, and has not done much to conciliate the Established Church, which was contented with the previous state. The Free Kirk now see in the Establishment a body of men who have the same privileges as themselves, so far as patronage goes, and have in addition the endowments from which they themselves are excluded. The serious thing politically is, that the Radicals have a close union, and a most able leader (Dr Rainy), while the Establishment Conservatives have "no leader, no cohesion, no defensive organisation."

May 3.—Took my seat. Question as to Bradlaugh's right to make an affirmation instead of an oath to be referred to a committee. It seems strange to require an oath from a Christian, and to dispense with it from an atheist. Would it not be better to do away with the members' oath altogether, and make the affirmation general?

May 8.—Left Wimbledon, and came down to Pynes. The papers are full of Fawcett's speech at Hackney, in which he charges us with having suppressed the bad reports as to the cost of the Afghan war until after the elections. This is of course untrue; but there has been gross laxity somewhere, and the whole system of Indian accounts must be overhauled.

May 10.—Received news of Harcourt's defeat at Oxford. It is important as a proof of the temporary and local character of the causes which led to our great defeat. Harcourt's success at the general election was mainly due to the over-confidence and consequent supineness of Hall's friends, who thought their man so safe that some did not trouble themselves to go to the poll, while others split their votes to bring in Harcourt rather than Chitty.

May 11. — We have had two Ministerial apologies. Fawcett has been compelled to withdraw his charge of the concealment of the Indian deficit, but has done so very ungraciously. Gladstone, on the other hand, has made a most abject and undignified apology to Count

Karolyi for his abuse of Austria in his Mid-Lothian speeches.

Our friends in the House of Commons continue hammering at the Bradlaugh Committee, contending that no such business as the appointment of a committee ought to be done till after the Queen's Speech. They are wrong. The House must be constituted, and for that purpose members must be sworn. If in the process of swearing them a difficulty should arise which the Speaker declines to solve, and which he remits to the House, as he has done in this case, it is clearly competent to the House either to resolve it at once by a direct vote, or to refer it to a committee. We shall not be bound by the committee's report, and shall exercise our own judgment upon it when it is made.

May 19.—Auspicious news this morning! We have won two more seats. Mark Stewart has beaten the Lord Advocate in the Wigtown Burghs, and Mr Crompton Roberts has carried Sandwich (on Hugessen's becoming a peer) by a majority of about 440 against Sir Julian Goldsmid. The Home Secretary and Lord Advocate are now both without seats. The wildest rumours are afloat as to the efforts being made to find an opening for the former. We shall see. The party meeting held at Bridgewater House. About 450 were present, including not only members of both Houses of the present Parliament, but also members of the late House who have lost their seats. There was an excellent and cheerful tone: Lord B. spoke for an hour and three-quarters reminding the party of former defeats, and of the great rallying power it has shown in the worst times.

May 20.—Parliament met for business. Grey moved Address in remarkably good speech, modest and in good taste, but independent in tone; Mason, the seconder, seems able, but very Radical. I followed them at once, notwithstanding a notice of amendment having been given by the Irish, and ran briefly over the topics of the Speech; saying that we should support in Opposition the same policy which we had promoted when in office; that we were glad to see that the general language of the Queen's Speech was in accordance with that policy, and with the recognition of established facts; but that we wanted fuller explanations, especially with regard to the meaning and character of Goschen's mission. Gladstone followed, and answered my speech, but did not throw much real light on the proposed policy in Turkey.. Some passages of his speech were significant, and seemed to point to the abandonment or revision of the Anglo-Turkish Convention. He spoke of the false impressions which it was necessary to remove from the mind of Turkey—one, that England had some such separate and overpowering interest in the maintenance of that empire, that her support might be counted on under any circumstances whatever; the other, that England was aiming at acquiring for herself a direct share in the government of Asiatic Turkey, and this latter delusion was perhaps fostered by the provisions of the Anglo-Turkish Convention. From what I hear, Léon Say is very much dissatisfied with the political prospect. He thinks proposals will be made to France which she will accept; amongst other things, that she will be invited to occupy Syria. He foretells the "joint occupation" of Constantinople by January or February. —— spoke to me most friendly in the lobby, and assured me that our foreign policy had done us no harm in the northern towns. Our defeat was mainly due to the distress and misrepresentations. We must notice that there had never been an election in which we had lost so many seats by such small majorities. He did not think the Government would last long. —— also spoke to me after Gladstone's speech, which he did not like. He commented on his saying nothing about Roumania and the Arab Tabia difficulty. He said, " You are in a strong position in the country: I have been down to Sandwich to help my friends, and I could not but see unmistakable signs of opinion in your favour. When an election like that is carried by 400 or 500 votes, it means something."

Went on to the House of Commons, where the Bradlaugh case was resumed. The Government were anxious to slur matters over by allowing him to take the oath without remark; but Wolff prevented this by raising his objection the moment the Clerk tendered the book. Dillwyn rose to order, but the Speaker ruled in Wolff's favour. Wolff made his case very fairly, but rather unwisely imported quotations from some of Bradlaugh's writings against the Royal Family, which did not really help his argument, and gave a too heated turn to the discussion. ·Gladstone then moved an amendment, which the Government had evidently prepared in anticipation of, and as a bar to, Wolff's motion, proposing to refer to a committee the question whether the House has a right to interfere with a member's taking his seat, if he is willing to take the prescribed oath. This form of reference obviously ignores the special circumstances and real point of the case, which is in short this, that a man offering to take an oath, and at the same time declaring that he regards it as an empty form, not binding on his conscience, does not really offer to take it at all. Gibson, our late Attorney-General for Ireland, made an admirable speech, to which the reports hardly do justice. When he took up the Testament and put the imaginary case of a man proposing to swear upon it, but at the same time saying, " I don't believe the first words, and I don't believe the last words of the book, nor any of its contents," he produced a great effect. The discussion ran on for some time, and was then adjourned till Monday, that we might see and consider the terms of the proposed reference.

The debate on the report of the Address then came on. Arthur Balfour raised some points as to the Goschen mission, and the intentions of the Government respecting the Anglo-Turkish Convention. Gladstone denied any instruction having been given for its abrogation. There were some unpleasant attacks made on the Government from their own side, especially a very bitter complaint by Leonard Courtney of their retaining Frere as Governor of the Cape. They were, he said, doing the very thing which they had been going up and down the country and abusing us for doing. The Radicals feel this very keenly.

May 22.— ——, whom I met in the Row, spoke very angrily about the conduct of the Government in the Frere case. I told him that he and his friends were like Falstaff and Pistol when they found that Henry V. threw over the associates of Prince Hal. He admitted the justice of the comparison.

May 24.—At Lady Mary Cecil's wedding in the morning. Afterwards walked down to Carlton Terrace with Sandon. We agreed to stand firm for Wolff's motion. It came on, and the debate was much in our favour. Randolph Churchill spoke very well and dexterously; Hardinge Giffard was excellent; Herschell weak and embarrassed; Watkin Williams practically with us on the main point, which is, that repeating the form of an oath, with a protest from the person who does so that he regards it as an idle and meaningless form, is not "taking an oath" within the meaning of the statute. The Government only got a majority of seventy-five in this their first struggle; and now we have got to see what the Committee will do. The consumption of leeks by the Government goes on merrily. To-night Cowen put a question to Childers as to whether they intended to give effect to the resolution which Hartington moved last year, and abolish corporal punishment in the army. Childers read an elaborate answer, amid roars of laughter from our side, that they fully accepted the spirit of Hartington's motion; but that they had to consider how it could be carried out, and what punishment could be substituted. He observed that flogging was now only used when an army was in the field, and that there might be "critical moments," &c., &c. In short, the matter could not be dealt with this year! Later in the evening, on a motion of Fowler's, Gladstone made an elaborate apology for not recalling Sir Bartle Frere, arguing that it was necessary to keep him at the Cape to carry confederation. I commended his policy, which was exactly our own, and only expressed a humble wish that he had thought of it a little sooner. —— said to Smith afterwards, "Did you ever follow in the tracks of a big animal through the snow, putting down your feet in his footprints? That's what the Government are doing with your measures." Terms of reference to Bradlaugh Committee agreed upon. Gladstone wants to nominate the late Committee, but I demanded some addition at all events, as Holker was our only representative, while they had Bright and their two law officers. We must have Cross and Gibson put on.

May 26.—Dined at Nobody's. My first election to the Club. Sat between Walpole and the Bishop of Hereford.

May 28.—Nomination of the Bradlaugh Committee. Gladstone's pretension to nominate on the principle of proportioning the numbers on the Committee to the strength of parties in the House. I protested at once against this assumption. If he tries to give effect to it, I must advise our friends to decline to serve. We are rather in trouble on account of Dyke's knocking up. He will not be able to take any more work as Whip this session. It is very difficult to make a new arrangement.

June 3.—There has been a good deal of difficulty upon the question of the nomination of Committees. The contention of the Government is, that the proportions to be allotted to different sections of the House in the arrangement of a committee should be somewhat the same as the proportions in which our parliamentary strength is now divided; and that a committee of twenty - three should be composed of twelve Ministerialists, nine Conservatives, and two Home Rulers. As the Home Rulers are commonly much more disposed to join the Government than the Opposition, this would usually put us in a minority of nine against fourteen. This is not at all in accordance with the practice of giving the Government a majority of one upon all the Committees, a practice which has been found very convenient hitherto. If it were not for the "Third party," our course would be clear; we should recommend our friends to refuse to serve upon Committees unless they were struck according to the old principle. But there is no doubt a real difficulty to be encountered. The Government may fairly refuse to reckon the Home Rulers as part of their forces, and might claim to nominate a majority out of the body to whom the Ministerialist Whip is sent. We may do the same. Then the Home Rulers would have no representatives on the Committee proposed by the two Whips. They would not stand this, and there would be a fight in the House, which would end in one of these ways—

either one or two Irish members would be added to the
Committee, or they would be substituted for one or two
of the members proposed by the Whips. In the latter
case, we should probably arrive at the solution proposed
by the Government, and the result would be the crushing
of the Conservative minority ; because it may be assumed
that the Government, having a majority in the House,
would support their own nominees on the Committee,
and would give the Third party their seats at the expense
of the nominees of the minority. If the other course—
that of adding two members to represent the Third party
—were adopted, then the Third party would have the
balance in their hands, and would be masters of the situation. The object of the Government seems to be to
reduce the Conservative Opposition to the level of a
"sect," more numerous than the sect of the Home Rulers,
but having no more rights than they. The Government
are to hold the position of an establishment. We agreed
last night, after a protest, to the appointment of the
Merchant Shipping Commission on the new principle ;
but we reserve our right to fight the battle again. The
speeches about Cyprus last night were suggestive and
amusing. The quiet way in which both Dilke and
Gladstone ignored all their old abuse of the island, and
their complete acceptance of it as almost a British possession, to be administered through the Colonial Office,
was highly edifying.

June 4.—The proceedings on the Employers Liability
Bill last night were highly edifying. The Government

have plunged into a thorny question without much consideration ; and, as they naively tell us, have taken up the most promising (as they thought) of the various bills presented last session, and ask the House to adopt its principle, explaining that by its "principle" they simply mean that the law requires alteration. They then propose to remodel it in accordance with all the hints and suggestions they may pick up in debate. Many of their supporters are furious with them, and the employers of labour throughout the country are much alarmed. The second reading we all allowed to pass last night, but the real fight is to come. Gladstone's reply to my remarks on the situation was curious. He had never said we were incompetent for domestic legislation ; on the contrary, I must be well aware that he thought me highly competent for it, and that his complaint was that we had allowed the time of the House to be taken up with other matters, which prevented our giving the necessary time to domestic affairs.

R. Grosvenor has agreed to form the Metropolis Water Committee on the principle of eight Liberals, eight Conservatives, and a member chosen by the Home Rulers. This arrangement is to be "without prejudice." It is quite satisfactory for the present.

I did not stay late at the House last night, and therefore missed a good deal of fun. The Opium debate was noteworthy, and Hartington caught it pretty heavily from "moral" friends on his own side. Gladstone had been dining out to meet the authoress of 'Sister Dora' (Miss

Lonsdale, who was very much alarmed by the rapidity and variety of his questions), and only came back in time to express his opinion that the House was too much influenced by feeling, and too little by judgment! It must be as good as a play to hear such sentiments from such a quarter. After this came the question of O'Connor Power's Land Bill, which is to give tenants "compensation for disturbance," when they are evicted for non-payment of rent. The Irish strongly pressed the Government to give them a day, which Gladstone had refused earlier in the evening; but it seems likely that they will have to give way. Whenever we come to a review of Gladstone's inconsistencies, we shall have to note (1) his apology to Karolyi, which is now disguised by his admirers as a virtual surrender of Austria; (2) his retention of Frere, which is now described as a virtual dismissal of that great man; (3) his retention of Cyprus, which is to be made more English than at present.

June 20.—It is almost impossible to keep up a journal when one is in the thick of the session, with all manner of questions to look up, a great many people to see, no books, papers, or secretaries at hand, and living at this distance from the House and the clubs. I hope to do better next year, when we have our house in St James's Place; meanwhile we are keeping up our spirits pretty well. The number of blunders which the Government have already committed is almost incredible, and there is a promise of a good addition to their difficulties. Harcourt's blundering, Gladstone's impetuosity, and Forster's vacillations have done much to disenchant the world, and it does not seem as if they had anything in store for us that will make up for the disappointment they have caused, and the alarm they have occasioned among their own friends.

It is possible that the Bill (Hares and Rabbits) may not come on for a long time. When it does, I think I must speak early, declaring myself personally ready to vote for one of the Whig amendments, and enlarging on the importance of upholding the doctrine of free contract, in view especially of the formidable invasions of the rights of property with which we are threatened in other particulars—as, *e.g.*, in the matter of rent; but I must make comparatively light of the probable division on the second reading, as we shall have the opportunity of amending the bill in Committee, and I shall say that we may regard the second reading in the light in which Gladstone (or Dodson) asked us to regard the second reading of their Employers Liability Bill—merely as an assumption that something ought to be done.

The course of the Government with regard to O'Connor Power's bill has been thoroughly discreditable to them. They began by refusing to give him a day for its discussion. Then, being pressed, they said they would think about doing so. Then they named a day, but gave no intimation as to their views as to the merits of the bill itself. Then, being pressed, they said they should oppose the bill; but that they would introduce into the Relief of Distress Bill a clause which should do pretty much what O'Connor Power proposes to do, but only for a limited time, within limited area, and at the discretion of the County Court Judges. Then, having given notice of this clause before the second reading of the Relief of Distress Bill, they propose to pass the second reading, but pretend that they can exclude discussion of the new clause at that stage, because it is not yet in the bill. The Speaker having ruled that they are wrong in this pretension, and that by placing so important a clause on the paper they have opened its principle to discussion, and Chaplin having moved that the debate on the second reading be adjourned, in order that the House may have time to consider this very important proposal, they again change front, and withdraw the clause, promising to make a new bill of it. The result was that (the House having agreed to the second reading on Thursday), when the Committee was called on Friday morning, Parnell moved the adjournment of the debate on the precisely converse ground from that taken by Chaplin the day before—viz., the change caused by the Government not proceeding with their proposed new clause. Gladstone, to get out of the momentary difficulty, said he would agree to the adjournment, and go to other business; but the Irish then started an irregular conversation, which lasted about four hours, and stopped everything else. At length the English members began to complain of the waste of time, on which the Irish suggested that the best way of saving time would be to refer the bill to a Select Committee consisting of all the Irish members. This proposal of course came to nothing, but it shows what is likely to be tried hereafter. The Relief Bill now stands over for the present, but O'Connor Power's bill comes on for discussion on Tuesday. The whole tone of the Irish speeches on the Relief Bill is ominous. They insist on representing the advances as being made for the benefits of the landlords; and there is an obvious determination to depreciate the landlord's rights, and the value of the land, which I fear the Government will rather favour than repress. The Challemel-Lacour business has been an unpleasant one.

June 21, 22, 23.—Monday and Tuesday nights occupied by the discussion on the Bradlaugh case. Labouchere having given notice that he would move, as soon as the Report of the Second Committee was received, that Mr Bradlaugh should be allowed to affirm, we decided on an amendment, which we placed in Giffard's hands, declaring, with reference to the Reports of the two Committees, that he ought not to be allowed either to affirm or to take the oath. The Government seemed much to dislike their position, and looked as if they wished to leave the discussion as much as possible to the House, till towards the end of the evening, when Bright made one of his characteristic speeches, vehement, intolerant, and at times so offensive that I was very near rising to call him to order. The debate would probably have been adjourned in any case, but this speech made it absolutely necessary. On Tuesday, Gladstone spoke early, and evidently under great anxiety. His speech, especially in its earlier part, was a very fine one, and produced a considerable impression. Towards the end, however, he refined far too much, and seemed a little to lose his hold of his audience. Gibson followed him with a very able and telling reply; but unfortunately the House had greatly emptied for dinner when Gladstone sat down. It is a favourite habit of his to speak into the dinner hour, so that his opponent must speak either to empty benches or forego the advantage of replying on the instant. The division took place at nearly 12.30. We had a majority of forty-five—a result wholly unexpected on our side, the more sanguine having only hoped for a close run, and being prepared to renew the fight by moving the previous question, and adjourning the debate on it. The excitement when the numbers were given was greater than I ever remember. There was shouting, cheering, clapping of hands, and other demonstrations, both louder and longer than any I have heard in my parliamentary life.

This morning (Wednesday) we have had a new act in the drama. Immediately after prayers Mr Bradlaugh came in, and proposed to take the oath. The Speaker thereupon read the resolution adopted last night, and added that he must retire in order that the House should consider the application, which he did. Labouchere then moved that he be heard, and Walpole added the words "At the bar of the House," saying that was the precedent in O'Connell's case. Gladstone meanwhile sent R. Grosvenor round to ask what I meant to do. I replied by asking what the Government meant to do. It was a critical moment, for some of our men were in a state of high excitement, and it was difficult to keep them quiet. It might well have happened that some one would rise and object to hearing Mr Bradlaugh; and, had a debate arisen, it was difficult to say what might have been its results. Gladstone's and my own mutual caution not to give the other a chance had the effect of keeping the House comparatively quiet for the moment, and the Speaker put the question, and it was agreed to. Bradlaugh accordingly made his speech, and a very clever one it was, and well delivered, with a good deal of dramatic effect. With much difficulty we kept our men from interrupting. When he had finished and had withdrawn there was a pause, and the Speaker asked whether the House had any instructions for him. Gladstone sat silent, and, after a moment of suspense, I thought it necessary to take the initiative myself, observing that I supposed Gladstone abstained from doing so on the ground that he did not feel himself responsible for the situation which had arisen from the proceedings of last night, which he had opposed. I said I saw nothing for the House to do, as Bradlaugh's speech did not seem to have introduced any new element into the case. Gladstone concurred with me, saying that he thought it better to leave the details of the proceedings consequent on last night's resolution to be suggested by those who were responsible for the resolution itself. A motion was made by Mr Labouchere for rescinding the resolution of last night; but it was obviously unfair to take such a step without notice, and on Gladstone's re-commendation he withdrew it. I had previously chal-lenged the regularity of making such a motion without notice; but the Speaker had ruled that, though ordinary res-olutions ought not to be rescinded except upon notice duly given, this restriction did not apply to cases of " privilege." There seems to be the same distinction between the rules for " privilege " and those for ordinary proceedings that there is between the rules for playing trumps and those for playing common cards. When Labouchere had with-drawn his resolution, the Speaker called in Mr Bradlaugh, and informed him that the House persisted in ordering him to withdraw. Upon this he stated that he must re-spectfully refuse to withdraw, holding that the House had no legal power to order him to do so before he had taken the oath. The Speaker then informed the House that he required its authority to compel Mr Bradlaugh to obey its directions. Gladstone still remaining silent, I made the necessary motion, which being accepted, the Speaker or-dered the Sergeant-at-Arms to remove Mr Bradlaugh. Captain Gosset advanced, and for a moment there was an idea that Bradlaugh would resist him, in which case the physical force would not have been on the side of the con-stituted authority. However, nothing unseemly took place, and Mr Bradlaugh allowed himself to be conducted below the bar, but immediately returned, and on being removed again, returned again, and again came to the table. The Speaker then appealed to the House for direc-tions as to the steps which should be taken to vindicate its authority. There were loud cries for " Gladstone," but he did not rise, and I therefore moved that Mr Bradlaugh be committed to the custody of the Sergeant-at-Arms for his contempt of the House. Gladstone concurred with me that this was the only course we could take. Leonard Courtney wished to insert words showing that Bradlaugh resisted the authority of the House, because he disputed the legality of its proceedings; but the Attorney-General held this to be an unnecessary and inconvenient addition, and the motion was not made. The Irish moved the adjournment but were defeated; and ultimately Mr Bradlaugh was committed. I don't see how we could have avoided the difficulty in which we are placed; but undoubtedly it is a rather serious one. The Government have done nothing to help the House out of it, and must suffer in their prestige in consequence.

June 24.—Meeting at Ridley's. Lord Beaconsfield, Cranbrook, Cross, Smith, John Manners, Sandon, Beach, Holker, Gibson, and Ridley. Talked over the situation, and decided that I should move for Bradlaugh's discharge, first, however, putting a question to Gladstone as to his intentions. I wrote a note to Gladstone, telling him that I meant to ask a question, to which he replied that he had been so busy with the details of his Budget that he had not had time to consider what he should do, and that he must therefore ask me to give notice of my question. I answered that I must persevere in putting it, and that, if he did not purpose to make any motion himself, I should take on me the responsibility of doing so. I put the question accordingly, and received from him a very curt answer, that he had not yet consulted with his colleagues on the subject. I thereupon proposed my resolution, saying that I had only moved the committal the day before in order to assert the authority of the House, which Bradlaugh had disputed, and to enforce order, which was being violated by his proceedings. Labouchere declared that Bradlaugh would, if released, immediately present himself in the House again. The motion was, however, adopted with very little discussion ; and though Harcourt and one or two others tried to raise a laugh, they were not very successful. There is much uneasiness as to what may happen to-morrow, when Bradlaugh will probably come to the fore again.

July 2.—The Bradlaugh incident has terminated, at least for the present. Gladstone found himself forced to bring the question under the serious consideration of the Cabinet on Saturday, and the result was that on Monday he gave notice of a resolution, to be brought forward last night, for admitting all persons who may claim a right to affirm to do so without question, and subject to their liability to penalties by statute. My first intention was to meet this by an amendment, declaring that if the House was of opinion that any steps were required to be taken, they ought to be taken by way of legislation rather than by way of resolution. Two or three of my colleagues in the House of Commons agreed in this view; but ——, whom we found in the House of Lords, expressed himself decidedly against any language which might be held to pledge us to initiate or to support new legislation, and I subsequently thought it safer to confine myself to a declaration against the virtual rescinding of the recent vote. I wrote to Lord Beaconsfield, telling him what I proposed to do, and asking him to telegraph to me if he had any objection. Not receiving any answer, I gave my notice at two o'clock on Tuesday, and I subsequently heard through Rowton that the chief entirely approved. I had some difficulty in restraining Randolph Churchill from putting down an amendment of his own ; and I could not prevent Gorst from giving notice that he would raise the point of order on Gladstone's motion, as being an infringement of the rule that matters once settled should not be brought forward again in the same session. He was technically wrong, though he argued his point with great ingenuity, and though in substance his contention was very much the same as my own. Gladstone's course was very unpalatable to many of his own friends, and is understood to have met with much opposition in the Cabinet.

July 3.—The Saturday sitting has not been brilliantly successful. The bill was not really through Committee at 12.30 Sunday morning. Our successors are beginning to find that the House is not so easy to lead after all.

July 9.—The Irish bill is becoming a very serious matter for the Government. We made as good a fight as we could upon the second reading on Monday, but were beaten by seventy-eight. We ought to have had at least twenty more of our own men. There was an unaccountable slackness among them, perhaps in part due to a feeling of hopelessness—partly, too, to bad whipping. However, we resolved to renew the fight on going into Committee, and after much consultation came to the conclusion that Pell should move an amendment limiting the operation of the bill to properties on which there had been ejectments during the period of distress. We had reason to believe that we should get some Liberal support to this. Meantime, and while our arrangements were being made, Law had put down a notice of amendment of his own, virtually providing for the extension of the Ulster custom to the distressed districts. This came about in the casual way in which the bill generally has been handled by the Government. During Gibson's speech on Monday he made a remark that the bill was so framed that a landlord could not even escape giving compensation for disturbance if he allowed the tenant to sell his interest in the holding. Gladstone shook his head, and made vigorous grimaces of dissent, declaring that he could; and then Law framed his amendment to give effect to his chief's interpellation. Anyhow this amendment came as a great surprise on the House, and had the twofold effect —1st, of puzzling the Whigs, and leading some of them to think that a great improvement was being made in the bill, and that they might relax their opposition to it, which was what the Government meant and hoped to do; and 2d, of irritating the Home Rulers, which was an effect wholly unexpected and very unwelcome to them.

This being the state of things, we met last night (Thursday) to proceed with the bill. The first thing we learned was that Lansdowne had resigned. This was startling and very significant. The Government were clearly in a very sore condition, and Gladstone and Forster had no temper to spare. Pell moved his amendment in a very short speech. Albert Grey seconded it, in a longer and a very able one; but he confined himself to a general attack on the bill, and said nothing about the particular amendment, except that he did not like it, because it gave too much colour to the bill itself. The Irish Solicitor-General (Johnson) rose to answer, and the Government probably expected a short speech and an immediate division. If so, they reckoned without Parnell, who rose with the Solicitor-General, and was called. He treated the amendment with contempt, but said the question really was, whether the bill was worth proceeding with, now that its character was to be so wholly altered as it would be by Law's amendment. For his part he should not take the trouble of voting for its further progress; but if it were carried on he should consider that the whole land question had been opened, and should move amendments to give it a proper form. Forster was much taken aback, and answered him with some irritation. Soon afterwards the Home Rulers retired to confer, and by-and-by Randolph Churchill came and told me that they had decided that if the division were taken on Pell's amendment, they should vote with the Government; but if it were taken on the main question, they would walk out. It was rather awkward to change front at that moment, but we contrived to ascertain from —— and —— that

the Whigs would not vote with us then under any circumstances, though they would support us in moving amendments in Committee, and, if necessary, in opposing the
bill on the third reading; so we got Pell to agree to
withdraw his amendment, and took our division on the
main question, on which we were beaten by 56, or 22 less
than on the second reading, though only two Whigs voted
with us instead of 21 as on Monday.

The Home Rulers seem to think that they have lured
the Government into a trap, and that they have got in so
far that they can't well get back. Then, if the bill is lost
this year, the Home Rulers will hold the Government next
year to the principles they have admitted now, and will
force them to carry them further.

July 11 (*Sunday*).—I went down to Hughenden in the
afternoon. Lord Beaconsfield sent his carriage to meet
me at Maidenhead, and I had a most charming drive of
twelve miles. The Sunday trains to Wycombe are inconvenient. Found the chief very well, and delighted to
see me. He has been quite alone with his peacocks, and
revelling in the country, which he says he has never seen
in May or June before. I gave him an account of the
parliamentary situation. His general view was, that we
ought above all to avoid putting our Whig friends into
any difficulty by making them appear to be playing a
Tory game. We must keep as clear as possible of any
Home Rule alliance, and we had better not move amendments upon the bill. He greatly doubted the propriety of
our supporting Law's amendment. We ought to make a

strong effort to defeat the bill on the third reading. The Lords, he said, were determined to throw it out,. and he hoped they would do so by a very large majority, a hundred or so. The effect of the proceedings upon next year would be salutary. After dinner we chiefly talked books. The chief is always at his best in his library, and seemed thoroughly to enjoy a good ramble over literature. He was contemptuous over Browning (of whom, however, he had read very little) and the other poetasters of the day, none of whom he thought would live except Tennyson, who he said was a poet, though not of a high order. He was much interested in my story of Sir R. Peel's consulting Monckton Milnes on the relative merits of Tennyson and Sheridan Knowles, when he had a pension to dispose of. He talked of Lord Derby's translation of Homer, and said he had given his opinion against rendering him in blank verse. It was ballad poetry. Pope's style was better suited to it, but was not the right thing. Walter Scott would have done it better than any one. I told him of Tennyson's telling me that Burns originally wrote "Ye banks and braes" with two syllables less in the second. and fourth lines, and that he had spoilt it to fit a particular tune. This was like, or rather the reverse of, Scott's treatment of the heroic couplet. The chief was warm against the Homeric unity, and considered that everything Gladstone had written on Homer was wrong. He agreed with my theory that no poet could be well translated except by a superior (or at least an equal) poet. I said Coleridge's "Wallenstein" was the most satisfactory

translation I knew, but then Coleridge was quite equal to
Schiller. "Yes," he said, "and better." He instanced
Moore's "Anacreon" as a success, and considered the
translator there quite equal to his original. He was very
laudatory of Theocritus, and quoted his line on Galatea
coquetting for the kiss as the most musical he knew in
any language.[1] He used to be fond of Sophocles, and to
carry him about, but did not much care for Æschylus.
Euripides had a good deal of fun in him. Lucian was a
great favourite, and he gave me the True History to read
in bed. He was very fond of Quinctilian, and said it was
strange that in the decadence of Roman literature, as it
was called, we had three such authors as Tacitus, Juvenal,
and Quinctilian. Horace, of course, he delighted in, and
Virgil grew on one; he was a great admirer of Scaliger
and of Bentley; Porson he did not think much of. He
agreed with me in being unable to see the point of "Now
Hermann's a German." He mentioned Bentley's correction
of "rectis oculus" as a good piece of criticism. Ben Jonson
he did not care for. I did battle for him, and he promised
to read him again. He gave me a good deal of information
about editions, and as to which were rising in price. Giffard's Ben Jonson was one which was going up wonderfully.
We lamented the disuse of classical quotations in the
House of Commons. He said he had at one time tried to
revert to them, but the Speaker (Denison) had asked him
not. "Why? Do you think they don't like it?" "Oh
no! the House rather likes it; but you are making John

---

[1] Καὶ φεύγει φιλέοντα καὶ οὐ φιλέοντα διώκει.

Russell restless, and I am afraid of his taking to it too. He gave us six or seven lines of Virgil the other night, which had not the smallest connection with his speech, or with the subject."

July 12.—Stayed at Hughenden till twelve, and had a pleasant walk in the garden with the chief.

He talked over the state of the House, and asked me many questions as to the progress of Harcourt, Chamberlain, Dilke, James, Herschell, &c., and also as to our own bench.

July 15.—The Irish Compensation Bill makes no progress. George Hamilton knocked a big hole in it on Tuesday by statistics, showing that the real number of evictions had been grossly exaggerated. In Donegal, out of 156 as stated in the Government return, there had been 45 cases in which the tenants had been readmitted as caretakers, and 93 in which they had signed acknowledgments and had not been disturbed at all, so that there had only been 18 cases of actual eviction, and of these, about half were due to the action, not of landlords, but of creditors. Gibson at the same time elicited a confession from Forster that the 3000 constables, said to have been employed in protecting process-servers in Galway, were not 3000 separate individuals, but a few hundred men employed several times over—like a stage army, as Plunket fairly said.

The oddest turn has been that of Parnell and his party, who are now beginning to take up against the bill, and are likely to join us in throwing it out on the third reading. The Government resemble Mr Pickwick going about with a horrid horse which he could not get rid of. Their floundering is quite pitiable.

July 28.—The Whigs disappointed us a good deal in the number they at last brought to the division on Monday. We had only sixteen of them. They were also afraid to take the lead in moving the rejection of the bill. But Charles Fitzwilliam seconded the amendment in the first speech I ever heard him make in the House of Commons, and Ramsden spoke very well for us. The majority was only sixty-six, though the great body of Irish voted with the Government. There had been an idea that they would stay away, and Parnell actually was absent; but T. P. O'Connor, while treating the bill with great contempt, said he could not take the responsibility of walking out, as he had intended to do when he came into the House, and so he and those present gave their votes for the Government. T. P. O'Connor speaks re-markably well.

July 28.—On going down to the House to-day I re-ceived a letter from Bradlaugh, complaining of the scurrilous language used about him at several contested elections, and especially of Sir John Hay's speech at Wigton, and of a card circulated at Scarborough. I re-plied that I could not undertake any responsibility for the proceedings of candidates, and still less for those of their supporters, as by doing so I should seem to approve everything which I did not distinctly repudiate, however much I might disapprove it. He made a very temperate reply, thanking me for my letter, and saying he did not wish me to undertake any responsibility; but that he wished to point out to me that, if the Conservatives did not repudiate such language as was used about him, they must be taken to approve it. I must say I think he has ground for his complaint. Our friends want a lesson from "Hamlet," how to use a man according to their own nobleness. News of the disaster to General Burrows's force on the Helmund. I fear this will seriously affect our position throughout Afghanistan. It comes most unfortunately, just as Abdur-Rahman was getting into the saddle.

To August 9.—We have passed a busy fortnight with the stirring events of the debate in the House of Lords on the Irish bill, and the scene of Gladstone's illness. It may be hoped that in both cases we have seen the worst of it, and shall be *quittes pour la peur.* The majority in the House of Lords was a crushing one, and the bill would have been defeated by the number of Liberals voting against it, even had no Conservative been in the division. Cairns's speech on the second night was the great one of the debate, though it was of course less lively and telling than Salisbury's. Lord Beaconsfield's does not seem to have been one of his best. He told me he was embarrassed by Gladstone's illness. There seems to have been no question of resignation after the defeat. Probably none of the Cabinet, except Bright and Chamberlain, liked the bill, or were otherwise than angry with Gladstone and Forster for letting them into the scrape.

Pyncs, September 7.—Note report of Gladstone's speech on Cowen's interpellation (Saturday, September 4). He misrepresents the action of the Powers in dissuading Greece from joining Russia against Turkey. It was in the interests of Greece herself that she was dissuaded from taking a course which would have exposed Athens to destruction by the Turkish fleet. Of course there would have been great pressure then put on the Powers, and especially on England, to interfere on her behalf; and Turkey might have been willing to attend to our remonstrances, but only with the condition that, if we held her back from striking at the ally of Russia, we should assist her against Russia herself. We did the best we could in obtaining for Greece a hearing at Berlin, and in then obtaining for her, without war, a claim and (so to speak) an international title to a revised frontier, such as she very likely might not have obtained had she gone to war. True, she is still left unsatisfied; and we are all ready to admit that Turkey may justly be called on to fulfil her engagements. But I should dispute the proposition that the action of the Powers in restraining Greece from joining in the Russo-Turkish war gave her a special moral claim on their consideration.

Mr Gladstone's remarks on the concert of Europe also deserve attention. He hints that the late Government broke up the concert and adopted a line of isolated action, having for its end British interests alone, and pursued it regardless of the rights and interests of others. He also says that it is " almost a moral impossibility that the whole of the united Powers of Europe ever can consciously act together in the pursuit of an object that is unjust. Errors may be committed, but injustice is hardly conceivable, whilst selfishness is totally impossible." Now it is clear, at any rate, that two or more nations may easily combine for unjust and selfish purposes, as Russia, Austria, and Prussia for the partition of Poland, or Austria and Prussia for the dismemberment of Denmark, and that the other Powers may, through timidity, indolence, or selfish indifference, allow them to act as they please; and so a virtual concert of the Powers may easily commit injustice. And this it was that we desired to guard against when we refused to join in the Berlin Memorandum in 1876. That was a nominally concerted action to be taken by all the Powers, but it would really have been a concert of three Powers only, acquiesced in through timidity or indifference by the rest, had not England dared to have an opinion of her own.

His closing observations on the unreasonableness of pledging the Government to summon Parliament before adopting any measure which can lead to coercion are very refreshing, and contrast curiously with his language in opposition.

Lord Granville's apology for Forster's language about the House of Lords is also well worth noticing. Clearly the Irish Secretary had had a good thrashing in the Cabinet. However he may explain away his words, there can be no doubt of the *animus* with which they were spoken.

CHAPTER XVII.

IN AND OUT OF PARLIAMENT, 1880-85.

CRITICISM IN OPPOSITION——SUMMARY OF POLITICAL EVENTS—— LETTER TO LORD BEACONSFIELD ON THE DEFEAT OF 1880—— PLAYING A LOSING GAME——REMARKS ON IRELAND——COERCION ——THE KILMAINHAM AFFAIR——THE PHŒNIX PARK MURDERS ——IS AN IMPERIAL DEMOCRACY POSSIBLE?——REMARKS ON THE TRANSVAAL——CANDAHAR——THE BOMBARDMENT OF ALEXANDRIA ——THE SOUDAN——HICKS——GORDON——THE REFORM BILL OF 1884-85——PRIVATE INTERVIEW WITH MR GLADSTONE——THE BUDGET OF 1885——CONSERVATIVES TAKE OFFICE——SIR STAF- FORD GOES TO THE HOUSE OF LORDS AS EARL OF IDDES- LEIGH——EXTRACTS FROM DIARY——TO BE " PRIVATE SECRE- TARY TO LORD RANDOLPH CHURCHILL"——SPEECHES OUT OF PARLIAMENT——THE NEW REVOLUTION FORESEEN——THE CON- DITION OF ENGLAND——ADVICE TO ELECTORS——AGRICULTURAL HOLDINGS——IRELAND——FAIR TRADE——THE NEW MOON AND THE OLD——STORMY WEATHER.

THE later years of Sir Stafford Northcote's life were crowded with great and momentous events. As to most of these, owing to the position of his party out of office, he occupied the attitude of a critic and of a teacher. In Parliament his business was to criticise, and his criticism was ever fair, and even generous. But criticism in politics is seldom perfectly well informed, and is seldom efficacious. For these reasons his action was not of such interest or importance as his conduct might well have been had he possessed other opportunities. Again, he was much occupied out of Parliament in journeys to distant towns all over the country, where he did his best to educate his listeners in politics as understood by him. In the chapter on Sir Stafford as a parliamentary leader, much of his activity has already been described. More as to his private impressions will be learned from the diaries which he kept at intervals from 1880 to 1886. In this chapter we shall endeavour briefly to describe his principal contributions to discussion in the House of Commons and on the platform. The events which he had to watch, the policy which he had to criticise, were extraordinary. There were the relations of the Liberal Government to Ireland in the first place. The Government, as is usual with new English Governments, made an attempt to govern without coercion, without renewing the Peace Preservation Act. Then came disorders. The Act was renewed, the Land Bill was also brought in—"A bill of Belial; there is no ruin to which it may not lead," said Lord Beaconsfield. Then came the " No Rent " manifesto; the imprisonment of Mr Parnell and many of his associates. Next followed their release—the " Kilmainham Treaty," or arrangement, or whatever it should be called. Mr Forster and Lord Cowper resigned on this, and presently Lord Frederick Cavendish and Mr Burke were murdered. A new period of repression or coercion followed.

Abroad we were not more tranquil. There was the rising in the Transvaal, the inglorious defeats, the convention with the Boers, and the surrender of the Transvaal. In Egypt there was Arabi's movement, the Alexandrian riots, the bombardment of the town, and Tel-el-Kebir. Russia gave us anxiety on the Afghan frontier, France in Madagascar. The Mahdi's propaganda threatened the Soudan and Egypt. Hicks was permitted to go to his doom; Sinkat and Tokar fell; Gordon was sent on his ambiguous mission, failed, was too long neglected, and the attempt to rescue him ended in the disaster of Khartoum. The Government accumulated unpopularity and misfortunes. The Reform Bill was introduced and carried; but the combined troubles of the Government ended in a defeat on the Budget. Lord Salisbury held a brief tenure of office. Sir Stafford was raised to the House of Lords, with the position of First Lord of the Treasury. The Conservatives were defeated at the general election. Mr Gladstone came in with his Home Rule Bill: it was outvoted; and in the new Government Lord Iddesleigh held the Foreign Office. In a very few months the resignation of Lord Randolph Churchill, the appointment of Mr Goschen to the Chancellorship of the Exchequer, and Lord Salisbury's choice of the Foreign department for his own, left Lord Iddesleigh without place in the Government. His death followed shortly afterwards — his old malady, an affection of the heart, suddenly declaring itself.

The record of these years, of these events, of this close to a long career, is sad, and shall be brief.

Sir Stafford bore the heavy blow of the defeat in 1880 with his usual good-humoured and courageous stoicism, as his diaries partly prove. To Lord Beaconsfield he wrote, when all hope was ended: "There is no use writing about the situation now. I suppose we made a mistake in dissolving; but I doubt whether we should really have gained much by waiting till the autumn, and we acted on advice which seemed good, though it now turns out that our advisers were greatly misled. . . . I hope you are pretty well. This great blow does not do any one any good; but I feel very little doubt that a reaction will come, and, even if it should not replace us in office, it will take the form of a juster recognition of your great services during the critical period we have passed through. The new Government will have some difficult nuts to crack, and it is yet to be seen whether their teeth will not be broken. I take for granted that, unless some external cause prevents it, they must bring in a Reform Bill either next year or the year after, so the Parliament will hardly be a long one." Later he speaks of hopes of further service " when the nation comes to its senses." The Liberal Government " seem to be finding out that they have heavier tasks than they expected."

Sir Stafford was unrivalled in the rare skill of waging a losing fight, playing a losing game, with courage and with good temper. He has been called an optimist; but it would be more fair to say that he deemed pessimism to be allied with cowardice. "Tyne heart, tyne a'" (lose heart, lose everything), says the Scottish proverb, with which he agreed. He never lost heart; and while we keep that, other losses may be reckoned, or would be reckoned in the stoical philosophy, as relatively unimportant. He had stated years before, in a speech at Exeter, when he assumed the leadership of the House of Commons, the nature and limits of his so-called optimism: "If the term optimist means one who thinks that everything at the present moment is as perfect as it can be, and that there is no need for us either to endeavour to improve or to take care lest damage should be done to that which we possess, then I altogether repudiate the title as one which is incompatible with me in every sense. But if it is meant by the use of that expression to describe one who is disposed rather to look on the bright than on the gloomy side, one who is disposed to give credit to his friends and opponents for the best rather than the worst constructions that can be put upon their deeds; if it is meant for one who is prepared to hold the view that though over-trustfulness is foolish and may lead to mischief, that over-suspiciousness may also be foolish and lead to harm; if these are the ideas that are associated with the word optimism, then I claim to be an optimist. I believe it is only by going on with one's work in a spirit of cheerfulness and hopefulness, in a spirit of readiness to acknowledge good rather than to distress ourselves by a possibility of evil, I believe it is only in that way that the real work of statesmanship is to be done.

I believe, myself, that is the spirit in which English statesmen should endeavour to act."

There was in him a good deal of the British soldier's
feeling, who, outnumbered and outmanœuvred, is said to
put his trust in " the luck of the British army." Pessimism is always easy in human affairs, especially in an age
with so troubled a present, so dark a future, as our own.
It may be combated by taking long views, and by believing that as good times, and bad times, and all times end,
ours, too, may some day pass into a brighter tranquillity.
Or we may try the other plan, Sir Stafford's, and, taking
short views, live in the day and for each day's work.

His own work in Parliament, as we have said, was the
task of criticism. For this he was eminently well adapted,
if criticism be the effort " to see things as they are." But
it is not this intention, so much as the desire to prove
them to be of one given complexion or the other, that
usually animates parliamentary criticism. For this labour
he was not naturally gifted; he trusted to reason more
than to rhetoric, and disdained noble opportunities of de-
clamation. Where it would have been easy to appeal to
passion, he preferred argument. He often almost studi-
ously understated his case, as when, in regard to the
Kilmainham affair, he said that the occurrence seemed to
demand " a good deal of explanation." He was less anxious
to embarrass his opponents than to guide them. He kept
insisting on the need of a reasoned policy, which would
at least try to consider all possible results of this conduct

or that situation. Such is the ideal policy of a leader of Opposition in a state formed by rational men.

In England, unluckily, we cannot reverse Voltaire's *mot*, and say that *la raison a tué le raisonnement*. Violent attack is preferred to sober counsel, passion has the preference over reason, and the mild wisdom of Sir Stafford was not to the taste of all his party. He remained true to his conception of duty, of duty and of respect towards himself and his political opponents.

When Parliament opened, in January 1881, even his optimism did not enable him, as he said, to take a rose-coloured view of affairs in Ireland. Later events made this endeavour yet more difficult. People in England, he complained, did not realise the condition of Ireland. They saw the rights of property and of individual liberty over-borne, they saw as if they saw it not. Mr Gladstone, when aiming at office, had done what Sir Stafford could not do, and had viewed the Green Isle through spectacles of rosy tint. He had spoken of "an absence of crime, a general sense of comfort and satisfaction." Consequently he had not renewed the Peace Preservation Act. Mr Childers had travelled in Ireland, and had described himself as "a passer-by." Sir Stafford was reminded of two other notorious passers-by, the priest and the Levite, "on the other side of the way." And now Ireland had two Governments, that of the Queen and that of the Land League. "Do not let us then be told that the Government has not broken down. The Government *has* broken down. They were now asking for larger powers. Why

did you not do it before? . . . You might have put out
the flame while it was small." The agitation in Ireland
was really directed against all holders of property, against
every class that opposed the Land League. More was
intended—legislative separation was intended. The revolution was political and social. Willing workers were
forbidden to work. The remedial legislation of 1870 was
mere "tinkering"—did not reach the root of the evil. If
people were not shot, they regarded being boycotted as
something rather worse (January 6, 1881). On a later
day (January 17) he repeated that Mr Parnell occupied
the position of a rival power, and aimed at "the ultimate
separation of the Legislatures of the two countries." He
demanded the vindication of order as the first thing need-
ful. He was not opposed to a revision of the land laws.
"We are most anxious that the land laws of that country
should be of such a nature as really to suit the necessities
of the people, and to provide, as far as possible, for the
proper cultivation of the soil, and for the maintenance of
a happy and contented population upon it." In criticising
the new Land Bill (May 19, 1881), he kept asking for
clearness of statement, definition of such a term as "ten-
ancy." "We never know exactly where we are: when
we try to express a supposed meaning we are told we are
wrong, and when we try another we are told we are
equally at fault. Do not," he said, "apply a false remedy.
What is it, after all, that Ireland requires? It requires
for its development the application of capital; it requires
the confidence which produces capital; and it requires,

what is still more, energy and wisdom in the application of that capital." "Moral restraint, enterprise, self-exertion," were needed; was the bill likely to bring these virtues in the folds of its clauses? If the changes did not produce a total revolution, "a total destruction of what is called landlordism," then the smaller changes scarcely touched the fringes of the question. Only confusion and quarrelling would be produced, he feared; and the fears have not been without justification. A revolution was to be intrusted to a Commission "of whose composition and powers we do not at present know anything." Many of his opponents seemed "to hate landlords more than they loved Ireland." The people of Ireland would be taught their true lesson backwards, taught to rely on Governments and Commissions rather .than on themselves. They would be taught that "when they are in difficulties there is a simpler course than work—that is, agitation." An old-fashioned maxim maybe; Sir Stafford had not moved with the times. Lord Hartington, however, thought he was moving with them, and that he no longer denounced "the three F's" as "Force, Folly, and Fraud," but was rather inclining to one of the three F's, "Fair Rent." Sir Stafford, however, was immovable in his opinion that they were passing "a bill which has never been sufficiently explained" (June 13, 1881.)

In the following year (February 8, 1882) he gave his views of coercion. If resorted to, it ought to be as a policy, not as "a hateful incident." Government had asked for powers, had obtained them: had failed at first to employ them, hoping that the mere threat would suffice. The Land Commission had not acted as it had been expected to act. "The interest of the landlords ought to be regarded like the interests of other classes. If not, why not?" Yet the real root of the evil had not been reached. Terrorism prevailed in Ireland: little result had come from imprisoning the Irish leaders. Then, "What are our prospects when we go back to the ordinary state of the law?" The Government could destroy, not reconstruct; and he quoted the words of Catherine de Medicis to her son, after the murder of the Duc de Guise: "*Vous savez tailler, il faut savoir coudre.*" They could slice, they could not sew. The Irish were being led to expect something more,—was it a Parliament of their own?

Probably no one knew exactly how much was intended, or what doors were being kept open. All this was opposed to Sir Stafford's constant appeal for a coherent policy that might be avowed and carried through. The release of the Kilmainham captives was another opportunity for similar criticism. What did it mean? On what, if any, conditions were the prison gates opened? On this topic it was often his duty to press questions which perhaps have not yet been satisfactorily answered. In their Kilmainham transaction, Sir Stafford admitted that the Government were consistent at least. "They are proceeding on the principles on which it seems to me that they have all along proceeded. These principles are somewhat those of a pendulum, which swings sometimes to the one side and sometimes to the other. . . . They are pursuing a policy which they have not thought out to its ultimate issues. . . . They are without a policy which they have themselves sought and decided on, and which they are prepared to recommend on their own authority to the House."

These remarks were made on May 2. On May 6, Lord Frederick Cavendish and Mr Burke were murdered by men who, in Mr Parnell's opinion, "must have absolutely detested the cause with which I have been associated," and who, in fact, must have done it to spite Mr Parnell and his allies (May 9, 1882). Sir Stafford in the House merely uttered a few words of sympathy with the victims of the Invincibles, and of support to the Government. In a debate on Irish policy (May 16), he returned to the subject of Kilmainham. The Prime Minister had said that there had been nothing in the nature of a negotiation. The Chief Secretary, Mr Forster, spoke of the strong objection which he felt to govern Ireland by negotiations with persons who had broken the law. It was now that Sir Stafford "felt convinced that there is a good deal which requires explanation. We know a great deal now that it is important we should know; but I do not even yet feel sure that we know all." His efforts to have the subject thoroughly examined were defeated.[1] He feared that submission had been made to the forces of dishonour. Holding these ideas, uttered out of Parliament as well as in it, as will be shown, he naturally resented Mr John Bright's speech at Birmingham, in which he said that the Con-

---

[1] Hansard, cclxvi. 107, 703.

servatives were "found in alliance with an Irish rebel party, the main portion of whose funds, for the purposes of agitation, come from the avowed enemies of England." Mr Bright had added that this unholy alliance made the work of the House of Commons impossible. These are charges which have too long been alternately bandied by either faction in the State, and the persistence with which they are urged may almost lead us to suspect the morality of our politics. They were not charges that could apply to Sir Stafford, who (June 18, 1883) made them the subject of a speech on breach of privilege. Mr Bright expressed his sense of Sir Stafford's courtesy in making his motion. He admitted that the word "alliance" was capable of being interpreted in a sense which he did not intend it to carry. He did not mean that there had been "any kind of arrangement." The dispute ended in a cruel display of Irish ingratitude, which he has doubtless forgiven, and even forgotten, towards Mr Gladstone. He was accused, by Mr Callan, of joining Mr Bright in hallooing "Mad dog"!

The Irish question illustrates the old controversy as to whether a democracy can be an imperial power—whether it can govern other States. History has still to show whether or not, on a large scale, a democracy can govern itself; whether its proper place is not in something like the Greek sytem of the πόλις, with its natural advantages and corresponding drawbacks. A democracy can have no better opportunity for the wider governing functions than under a really trusted leader, such as, in widely different historical circumstances, and with aims and characters leagues apart, Pericles was in Athens, and Mr Gladstone in England. Yet it was under Mr Gladstone that the constant lack of a stable, and far-sighted, and consistent policy displayed itself. The affairs of the Transvaal, of Egypt, of the Soudan, evoked from Sir Stafford precisely the same sort of criticism as the affairs of Ireland. The difficulties were, indeed, immense, and not to be overrated. We showed, as Sir Stafford declared, want of power, want of grip, want of consistency, in the Transvaal. He could easily defend the Conservative Government from the charge of having caused the Transvaal troubles by the annexation. The annexation, at the moment when it was made, probably saved South Africa—above all, the Dutch parts of South Africa —from being swept by the Zulus, and from what would have made that calamity possible, internal anarchy. It turned out that the Boers, after we destroyed the Zulu military organisation, no longer needed nor wanted our presence. The Conservatives, Sir Stafford argued (June 25, 1881), had been anxious to give to the Boers "that measure of representative institutions, and that measure of local self-government, which might be reasonably desired by them." But his party was expelled from office. The Liberals might then have peacefully reversed the measure of annexation. Or they might have maintained British authority at any cost, later. But they did talk of the iniquity of shedding blood, almost all the blood shed being that of gallant British soldiers, sacrificed by the most insane leadership that ever courted disaster. "Arguments of that sort," about bloodshed, "are among the arguments that make one ashamed of one's self. . . . We say your policy was faulty as a whole." If the soldiers had only been allowed to charge at Majuba when they wanted to charge; when Ian Hamilton repeatedly crossed the line of fire to ask General Colley for a charge,—Privates Helmsley and Boyle actually charged alone, and fell,—then we might have held Majuba, and then it is probable that the Transvaal would never have been given up. But some blindness of fate overcame General Colley; we were defeated without fighting, and then it was that the Government, which began the war, talked of "bloodshed," and surrendered. Even afterwards to conquer the Boers was not beyond our power. But the Government, as Sir Stafford said, conducted the negotiations "with divided minds." They ruined confidence in England. They did not, as Sir Stafford told them, remember the advice of Polonius :—

> " Beware
> Of entrance to a quarrel; but, being in,
> Bear it that the opposer may beware of thee."

But, now that negotiations had gone so far, he "should be sorry to say anything that would still further weaken the hope of a satisfactory settlement of this matter."

In the affair of withdrawing from Candahar, Sir Stafford had to defend his old agreement with Sir John Lawrence's policy, as not inconsistent with his present disinclination to leave Candahar. Circumstances had altered, by the nearer neighbourhood of Russia to Afghanistan. We were told that Russia had been justified in her overtures to the Ameer. "Well; but if she were justified, that proves our case: it proves that though you are not afraid of Russia when you are at peace with her, . . . yet that if you ever come into difficulties with Russia, it is in her power to interfere with you in a very inconvenient way in Afghanistan." He was not to be accused of wishing to enlarge our empire. "I can only say for myself it is that which I most shrink from if it can in any way be avoided." He appealed to the authority of Lord Lawrence, who held that it would be our duty to interpose, in case of Afghan dealings with Russia. He did not believe that the Government, in quitting Candahar, had thought the question out any more than they usually did think questions out. He asked if our Indian policy should be at the mercy of every general election. "In adopting such a course, you are attempting one of the rashest and maddest feats that are possible."

Such, however, is the nature of a democracy that would be imperial. He believed that if the Liberals were in power for twenty years, "at the end of that period there will be very little of the British empire left for them to govern." That seems highly probable in any case, for democracies have never yet succeeded in being imperial. They have other aims, other ambitions, inconsistent with empire.

On the Egyptian troubles, the wildly mismanaged bombardment of Alexandria, Sir Stafford had to remark (June

27, 1882), that "the Government are attempting to make war upon peace principles, and such an attempt must always fail." As to our "military operations," which were not war and were in self-defence, he examined that argument from the point of view of Arabi; "was *he* not entitled to defend himself against the ships which were coming against him?" These arguments of the Government weakened their case, and reflected very severely on their ally, the French. The Conservatives would support the Government "on the ground of national interests"; but retained the right to criticise and disapprove of their policy, their miscarriages and shortcomings, their wanton sacrifice of the influence of the Porte. Government at once hampered and isolated us, for example, by not being able to land troops in the seething tumult of bombarded Alexandria. Mr Gladstone found these charges "too vague and general."

Opportunities of criticism less vague were unfortunately frequent in the miserable business which began with General Hicks's march against the Mahdi, and went on through the series of disasters at Sinkat, Tokar, El Teb, Suakim, and Khartoum. On February 12, 1884, Sir Stafford had to move a vote of censure on Government. Their main fault had been the shirking of responsibilities which could not be shirked. England, like Pontius Pilate we may say, was trying to wash her hands of guilt which clings to her. If the Conservatives had been responsible, as they were told, for the misdeeds of Turkey, much more were the Liberals responsible for the misfortunes of Egypt and our own. "I venture to think that the treatment which

General Hicks received, beginning from the time when he was first brought into communication with Lord Dufferin, to the time when his life was sacrificed, was of the most extraordinary character, and amounted to the sacrifice of General Hicks." "The Government would seem to have more regard for their responsibility than for their honour."

Why continue this criticism, so unfortunately obvious, so undeniable, as one is reluctantly compelled to feel, and yet so impotent at the time, so unavailing now? Gordon had been sent alone, unaided, on his dubious effort, and Sir Stafford could only hope that Gordon was not to be treated like Hicks; that his position was not to be " confused." Sir Stafford had never felt any confidence in Gordon's mission. He wanted to know (April 3, 1884) whose servant Gordon was to be. " No man can serve two masters." The " plans," doubtfully attributed to General Gordon, " had always seemed to him rather vague and extravagant." Mr John Morley, when Gordon had fallen, turned this phrase of Sir Stafford's against him. He had a perfect right to entertain these opinions, nor do they at all clash with our admiration of the best, the bravest, the purest of men. Gordon's mission was not of Sir Stafford's sending. In various points Gordon was, if not " extravagant," at all events too much outside the common course of mankind to be a cautious cold negotiator. Every one who knew him at all, knew that he loved honour more than any earthly reward; that once sent, unsupported, to do his best, he would relinquish anything sooner than honour. Those who knew this should either not have sent him out, or

should have trusted and supported him. He was not the
man to make a cat's-paw of: it was by no means safe to
imagine that he would take measures first for his own
safety. He carried the honour of England, as he understood it, a stainless shield without which he would never
return from any fray. In vain Sir Stafford kept asking
the Government for their policy. "Is it their policy to
let things drift entirely, or are they going to stir?" Mr
Gladstone resented the occupation of many nights (seven-
teen) with this question. "They will have made a
precedent of pushing a question of this kind in a measure and to a degree to which I declare, so far as my
knowledge goes, there is nothing approaching a resemblance in the whole history of the House of Commons."
Mr Gladstone thought Sir Stafford's assertion that General
Gordon's plans had failed (he had been refused Zebehr,
with Sir Stafford's approval) was not "beneficial." Was
it premature? Had he "anticipated the fact"? History
knows, and knows, too, that if aid was sent too late to
Gordon, if the blood and labour of our bravest men was
spent in vain, the fault did not lie with Sir Stafford Northcote. Speaking at Barnstaple, as a candidate for that
division of North Devon in 1885, when Khartoum had
fallen, when Gordon's body lay on the sands or tossed on
the Nile, Sir Stafford said: "This nation has exerted
itself to prevent, and to crush in its cradle, the slave traffic
in the interior of Africa. It was for this purpose that
that gallant hero whose name will always be a household
word in England—great and good General Gordon—it was

to crush that traffic in its cradle that he sacrificed his time, his energy, and in the end life itself. It was because he loved those nations who were suffering as he knew from the great evils which civilisation and religion alone could cure—it was because he sympathised with these nations, that he placed his services at the command of the British Government, and that he undertook a mission which few others, or none, would have dared to think possible. He undertook that mission in a spirit of reliance upon God and of trust in His providence, and in reliance upon the hearty support of his countrymen, which carried him through the greatest dangers and difficulties, and which, as I firmly believe, would have enabled him to accomplish his object, had the expected succour been in time. I said just now that his was a name which we should always regard as a household word, and to which we should point with gratitude and pride ; but at the same time I fear we must add that it is a name which will call a blush to our countenances when we think how that great and good man was abandoned, when we think of the last months of his life, struggling against desperate odds, and always hoping against hope that England would in due time come forward and rescue him."

This is a theme from which one turns with an inextinguishable shame and regret. Years have passed, feelings have lost their edge : it scarcely becomes us now to use Gordon's name—it never became us to use it as a party watchword—as a reproach to this individual or that. We were all to blame. He asked for Zebehr, and we refused him. The country, too, might have done more to save him and his charge, but for party. Gordon is our common shame and our common glory; his glory alone is shared by the gallant men who, to save him, gave their lives too late, suffered all extremes of labour and of distress, and were vanquished only by space and time. The names of our soldiers are untarnished by this dishonour. Gordon lives yet in our hearts, a light to lighten our conduct, and aid those who lack his courage and his force, to try at least to imitate in their lives his purity, his piety, his goodness, his contempt of wealth and fame and death. He deserves better than to be the hero or the reproach of a party. "A man," said Sir Stafford, "of whom it has been truly said that he was of a heroic character; a man who was above all things loyal, unselfish, earnest, fearless, devoted to the duties which he undertook, and ready to spend and be spent in the honour of God and his country" (February 23, 1885).

In the affair of the Reform Bill of 1884-85, Sir Stafford's most interesting part has been recorded by himself in a note, a portion of which may be published for its curious interest :—

"The main lines of the discussions on the Franchise Bill of 1884 and the Redistribution of Seats Bill (1884-85) are sufficiently known. The autumn agitation was directed by the Liberals, not so much to the passing of the Franchise Bill, as to which there was at least a profession of agreement on all sides, as to the exciting public feeling against the House of Lords. The results of the meetings held throughout the country seemed to be these : 1. That the passing of the Franchise Bill was adequately desired (though there cannot be said to have been any ardent demand for it), on the part of a large number of persons, especially in the north of England and in Scotland. 2. That it was generally admitted that the extension of the franchise ought to be accompanied, or immediately followed, by a redistribution of seats. 3. That the animosity of the fight was directed against the action of the House of Lords.

"It seemed probable, when Parliament reassembled in October, that the House of Lords would again receive the Franchise Bill in the same spirit as that which they received it with in July; but they had pretty well agreed to give it a second reading, and then to fix the next stage for a distant day (in March or April), so as to give time for the Government to introduce their Redistribution Bill and pass it through the House of Commons before the Peers proceeded further with the first bill. What course the Government might take upon this was of course uncertain; but it was hoped by some, and feared by others, that they would throw up the bill, dissolve, and set on foot a more violent agitation against the House of Lords.

" I never shared the extreme anxiety which was felt by so many on both sides; but it was obvious that the alarm was of itself likely to cause danger, as the cry of ' Fire ' does in a crowded building. . . .

" Already in the early autumn some communications

had been opened with the Opposition leaders through the Duke of Richmond; but these had led to little more than a conference between the Duke, Lord Salisbury, and Lord Cairns, and to a substantial agreement between them as to the course to be taken in the House of Lords. When we reassembled (October 23), and when I opened the debate on the Address in terms of studied moderation, Mr Gladstone replied to me in a speech of no compromise, and of menace to the House of Lords.

" On Sunday, October 26, Lord Norton came to me with a letter which he had received from Gladstone, referring to a conversation they had had at Grillion's in July or August, when Gladstone had asked him what it was that the Conservatives wanted,—if it was that the urban element should be kept as much as possible out of the counties, he (Gladstone) agreed with us. Gladstone had now noticed some expressions of Carnarvon's at some public meeting, and taking a hint from them, he suggested some kind of intermediaries who might draw the scheme of redistribution. This had brought Adderley [Lord Norton] to town in a hurry, and it was obvious that Mr Gladstone expected him, for we were all three in the Chapel Royal, and I observed some significant glances as he saw Norton come up to speak to me. We called in Arlington Street, and had a talk with Salisbury; but the whole matter was very vague. Reference was made to Sir Erskine May, who had been staying at Highclere, and who had been in communication with Gladstone. Norton went to see him, and on subsequent days I also saw him; but everything was vaguer and vaguer. I have a memorandum, dated October 28, giving the substance of my first conversation with him, and another, without date, of a further conversation after he had seen Sir C. Dilke. It may be observed that various communications had been proceeding between Sir M. H. Beach and Lord Hartington, of which I was only partially cognisant, as we did not wish them to commit us as leaders of the party. The advantage we anticipated from these communications was, that we might disabuse the Government of the idea that we only wanted the Redistribution Bill produced in order that we might break up the whole Reform scheme by means of it. That this idea existed among them was evident from some conversations which I had with Lord Tollemache, who, while a staunch Conservative, was in close personal relations with Mr Gladstone and ——. He showed me a ridiculously alarmist letter from the latter, to which I wrote a soothing reply."

A private meeting with Mr Gladstone himself was finally arranged.

" On the 13th November my eldest son came to see me, and gave me to understand that Algernon West and he had been speculating about my views of the position. I said to him what I had been saying all along — to Lord Tollemache, to Mr Peel, and others—by some of whom it must have been communicated to the Ministers —viz., that in my opinion if the Government would introduce the Redistribution Bill all would go right. He asked me whether this might be communicated to Mr

Gladstone as my personal opinion? I said, 'Yes.' He then went away; but in the course of the afternoon he came down to the House of Commons and told me that, as soon as West had mentioned this to Lord Granville, Lord Granville had gone over to see Mr Gladstone, and then desired West to acquaint me that Mr G. would like an hour or two to consider so important a communication, and in the meantime Lord G. and Mr G. would think it most desirable if, on the grounds of old private friendship, I would meet Mr Gladstone for a short conversation either at West's house or Lord Granville's, or elsewhere. I said I must take a little time to consider this request, and I went into the House of Lords and consulted Salisbury. We agreed that I had better hear what G. had to say. I told Walter of this, and he went away, and came back with a message that 'Mr G. is nervous about meeting in the daytime, as so many people watch him. He dines with West to-night (in St James's Palace). Could I meet him there about eleven o'clock, when the guests will have gone?'

"I went accordingly at eleven o'clock, and was let in by Mr West. I found Gladstone alone, and remained with him about half an hour. The substance of our conversation is in my letter to Lord Salisbury (November 13), of which I have kept a copy."

The result of this and other negotiations was the announcement of the Government's willingness to communicate with the leaders of the Opposition on the details of the Redistribution Bill. The proposed conference was accepted, and comparative peace was restored.

The main lines of Sir Stafford's conduct as a critic of Government during his last years in the House of Commons have now been traced. On June 8, 1885, Government were defeated, on the second reading of the Customs and Inland Revenue Bill. In his speech Sir Stafford objected chiefly to taxing a falling revenue in beer and spirits, and to confusing a moral and a fiscal tax. Taxes should be fiscal; but the Government seemed to think that beery and spirituous men were their opponents' chief supporters, and therefore meant to hit them in their pleasant failings. He did not know that there was anything very novel or magnificent in his own principles of taxation, which were that you should raise money in the form most to the advantage and least to the disadvantage of the community, and that you ought, as far as possible, to keep your taxation steady. Mr Gladstone spoke of those principles as possibly deserving to be called truisms and platitudes. He also fell back on the celebrated surplus which was frittered away, and styled Sir Stafford " the author of habitual deficit." In opposition to Sir Stafford, he himself laid down the duty of " Pay your way," and found the real cause of opposition to the Government's proposals, not in compassion for the beer-drinker, but in dislike of the death duties. These arguments and amenities ended in the defeat of the Government by twelve votes.

On the following day, rumours already prevailed that Sir Stafford was to go to the Upper House as First Lord of the Treasury. Of the influences and motives for this change enough will be learned from the following diary,

or at least as much as is deemed desirable.   On July 6,
Sir Stafford took his seat in the House of Lords as Earl
of Iddesleigh, the name derived from a family estate in
Devon.   This was a sacrifice of himself to his party.   His
career had been in the Commons: in the Lords he occupied, for a few months in 1885, the position of First Lord
of the Treasury, and in 1886 held the important post of
Foreign Minister.   On all these matters extracts from the
diary of 1885 may now be given.

June 6, 1885 (*Saturday*).—Came up from Pynes this
evening with Amyas.   Very tired.

June 7.—Prepared scheme of speech for Budget debate
to-morrow.

June 8.—The great debate came off to-night.   Beach
made a good speech; but was unlucky in what he said
about a tax on tea.   His words were greedily caught up
by Sir C. Dilke, and I had, later, to do my best to explain
them away.   The result (a majority of twelve against
the Government) took the House generally by surprise, though we ourselves had reckoned on a victory
by three or four votes.   About forty of the Parnellites
voted with us.   The excitement on the declaration of
the numbers was very great, and displayed itself rather
indecorously.   Randolph Churchill jumped upon his seat,
and stood waving his pocket-handkerchief, and shouting.
Walter [his eldest son] left the House with Algernon
West, and said something about this being a curious
end of Gladstone's career.   West said, "Ah, this can't

be the end now; you will see him come out more energetic than ever."

June 9.—Went to see Salisbury. I was strongly in favour of accepting office, considering that, with all its disadvantages, it was the only honourable course open to us after our action in turning out the present Government. I thought if we declined the responsibility now, we should be held to have justified the taunt that we have no policy and no men.

Had a good deal of talk with friends at the Carlton and elsewhere: opinions as to our taking office a good deal divided; but preponderance in favour. The real *crux* is in the question of Ireland. —— strongly urges the duty of proposing a continuance of the present Crimes Act for one year. If the proposal is defeated, we can't help it, and must go on as best we can; but if we don't make it, we shall be held guilty by the whole of North Ireland.

June 10.—Report that Gladstone had gone to Balmoral, but this is incorrect. He was going, but is stopped by his doctor. The " dutiful communication " has been sent by messenger. Dined with the Middle Temple, to meet Prince of Wales and Prince Albert Victor on the latter being admitted to the Bench. Large party, and the hall full of barristers and students, who cheered several of us as we drank the loving cup, especially R. Churchill and myself.

June 11.—On coming home from a drive about seven, I found Cranborne waiting for me with a message that his father wished to see me, as he had been summoned to

Balmoral. I found Beach with him. He asked me what I thought about taking office; and I replied that I still held that we were bound to make the attempt. Beach urged the importance of making it quite clear to the world that we had no alternative. This is, of course, quite true, and it bears on the question which may arise as to dissolving on the old franchise, in case we are unfairly thwarted in necessary measures, after having been forced to take office. The more I think of the heads of Salisbury's scheme, the less I like it.[1] The point on which it will be necessary for me to insist is, that I should see all the Foreign Office despatches as if I were Prime Minister, otherwise we may be exposed to serious trouble.

June 12.—Telegraphed to Salisbury that the cardinal point of the constitution of the Cabinet seemed to me to require more consideration, and that I must ask him not to pledge me till I had seen him. Several visitors to-day, among them Sir —— ——, warmly thanking me for my services to the party, and hoping I would not desert them, at the same time offering his own if required. To House of Commons, where Gladstone stated that he and his Government had tendered their resignation on account of the defeat on the Budget, and *for no other reason,* laying some stress on the last words, whether as an answer to the charge of " riding for a fall," or whether to hint that the ground of the resignation was not a vital one, had they

---

[1] This scheme was, that Lord Salisbury should be Prime Minister and take the Foreign Office, and Sir Stafford Northcote be First Lord of the Treasury and leader of the House of Commons.

been pressed to withdraw their tender. The House remained sitting till the House of Lords sent down their amendments on the Seats Bill. Gladstone would have liked us to go through them at once, and I should not have objected; but some of our friends thought it better to wait till the amendments were printed. Coming home to dinner, found a telegram from Salisbury asking me to state in detail my difficulties as to the construction of the Cabinet. Wrote memorandum that the separation of Premiership from office of First Lord of Treasury being novel, there would be no precedents to guide us in distinguishing the functions of the one and of the other—*e.g.*, was the First Lord to be in distinct personal communication with the sovereign? Was he to be entitled to see all the Foreign Office despatches, as the Prime Minister is under the settlement of 1851 (Russell, Palmerston)? What appointments were to be at his disposal? I pointed out that in present state of affairs it was essential that the leader of House of Commons should be fully in possession of the foreign policy of the Government. Other matters, such as the *personnel* of the Treasury and offices connected with it, might be settled hereafter. A "scientific frontier" wanted.

June 13.— ―― this evening told me of the wish of the Carlton that I should go to the Upper House. With some of them it is a wish to get rid of me; with others it is anxiety for my health.

June 15.—Meeting in Arlington Street. Salisbury, Richmond, Carnarvon, Harrowby, Cranbrook, Cross, Smith,

Beach, Manners, G. Hamilton, and myself. Stanley had gone to Lancashire. Question whether we should take office put by ——, and answered affirmatively by all, except —— and (in part) ——. House met, and Gladstone announced that he had authentic information that Lord Salisbury was engaged in forming a Cabinet, and that he wished the House to adjourn till Friday; Gladstone, however, thought that we might go through with the Lords' amendments on the Seats Bill, and might read the Princess Beatrice's annuity a third time. To this I assented, and the question that the Lords' amendments should be taken into consideration was put, Dilke explaining that the principal additions were for the purpose of expediting the dissolution, and that they had been inserted on the suggestion of Lord Salisbury. I confirmed this statement; but Gorst and the Fourth party objected to the House being hurried into the discussion, and moved the adjournment of the debate, which was, however, defeated by 333 against 36. Salisbury's present idea is, that I should take the post of First Lord of the Treasury, and lead the Commons, with F. Stanley for my Chancellor of the Exchequer. I have offered either to do this or go to the Upper House, taking the India Office. I have offered to do whatever he thinks best. I have not much heart in the matter. This has apparently been my last night in the House of Commons. I have sat in it rather more than thirty years, and it has become part of my life.

June 19.—To the House at four o'clock. A most remarkable reception when I entered: it was difficult to say which side cheered me most. Speaker read Bradlaugh's letter. I asked Gladstone what counsel he meant to give on it. He replied, "None—at least none at present." I might then have moved the renewal of the order excluding Bradlaugh from the precincts of the House; but I did not like to mark my last appearance by the exclusion of another member. Great dinner at the Mansion-House to Conservative candidates. We had no reporters. Cranborne spoke very well, responding to toast of his father's health.

June 20.—The hitch still continues, and it seems to me likely to prove very injurious to our cause.

We are pestered by reporters, who cross-question the servants. Smith (the butler) was asked the other day what office I was to have ? "After much consideration the Cabinet had offered me the private secretaryship to Lord Randolph Churchill."

June 24.—Went to Windsor by special train at 3.15. All the Cabinet except Richmond, who had hurt his foot; also Balfour (Local Government Board), Chaplin (Duchy), Dyke (Irish Secretary), Wolff (to go to Cairo), Selwin Ibbetson (a complimentary Privy Councillor). Returned by six.

June 25.—Began work in Downing Street. Appointed A. Saumarez and J. F. Daly private secretaries. Gladstone, whom I met on the stairs, was very civil, and presented me with three of his books on Homer.

Party meeting of both Houses at Carlton. Salisbury explained his reasons for taking office. I said a few words, and so did Beach. Several of our friends expressed regret at my leaving the House of Commons, while the Duke of Northumberland and others warmly welcomed me to the House of Lords.

These extracts are, of necessity, most fragmentary. Among the passages omitted, is one in which,—there can be no harm in quoting it, and it is perhaps a proof of Lord Iddesleigh's personal fairness,—Lord Randolph Churchill is described as "certainly the shrewdest member of the Cabinet" which was presently evicted by the general election.

We have followed Sir Stafford's critical work in the House, from 1880-1885, the House which he left in the latter year. A few words may be said of his reception in Exeter and at Pynes, after he was raised to an earldom. Lord Iddesleigh's new honours were welcomed by his neighbours near Pynes and in Exeter. He arrived from London on the 13th of August: his tenantry and the people in the neighbourhood were bent on congratulating him, and the Conservative working men in Exeter were not backward in the same resolve. The local Liberals, also, were not displeased, and, with bunting and music, a very pretty display was made on the railway platform. A *feu-de-joie* of fog-signals was arranged as the train came in, and a happily phrased address was delivered. Lord Iddesleigh, in reply, feared that he could scarcely make himself heard by so large a gathering, and preferred to look on his welcome as personal rather than political. Speaking of Lady Iddesleigh, he remarked that she had shared the labours of his life, having received from her not only " comfort, support, and sympathy," but often having had " recourse to her pen " in order to ease him of the work that was more than a single hand could accomplish. As to the political situation, he remarked that the Government, like most Governments, had fallen, not under the attacks of the Opposition, but self-destroyed. The Conservatives would do their best. " You ought not to think so much of who is to have the honour of doing the thing, as to see that that which is necessary and right for the country is done :" a counsel of perfection this, which, if acted on, would introduce something better than that most imperfect institution, party government. Resisting the temptation of cries to " Go on," he spoke a few last words in acknowledgment of the general kindness. There was a long procession to Pynes, passing under arches lit with coloured lanterns, and the people took out the horses and drew the carriage—near neighbours succeeding to admirers from Exeter,—an attention which a recipient of it once described as " perhaps most grateful to the horses.". So the procession reached home at last, among showers of flowers, and with singing, a happy example of a stainless popularity, honestly gained, and never lost. " If I felt I could command myself," Lord Iddesleigh said, in replying to an address from his neighbours of Upton Pyne and Bramford Speke, " I would like to say a few words of Lady Iddesleigh, and for her; but I know that I could not. I know you all know her and love her so well, that it is quite unnecessary for me to try to put into language that which is in all your hearts. She does thank you most sincerely and cordially for this, the latest act of kindness—I will not call it the last—in coming to meet us on a day which must always remain in our memories."

To every man, however indifferent to fame, the dearest honours he can receive are those which come to him in his own country, from his own people, and Lord Iddesleigh was rich in this kind of honour, proverbially rare.

But he was almost as busy in the country. He spoke in many distant places, Aberdeen, Edinburgh, the north of Ireland, Birmingham, and elsewhere. He was endeavouring to teach the new electors his confirmed doctrine, the doctrine of improvement on old lines, of honesty, steadiness, industry, all that could give confidence in England. He called himself an optimist, but in those speeches he faced facts, and a future that even to him seemed gloomy. To these tasks he devoted his last years, and did not spare his health, which was no longer what it had been. He never had Mr Gladstone's robustness, but he had great energy, and he expended it. He was not an eloquent orator, though his voice was clear and pleasant in conversation or in reading aloud. He was, by instinct, taste, and habit, no dealer in perorations; even before a popular audience he did not appeal much to sentiment, nor at all to passion. Yet he was popular on the platform. He had a telling knack of anecdote, and humour never divorced from good-humour. He did not hide his apprehensions, with all his courage and buoyancy.

He ventured to say what he saw, and to forecast things that, perhaps, may come to pass, as they have often come to pass before in history. Speaking in Edinburgh, in 1884, he said: "I am afraid that the Government will take far too much to the numerical principle, and if you take to the principle of mere numbers, depend upon it you will be introducing the most dangerous change into the Constitution. The first effect of an appeal to the masses would probably be an agitation and then disappointment, and then what would flow from that? Personal rule. Then follows a system under which an individual would obtain a position in which he had, or in which he would exercise, personal authority which there would be no power of resisting. There is a curious saying I was reading the other day in a clever play written some years ago, describing the peculiarities of a government in which there was a constitutional monarch who found himself ultimately in the hands of a man who had begun with the most extreme doctrines of exaggerated Radicalism till, seeming likely to become the Minister of the Prince, he startles him with the following claim, 'Why, if you refuse me absolute power, how in the world can you expect me to establish freedom?' That is the language that has been used and is being used now with regard to our great Prime Minister. They say, 'This is the man, and we are content to support him whatever he may say or do.' If you come to that, it will not be very long before the system produces a reaction, and you will find that there will be agitation meetings of trades-unions, and after that there will come a bureaucratic despotism; that is to say, the permanent officials will take the management of affairs into their hands, and Parliament will have little to do, and the great mass of the people will have little to do, and you will have all the evils of a bureaucratic Government; that is a very dangerous state of things, and one which we do not like to contemplate. I admit that I am travelling into the region of the future, and am giving you opinions which have yet to be verified. But depend upon it that is the course which things are likely to take if you throw up the power of the Constitution. If you destroy or neutralise or turn into a mere sham the independent existence of the House of Lords, and if you proceed, as you would have to proceed, and as you have had plenty of suggestions you would have to proceed, to deal with the House of Commons upon equally stringent principles, we shall find that the power will pass away from our old parliamentary institutions, and that it will fall into the hands of personal Government and what I call an autocracy tempered by despotism."

This may be, no doubt, but it seems likely that much will be suffered before we suffer anything like a personal despotism. More certain is another prophecy of his, that we shall have "a second chamber in the streets." That we have already, indeed; and, of all governments, government not by the people but by the mob is the least desirable. This is how he stated an obvious view: "You will have the trades-unions developing their power, carrying on not only that which is legitimate and desirable—

namely, the consideration of the proper interests of their own trades—but carrying on political business, and also interfering to overrule the elected representatives of the people. That is a danger which those who read history, and especially who read the history of that great revolution in France which took place now about a hundred years ago, will very easily appreciate and understand."

From these modes of popular sway, Sir Stafford expected, or feared, the overthrow of the English character for steadiness and honesty, the flight of capital. But where is poor capital to find a refuge? International disturbances will leave no land where capital can find security, and this was, perhaps, an element of the future which he did not foresee. Talking on this topic at West Calder, in November 1885, he spoke as follows:—

"There are some people in this country who are always prophets of evil. There are some who think the greatness of Great Britain, of the United Kingdom, has now culminated, and that we have before us a terrible period of decline. .I don't believe a word of it: I believe myself that our fate lies in our own hands. I believe, under Providence, that the energies of the people, if they are rightly directed, if they are allowed fair play, will pull us through all the difficulties of our situation, and will improve, instead of diminishing, the position of this country. Don't allow yourselves to be led away by the sort of teaching you hear from some quarters, that the great imperial questions don't concern the mass of the people— that what the masses of the people have to look to is the improvement of their houses, of their food, of their wages, and of their employment, and perhaps of the education of their children.   These are all matters of the highest importance, I admit.   But you must not separate them and set them against the other calls upon the energies of the empire, because you may depend upon it if you do you will find you are only injuring and ruining the very classes in which you are interested, by bringing about the ruin and fall of the empire.   Remember what a peculiar position this country stands in.   We are not in the position of the United States of America, which our friends are pointing to and urging us to take as an example.   We rejoice to see the prosperity which is to be found in these countries, but we are in a different position.   We have not all that expanse of land—at least not within the four seas.   We have not that unlimited power of disposing of the population; we have not the growth of the materials of manufacture which some countries enjoy.   If everything were to begin again, you would only have one or two points on which you would be able to trade and hold your own in the intercourse with nations.   But you have —and this is your great advantage—an established character; you have established the character for this country, that it does its work honestly and well, that it is to be trusted in all that it turns to, that it is to be trusted in all its relations.   You have this advantage.   It has already established such a large connection that it has become the centre of credit, that it has become a sort of depot for the trade of the large population of the world; and that as long as it fulfils these conditions, which have given it these advantages—as long as it takes full measure of that great accumulation of trade and credit which was set up by our forefathers—so long there will be in this country a state of things in which working men will be able to obtain employment, and the various classes of society will find that they share in the general prosperity.

"It must be taken into account that we have accumulated in this little island so enormous a proportion of the population of the world, and in that way have gathered together much energy, which is displayed in our numerous industrial establishments. Think what it would be if that were taken from us; if the great mass of the people here were left without employment—without that which has been created and maintained by our system of credit, and our system of commerce, and above all, by the character you have obtained for honesty. Remember that, and do not be short-sighted enough—I put it only upon that ground—I do not speak of honesty or dishonesty; but who will be short-sighted enough to risk and jeopardise the general interests of the empire for the sake of these class interests?"

The end of all these things is not to be foreseen. The current runs ever swifter to the fall; and how the vessel is to bear herself in the gulf below, whether she is to be swamped, or to sail into smoother waters, no man can foretell. We are to have a new morality. Sir Stafford spoke for the old beliefs.

We have indicated the sentiments of Sir Stafford as to the Social question, the great question. He did not look forward to any vast change in human affairs, any complete reconstruction of society on a new and untried principle. To him it was a choice between bettering the world on the old lines of capital and employment, or, apparently, of mere chaos, without any escape save through autocracy. For example, he does not discuss the idea of "nationalising" land and capital, the aim of extreme reformers. On the matter of small agricultural holdings, a scheme which would be rejected by the extreme Left, he spoke thus, at Lynton, in May 1885 :—

"I have no doubt that a great deal might be made out of a movement, wise and judicious, for creating small holdings when the country is capable of supplying them, and when you have those who will be able to cultivate them well. But let me ask any good and sensible labourer what size the holdings should be, supposing it was decided to give them ? I was told some time ago that there were thirty millions of people and sixty millions of acres of land, and that therefore everybody ought to have two acres apiece. I should like very much to have two acres in the heart of London, I think it would pay very much better than on Dartmoor or elsewhere; but we cannot all have our two acres in London, and let us suppose that some honest labourer were to have two acres of his own on Exmoor, what is he to do with it ?

"It is not the possession of land but the possession of the power of working the land that you have to consider.

A man must expend a good deal of capital in order to get the means of working even two acres of land. If he has to buy a spade and hoe there is capital required, and if he has to get credit in order to supply himself with necessaries, and if he has got to wait in order to sell his produce, he is in great trouble and difficulty; but when he has got the property, is he to be more secure in his property than anybody else? Depend upon it, if you diminish the security of property the people who will feel it most will not be the rich, but the poor. The great support of sound agriculture is the capital which is expended upon it; and if there is no security for expending the capital it will not be expended; and if the capital is not expended, England will not be as productive as America or many other countries that could be named."

These remarks would be an answer to a scheme for giving everybody two acres of land of his own, but are not an answer to a scheme for making the State the owner of all land and of all capital. On Irish questions, too, he could merely say, in his own words, and with his own illustrations, what has been said so very many weary times. [Thus at Paisley, in May 1886, he admitted that, in matters of commerce, Ireland had been very badly treated. England had behaved "in a most unworthy and selfish manner in crushing and keeping down the industries of Ireland." But he saw "no compensation in Home Rule."] He thought Mr Gladstone would grant the demand of the Irish to their ruin, as the gods ruinously answer men's prayers, *poscentibus ipsis.* [The sketch of

Home Rule was a pretty sketch, not a practicable architect's plan: "I remember quite well seeing once a very beautiful design—an elevation for a front of a house that was going to be built. It was the west front, and it was a very beautiful elevation; but when the house came to be built, it appeared that the east front showed in a remarkable way behind the west front—that the whole did not fit together—and the result was that the whole thing was unsatisfactory indeed.. The architect's defence was, 'I had nothing to guide me in drawing the east front. I drew it from my view of the west front, and therefore I saw nothing of the inconvenience that arose.'

The old system of life, more justly and liberally worked, was his idea of a remedy for Ireland. 'Ireland requires many things; but one thing she requires certainly—she requires to know she is governed."[1] This, it must be repeated, this and no revolutionary change, nor in finance any attempt at bringing back the mastodon of protection, whether under the name of Fair Trade or otherwise, was all his policy. "I do not believe in some of the suggestions" (as to reciprocity and fair trade) "that are put forward by friends on my own side." He knew that Mr Cobden's ideal future of universal free trade had not arrived. It is very long on the road. "That which Mr Cobden asserted was bad for England and bad for the world, we say is bad for the foreigner and bad for the world also; but the difficulty lies in this—how are you to gain your end? When they were agitating they

[1] Hansard, May 16, 1882.

had an easy task comparatively—they had to convince the Parliament and the Government of England that it was desirable to put down the protection that then existed, and the thing was done. But how are you going to operate on the minds of the foreign countries and get them to do the same thing? That is the problem. Let us just look back for a moment at the history of the manner in which our free-traders have dealt with the question. When first they got the protective duties taken off, and the productions of England thrown open, they believed that all other nations would abandon their protective duties and that their hostile tariffs would fall down, as the walls of Jericho fell at the sound of the trumpet. The prevailing belief that was in the minds of those men at the time was this—that England was the great obstacle to the free trade of the whole world, and that the landlords of England were the obstacles to that difficulty being removed in England. That was the view they took; but somehow or other the walls of Jericho did not fall down, and for some years, although we had very great prosperity, owing to the great reduction of our own tariffs, we did not find that the foreign markets were opened in the way that was expected."

Much worse than the evils we know, he thought, were those we fly to in "false remedies." This, in regard to all the new difficulties, which are only the world's old difficulties, far more widely felt by a more educated people, far more violently resented, was Sir Stafford's attitude in these late years of his life. He indulged in no dreams and no delusions. Fair trade, a specific of the moment, was "a pious opinion," not a practicable policy. The newer remedies meant national ruin. He disliked the signs in the heaven of politics, the strange conjunction of planets in the sky above England. At Aberdeen, in 1885, he happily and appropriately illustrated these from the ballad of "Sir Patrick Spens": "Mr Chamberlain is not the leader of the party. The leader of the party is a much abler, much greater, and much more dignified person than Mr Chamberlain. I am prepared, from a long acquaintance with him, both as a friend and as an opponent in Parliament, to bear the highest testimony to the great abilities of the late Premier Mr Gladstone; at the same time, I think he is about the most dangerous statesman I know. What signs of danger are there? What signs of bad weather are there which you sometimes notice when storms are coming on? It always seems to me that the worst sign of bad weather is when you see what is called the new moon with the old moon in its arms. I have no doubt that many of you Aberdeen men have read the fine old ballad of Sir Patrick Spens, who was drowned some twenty or thirty miles off the coast of Aberdeen. In that ballad he was cautioned not to go to sea because his faithful and weather-wise attendant had noticed the new moon with the old moon in its lap.[1] I think myself that that is a very dangerous

---

[1] "I saw the new moon late yestreen,
    Wi' the auld moon in her arm ;
  And if we gang to sea, master,
    I fear we'll come to harm."

sign ; and when I see Mr Chamberlain with Mr Gladstone, the old moon in his arms, I think it is time to look out for squally weather." Many a threatening new moon has held Mr Gladstone in her arms since his alliance with Mr Chamberlain went where the old moons go. But,

> "Be it wind, be it weet, be it snaw, be it sleet,
>   Our ship maun sail the faem."

Such, and of such tenor, were his popular addresses. The following chapter will contain extracts from his diaries, and other accounts of his Irish journey, and his expedition, in a non-political character, to Edinburgh, at the Tercentenary of the University.

CHAPTER XVIII.

HOLIDAYS AND HOLIDAY TASKS.

CRUISE IN THE PANDORA—BAD WEATHER—SHAVING ON BOARD SHIP—SOTOMAYOR—GIBRALTAR—" EXCEPTIONAL WEATHER " —MALAGA— PORT MAHON — SARDINIA— SORRENTO — CARTHAGE — SYRACUSE — SNIPE ON THE ANAPUS — NAPLES— MENTONE—HOME—POLITICAL REFLECTIONS—DIARY—VISIT TO IRELAND — BELFAST — FRIENDLY MOB — SPEECHES — IN WALES—RECTORSHIP IN EDINBURGH UNIVERSITY—SPEECHES —TERCENTENARY—THE WEST COAST—BALMORAL.

EVEN the weariest statesman is allowed a few holidays, especially when out of office. Sir Stafford's holiday-time was occasionally occupied by holiday tasks, as when he visited the north of Ireland in the autumn of 1883, and made political speeches. But his voyage to the Mediterranean in the Pandora, Mr W. H. Smith's yacht, in 1882, was purely unpolitical. Of both the Irish and the southern trips he kept diaries. Unluckily the brief notes on the Mediterranean cruise tell us little of what he thought and felt in Sicily, at Pompeii, in Carthage, and other scenes whose interest can only die with human memory of the past. The cruise was ill served by weather, and the diary once more makes us marvel at the courage of ladies, who are " not good sailors," and yet go down into the deep. Lady Northcote, Mrs Shelley (Lady Margaret Shelley), Mr Henry Northcote, Miss Smith, Mr John Northcote, and others, were the party which started from Portsmouth in the Pandora, on November 27, in stormy circumstances. The early part of the voyage was a series of puttings into havens, out of the rage of perilous seas. They began to think that they would never reach the " tideless dolorous Midland sea," and the shores where Carthage lies forlorn. Quoits on deck cheered the leisure of the vigorous. The less vigorous possessed their souls and kept their berths in patience. On December 2, the diary announces better things :—

" *Dec.* 2.—We were cheered by the first news of the morning (about 7 A.M.) that C. Finisterre was in sight. As the day advanced the sea became much calmer, and we had a beautiful run to Vigo, which we reached before 4 P.M. A quite magical change took place in our two invalids as soon as we got into smoother water. They got up and were half dressed before we cast anchor. We had a very lively dinner and evening. The health officers came on board, to give us *pratique* and to be entertained with champagne. They were very courteous and dignified.

" *Dec.* 3.—A quiet Sunday, for which all very thankful. Careful shaving of the crew in the forecastle, and scruples as to the use of the blunt side of the razor. Service on board. Short walk on shore in the afternoon. Not much struck with the town. The commandant of the fort (Señor Llorentes) called on us, reminding me that I had given him permission to accompany the Abyssinian Expedition in 1868. He was very friendly, and recommended us to take a drive either towards Bargona (which would be nearly in the direction we shall take in sailing to Lisbon) or to Sotomayor, lying inland about fourteen kilometres. Señor Sagasta's house is in that neighbourhood. Quiet evening. The roll in the harbour indicates a good deal of wind outside. Voted that we would stay here another day before going on to Lisbon.

"*Dec.* 4.—Ordered two carriages to take us to Redondela, the station two or three miles short of Sotomayor. The steward found us a smart young man to go with us as guide and interpreter. He combines this calling with that of a butcher or a purveyor of meat. We did not exactly make out his name: it was something like 'Thomas.' He had been in England, and received part of his education at the Brighton College. His father is said to have been a purveyor of meat to the British navy. It was a rather showery stormy day at times, but mild, and beautiful between whiles. Lady Northcote, Helen, and I went in one carriage with the guide on the box; the others went in the other carriage, Harry acting as conversation-master. We took our lunch with us, and found a very clean, tidy sort of *posada* at Redondela, where we got a room and refreshed ourselves. The younger members of the party went out for a walk, while Lady Northcote and I amused ourselves looking out at the window. It is a queer little place, but has a thriving air. We observed a great many houses in which the lower storey was devoted to cattle and pigs, while the upper one was neatly got up and formed the habitation of the family. There is an air of politeness and even of dignity about the people. We were much struck with their quiet manner, not staring at our party, although we must have imported a good deal of strange life into the place. We got back in the afternoon, and spent the rest of the day on board. The wind still very high."

The weather continued to be most unruly; but on December 9 they found themselves at Gibraltar, where Lord and Lady Napier showed them no little kindness. The diary runs on :—

" The weather is now what Gibraltar calls cold. We should call it fresh. From the telegrams we learn that there is severe frost and fog in London. Mr Pender has been very kind in directing the agents of the Eastern Telegraph Company to furnish me with the summary of English news every day at all the stations in the Mediterranean which we may visit. This is a very great boon. He also gives me the privilege of sending messages free of charge, as ' service messages.' Had service on board. After luncheon the younger members went on shore for a walk. Weather very ' catchy '; and several sharp showers. Read aloud the fourth book of ' Paradise Lost ' in the evening.

" *Dec.* 11.—A rainy day. We all went on shore and got safely to the Convent, where Lord Napier showed us over the house and tried to show the garden ; but weather did not permit. So Margaret and I settled ourselves to a game of billiards, and the others looked over photographs, and otherwise amused themselves with the A.D.C.'s, Major Napier, Major Gilbard, and Mr Napier. After luncheon the younger members attempted a walk and donkey-ride, and succeeded in seeing the galleries, and in getting wet. Lady Northcote and I took a drive in a close carriage to the North Front, and afterwards to the Governor's Cottage at Europa Point, so as to get a general idea of the place ; but the rain greatly marred our enjoyment. The 'West Indian Aloes' or 'Socotras,' and the 'Bougainvilleas' were most beautiful. The exceptional character of the weather was strongly impressed upon us. I remembered that it was exceptional when I was here in 1869, and am inclined to suspect that it generally is so. Perhaps the rule proves the exception, just as the tail sometimes wags the dog. Lord Napier told me he always insisted on tanks being put up at every house which the Government let to any one, as he seemed to think the supply of water very precarious."

On this occasion the supply of water was vastly in excess of the demand. They gleaned the impression of Gibraltar, which Charles II. derived from Taunton, that it is always raining there. Indeed, if the weather was exceptional, it persevered in being "still more exceptional" day by day, and, as in another case of bad years in finance, "not to be exceptional was the exception." They were told that Tangiers would prove a haven hard to win, and were warned as to the strength of

> "The running seas
> Between the Pillars called of Heracles."

" *Dec.* 13.—No Tangiers to-day. The rain has taken courage, and the wind is following its lead. We spent all the morning on board; but were able to go on shore in the afternoon, and to pay a very long visit to Mrs Ramaggee, the great lace-dealer, who delighted our ladies with a great many beautiful specimens, giving me a Newfoundland puppy to play with meanwhile, that I might not become impatient and carry off her customers too quickly. They made several purchases, and then Jack and Helen started for a walk up the Rock, while Lady Northcote, Harry, and I went to Benoliel's shop, where, however, we were rather disappointed with the much-vaunted collection of Moorish ornaments. We made a few purchases, and returned to the yacht.

" *Dec.* 14.—Started at 4 A.M., but were not energetic enough to get up to see the last of Gibraltar. When we did come on deck we found ourselves approaching Malaga, with a brilliant sun and fresh breeze in our favour. The Sierra Nevada and Sierra Ronda are great features in the scene; and Malaga itself is picturesquely situated, though a dirty and unattractive town when you are in it. The old line of fortifications looks well, and the cathedral is well placed. The officials were rather troublesome, and the doctor who came with them was anxious to put us in quarantine because our captain had gone on shore with the ship's papers. They asked us pointedly whether anybody on board was ill. Our ladies are now such good sailors that there was no scruple in answering for them; and I judiciously suppressed the fact that I was 'travelling for my health,' as it would have given our friends a grand opportunity for displaying their authority. The British consul, Mr Bidwell, came on board, and was very useful to us. He accompanied us to shore and to the Protestant cemetery, where we visited his poor brother Mowbray's grave. The cemetery is beautifully kept, and there is an air of peace about it, with its lovely flowers and beautiful sea-view. We came back to the yacht at twelve, and hastily wrote a few letters, as the post goes at one. Off again about 1.15, and had by far the pleasantest day's sail we have yet experienced. It seemed as if all our troubles were over, and that we were really going to have a good time. The coast very fine, and the sunset most beautiful. In the evening began to read aloud the 'Bride of Lammermoor.'

"*Dec.* 15.—'Varium et mutabile semper.' All our hopes dashed by a storm in the night, and a high sea all day. Found ourselves abreast of C. Palos when we got up to breakfast. Kept along the Spanish coast as far as C. Nao, and then began to strike for Iviza and so to Port Mahon.

"*Dec.* 17 (*Sunday*).—In Port Mahon. A splendid resting-place. We appreciated Andrea Doria's saying that there were four good harbours in the Mediterranean, June, July, August, and Port Mahon. After service the guide (Francis Prieto) came on board, and we desired him to order a carriage. After luncheon, Lady Northcote, Margaret, and I went for a drive in an open carriage drawn

by two mules, with the guide on the box. The rest of the
party went for a walk. We drove through the curiously
paved town at a very rapid rate, so that we were more
shaken than if we had been in the Gulf of Lyons. Our
guide made us first go and call on the consul, M. Segui,
a gentlemanly man, with whom I sat for a short time, and
who, coming down to see me off, and finding I had ladies
with me, insisted on sending for his baby, of whom he was
enormously proud, he having been married for eight years
before attaining to the honour of parentage. The baby
was a nice little girl of eight months old, wearing already
a pretty little pair of earrings. After paying this visit we
took a drive into the country. We were struck with the
apparent comfort of both town and neighbourhood, though
there was no very striking beauty in the scenery. The
fields are very small, not more than from half an acre to
two acres in size, and separated by enormous stone walls,
the materials for which were not far to seek, for the whole
ground is a mass of rock, with little interstices of earth,
which in some places have been enlarged by grubbing up
the stone. There was a good deal of young wheat making
its appearance in some of these little patches. Others had
a little vestige of grass, on which cows, sheep, and donkeys
were feeding. There was a good deal of the prickly pear,
and a quantity of ilex, olive, orange, and other trees. The
guide stopped the carriage for a moment as we passed a
nice-looking house; and saying something about gathering flowers, ran into the garden. Our driver, who I suppose would not even have understood Castilian Spanish,

only the Minorcan *patois*, went slowly on, and we began to feel ourselves at his mercy ; but at length the guide came up with two really beautiful nosegays of geraniums, carnations, and other flowers, and a branch of orange with four young oranges on it for me. We drove on till we came to an ilex, hanging over the road; when our guide, exclaiming 'Oak!' jumped up on the box-seat, and seemed likely to share the fate of Absalom among the branches. He was looking for some edible acorns, but did not find any, and murmured that somebody must have been ransacking the tree already. We came back to the yacht much pleased with our excursion. There are some Spanish men-of-war lying in the harbour. One of them sent this morning to inquire whether the Pandora was not an English gun-boat with an admiral on board.

" *Dec.* 18.—Started after breakfast, and made our way out of harbour, dipping to four Spanish men-of-war as we went out; but only three returned the compliment. A tolerably good day, but not exactly suited to our ladies. Wind got up in the night, and on

" *Dec.* 19 we woke to find that we were to stop at Cagliari, as the captain thought we should find the passage to Naples rather disagreeable. The coast of Sardinia is very beautiful about Cape Spartivento, and thence to Cagliari, which is itself a striking town. Having sent a note to the consul (M. Pernis) asking him for a guide, we prepared to go on shore after luncheon and see the place. At this conjuncture a brilliant thought occurred to Lady Northcote. With the intuition which pointed out to Columbus the great truths which lay beyond the Atlantic Ocean, she seized the fact that Palermo, the promised land to which we have so long been looking forward, was now actually nearer to us than Naples itself, and she suggested that we exchange the roundabout course for a straight one, and make direct for the great Sicilian harbour. The idea was received with acclamation by the whole party, including our commodore (Helen), and we felt like Tennyson's crew, when some one proposed that they should put an end to their voyages in the happy Lotos-eaters' land.

> 'We have had enough of action and of motion we,
> Rolled to starboard, rolled to larboard, with the surges seething free.'

So we telegraphed home, and to the Stanhopes, and to the consul at Naples, to say 'Palermo direct,' and to ask that our letters might be sent on there. Having taken this great resolution, we prepared to go on shore; but as Lady Northcote did not much care for stepping into the boat in the then rolling condition of the sea, we left her behind. The rest of us found a carriage which Mr Antonio Cugurullo (one of the clerks of the consulate) had got for us, and some in it, some on foot, we visited the public garden (from which there is a magnificent view), the old Roman amphitheatre, and the cathedral. A quiet night, though with a good deal of rain."

Indeed, the voyage, so far, was like Lord Tennyson's tour in northern Italy:—

> " Remember what a plague of rain
>   Beset us on the Lombard plain.
>   Of rain at Genoa, rain at Parma,
>   At Padua rain, Piacenza rain ! "

On December 22, still fleeing from the cloud Harpies like the sons of the North Wind, they reached Palermo, and " kept Christmas there very properly." On the 28th they were in a position to appreciate Saint Beuve's line—

> " Sorrento m'a rendu mon doux rêve infini."

" *Dec.* 28.—(Helen's birthday.) We made our excursion to Sorrento, driving all the way, as a pleasanter manner of going than by the train, which would have taken us to Bagaria. Visited the curious Villa Butera, where there is a sort of sham convent, built in the seventeenth century, with wax-work figures of monks and other personages. The old lady who showed it gave us an account of two of the figures, representing a monk and a nun, who had retired into the convent for the purpose of being next door to one another, and had contrived an access to their rooms through the partition wall. This afforded our show-woman great amusement. Lunched on the hill going up to the old city, and then Lady Northcote, Margaret, Helen, and I seated ourselves on a beautiful point of the mountain, while the rest went to the top. The shepherd girl who had lost her kerchief, her brother with the newly born lamb, and suchlike sights, entertained us till the return of our party. Visited the palace of Prince de Villa Franca ; beautiful terrace and gardens. Got home about

5.30. This was a most enjoyable day. Sicily is a charming country, but the people have an appearance of great poverty, strongly contrasting with the well-to-do, handsome Minorcans whom we saw in our drive through the rocky country about Port Mahon. For natural fertility Sicily has an advantage of ten to one, but the populations are in quite an inverse ratio so far as comfort goes. The heavy taxes on food, &c., tell very severely on the Palermitans."

On the 30th they reached Goletta:—

" *Dec.* 30.—Having got *pratique*, we went ashore (all except Lady Northcote) in time for the twelve o'clock train from Goletta to Tunis, which is ten miles off. Our guide, who repeatedly impressed upon us that he had lived here twenty-seven years, accompanied us. We went to the Hotel de Paris, or Bertrand, where we had an excellent luncheon, and then went on to the bazaar quarter; but the time when it should be visited is from nine to twelve, when what is called the bazaar—*i.e.*, the open buying and selling—goes on. This being Saturday was also a bad day for a visit, as many of the Jewish shops were closed. We were, however, taken by our guide through a courtyard, filled with palms and other plants, and up to a long room, where we were courteously received by the proprietor, who shook hands with us, made us sit down on some handsome mother-of-pearl seats, and offered us a cup of coffee apiece. I thought it very good, though too sweet. Meanwhile we had every sort of burnous, shawl, scarf, &c., to choose from, and we made several purchases, on which we presumed that our guide got his commission. On our return we had the honour of travelling in the same train as the Prime Minister of Tunis.

"*Dec.* 31 (*Sunday*).—The consul came to lunch, and afterwards took the gentlemen of the party to Carthage, —none of the ladies caring to go. We drove first to the College of St Louis, which occupies a site on the Citadel (the ancient Byrsa), and where all the best things found in the ruins are said to be deposited. Unfortunately the priests who attend to them were absent, and we could not (or at least did not) get in, though Stanhope showed his agility by climbing in at an open window, and would have opened the doors from within if we had not feared a scandal. The French call this site that of the Temple of Æsculapius; but the consul says that is not the general opinion of antiquarians. We went on to the great cisterns, which supplied this part of the city with water. There are some still larger ones on the side near the Goletta, which we afterwards visited; and many of the houses had cisterns of their own. The cisterns were supplied by an aqueduct of some 50 miles in length, of which there are many traces, and which is said to be quite perfect for several miles of its course; but in Carthage itself the remains are very shattered. The great features of the place are: 1. The much larger extent of the city than I had in the least expected; 2. The great beauty of the situation; 3. The utterness of the destruction of every building of any sort or kind, except the remains of the cisterns and some traces of an amphitheatre.   The ground for miles is covered with stones, the *débris* of the ruins—but it is but the shadow of a shade that remains of Carthage itself.

" The consul took us to see his own country-house—very charming ; and showed us some of the palaces of magnates, including that of the Bey himself.   He praised the Tunisians ; but he is such an Arab himself that he was sure to do this.   He said there had been great sympathy with Arabi, and that if he had escaped from Egypt and reached Ben Ghazi, the whole of the north of Africa would have been in flames.   The game is now considered to be up ; but the English are less popular here than they used to be.   The French, he thought, were not likely to attempt the annexation of Tunis, but they were trying in every possible way to extend their influence and to exclude other countries.   It would suit them very well that there should be occasional troubles, which would demonstrate the feebleness of the Bey's government.

" *Jan.* 1.—We all wished one another a happy New Year. It opens with a most lovely day, very bright and rather fresh.   The consul says rain is much wanted, and the season is exceptionally dry.   We cannot bring ourselves to regret this as we ought.

" The younger members went on shore and had rather a tiring day.   They brought back the news of Gambetta's death.   Lady Northcote and I remained quietly on board, and read Chaucer and a little Italian collection of popular stories which we got at Palermo, and which is curious as showing the bitter anti-aristocratic feeling of the Sicilians.

" *Jan.* 2.—Started for Malta after breakfast. Lost a couple of hours by a mishap to the engine, and did not reach Malta till about ten next morning. Good passage.

" *Jan.* 5.—The weather having prevented our sailing last night as we had intended, we spent the day in a charming expedition to San Antonio and Verdalla, the two country residences of the Governor; and were much struck with the beauty of the gardens at the first, and that of the situation of the second. We dined and went to bed in good time, having to start for Syracuse in the night. We did start accordingly about 11.30, and after a fairly quiet passage found ourselves—

" *Jan.* 6—at Syracuse about 8.30. Just as we had finished breakfast came the health officer and doctor, who would not give us *pratique* till the whole of our party had been paraded before them. Lady Northcote had to put hasty finishing touches to her toilet, in order to display herself. They departed satisfied. The vice-consul (M. Pisani) then came on board, having already sent my letters, but none for any other of our party. In the course of conversation I mentioned Stanhope, when he immediately remembered that a packet had come for him; and then I mentioned Mr Smith, when it appeared that he had letters for him which had been waiting eight or nine months !

" After luncheon we took a couple of carriages, and, declining the assistance of a guide, started for Epipolæ and Euryalus, where we were rewarded by a magnificent view of Etna, Hybla, and the northern part of the island, and of the great harbour, Ortycia, Achiadina, and other well-known scenes of the great Athenian siege. Harry, Stanhope, and Helen made a short cut on foot, rejoining the road near Timoleon's Villa, where we had left one of the carriages to wait for them. We were struck with the more flourishing appearance which the people here present than that of the Palermitans.

"*Jan.* 7 (*Sunday*).—Service on board. After luncheon went on shore, and saw the fountain Arethusa (either a natural spring of fresh water within 9 or 10 feet of the sea, or a basin supplied by a submarine shaft connected with the aqueducts of Achiadina), the cathedral (with some traces of the old temple of Minerva), and the museum.

"*Jan.* 8.—Most of the party went on shore after luncheon, leaving Lady Northcote and Mrs Stanhope on board. Drove first to the Latomiœ di Paradiso, and the cavern called Dionysius' Ear. Then saw the Teatro Greco, and then the Amphiteatro Romano — both very interesting. Then drove to the Catacombs, and went through a portion of them; and ended by visiting the Latomiœ di Capuccini, where the 7000 unfortunate Athenian soldiers, captured after the great siege, were imprisoned, and underwent such terrible suffering. The place is now a lovely spot, thickly planted with oranges and lemons, some of which our guide gathered and presented to us.

"*Jan.* 9.—Stanhope, Harry, and Fred went off after breakfast to explore the Anapus and to shoot snipe, of which, however, they only got one. The ladies went ashore with me after luncheon, and we went over the theatre and amphitheatre, and Dionysius' Ear, which they had not seen yesterday.

"*Jan.* 10.—Left Syracuse soon after 10 A.M. A perfect day for our sail to Catania, which we are now approaching (12.30). Etna is rather lost in the clouds. It showed very well an hour ago.

"*Jan.* 11.—Started at 10.30 for a drive in the country, with the original intention of going to Nicolosi; but, being anxious to get back in time to sail at three, we cut short our expedition, and lunched in a field near Punta San Giovanni, having first seen and declined a 'back garden' in the town, which was kindly offered for our accommodation, but which was not tempting. The spot actually selected commanded a most lovely view of Etna, and we lay under some trees on a knoll in the corner of the field, enjoying the shade, for the sun was very hot. We got back by three, much charmed by our day, but not so much so with our guide, who was rather. stupid and very extortionate in his charges, though he had good manners, and thought himself a smart fellow. At three we set sail for Taormina, which we reached in about two and a half hours of lovely coast scenery. The day was delicious; but we noticed ominous signs in the 'glassy' look of the sea (Lady Northcote's comment), the 'old moon in the new moon's arms' (mine), and the wild look of the sky at sunset (Mrs Stanhope's). The night was a rather rolling one."

On the 12th they visited Messina, and some of the party viewed the ancient theatre at Taormina. Rain now gave place to the fine dust of the *sirocco*.

"*Jan.* 15.—We had planned an excursion to Castanea; but the rain was so teasing, with fierce showers occasionally, and the sky so overcast that we gave it up. Lady Northcote, Harry, and I, stayed on board all.day. The rest went for a short walk in the afternoon.

"*Jan.* 16.—Took a drive this morning, and went first to the Capuccini, where we had a beautiful view, and then to the Villa Guelfonia, also beautiful. Vice-consul Rainford came to call after lunch, and told us the people were very much worse off now than before the days of Italian unity, the taxation being enormous. Started for Naples about 4.20. Not very good views. Rain.

"*Jan.* 17.—Reached Naples about eleven. Had a beautiful view as we passed Capri early in the morning, but the clouds had settled down again before we cast anchor. Got our letters, and had luncheon; after which we all went on shore. Helen and I went to the museum, where we spent the whole of our time; the rest went shopping in the direction of the Chiaja.

"*Jan.* 22.—After breakfast started for Castellamare, which we reached at eleven, and immediately went on shore and took carriages to Pompeii. Had a most charming day, and a picnic near the house of Sallust. Development of a new crater on Vesuvius, which presents a grand appearance in the evening."

The rest of the cruise was in familiar waters to Mentone, without even stopping at Elba. They did not try fortune at Monte Carlo.

"*Jan.* 30.—On our way back we came across a French cavalry drill, and were much struck by a new method of dismounting. Each trooper threw his left leg forwards over the saddle, turned so as to sit sideways on the off side of the horse, then threw up his legs, *turned a somersault backwards*, and alighted on his feet on the near side. Lady Northcote holds that all this drilling means that France is preparing for war. All of us went on shore for a walk after luncheon.

"*Feb.* 1.—Started after breakfast for Cannes; a most beautiful sail along the coast, with grand views of the Alpes Maritimes. Quite understood the French idea of the *revendication*, for which they made the war of 1859. Found Cannes harbour so crowded that we turned back from it, and ran into Antibes, where there is a delightful little haven, with hardly any vessel of any kind in it. We preferred it to Ville Franche. Its situation is certainly much more beautiful. Walked on the ramparts.

"*Feb.* 2.—After breakfast sailed for Nice, where we landed the younger members of our party to go to lunch with Dr Rollit, and to see the Carnival procession from his windows. Remained ourselves on board till after luncheon, and then strolled to the promenade, where the procession was forming, and where we saw a good deal more of it than our friends did from their window. Returned to Antibes in the evening.

"*Feb.* 3.—Sailed to St Raphael, where we landed, and went to lunch with the Salisburys at Villa Marguerite (Valesclusa), situated in very pretty country, which will probably ere long become covered with villas. After lunch, Lord and Lady Salisbury, and some of their party, walked down to the harbour with us, Lady Galloway going down in the carriage with Lady Northcote and visiting the yacht. Returned to our favourite harbour, Antibes."

Friday the 5th was their last day on board, and they were at home on the 10th, after a rather unlucky cruise, as far as weather was concerned.

The next diary is the story of a trip less pleasant and stormy in its way, a political tour in North Ireland, in the autumn of 1883. Sir Stafford's own version may be given first as it appears in his journal, with additions from his speeches, and from other accounts.

"*Aug.* 24, 1883.—Came home to Pynes after the practical close of a very tame and unsatisfactory session. We have not found much benefit from the new Rules of Procedure, except possibly in the working of the Grand Committees— or at least of one of them, for the Law Committee was rather a failure. The Bankruptcy Bill has been well discussed, and the House have accepted the work of the Grand Committee with little debate except on the question of the extension of the bill to Ireland. It remains to be seen what other measures can be dealt with in the same way; probably not many. As regards the behaviour of members in the House itself, the less said the better.

The Government have not distinguished themselves much. The Agricultural Holdings Bill is rather a sham, which will do little good or harm. What will come out of the Corrupt Practices Bill is a question. It will render it necessary for us to develop voluntary action much more than has yet been done, for there will be little money to spare for paid agents.

" The foreign and colonial questions left in a state of confusion are (1) Egypt; (2) Suez Canal; (3) South Africa, comprising the Transvaal and Bechuanaland, the Basutos and the Zululand difficulties; (4) Madagascar, the treatment of Consul Pakenham, the arrest and detention of Mr Shaw the missionary, and the insult offered to Captain Johnstone and the Dryad; (5) the Congo; (6) Afghanistan, and the subsidy to the Ameer Abdul-Rahman; (7) the New Guinea annexation.

"*Aug.* 31.—Letters from Lord A. Hill and Lord Rossmore, who want me to visit and speak at Monaghan. I must not, however, undertake any more Irish work. Dublin will be affronted as it is. Note Parnell's speech, reported in papers of yesterday. His moderation is ominous, and prepares one for some fresh 'transaction' on the part of the Government. It would be unpolite to say that it points to a new treaty of Kilmainham. But the Gladstonian legislation for Ireland is Danaidal. Note Bright's speech at opening coffee-house at Birmingham, and his suggestion that the excise duties collected within the municipality should be handed over to its management.

" *Sept.* 1.—News of young Lowther's victory in Rutland.

Very satisfactory, as showing the temper of the farmers, and administering a snub to Mr James Howard and the Farmers' Alliance. Letter from ——, deprecating my visit to Belfast as likely to affront and alienate the Catholics, by indicating an exclusive alliance with Orangeism. Told him I hoped he would find himself mistaken; that I wanted to infuse a rather more imperial spirit into the party, and to draw them a little away from the disputes among themselves to the great questions which affect the whole empire. Undeveloped Conservatism needs to be fostered into life. Great interests at stake, equally dear to Catholics and Protestants. Parnellites the common enemy, and manner in which present Government has dealt with them makes me very suspicious of further concessions.

" *Sept.* 4.—Read Fawcett's pamphlet on State Socialism and Nationalisation of the Land. Very good and suggestive. Perhaps a little too adverse to the principle of State aid; but that is necessarily so in an attempt to check the spread of dangerous doctrines. He is champion, ἐπὶ τὸ κάμνον.

" *Sept.* 5.—Wet day. Went to meet of the stag-hounds. But it was too wet to make a ride on the hills pleasant; so Fortescue and I rode home again, leaving the huntsmen to enjoy themselves as they might. They did little; and Ebrington is growing impatient to kill a few more stags, as they are increasing too much, and doing damage to the farmers. As we got near home, my horse came down with me, and broke her knee rather badly. We were on level ground, and going quite gently. I was not hurt, except for a little sprain of the back.

"Note Hartington's speech at Sheffield, and good article upon it in this day's 'Standard.' Note also Chamberlain's short letter to the Battersea Radical Association. 'I have always assumed that the first step in the direction of reform would be an assimilation of the county and borough franchise. Public opinion must ripen considerably before it would be possible for any Government to go further, and the final settlement of the franchise question must of necessity be postponed until there is evidence of a general agreement on the subject.' Compare this with the 'daring duckling's' speech at the Cobden Club dinner, and contrast with Hartington's.

"*Sept.* 20.—Started for cruise in Pandora [to Ireland ultimately]. J. S. N. and Hilda, Fred and Margaret Shelley, Frank Farrer, and Lady Susan Fortescue went with me to Dartmouth, or rather to King's Wear, where we found the boat waiting to take us on board.

"*Tuesday, Oct.* 2.—A deputation from the County and City Conservative Association came on board before breakfast and presented an address. I express my regret at not being able to visit Dublin on this occasion. Hope to do so another time. A few words of encouragement. Start for Belfast by two o'clock train, Tottenham with me. Ladies, with Fred and Frank, remain on board. Jack is on his way, *via* Greenore, to Belfast. At Portadown, and again at Lisburn, there are deputations with addresses, to which I make brief replies. Reach Belfast about 6. 30, and find

ourselves in a whirlpool of excitement. Fearful crush at
the station, through which Sir T. Bateson and Lord Arthur
Hill with difficulty get me to the carriage.

"Everybody, however, is disappointed at my not having
come by sea and landed at Carrickfergus, where thousands
of people had assembled to meet me, and to make a trium-
phal entry into Belfast. We drove round some of the
streets of Belfast to see the decorations, and then out to
Belvoir, where a deputation met us at the gates of the park
and brought us to the house.

"*Oct.* 5.—Began by receiving deputations from the Oddfellows, and from the advocates of Women's Suffrage.
Then drove to Carrickfergus, the road by which we ought
to have come on our arrival. Lunched with Mr Greer,
M.P., were photographed, visited the Castle, and stone on
which King William landed. Came back to Belfast in
the Pandora, which had taken a certain number of the
party down to Carrick. This evening was the unlucky
torchlight procession, which was organised in spite of remonstrance from Sir T. Bateson and myself. It was generally well conducted as far as its members went; but
some of the lower people and boys attracted by it were
rather riotous, and some windows were broken, both at the
newspaper offices (both sides) and at a convent where the
Lady Superior was actually dying. There is no reason to
suppose that her death was in any degree accelerated by
the disturbance, or that she was even conscious of it. But
the circumstance will be much magnified by our opponents;
and it is an illustration of the mischief of these processions.

"*Oct.* 6 (*Saturday*).—Most of our party went in after breakfast to attend the laying of the first stone of the new Orange Lodge by Lady Crichton. It had been suggested that I should be asked to do this; but I had prevented the request from being made, as I was most anxious to avoid giving an Orange character to my visit. It has, however, been impossible to keep clear of that character. Orangemen have crowded round me everywhere. Their bands and scarves have been conspicuous in all the meetings. It would have been impossible to repel them, and serious injury might have been done had I attempted it. Waterford, Jack, and I started late from Belvoir, and drove to the Botanic Gardens, where an enormous crowd had assembled. There were probably about 40,000 people present and within sight of the hustings. As to the hearing our speeches, the less said the better; for in addition to the difficulty of the numbers, we had to contend with the various Orange bands and their music. After the meeting we went with the Duke of Abercorn, the young Hamiltons, Crichtons, Tottenham, Macartney, Ion Hamilton, King Harman, Somerset Maxwell, and the Batesons, to Baron's Court. Several addresses were presented at different stations. Between Dungannon and Pomeroy a stone was thrown at the train, which broke the window of the compartment next our own, and struck Lady Crichton sharply on the back. She was a good deal hurt, though not seriously injured. We arrived at Newtown Stewart, and were escorted from the station through the town by a torchlight procession and band, organised by Captain Maturin. We reached

Baron's Court late, and found the Duchess, Lady Lansdowne, Lady Blandford, Lord and Lady Winterton, Lady G. Hamilton waiting dinner. Hasty toilet. Pleasant, reposeful evening.

"*Oct.* 7 (*Sunday*).—Drove to church in the morning. Jack assisted rector (Mr Winn) in the service. Walked back, and after luncheon took a walk with the Duke and Duchess round the garden and up to the home-farm. Very much charmed by the whole family.

"*Oct.* 8.—Drove with the Duke to see some of the neighbouring farms. Returned to late luncheon. Went out to play at salmon-fishing, but without result. On the following day there was an enthusiastic meeting at Newtown Stewart. Coleraine was visited on the 10th, and the Giant's Causeway on the 11th. On the two following days there were more orations, the 14th was Sunday, and a blessed day of rest.

"*Oct.* 15.—A wet wild morning. It cleared a little before the time came for our landing, but was still so bad as to make us abandon the attempt to land at the outer steps of the pier, where great preparations had been made for our reception. We rowed to the inner steps, and hastened to the hotel (Olderfleet), where I first received, and replied to, several addresses, then lunched with a large party and made them a speech, and then 'said a few words' to the people outside. I believe all this failed to satisfy them for my not having landed on the red cloth under their arch, and listened to the addresses given from a sort of pulpit erected for their better delivery.   Drove out to Magheramorne (Sir J. M. Hogg's) where again a band, an address, and some more 'few words.'   In the house, besides the family, including A. Saumarez and wife, were Mr and Lady Mary Cooke and Mr Des Graz.

"*Oct.* 16.—Tullymore is certainly one of the most beautiful places I have seen.   We had first a charming walk by the river-side, and then a drive among the woods, before luncheon.   Afterwards we drove to Castle Wellan (Lord Annesley's) where we were to have stayed, but had found it necessary to give up our engagement.   Lord Annesley met us at his garden gate, showed us some of his planting, and made me put in a tree.   Then he drove us round his beautiful lake, and brought us back to tea.   Back to Tullymore to dinner.

"*Oct.* 17.—Started about eleven to drive across the Mourne Mountains to Rosstrevor, where the yacht had been sent to wait for us.   It was a striking drive through a wild country.   The chief properties through which we passed were Lord Roden's, Lord Annesley's, Lord Downshire's, and Lord Kilmorey's.   The houses on Lord Roden's and Lord Downshire's estate seemed superior to the others. We noticed a large number of unroofed and deserted cottages, which the driver told us had belonged to men who had sold their tenant-right and emigrated.   Lord Roden afterwards told me that this was a beneficial process, so long as the landlord had a voice in the matter, for he could put two or three evacuated holdings together, and make adequately large ones of them.

But under the new Land Act he can do nothing, and what happens is that the more energetic man sells his tenant-right to the less energetic, emigrates much to his own advantage, but leaves Ireland all the worse off for the exchange."

The rest of the Irish diary merely records movements in the direction of Wales, where he had to attend meetings. A more complete view of the Irish tour, and of Sir Stafford's speeches there, may be gleaned from the following incidents.

I wish [writes Mr John Northcote to Lady Northcote, on October 4] you could have seen the greeting which my father received. They yelled and screamed with delight, and rushed at him the moment he got out of the train, and pushed and crowded and fought to get near him, until I really began to be afraid he would be hurt in the crowd; but Lord Arthur Hill got behind him, and kept them off, and we slowly struggled through to the carriage,—one man patting him vigorously on the shoulder, and crying, "Hurrah! you're the boy." Then we drove about amidst a continuous crowd of shouting, enthusiastic working men, and finally came out here just in time for dinner.

Sir Thomas Bateson had made a mistake, for he had invited enormous crowds to meet my father at Carrickfergus, and in the city, in the morning, and had not told my father, and so they all missed seeing him. Many had come from great distances, and many workshops had a whole holiday—and so people were very angry, and inclined to blame my father for not coming; but I am happy to say I have put a considerable number of them right about the matter. The town is much decorated, and among the placards there is one I particularly

like, which is "Our Leaders — Northcote and Salisbury."
Father was in very low spirits the first evening, but he is more
cheerful now, and keeps very well, although they keep him hard
at it.   He made a capital speech yesterday.

"They say I did well yesterday.   I was only moder-
ately satisfied," says Sir Stafford.   From Belfast, as we
have seen, he went to the Duke of Abercorn's, at Baron's
Court, Newtown Stewart.   He received deputations of
Oddfellows.   "You are the best British baronet that
ever crossed the Channel," their spokesman said.   A
deputation of "strong-minded women" was also received
—a trying encounter for any man.   A big blue banner
was raised in welcome, with the legend, "Long live Sir
Stafford Northcote, the Opponent of Atheism"—a rather
unexpected theological testimony.

At 'Derry their "marvellous reception" was tempered
very much by regret for some local window-breaking by
roughs at Belfast, which had a melancholy sequel.   The
Lady Superior of the convent assaulted by the mob died:
she was dying when the disturbance began, and may
never even have been aware of the riot.   But the event
was terribly painful.   Such are the doings of mobs, however loyal.   "The window-breaking," says Sir Stafford,
"was not done by any of the procession; but of course
the procession led to the crowd of idlers who actually did
it, and I am very unhappy about it."   This led to the low
spirits which made him at one time doubtful of his
own success.   The enthusiasm of Coleraine and Larne

failed to cheer him much. "However, I believe I have done some good," he adds, on mature reflection.

In his speech at Belfast (October 4), he made the following remarks on the policy of Mr Parnell and Mr Gladstone, with a humorous and too appropriate illustration: "There is a tendency on the part of Mr Parnell's party to draw towards Mr Gladstone's party and the Liberal Government, and to endeavour by association with them to gain something which will forward their object. I can well believe that between the skill and patience of Mr Parnell and his readiness to accommodate himself to the peculiar weakness and characteristics of the Prime Minister, the Government may be led into concessions which may be enlarged into measures of a fatal character; but remember this, whatever blows Mr Parnell strikes, he strikes not a particular institution, but at the English connection altogether. I do not know that it would be fair to claim for Mr Parnell community with the great leaders of the Irish people centuries ago. There is a story told of the Earl of Kildare, who, in the reign of Henry VII. or VIII., was in arms against the British power, and who was particularly at enmity with the bishop of his diocese. The Earl burned down a church in the diocese, and when questioned afterwards, and asked how he could have done so horrid a thing as burn a church, he said he never would have done it if he had not thought the bishop was inside. I believe the same is the case with Mr Parnell, and there are many institutions which he only attacks because he thinks that the

British power is inside them. I hope that he may be frustrated in his attempts."

As to the *trop de zèle* which breaks the windows of quiet religious ladies, he had uttered his warning: " I believe the time is coming and is not far distant when we shall be called upon to fight, not with our hands—as Irishmen are perhaps sometimes a little too ready to do—but with our voices, and our energy and our organisation at the poll, to which we shall have to go, and where that contest will be waged. Gentlemen, I hope you will keep your powder dry for the occasion; and when I say that, I do not speak literally with regard to powder, for I am told that I expose myself to being brought up under the Crimes Act for having used such a word. I speak metaphorically, and I say you must keep yourselves ready. Your oratory, your eloquence, your zeal in fighting your battle, you must keep ready to use when the moment for action comes, as come it will. . . . But remember, *no offence against those who differ from you,* no offence that can give them an opportunity of complaining that you are yourselves breaking the law and the order which you profess to support; and don't forget that, though the great strength of our party may be amongst the northern Irishmen, and amongst those of whom I have been speaking, do not forget that they are by no means the whole strength of the Conservative and Union party throughout Ireland. Do not forget that there are others who, differing from you in not immaterial particulars, yet will be ready at the right time, ready to stand by the old cause. Do not forget to recognise all that is earnest and good in them. Do not forget, too, that they are the allies you must have if you wish to maintain that which is your true character, that which is the character of the true National party in this country. Do not allow yourselves to be lowered into a section, do not allow yourselves to be carried away by regard for mere sectional individual interests, but stand by the great cause, and stand by the old banner, and stand by it in company with those who are prepared to stand with you."

At Larne his remarks on the Land Act were assuredly not violent nor incendiary: "But I am quite prepared to say that I consider the great principles upon which all legislation should be founded are the principles of justice and fair treatment; and with regard to the Land Act in particular, I say that in so far as that Act was intended and framed for the purposes of giving proper security to the capital invested in. the. cultivation of land—now that I have seen something of the agriculture of this country, and what the conditions are under which that agriculture is conducted—I say that is a sound and right principle, and that everything should be done that can give fair encouragement and confidence to the tenant-farmers. At the same time that can only be done by doing justice to them, and doing it in such a way that you do no injustice to others. If it is to be in the nature of a boon to one class of those who are engaged in agricultural pursuits at the expense or with injustice to other classes—I care not whether those other classes be the owners of the land or the labourers on the land—if it is to be a measure pressed in that spirit, it will not succeed in the object aimed at, and there will not be the result which is desired from it. If there is a feeling that justice is being done to all, and done impartially, then I venture to think that we may expect better results from this sort of legislation. But here again is just one of those questions on which so much turns upon the administration. The value and importance of such legislation as contained in the Land Act does now greatly depend upon the method of its administration. 'It sometimes reminds me of the figure which was seen by the king in his dream, and which was expounded by the prophet—the figure which had feet partly of iron and partly of clay. The Land Act seems to me to rest on such a foundation, the question being whether you have got an iron and permanent footing, or a clay footing which will be carried away. So far as it is a measure of justice and equity, it rests upon iron; so far as it rests on injustice, it is a foot of clay, which will in time be carried away."

When once the Irish expedition was over, Sir Stafford's next task, following almost without a break, was a tour in gallant little Wales.

"*Oct.* 22 (*Monday*).—Evening meeting at Carnarvon. Drove there. Enthusiastic reception; but of course tame after Ireland. Spoke in the Pavilion to about 5000 or 6000. Thought to have done well and to have avoided treading on the toes of the moderate Liberals and Dissenters. There is a very up-hill battle to fight in Wales, but something to be done by showing the people what Conservatism is. No Conservative of Cabinet rank had ever spoken in North Wales before, nor any one (except myself at Brecon) in South Wales. My own good reception was of course largely due to civility to a stranger; but Mr Douglas Pennant was warmly welcomed too, notwithstanding his having been told that no Welsh audience should ever listen to him again, on account of some remarks of his reflecting on the national character.

"*Oct.* 28-30.—Reflected on my expedition. I think it may fairly be called a successful one, though I do not share the enthusiasm with which some of our friends regard it. The amount of loyal feeling displayed in the north of Ireland was mainly due to causes unconnected with my visit, such as the growing irritation of the Orangemen, who thought themselves abandoned by the country to which they wished to remain united, the boastful language of the Parnellites, the Monaghan election (Healy), and the 'invasion of Ulster' at Dungannon and elsewhere. My presence was of the sort of use that a lightning-conductor is. It gave a comparatively safe means of escape to the electric fluid with which the air was heavily charged. I did what I could to direct the energies of our friends to the registration courts and the organisation committees. How far I have succeeded time must show. As regards other matters, it is possible that my visit may have added a little to the excitement, but it let off more steam than it generated; and a good deal of zeal was expended in cheering me which would otherwise have gone to breaking heads and discharging revolvers. On the whole a good stroke of work has been done, in showing England and the world that there is a party in Ireland heartily loyal to the Union.

"*Nov.* 3.—Elected Lord Rector of Edinburgh University, against G. O. Trevelyan and Professor Blackie. This seems to excite our friends very much, and I suppose it has a good appearance, which is a good thing for the party."

Whether the appointment was or was not a good thing for the party, for the University of Edinburgh it was a good thing. The rectors of the Scottish universities have not, as a rule, very much to do. They are represented by an assessor in the councils of the College, and their chief functions are to give a prize, to utter a speech—and, above all, to be elected. The constituency is the students, and they get an extraordinary amount of entertainment from the struggle. There is usually a Liberal party, a Conservative party, and an Independent party among them, but the latter seldom carries its man. The others select some celebrated persons, often not unconnected with letters, and they canvass, and intrigue, and expend their wealth on printing pamphlets and squibs. Many meetings are held, much young rhetoric bubbles over, and not infrequent peas and other missiles are thrown about. But the essence of the election is usually political, though it would be difficult to name the party which Mr Carlyle, for example, represented. The rectorship gives eminent men a title not to be disdained, and brings them pleasantly into contact with the young. During Sir Stafford's tenure of this office he had far more work to do than commonly falls to Lord Rectors, for the Tercentenary of Edinburgh University was celebrated in the spring of 1884 with much festivity, and in the presence of many distinguished aliens. The Principal, at that time, was the late Sir Alexander Grant, editor of the 'Ethics of Aristotle.' He had just written a history of the University, the youngest in Scotland. In the Rector and the Principal this Alma Mater was peculiarly lucky, for no two men could have been found better qualified to grace the ceremony and to please and charm the visitors from abroad. But this is anticipating. Sir Stafford went to Edinburgh on January 29, 1884, and it is understood that he grumbled less than Mr Carlyle did of the discomforts attending the journey. The collar of his shirt may have been blackened in the train, as Mr Carlyle complained in his own case with much vigour of invective. The new Lord Rector did not think it necessary to mention this detail; but he did " expect fun from the symposium to-morrow." He was warmly welcomed by the students, on this or another occasion, at a social gathering, where he told some of his Devonshire stories. In his rectorial address he discouraged the tendency of literary persons to abstain.from political life. The students in Scotland do not carry to that pitch their exclusive devotion to letters. " With us the object of the University is not merely to protect scholars, but to form citizens." Turning to the studies of the place, he denied that the time spent on the classics was time wasted: "No doubt there have been many young men who, when they came to compete in the examination halls, or still more in the actual walks of life, with contemporaries prepared upon a different system, have felt an inferiority in practical and directly, useful knowledge, which has placed them at a considerable disadvantage. But for all that, there is in the old learning a charm which carries us away from the bonds and fetters of the workaday world, refreshes us when we are weary, elevates us when our aims are sinking, cheers us when we are despondent, calms us when we are agitated, moderates our minds and thoughts, alike when we are in prosperity and in adversity, sets before us high examples of courage and patience and wisdom and unselfishness, and does us, too, the inestimable service of renewing in our own hearts the memories of our nobler though probably less practical selves—such as we were when we began to look eagerly forward to the race in which we had not yet engaged, and which we have since found so absorbing of our energies."

He ventured on a defence of Greek literature; not unnecessary, for apparently universities will soon need to be told that screws, iron plates, chemistry, and the development of the electric light of the streets, are not the only things worth study—that the best words and thoughts of an age which cared for none of those things are also worth attending to. Greek is in a tottering condition, not for lack of the best of teachers at Edinburgh, but because Greek is thought, here, as in America, not to be "practical," not actual enough. It was thus that Sir Stafford commended a kind of learning which, if not practical, is disinterested, and if not actual, forces us to say, " So much the worse for minds to which it seems lacking in .actuality ":—

" It might be said of the best period of Athenian history, that it was a democracy tempered by comedies; and what comedies they are! It is not easy to convey to you young men any adequate idea of the delight with which, when one is wearied with long sittings in the House of Commons, one takes up the ' Knights ' or the ' Clouds '; and then there is the more serious tragic poetry, which, while it tells the tale of Grecian thought and breathes the spirit of the Grecian muse, opens to us from time to time the depths of the universal poetry of mankind, and startles us at moments with its religious, its almost Christian sentiments. When we listen to the noble pleading of Antigone, her piety towards her brother, her resolution to obey the higher law of God rather than the law which condemns her to die for the discharge of a sister's duty, and her somewhat haughty refusal to allow her younger sister to involve herself in her fate, we feel as if we had before us one who might fitly take rank with Shakespeare's Isabella, nay, whom I would not hesitate to place above her for dignity and greatness of character, even though there are wanting in the older play those more distinctly Christian touches like the celebrated passage that 'all the souls that are, were forfeit once,' which gives to ' Measure for Measure ' its chief flavour of superiority."

The Rectorial address was very much liked, but the Lord Rector's hardest holiday work had to come. On April 16 he was again in Edinburgh, at the assembly which gathered to celebrate the Three Hundred Years' life of "The Town's College," for Edinburgh University is civic, and owes nothing to popes and saints.

Sir Stafford briefly described the scene to Lady Northcote: "Just a line to say it is hopeless to think of writing. Yesterday was a very striking though tiring day. I wish you could have seen the congregation of all manner of gowns and hoods which assembled in the old Parliament House and formed the procession to the old Cathedral of St Giles, which has now been very well restored. I have ordered a 'Scotsman' for each day, so you will get the account. I struck work after the evening reception, and declined to go to the ball. The M——'s are most kind and considerate—and don't ignore the 'cravings of youth.' But it is an advantage to be with people who can sympathise with the infirmities of age. 'Si jeunesse savait,' they wouldn't overwork me, and 'si vieillesse pouvait,' they could not; for I am very anxious to do all they ask. I hope to be of some use in the matter of their meeting the foreign delegates on Friday, which they could not well have managed without me. I went to their dramatic performance for part of the time. They had taken too heavy a piece in the version of 'Nigel,' but had got it up well, and the man who acted Trapbois was really clever."

Though he talked lightly of *la vieillesse*, he really was be-

ginning to feel hard work of this kind as a strain. He
had almost given up shooting, for which, perhaps, he never
greatly cared; and his Irish tour, though it did not actually
harm his health, had warned him that he might be over-
wearied. This is recognised in the following letter of
April 18, describing a beautiful and interesting ceremony.
When collegiate people do dress in their academic best,
and when the variegated hoods of a hundred colleges
are displayed, the scene proves that men of peace can be
almost as gorgeous, and " in their attire do show their wit "
as magnificently, as men of the sword. This was the most
magnificent academic festival which has been held for
very many years; and with the old grey Grassmarket and
St Giles' for a background to the reds and blues and
greens of the robes, Edinburgh needed not to fear rivalry
with Bologna.

"The best thing is that I hope to be with you on the
same day with this letter. Look out for me (or my ex-
hausted carcass) by the train reaching King's Cross at
seven.

"Yesterday was a very remarkable day. I wish you
could have seen the sight in the great hall where the
degrees were conferred. The masses of colour were quite
like a flower-bed, and the ladies in the gallery must have
been much exercised between admiration and jealousy.
Some of the French robes were the most striking. The
banquet was less gay, as gowns were not worn; but it
was a most striking sight. To-day is my day. I am just
going to hold an assembly of the students, to give them

their turn of the great gathering. They are very much pleased, and I hope will forgive my not going to the ball on Wednesday. There is their symposium in the evening. Altogether it will be as hard as any day we have had.

"Now I must go. The M——'s are very kind, though the N——'s think they keep me away from the festivities too much. I should die under the energetic system; as it is, I can only just get along."

In his speech at the Tercentenary he made one of the classical allusions in which he excelled: "I feel assured that this University is destined to exhibit in its future career the same high qualities which it has exhibited hitherto. I was staying a very short time ago in an old house in the country that belonged to the family of the Mores. There were badges upon the walls, and the badge was the mulberry-tree—the morus; and this was the inscription: 'Morus tarde moriens, morum cito moritur '—The mulberry-tree is slow in death, the mulberry fruits die quickly; and so it may be with us and all of this University. The individuals may pass away, but the stock will remain. It is a consolation which all who are connected with such a body as this may take to themselves, that though the work they do in this life may be short, and the art may seem to be long in comparison, though their life is short, the life of the body to which they belong is not short; and we may fully trust and believe that the future of this University will be connected, and will be proudly connected, with the history of our country and the prosperity of the English nation."

Edinburgh never in the illustrious roll of her Lord Rectors had one more popular, one who better graced a graceful office, than Sir Stafford. He visited Scotland again in the autumn of 1884. He voyaged along the beautiful west coast in Mr Smith's yacht, the Pandora, which had frequently, and with great benefit to his health, been placed at his service. His best holidays were due to the kindness of Mr Smith. At Glasgow he had rather more publicity than he liked. He writes from Oban: " One enthusiastic gentleman came and talked to me at the station, expressing his great disappointment that there were not more people there to see me off. I had a newspaper correspondent who came and seated himself by my side at breakfast, and interviewed me so energetically that I cut short my meal."

Such are the holidays of the conspicuous : and even at a Scotch breakfast the interviewer comes with the porridge and stays till the marmalade. They saw Iona in the wet (there are English people who complain that the west coast is wet; it is not nearly wet enough for salmon and sea-trout), and they beguiled time at Tobermory with readings from " The Lord of the Isles," and, less appropriately, from Mr Mallock. In Glencoe, too, it rained; but the glories of the Sunbeam, Lord Brassey's gorgeous yacht, were viewed and admired at Oban. On beholding this portent the muse awoke—as well she might ; for, since the Sicilian tyrant's days, or the seafaring of Cleopatra, never was there a barque like the Sunbeam— and Sir Stafford's hand touched the lyre of Ingoldsby.

It had poured at Oban, it streamed at Strome ;
When we tried to go out the rain drove us home ;
At Tobermory it was still the same story,
And at Ballachulish it made us feel foolish ;
But when we had reached the magnificent Strome
    Ferry,
   We saw a sight
   Which made us quite
    Merry ;
    Very.
We saw a vessel of brilliant whiteness,
And a company bowing with great politeness,
   And we shaded our eyes
   In glad surprise,
And said to one another, " Now what's to be done ?
   That's the Sun-
   Beam.
   How bright it doth seem !
   And who's on board ?
   Why, upon my word,
When I look again, how silly I am
Not to have known Sir Willyam
   Harcourt,
Pride of the Home Office and the Bar Court ;
   And there as I reckon,
   Beginning to beckon,
Is Mr Gwynne Holford, late member for Brecon."
But oh ! what an outburst of welcome broke from us,
When there came to our gangway a boat with Sir Thomas
   Brassey,
With many a lady and laddie and lassie !
It was quite " too too " with " How d'ye do ? "
And in such a blare of universality,
We seem to lose individuality,
While never was known such hospitality.

They asked us to dinner, they asked us to tea.
"But nothing of that sort will do," said we;
"This night we have marked for a musical swarry,
And to disappoint our crew we'd be sorry.
We've the Well of St Keyne, and the Nancy Brig,
And Miss Mabel is ready to play us a jig;
But if you'll allow us, your sails being furled,
We will visit the vessel that went round the world."
But oh! how Columbus and Francis Drake
With envy in their graves must shake!
And sure the ship Argo had ne'er such a cargo;
Nor that which was built in Sicilian waters
For the ancient tyrant, his sons and his daughters,
Which had gardens and bowers, and goldfish and flowers.
No; nothing can match the Sunbeam gay,
Or the motes that people its brilliant ray.
There are schoolrooms and smoking-rooms, bedrooms and baths,
    With hot and cold water turned on;
And we wander through passages, doorways, and paths,
    Till we can't make out where we are gone.
Through dining-room, drawing-room, boudoir, and study,
I pass till my brain is quite mixed up and muddy;
With silk and with satin and velvet arrayed,
And china and shell-work and ivory displayed—
Gifts from this Royal Prince, or that Maori chief,
And from Japs and Chinese: it was quite a relief
To escape from such splendour, and, wiping my pen,
To sit down in the dear snug Pandora again.

From Oban they sailed north, by the cliffs and moul-
dering castles—

    "Each on its own dark cape reclined,
      And listening to its own wild wind"—

and they stayed at Dunvegan. Here they were on familiar

ground, and saw familiar sights,—Flora Macdonald's stays, the sword of Rory More, and the mysterious Fairy Flag, which brings victory to the Macleods.

Early in September they sailed south, and, after a few brief visits to Stobo, Pitlour, and other houses, Sir Stafford went to Hopetoun and made Conservative speeches at a Conservative gathering. The Provost of Edinburgh, although a Liberal, met him at luncheon at the Conservative Club, and took him to view Heriot's Hospital, the foundation of " Jingling Geordie." Sir Stafford visited Dalkeith, stayed at Birnam, at St Mary's Tower, and then crossed the Tweed.

He had a great deal of political work in Scotland, late in 1885, after an official visit to Balmoral. Staying at Blythswood he spoke at Glasgow : " It was an enthusiastic lively audience, sometimes a little noisy, but very good-humoured. The most striking thing was the way they cheered Lord Beaconsfield's name. It was an interruption of quite. two minutes." He was nervous at having to speak in a hall built specially for Mr Gladstone, whose voice fills a very considerable amount of hall. Next year, in June, he spoke on the Union with Ireland, at Paisley. In September he visited Balmoral, and this was the last time he crossed the Border, or saw the heather, of which Sir Walter Scott said that if he did not see it every year he thought he should die. For Sir Stafford, holidays and work were very nearly over : he had one last trial to bear, and then his earthly task was done.

CHAPTER XIX.

LAST DAYS AND DEATH.

TESTIMONIAL FROM HOUSE OF COMMONS—COMMISSION ON DE-
PRESSION IN TRADE — LORD RANDOLPH'S RESIGNATION—
LORD SALISBURY AT THE FOREIGN OFFICE—NEWS OF THIS
CHANGE—LORD IDDESLEIGH'S HEALTH—HIS DEATH.

IT has been seen that, on the defeat of Mr Gladstone's
Government in 1885, and the accession of Lord Salisbury's short-lived Cabinet, Sir Stafford Northcote went
to the House of Lords with the title of Earl of Iddesleigh,
and with the office of First Lord of the Treasury. As he
said later, when a splendid testimonial was offered him by
members of both parties, in March 1886, "For thirty
years the House of Commons was his home." Thirty
years see, in most cases, the life's work of a man; for
him little more was left of life and work. "The House of
Commons was his love, that was the place his heart went
out to, and he could not get rid of his feelings. He
always knew that he should greatly feel leaving the
House of Commons, and he could only say that he had
felt the separation a great deal more than he had thought

he should." His departure was not, one may venture to say, of benefit to his party, nor to the House. An admirable example of patriotic conduct and courtesy was lost, where it could ill be spared. One of the last barriers to partisan rancour was removed. Even the official journals of his party felt and deplored the loss and the change. For his own part, Lord Iddesleigh was at once engaged in the kind of work which he had often done so well; he presided over the Commission which examined into the Depression in Trade. This Commission was appointed by the Conservatives as soon as they came into office, in 1885. Its report, or rather its reports, were not issued till a few days after its President's death in 1887. Lord Iddesleigh's unrivalled financial experience, and the sagacity of his views on trade, naturally marked him out as the President.

The Commission was doubtless appointed for a political reason. The "bad times" since 1875 had, as we have seen, been pretty freely attributed to the Tories. The justice of these charges we have examined: they were partly superstitious, an affair of belief in luck, partly they rested on the foreign policy of Mr Disraeli's Government. It has been said that another foreign policy might have avoided certain expenses; but no policy could have altered the general conditions which depress business. There were Conservatives, however, who believed in "fair trade," in a commercial league between England and her colonies, and in other specifics. It was well, at least, to hear what they had to say, and to collect information.

" One-sided free trade" was being denounced, not un-
naturally; but Lord Iddesleigh had never any confidence
in the talk about reciprocity. The reciprocity that was
wanted was what could not be got, he said, and what
could be got was not reciprocity. Still, the Conservatives
were expected to do *something*, and they could, and did,
appoint a Commission. Lord Iddesleigh was not ill
pleased to be at its head. He saw that all the remedies
put forward were more or less modified forms of protection. He foresaw that the Commission, or the majority
of it, would find that the depression had been exaggerated, and that the results of the inquiry would, in the
long-run, be favourable to free trade. He did the work
with his usual energy and conscientiousness. It was
long and even laborious, ending much as he had expected. The report of the majority, drawn up by Lord
Iddesleigh but issued after his death, found that trade,
since 1875, might fairly be called depressed. There
was a diminution of profit and of employment. This
was caused by over-production, by "appreciation" of
gold, by restrictive foreign tariffs, by foreign competition
in all markets, and, among other things, by our defective
education, both technical and financial. The civilised
nations, in short, are now engaged, as never before, in a
struggle for existence. England was the first earnestly
industrial people: for long we had a kind of monopoly of
trade. But in the last forty years most of Europe has
taken to making things to sell. It is not so much that
we make things worse than we did, as that every one

can make them as well, and often more cheaply. The struggle for the cheap produces cheapness, and that is depression, or part of it. There is, to be sure, the consolation that the poor can get more for their money; no great comfort when, for want of employment, they have no money. The state of agriculture is notorious. "Sir James Caird estimates the loss in the purchasing power of the classes engaged in agriculture at £42,800,000 during the year 1885," a calculation which means incalculable misery and peril. The majority did not think that legislative restrictions on labour, and that strikes, had "materially affected the general prosperity of the country." They did not believe in longer hours of work as a remedy, and "feel satisfied that public opinion in this country would not accept any legislative measure tending to an increase in the present hours of labour." Legislation is likely to be in the contrary direction. They believed that the condition of the working classes had been immensely improved in the last twenty years: the share of labour in wealth was greater than it had been. But there would come a time, as profits fell and wages rose, when capital would be driven out of the field. What would happen then, the Commission did not prophesy. They did not blame, but rather praised, the trades-unions. They admitted, as well they might, that "the number of the unemployed is a matter of serious importance." They thought agriculture must be depressed "until the competition of soils superior to our own has been worked out." Profits would fall, till there was some corresponding expansion of trade, or " some destruction of wealth, such as is caused by a great war." We might seek new markets, and adapt our wares more to wants, and educate more, both technically and in the knowledge of foreign languages. They thought they were " encouraging a more hopeful view "; indeed, a minority of the Commission regarded theirs as too optimistic, and yet one thinks they had

> " Close-lipped Patience for their only friend,
> Sad Patience, too near neighbour of despair."

" If our position is to be maintained, it must be by the exercise of the same energy, perseverance, self-restraint, and readiness of resource by which it was originally created." Professor Bonamy Price, in the name of free trade, protested that " shorter hours of labour tax the community with dearer goods in order to confer special advantages on the working man. They protect him, and that is a direct repudiation of free trade." The class in power has usually managed to protect itself. The Commission, as was to be expected, did little to lighten the burden of the world, and produced no scheme for giving all profits to labour. We have still to see how that plan will work. Meanwhile, this was the last heavy piece of official work which Lord Iddesleigh did, except at the Foreign Office, which he held from the end of July 1886 till Lord Salisbury took it. Among the " pantomimic changes " of his brief tenure of office, the most amazing was the kidnapping (August 21) of Prince Alexander of Bulgaria. But a brief reply to questions in the

House of Lords was Lord Iddesleigh's only public remark
on this occasion. His heavy work, on which, of course,
it is not possible to comment here, was deeply interesting
and even refreshing to him. He went up to town from
Pynes at the very end of December 1886. Lord Randolph
Churchill had resigned the Chancellorship of the Exchequer on December 23, from "a little temper on both
sides," Lord Iddesleigh supposed (letter to Lady Iddesleigh, December 28, 1886). His own resignation followed
shortly, in circumstances which shall be stated as shortly
as possible.

On the sudden and unexpected withdrawal of Lord
Randolph Churchill, Lord Salisbury entered into negotiations with Lord Hartington and the Liberal Unionists.
Lord Iddesleigh, with his wonted unselfishness, placed his
seat in the Cabinet at the Premier's disposal. On Tuesday morning the 4th of January he learned from an
announcement in the newspapers that his offer had been
accepted, and a telegram in cipher from Lord Salisbury
reached Pynes in the afternoon of the same day. Mr
Goschen had joined the Government, and in the course of
the new combination Lord Salisbury found it desirable to
go to the Foreign Office, Mr Smith giving up the War
Office to become First Lord of the Treasury and Leader of
the House of Commons. A letter to the same effect was
received on the next morning. Lord Iddesleigh replied
that he cheerfully accepted Lord Salisbury's decision.
No proposal of another post had been made to him,
and he regarded the transaction as completed. He then

received a telegram, offering. him the Presidency of the
Council. Not being anxious "to have more political
bother," immediately after resigning duties in which he
was interested, he declined, and continued to decline
after receiving "a kind letter from Lord Salisbury." To
have accepted would have been to suggest various obvious misconstructions of his position, powers, and character. He hoped to be better able to serve his party
outside than in a new office.

It is not correct to state, as was stated at the time,
that Lord Iddesleigh's resignation was due to a. conscious-
ness of failing health. His old enemy, an affection of
the heart, of thirty-six years' standing, was present with
him; but the work he had done in the last two years
had not brought it, as yet, prominently into his own
notice. We have seen how busy he had been with
speaking in many distant places, and in his canvassing
tour in 1885 he often addressed large audiences in the
open air and even in the rain. His work at the Commission on Trade kept him in town in 1885, till his visit
to Balmoral, whence he went to speak at Aberdeen. He
spoke later at various places, and his lecture at Edinburgh
on Desultory Reading (November 3) certainly gave no
sign of failing power in body or mind. The year 1886
found him speaking at many public meeetings, and a brief
visit to Balmoral was almost his only holiday. He wound
up the Trade Commission on December 8, and, as we saw,
was busy in town at the end of that month. It was not

till January 4, 1887, that he had a feeling of faintness on climbing the Castle Hill, when he was attending sessions at Exeter; but this attack seemed so unimportant that, in the afternoon, he attended an oratorio in a village near Pynes. All this distinctly shows that he had been in his usual health, and even more than usually active. Nor did the passing illness of January 4 at all give him cause for serious thought about his condition. After his resignation, on January 7, he presided over a large county meeting in Exeter, and spoke on the Prince of Wales's scheme of an Imperial Institute, in commemoration of the Queen's Jubilee. He occupied this position as Lord Lieutenant of Devonshire, a post which he had held since January 1886. At the meeting which the Prince of Wales was to preside over in the following week, he was not destined to attend, though he set out for it. His work had ended ere he reached it. To be brief, his days were numbered; but he was unwarned of this, and felt full of power and readiness to work. All this is mentioned merely in contradiction of a report published in the 'Standard' of January 7, that Lord Iddesleigh was extremely ill and dejected, and suffered from the work of the Foreign Office. That he first heard of the change at the Foreign Office from the newspapers was a circumstance to be explained, no doubt, by clumsiness or haste, but it was a circumstance deeply to be regretted.

The sudden close of the life of Lord Iddesleigh is too

familiar to need a long repetition. On January 11, he went up from Pynes to London, where he was to speak at the Mansion House on the Prince of Wales's scheme of an Imperial Institute. On the forenoon of the 12th of January, he went to the Foreign Office, and had a long talk with Sir James Fergusson, the Under-Secretary, to whom he said that he hoped his separation from his old colleagues would not be permanent. He was to call again at 6 P.M., and see Mr H. M. Stanley about the expedition to relieve Emin Bey, in which he was much interested. He then walked to Downing Street, to see Lord Salisbury. On reaching the anteroom, he sank into a chair, where Mr Henry Manners and Lord Walter Gordon Lennox found him very ill, and breathing with difficulty. He never spoke again, and died at five minutes past three, in the presence of two doctors, of Lord Salisbury, and of Mr Henry Manners.

It was a death-scene brief and painless, "a sleep and a forgetting." He died at peace, but with his mind still busy with national affairs. The notes of the speech which he was never to deliver were found in his pocket, and among the notes a brief classical quotation, *India mittit ebur;* a trace of his old and dear studies. About such a death— a euthanasia to himself, a shock intolerable to his nearest survivors, a sorrow to the whole country—eloquence were impertinent. The day before he had said, about his official work, "I shall leave no arrears." His work was done, and well done.

> " ' A very perfect, gentle knight,'
> In fields whence Chivalry has fled :
> He lived in honour's clearest light,
> He lies with England's noblest dead." [1]

The regret for Lord Iddesleigh's death was universally felt, was universally expressed : by the Queen, with her usual warm sympathy ; by his countrymen of almost all ranks and creeds. At the same moment as the funeral rites were paid amongst those who had been most dear to him at his own village of Upton Pyne, services were held at Westminster Abbey, Exeter Cathedral, and St Giles' Cathedral, Edinburgh, at which public men of all parties and professions paid their last tribute to the honoured statesman. He rests in the place he had chosen, by the church in which he had worshipped from the happy days of his boyhood, and which he loved as a part of his home.

[1] 'Daily News.'

CHAPTER XX.

LITERARY PURSUITS—DOMESTIC LIFE.

TASTE FOR LITERATURE—REFUGE IN A TREE—DESULTORY READING — FAVOURITE BOOKS — THE ANCIENT CLASSICS — SIR WALTER SCOTT—DICKENS—DANTE—MOLIÈRE—CHAUCER—LADY NORTHCOTE'S CONTROVERSY WITH MR GLADSTONE ON HOMER AND TASSO—LORD IDDESLEIGH'S WRITINGS—LITERARY DIVERSIONS—HIS "HAMLET"—PLAYS—POEMS—ART—DOMESTIC LIFE—SPORTS—HOME—LOVE OF DEVONSHIRE—DEVONSHIRE STORIES—EXAMPLES—CHILDREN—RAILWAY ACCIDENT — MOBS — MEETING WITH MR GLADSTONE — CONCLUSION.

LORD IDDESLEIGH was one of those men of affairs, or of action, whom Nature has half intended to make bookworms or men of letters. As a boy, his relations remember that he had a favourite retreat under a tree, where he would take refuge when strangers came, happy, like Thomas à Kempis, *in angulo cum libello.* His father and grandfather would even implore one of his sisters to rout him from his "nook and his book,"[1] and make him

---

[1] In omnibus requiem quæsivi sed non inveni nisi in *nocxkins ond boexkins.*—A Kempis.

play, or ride, or shoot. It was only in later life that he who had been famous as a rowing man attained respectable skill as a shot or a rider to hounds. In boyhood, field-sports came seldom between him and his books, and he practised with pleasure what he praised without paradox —the art of desultory reading. For the rector of a Scottish university to tell his undergraduates that they might read (as the Scotch laird swore) "at lairge," was rather a bold act. He likened himself to the Matinian bee, which in a desultory fashion "employs each shining hour," rather than to the soaring, and possibly singing, swan of Dirce. Neither in precept nor in practice did he "confound desultory work with idleness." He read much and in many directions, and in part perhaps, like Emerson and Dr Johnson, "with his fingers," because his active mind found repose as well as enjoyment in variety of study. The very word "desultory," as he mentioned in his address to the Edinburgh students, implies etymologically the leaping from one horse to another.

The steeds he rode in this light Numidian fashion were many. Theology, History, Poetry, the Drama, Romance, and Science were all in his stable. Like a true friend of books, he was no great lover of epitomes and "cribs." If he had not read the league-long Mahabharata and Ramayana, still less, if possible, had he improved his mind, as Sir John Lubbock recommended, with Wheeler's condensations of these gigantic epics. It is odd to find him telling Sir John Lubbock, in a discussion of the "Hundred Best Books," that he has never read Marcus Aurelius. But the

reason of this probably was that the Greek of the Stoic
Emperor is crabbed and corrupt, and that Lord Iddesleigh
had a scholarly dislike of translations. Now there is a
medium between Emerson's belief that Plato is sufficiently
Attic in the prose of Bohn, on one side, and a total rejection of "cribs" on the other. The New Testament we
are mostly content to read in English, and probably there
is no disgrace in preferring for everyday use the English of Mr Long and the anonymous translators of the
eighteenth century to the Greek of Marcus Aurelius.
But Lord Iddesleigh appears to have been of another
mind, and scholars will be the last to condemn him unless
they have written translations.

In the spirit of his own Edinburgh lecture, he re-
nounced the idea of being a bookman like "our old giants
of learning, of whose powers of reading we hear so much,
and of whose powers of writing we see remaining so many
substantial proofs." Only while reading ten or twelve
hours a-day for his class, could he emulate the toil of
Buchanan or Casaubon. But in that very period of solid
study he read more novels than at any other time in his
life. The man who worked through the 'Arabian Nights'
during the evenings of the week when he was "in the
Schools," gave proof of that mental activity which finds
repose in variety of interest. But this is not desultory
reading in any invidious sense.

There are people who will and must read, who, as Scott
when a child defined the *dilettanti*, "will and must know
everything." There are others to whom all reading is a

task and a weariness. These two classes will never understand each other. Lord Iddesleigh was an excellent specimen of the first class. He read all round him; and his memory, which nearly equalled Macaulay's, enabled him to remember most of what he read. His reading was not, and could not be, "indolent reading": it flowed not idly and wastefully through his mind, but left a golden deposit of knowledge, and of bright and apt illustrations. He could amuse and instruct his Edinburgh undergraduates with ancient instances from Seneca and Lucian, as easily as with anecdotes from Mr Pepys his Diary. He shared Mr Lowell's and Mr Matthew Arnold's distrust of new books, "which, like new bread, bring one to mental dyspepsia." Probably Lord Iddesleigh will remain one of the last of English statesmen who knew the literature of Greece and Rome widely and well. New times, new manners. Soon there will be no scholars but scholars by profession. The ancients, it seemed to our fathers, keep a school of taste and knowledge, because they reached the heights and depths of human wisdom by paths not ours, and in lives lived under very different conditions. To know the literature of Greece and Rome is to be wise with a threefold experience, the experience of many ages, of varying civilisations. This knowledge, too, should teach discretion and limit in style. Lord Iddesleigh usually kept in his pocket a small volume of one of the Greek or Roman writers. Like Cicero or Macaulay, he might have said that they were his companions by night, by day, in town and in the country. Perhaps from this constant

companionship with the best minds and the best styles
(the more impressive because foreign and old), he learned
to shun fine writing, fine speaking, eloquence for the sake
of sound, and parliamentary wit, which is apt to turn to
waggery. It was his opinion that "funny speeches are
not difficult to make, but it is difficult to make them and
retain the respect of the hearers." The plain manner of
Lord Iddesleigh, in writing and in speaking, seems to have
been derived, then, from that sense of appropriateness
which the classics ought to teach, though often they fail
to teach it. . In all his many letters he never makes a
needless point; he never aims at literary brilliance; he
never attempts display; he is never fantastic. They are
often more like a woman's letters, in their fulness of
domestic news, than like the compositions of a wit at
rest, and yet constrained by habit or inclination to be
diverting. This unusual sobriety may be partly due to
a perpetual familiarity with what the classics teach, and
what many of their assiduous readers fail to learn. Some
of the most florid and "Asiatic" writers of our age are
those to whom Greek is most familiar. They miss, with
all their ornament, what Lord Iddesleigh did not miss, the
great and difficult lessons of Greece, the lessons of appropriateness, of moderation, and of dignity. Nor is it easy
to see whence, save from the classics of the world, these
lessons are to be learned by politicians in our age, which
neglects the past, and is deafened, like the Black Knight
at the siege of Front de Bœuf's castle, by the noise of the
blows it deals at every bulwark of antique renown. To be

sure it might be replied that moderation and dignity were not exactly the merits of Cicero, nor often of Demosthenes and Æschines, in their political harangues. We need not all be politicians; and those who are or who are not may still retire on Lord Iddesleigh's favourites, Sophocles and Shakespeare, Molière and Lucian, Rabelais and Sir Walter Scott.

In fiction, Lord Iddesleigh knew Sir Walter above all others. Perhaps he too, like a living critic, thought 'Count Robert of Paris' better than any novel that has been written since. Almost the last exercise of his pen, in the days which preceded his death, was to jot down the heads of an Edinburgh lecture on the parallel characters in Sir Walter Scott. Almost the last book, perhaps the very last book, which he read with pleasure, was a volume that contains more of the spirit of Scott than any other in English fiction, Mr R. L. Stevenson's 'Kidnapped.' Lord Iddesleigh was a very warm admirer of Mr Dickens, and he did his best, but unavailingly, to make Mr Disraeli appreciate the fun of 'Pickwick.' On the other hand, Lord Iddesleigh had no sympathy with the works of Mr Thackeray. Nature has made many people Dickensites or Thackerayans, as we are all born either Aristotelians or Platonists, and they are few to whom our two great humorists shine like double stars, Gemini in the skies of literature.

It is no inconsiderable pleasure to a biographer, separated from the topic of his study by so many differences of life, interest, and habit, to find that in literature, at

least, he and his hero are at one. If Scott was Lord
Iddesleigh's favourite novelist, Molière was his favourite
comedian. By "favourite" one means the comedian whom
he chose out of all the world for his own delight, because
Shakespeare is imposed upon all of us, no less by patriotism than by natural bent of taste. But in Shakespeare's
comedies, the poetry, after all, outshines the humour and
the wit. Molière's wit, let his most ardent English friends
confess, has little to dread from the competition of his
poetry. As Lord Iddesleigh said, "Comedy has been defined as the *bienséance* of society," or rather as the humorous representation of that *bienséance*. Of the world's
three chief comedians this narrow definition almost excludes Shakespeare, quite excludes Aristophanes, and is
only filled by Molière.

A very fair idea of Lord Iddesleigh's literary taste and
of his humour may be gathered from a correspondence
between him and Sir John Lubbock in 1885. Sir John
Lubbock was preparing his famed list of one hundred
books, though why any one should select the best hundred, more than the best eleven, or the best thirty books,
it is hard to conjecture. His list, at all events, he submitted to the criticism of Lord Iddesleigh, who decidedly preferred Theocritus (omitted) to Wake's 'Apostolic
Fathers,' which was included by Sir John Lubbock. He
confessed, as we have seen, his ignorance of Marcus Aurelius, of Wake, of Confucius, of the Indian epics, and of the
'Shahnameh.' He complained, on the other hand, that
Livy, Tacitus, Lucretius, Ovid, Juvenal, and Chaucer

were left out. Of Chaucer he says, "I really don't know a writer with so many charms, or one who so brings home to you the life of his day, or who touches the tender feelings so effectively, or who has such an eye for the beauties of nature." Perhaps it would be impossible to sum up Chaucer's merits more briefly. Of Lord Iddesleigh's own favourite things in literature, a list has been compiled by Lady Iddesleigh. If it be true that when one knows a man's literary friends—the bookish company he keeps—one knows the man, Lord Iddesleigh's character will stand high enough. Like Mr Gladstone, he was devoted to the "Divina Commedia" of Dante; unlike him, he thoroughly appreciated the creator of "Tartuffe." As he had a love of reading aloud, he perhaps took more pleasure than most people who are not poets in the Elizabethan drama, above all in Ford's "Broken Heart," which was an especial favourite, and which he could scarcely read without tears. He was devoted to Ben Jonson's "Volpone" and "Alchemist." Marlowe and Shakespeare did not, in his mind, oust Sheridan and Goldsmith, and he knew by heart "Chrononhotonthologos," a great admiration of Sir Walter Scott's. Of Scott's novels he preferred the 'Antiquary,' where all were dear; and of Miss Austen, 'Pride and Prejudice.' Lamb and Crabbe were often in his hands; he was one of the last readers of Southey's "Thalaba," and he was familiar with the plays of Goethe, with Jean Paul Richter, Swift, and Sterne. I do not find that French literature attracted him much, except in the works of the most English-natured of Frenchmen, Molière and Rabelais, and in Sardou and Voltaire. His opinion of Tasso, of Homer, and of Pope's version of Homer, may be gathered from an interesting letter to Lady Northcote. Much as Scott, when, in his boyhood, he was called "the Greek dunce" at Edinburgh University, wrote an essay to prove that Ariosto was a greater poet than Homer, so Lady Northcote had challenged Mr Gladstone to a comparison of Homer with Tasso. Concerning this her husband wrote, February 23, 1857: "I like your criticism on Tasso very much, and hope you will complete it for Gladstone's benefit, as you are sure of a characteristic reply from him. You must bear in mind that the subject of the Iliad is not the siege of Troy, and that in point of fact Troy is not taken in it. Homer concentrates your interest on the individual Hector among the Trojans, just as Tasso does upon the individuals Clorinda, Armida, and others among the Pagans. Again when you speak of the beauty of particular passages in Tasso, you must recollect that you have not the means of comparing them with particular passages in Homer, and at least you must compare Hook's or Hunt's translation (and not the original Italian) with Pope's miserable version of Homer. Subject to these cautions, I think you may make something of a case for Tasso. A strict comparison is not admissible, because the subjects are different,—the wrath of Achilles is not the same kind of subject as the siege of Jerusalem. Rinaldo is a poor creature, and you must give him up; but in Tancred you have a fine character of a Christian warrior and a chivalrous knight to set against the pagan heroism of Achilles. In so far as the Gerusalemme is the development of character, Tancred is by far the most important personage in it, and there are many points in which he contrasts favourably with Achilles. Of course the question is not which of two heroes one likes best, but which of the two poets describes best. The character of Achilles, whether you like him or not, is wonderfully drawn. Is that of Tancred equally so? As regards Helen and Armida, Gladstone disputes Helen's being a consenting party to her original abduction, but she appears to have acquiesced in it by the time the poem commences, and does not, I think, show any desire to return to Menelaus. She is, however, very skilfully treated, and kept in subordination to the plot; and no attempt is made to create any interest in her beyond a gentle pity, not wholly unmixed with a feeling that she is partly to be blamed, while Paris is always held up as contemptible. Armida, on the other hand, is thrust upon our notice, and all the blots in her character are patent."

To call Pope's Homer "miserable" is, no doubt, to speak hastily, as in a private note, not in a public essay. The rhetoric of Homer's speeches has always an incomparable rendering in the famous English version. But in the many passages where Homer is not rhetorical, doubtless we feel in Pope a lack of the magic, the simplicity, the truth of the "Ionian father of the rest," the first and greatest of all poets. In comparison with him, what translation is not "miserable"? Mr Gladstone, in his apology for Helen, has omitted, I think, the curious tradition in Eustathius which tells us that Paris deceived her, as Uther, Arthur's father, deceived Ygerne, by magically putting on the shape and semblance of her husband. Perhaps Homer knew this tradition, and alludes to it, where Penelope, after the slaughter of the wooers, still declines to recognise Odysseus.

What manner of writer Lord Iddesleigh might have been if literature had conquered in his mind the attractions of politics, it is impossible to say. His position made it wholly needless for him to adopt literature either as crutch or staff. He had not that studious fervour which compelled Gibbon, Mr Grote, and other men like them, to live laborious days of learned application. When he wrote it was either on some political or social question in the 'Quarterly Review,' for example, or for the purpose of pleasing his friends at Exeter, or his undergraduates at Edinburgh, or, finally, for his own diversion and the diversion of his children at home.[1] His lecture at Exeter on "Nothing" was a most successful and playful *tour de force*, and the more original, as he doubtless knew nothing of a rare work on the same topic by "Nobody," a book of the early part of the century. Nobody could have spoken better on "Nothing," a topic which might even have taxed the practised ingenuity of Swift. Lord Iddesleigh's genial activity found scope in producing articles,

---

[1] It was no doubt to oblige a friend and former secretary of his own, Mr Marwood Tucker, that he wrote at one time in the 'Globe.' Mr Tucker mentions that Lord Iddesleigh asked him to cut about his articles as freely as if they were those of the youngest contributor.

verses, parodies, charades, fireside plays, and often pieces of pure nonsense—indeed in the difficult field of nonsense he had very considerable skill. It was the custom at Pynes for the family to act plays during Christmas-tide, and to enjoy a mild feast of Unreason. For these games Lord Iddesleigh used to contrive dramas sufficiently unreasonable. In 1878, his play (written in collaboration with Mr John Northcote) was "Hamlet, with Hamlet Omitted." Among the "properties" one finds "skates for Ophelia." It seems that Ophelia has been affrighted by the Ghost, who "is mad for her love," and the stage manager seizes this opportunity to "place" a "real ghost-story." Polonius, most naturally, inquires of Ophelia what her shadowy wooer was like, and receives the no less natural answer, "Why, very like a whale." It appears that the Ghost is also mad, Ophelia having repelled his addresses. The spectre carries his infatuation so far as to stab Polonius, whereon Laertes threatens to kill the Ghost, who replies with candour, "I wish you would, for killing a ghost would make him come alive again." Yet this is rather the inference of a ghost new to his business than a sound spiritual theory, as any one may learn from "Grettir *v.* Glam" in the saga. Nothing can be more proper than the precaution taken by the King, who habitually wears great quantities of cotton-wool in his ears. "'Tis conscience that makes cowards of us all," and as the King says—

"They'll poison me in the garden for my estate. They'll pour it into my ears. That's what happened to the Ghost. I'll take care it shan't happen to me.

> *Enter* OPHELIA (*with a pair of skates*).
> QUEEN : How now, Ophelia ; are you come to sing to us ?
> OPHELIA *declines to sing, says she is going to skate.*
> QUEEN *says she must be mad, as it's thawing.*
> OPHELIA *admits that she is mad, but that is of no consequence,*
> *as everybody else is.*"

The drama concludes (happily) in conformity with the Aristotelian unities. Finally Laertes kills the Ghost, Ophelia comes alive again, and Hamlet, making a tardy appearance, leads her to the altar.

" The Senior Wrangler " (1870) was a play with more of a plot, and was cast for three chief characters, *Sir Marmaduke Mouldcastle* (Sir Stafford Northcote), *Lizzie Mouldcastle* (Miss Northcote), *Tom Mouldcastle* (Mr John Northcote). The scene is Newmarket, where Sir Marmaduke is staying at a hotel with Lizzie, and threatening to disinherit Tom if ever he has visited " headquarters." At this moment enter Tom, who adopts the old plan of pretending not to know his relatives, and to be some other person. Tom gives himself a splendid character for industry, and this, it appears, he deserves, for he has fled to Newmarket, not to bet, but to avoid congratulations on being Senior Wrangler. This *dénouement* is not reached without many excursions and alarms. The drama has the peculiarity of being a Cambridge play by an Oxford man.

The latest of all Lord Iddesleigh's essays in pure literature was interrupted by his death. It was of a character not familiar to him, the editing for the Roxburghe Club of

PYNES

"The Triumphs of Petrarch," a reprint of the translation by Henry Parker, Lord Morley, of 1554. The Roxburghe Club is an association of bibliophiles, and was founded in memory of the great collector immortalised by "Froggy Dibdin." Lord Iddesleigh was elected in 1885: though a lover of books, he could not be called a bibliophile, still less a bibliomaniac. His library was that of a reader, a student, not of a collector. It contains hardly any rarities, and might perhaps be ransacked in vain for scarce examples "on large paper," for first editions, and bindings by Derome, Le Gascon, Padeloup. But, having been elected to the Roxburghe Club, he determined to do his duty therein, and set to work on his edition of Morley's "Triumphs of Petrarch" from a transcript once in the possession of the late Mr Payne Collier, the well-known Shakespearian. Two days before his death, when on the point of leaving Pynes for London, he said to Lady Iddesleigh, "When these few days are over, I shall take up my preface to "The Triumphs of Petrarch.'"

In a note by Mr Berkley, Vice-President of the Roxburghe Club, he says that Lord Iddesleigh probably chose Lord Morley's old work under the influence of his "strong Devonshire feeling, he being apparently under the impression that the Parker, Lord Morley of the Tudor period, was in some way connected with the noble Devonshire family now bearing the same name and title." The present Lord Morley, however, disclaims any traceable connection between his name and that of the old translator of the "Triumphs of Petrarch," who remarks, " I thoughte in my mynde howe I, beynge an Englishe man, myght do as well as the Frenche man," the author of an earlier version. And yet this Englishman could call the tale of Robin Hood "some dongehyll matter" in comparison with Petrarch. From this view Lord Morley's editor would probably have dissented, but, unfortunately, a few notes on the influence of Petrarch on European literature are all that Lord Iddesleigh has left. The "Triumphs" were presented by his son, the present Earl of Iddesleigh, to the Roxburghe Club.

Lord Iddesleigh, like most people, wrote verse at times. His themes were usually either light political skits, or matters of domestic interest, a narrative in rhyme of some pleasant adventure, as in the encounter with the glories of the Sunbeam, already quoted.

Of "Skye Castle" he also rhymed, and of Dunvegan,—

> A Viking here, a Chieftain there,
> Seems rising o'er each crag;
> An ensign bold floats on the air,
> But where's the fairy flag?

More serious and very charming verses were written by Lord Iddesleigh early in life; but they were meant for the eyes of few, and need not be given to the world. This brief review of his πάρεργα in literature may include his lines on Marly, where among the beauties of the South he longed for home, and for Devonshire, which was so dear to him.

MARLY.

As Marly's bright green leaves give place
　　To tints of rich and mellow glow ;
As close the shortening autumn days,
　　Whilst summer lingers, loath to go ;
Quick rises each familiar scene,
　　And fancy homewards turns her gaze ;
Such are the hues in Oakford seen,
　　And such a light o'er Iddesleigh plays—
Methinks the oaks of dear old Pynes
　　With richer brown delight the eye,
Nor would I take those reddening vines
　　For our wild cherry's crimson dye.

A particularly pretty set of lines were those which he wrote to Lady Iddesleigh, enclosed in a bottle, and threw into the Exe at Exford, on the chance that the water might carry them to Pynes. This was done at an open-air luncheon, during a riding tour in 1873. When the party reached Knightshayes, some of them caused another bottle, with the same poem, to be brought in, as if it had just been found in the Exe. Sir Stafford was delighted at the chance, but had to be undeceived. This was the poem :—

"Go, lovely rose," so runs the ancient song,
But humbler themes to my poor Muse belong :
Go, lovely bottle, down the stream of Exe,
To *her*, the gentlest, dearest of her sex,
These lines, a tribute of affection bear,
And tell her what we do, and how we fare.
Tell her, where Lynton looks upon the sea
Where over Exmoor heights the deer run free,

Where in the vale the meeting waters flow,
Where the great beacon towers o'er all below,
By fair Glenthorne, and Porlock's lovely bay,
By the Doone valley, where the phantoms stray,
And wake the memories of an older time
With many a tale of love, and many of crime,—
Where'er we roam, o'er hill, or vale, or plain,
One image fills my heart and rules my brain;
And say, "Each beauty pleases, for to me
The sight of beauty ever calls back thee."

The days at Washington, during the arrangement of
the treaty, were filled with poetry, chiefly on the diplomatic arrangements. The lost Fourth Article had an ode
to itself, and there was a capital parody of Mr Lowell's

"J. P.
Robinson he
Says they didn't know everything down in Judee."

In much earlier days, when he first came to London,
Sir Stafford versified on the Duke's statue opposite Ashley
House. The gods decree the ugly image—

Bear it to Hyde Park Corner straight,
And set it up before his gate,
That so the thought may often strike,
"That's what the people think I'm like."

Sir Stafford was a great victim of the Album:—

Remember, ye poets, its marvellous virtue,
Since ye cannot avoid it, submit to your fate;
The sooner you write in't, the less it will hurt you,
And be sure you must write in it sooner or late.

Thus literature, on the whole, was his pleasure, his diversion, his consolation. But it never could well have been his business. "To live in ease and tranquillity may be man's wish," he says in an early essay (1840), "but it can never be the legitimate object of his life; nay, if he aim at it as an end, he will in all probability miserably fail." He certainly never made the "passionless bride, divine tranquillity," his choice; but took his part in the fray, declining "that which is too often the object of the purely literary man, individual and selfish pleasure." Nor was Art a matter of great moment to him.

Though he had much to do with fostering schools of art, and had devoted attention to them since his tour of inspection in 1849, Lord Iddesleigh, in his correspondence, seldom says much about pictures as they affected himself. I extract the following description of the Royal Academy in 1865, from a letter to Lady Iddesleigh, written after the private view.

"Mary and I have been to the Exhibition this morning, and thought it a good one. There is an excellent portrait of Sir E. Landseer by himself, with two dogs looking over his shoulder and criticising his painting. Also there is a good Marks of 'Beggars are coming to town.' There are some Millais which I like pretty well. I think the best is a Joan of Arc; and there is a striking but disagreeable one of the enemy sowing tares, with a sky something like that in the gravedigging nuns. It is a wonderful contrast to a beautiful, sunny, simple, but expressionless picture by Herbert of the man sowing the good seed.

They are not in the same room.   I almost wish they were. Then there is a dear little thing by O'Neill, called the 'Anxious Mother,' representing Peg sitting by a bed in which she has put four dolls to sleep (with their eyes wide open), and holding up her finger to enjoin silence.   There are some wonderful pieces of colour by Leighton—one of Helen of Troy, which I should admire if it were intended to represent a statue of her, for the effect is as of marble flesh, marble drapery, &c., well coloured and very lifelike, for marble.   There is a bull-fight scene by Burgess, not representing the fight, but the people looking on at a critical point, which I thought very clever ; but Lady Eastlake was disgusted with me, and said that was not art.   There is a delicious Hook, ' The Seaweed-Gatherer ' ; and there is a picture called the ' Marble Seat,' by that young Moore, which I thought very good indeed, in point of drawing, though the absurd effect of pre-Raphaelite daisies and checkered lights spoils it."

It is when he tries to describe the manners and daily life of Lord Iddesleigh that a biographer feels most the lack of personal acquaintance with the subject.   The following remarks are based chiefly on notes furnished by Lady Iddesleigh, and by other members and friends of the family.   The personal appearance of Lord Iddesleigh was for many years familiar to most people from his portraits, and from the excellent drawings of Mr Tenniel and Mr Sambourne, in ' Punch.'   He was of rather more than middle height, of complexion extremely fair, with blue eyes, and with a beard, worn after a bumping ball from a bowler on a rural wicket cut open his lip. Phrenologists and artists are said to have seen in his head some resemblance (which I confess that I cannot discover) to the head of Sir Walter Scott. The brow, the "peak" of old Sir Peveril, was of a commanding altitude, and a shape which survives in one of his descendants, though seldom met with among men. But, if this resemblance was fanciful, it may be a less arbitrary imagination which detects in Lord Iddesleigh's character and ways certain likenesses to those of the author of 'Waverley.' What these two men, so unlike in genius and in career, possessed in common were the characteristics of the best sort of country gentlemen,—the love of books, and "desultory" reading; the retentive memory; the liking for country anecdotes, and the art of telling them well; the fondness for sports, and for military exercises; old-world loyalty, generosity, a certain large way of living; and a singular goodness, kindness, and loyalty of disposition. It is perhaps this last and most important note of character which has most frequently brought back, to a reader of Lord Iddesleigh's domestic letters, the character of Scott. But in many ways I have seemed to see, in the younger man, the Devonian, with Border blood in his veins, traces, as it were, of a family likeness to the great Borderer. Both were undeniably akin in this, that they loved their country well, and their own country - side, if possible, better. This local patriotism was not less strong in the owner of Pynes than in the scion of Harden's line. But

Lord Iddesleigh, unlike Scott, was little of an antiquary. The house of Pynes, built under William and Mary or Anne, has nothing romantic. Here is no Border keep, frowning over the dark and narrow glen where Harden kept the cattle of his Southern neighbours, or even of Elibank. There is little to foster archæological tastes; there are few or no legends, no memories of feud and fray. The neighbourhood boasts some Roman remains of a summer camp; but has by no means that richness in tradition and in relics of every age which inspired Scott beside the Catrail, or near Newark, or Smailholme Tower. A taste for heraldry was almost the only archæological taste of Lord Iddesleigh's. The traditions of his family had also their interest, and we have extracted a passage from a letter about that curious old card-table which is thought to record an ancestral victory at cards.

Even if the old Justice Northcote of the story was a gambler, "a plunger," Sir Stafford did not inherit the passion with the farm. He was very fond of almost all games, but he speaks disparagingly about his own performances at whist. He may not have been a worse player than Mr Forster, but he played in much less exacting company. He mentions having won a good many points from Lord Houghton, and "hopes he will be paid"; but the points were probably the domestic sixpences. He was also attached to piquet, and to the oracles of Patience, which he was rather addicted to consulting. Once Patience foretold that the poor Prince who fell in Zululand would inherit the throne of France—a very unlucky guess. Charades and acrostics were also favourite diversions of Lord Iddesleigh's leisure; they are amusements almost too active for intelligences easily fatigued, but he was as skilled in making as in solving acrostics. As to athletic sports, he was fond of all of them, but distinguished in none. He once showed Lady Iddesleigh the place in Windsor Forest where he and Colonel Anstruther Thomson of the Fifeshire Hounds used to set springes for pheasants. All boys, all natural people, are sportsmen, and born poachers. He did not take to shooting much till he was thirty, and as his eye was never very good, he was not a crack shot. The same defect was inconvenient, as it made him slow to recognise faces, and, as hath already been mentioned, prevented him from excelling as a cricketer, though he encouraged the village club, played in country matches, and commemorated the feats of Mr Webbe and Mr Alfred Lyttleton in verse. He was an excellent runner in his youth, and it seems not unlikely that the beginning of a weakness of the heart was caused by his running swiftly down a steep descent in the Lake Country, with his oldest boy on his shoulder (1849).

As becomes a country gentleman, he was interested in farming: he wrote a short treatise on "the Draining of Catch Meadows"; he was on the council of the Royal Agricultural Society, and steward of cattle (1855, 1856) at Carlisle and Chelmsford.

Hunting was his chief winter pastime. He was not a scientific pursuer, but he delighted in the perils of the chase, and he might even be described as a reckless rider. His plan was "to throw his heart over first," and his favourite horse, an extremely accomplished fencer named Nimrod, usually managed the rest. Nimrod was his favourite mount in 1860, when one finds careful injunctions as to warming his loose-box: "Perhaps it would be a good plan, if he does go into the box on the first night, to let White Rook stand by the stall by its side, in the same stable, so as to warm the air a bit." He was master of the Pynes Harriers,—the Hunt wore a green coat with brass buttons, marked P.H.,—and a writer in the 'Sporting Times' (February 5, 1887) remarks that "few rode straighter to hounds than the master in his spectacles." The same writer mentions how his own horse, "a big powerful brute," once cannoned against Sir Stafford, and knocked old Nimrod against a gate. "Of course I expected to be greeted with some such remark as, 'Where the devil are you riding to?' but no; Sir Stafford never lost his self-control. He simply said 'Take care,' though most masters would have 'sworn at large.'" After old Nimrod died, and was honourably buried, his master hunted but little. The description of his recklessness in his saddle once more reminds one of him to whom Archibald Park said: "Shirra, ye'll never rest till they bring you hame feet foremost!"

In the life at Pynes, as of old at Ashestiel or Abbotsford, there was a happy tenacity of old traditional usages, a friendly and feudal hospitality to tenants as well as to friends. The mummers still came round at Christmas with their play, and the Yule-log was lighted, with an accompaniment of " wishes," as at the Scottish sports of Hallowe'en. The master of the house, the children, and the guests took part in writing and acting charades,—examples of these diversions have been given. Sir Stafford would occasionally patronise the Exeter Theatre for a night, when a speech from his box was part of the pleasure of the evening. We have already seen that he was an officer in the local Yeomanry; and he encouraged the Volunteers. From his days with the Yeomen he picked up the excellent anecdote, already quoted, of going straight in politics.

As a good Devonian, Sir Stafford was a great believer in the county of Drake and Raleigh. "I had it from my childhood, from my ancestors; the love of this place, the love of this country, the love of this county, and the love of all my Devonshire friends," he said, when he was welcomed at Exeter, after being raised to the House of Lords. It is recorded of him that he once met a young lady out of Yorkshire, the daughter of a contemporary politician, who challenged him to number eminent Devonshire men against those of her own county. Sir Stafford went through a list of worthies, and asked the lady to cap them. " Well," she said, reflectively, " well, there's my father," nor could she add to the list. As a Devonshire man, Sir Stafford was rich in Devonshire stories, which he told with a great deal of humour, and with the accent of the county, so disliked by Herrick and Keats. They lose a great deal when taken out of their oral form and set forth in print, but as almost everybody who has heard of Sir Stafford has heard that he was famous for Devonshire stories, I offer two or three of them.

A Case of Horse-stealing.

A man of the name of J. B. was accused of having stolen a horse, and one of his neighbours had been summoned to attend the trial as a witness. The lawyer, after having asked him a few preliminary questions, proceeded thus in cross-examination :—

Lawyer. You know J. B. ?

Witness. Yes, your Honner.

Law. Did he ever say anything to you about the horse ?

Wit. Well, I'll tell your Honner just how 'twas. The other day I said to him, "How about the horse ?" and he said to me, "He didn't know nothing about the horse."

Law. Stop now, witness, that's very important ; tell me what he really did say ?

Wit. It was just that, yer Honner. I said to him, "How about the horse ?" And he said to me, "He didn't know nothing about the horse."

Law. He didn't say *he* did not know anything about the horse.

Wit. Yes, he did. D'ye think I'd tell yer Honner a lie ?

Law. You don't understand what I mean ; he did not speak to you in the third person.

Wit. There weren't no third person there, there was only him and me.

Law. No, no ; but I mean, I suppose that he spoke to you in the first person.

Wit. No, a didn't ; I was the first person spoke to he, and I says to he, "How about the horse?" And a says to me, "A didn't know nothing about the horse."

Here the judge thought it time to interfere and clear up the difficulty, and he said, "Stop. Now, witness, attend to me ; this is what I suppose took place. You said to him—How about the horse?"

Wit. Yes, yer Honner, I did.

Judge. Well, then he said to you, "*I* don't know anything about the horse.

Wit. No, yer Honner, he didn't ; he never once mentioned yer Worship at all.

·The Cornish Jury.

One day as Mr Hicks was going into Bodmin he met Mr ————, a farmer who lived near Launceston. "Marnin', Mr Hicks." "Good morning, Mr ———— ; why, I thought you always kept Launceston market?" "Well, so I did till Vicky Donnell's trial." Now Mr Vincent Donnell was a veterinary surgeon who had been tried on the accusation of having poisoned his mother-in-law, an old lady who had died rather suddenly after a hearty supper on rabbit and onions. Vicky Donnell was acquitted, to the great astonishment of the world at large. "Ah, that's another question," said Mr Hicks; "you were fore-man of the jury, how came you to let Vicky Donnell off?" "Now, Mr Hicks, you'me so bad as the rest of them ; they're always asking why we let'en off, but I'll tell you how 'twas. We were shut up in a dark room without food, fire, or candle, and told we must find a verdict; so when we'd talked some time, 'Genelmen,' I says, 'we can't sit here all night, that's certain, so we'll take opinions. What do you say, Mister ————?' We was sitting all roun' a long table, you know, and I spoke to the nearest. 'Why I think the man's had very hard measure; I don't think he did it at all. She died of the rabbit and inions; what bizness had an old 'ooman like her to be ating rabbit and inions at that time of night?'

" 'Well,' says Mr Pengelly, who sat next, 'I think 'twas the arsenic did it; they doctors be so frolicsome with their arsenic, always trying things on; still as 'twas to be experimentin' like, I think 'twas much to his credit that he took an old woman to try it on; he might 'a took a young one.'

" 'So I think,' says Mr Boase; 'I should not like to hang Vicky Donnell for the likes of her; I reckon she was a very tadious sort of old 'ooman.　She's not the first tadious sort of old 'ooman that's been put out of the way, not by many a wan. I shouldn't like to hang Vicky Donnell for the likes of her.' 'No more shouldn't I,' says the next, 'for Vicky Donnell he saved my wife's life in the scarlet fever; she'd 'a died else.'

" 'Yes, and he saved my pig in the measles,' says the fifth, 'so there's two lives for one, take it how you will.'　'Well,' says the next, 'I do not think us ought to let him off altogether; I think us ought to give him six months on the debtor's side.'

" 'Oh, you can't do that, mister,' says I; 'it must be neck or nothing.'

" 'Well then,' says he, 'I'm for nothing, I'm sure.'

" 'Well, Mr Hicks, I thought there was a good deal in it, Mr Hicks—a good deal; but I didn't like quite to make up my mind, so I called down the table—for 'twas grown so dark you couldn't see your hand—to Abraham Smith of Grampound,— him with the squeaky voice, you know—us calls him Winnick, for short; 'Mr Smith,' says I,—'for you know, Mr Hicks, being foreman of jury, I could not call him by his short name,—'Mr Smith,' says I—'Winnick,' I adds, that he might know who I was a-speaking to—'what do you say to it?　I've as good an opinion for your judgment as of any man at the table, and you live over against the man opposite side the water as 'twere, so you must know; what do you think?'

" 'Well, mister,' says he, 'what you zay, I zay tu.'

" ' Sir,' says I, ' Winnick,' says I, ' I shall respect your judgment the longest day I have to live.' Then I asks the next two, and they said they'd go ' with the majority.' ' Well,' says I, ' you go with us and you'll be the majority.' So they went with us and we were the majority. And that's how Vicky Donnell got off."

THE ELOPEMENT.

When the late Alderman ———— of Exeter married for the second time a Miss Mary Glendinning, a friend of the bride's mother gave the following graphic account of the elopement, for such it was, which had taken place after the Friday market in Exeter :—

" Now, I'll tell you how 'twas, sir. About a month before, Mrs Glendinning gave Mary a new gown; 'twas an innocent-looking pattern—'twas silk—'twas a blue. Now Mary was that cunning she meant to be married in it, but that her mother might not suspect anything, she took to wearing it mornings; and Mrs Glendinning she says to her, ' Mary, my dear, why do you wear your best gown, mornings?' But Mary, she was that artful like, she says, ' Mother, I've took a fancy to it.' And Mrs Glendinning her says, ' Oh, very well, my dear, if you've took a fancy to it.' Now on Friday Mrs Glendinning was going to market, and she says, ' Now, what shall I bring home for dinner, Mary, my dear?" she says; ' you shall choose, for it's your turn :" and Mary, she says, " Well, mother, if you ask me, I should say a fore-quarter of lamb.' Now, mark the artfulness, sir, for she knew she wouldn't be at home to eat it; for as soon as Mrs Glendinning turned down the street to the right, Mary she popped on her bonnet and went down the street to the left, and there was Mr C———— waiting for her in a post-chaise round the corner, and so they went off and were married."

In addition to his Devonshire tales, Sir Stafford was a great *raconteur* of fairy stories to children. Of *them* he was unaffectedly fond, and they knew it, and would severely tax his memory or invention. From babies upwards he had a tender heart for all young people. At the close of his life, on a wet day, he was amusing some children with stories. The rain ceased. "The clouds have stopped to hear grandpapa," said one of the little audience.

He had a very unusual understanding and tolerance of the characters of boys. This showed itself even when he had just ceased to be a boy himself, in his advice as to the studies and treatment of a younger brother at Eton. Several of his letters to his sisters, when they were all young, to his sons in his later life, were intended to make easy and plain some difficult points in French grammar and French history. Thus, on September 20, 1860, we find him encouraging his son Harry to try for a French prize at school, and giving intelligible rules for the declension of the past participle, and the use of the definite article, also for *de* and *du*, the despair of Englishmen. No lessons could be more lucid and helpful. Girls found him as good company and as sympathetic as boys. He was reading bits of 'Pickwick' to children when he received the telegram which asked if he would accept a minor office, after leaving the control of foreign affairs. He glanced at the message, answered, "No, I think not, and went on reading 'Pickwick' aloud.

The stories he told children were sometimes traditional, sometimes were adapted to infant minds from the 'Arabian Nights,' the 'Iliad,' and the 'Odyssey.' The last poem he knew almost by heart, for he had the memory of a Rhapsode.

Of his kindness to children, which was extended even to babies, it is told that when one of his elder children was an infant, and in bad health, the nurse who attended the child had brought with her a baby of her own. This was a most pessimistic and wailing baby, whom nobody could soothe. Lord Iddesleigh took it in his arms and walked up and down with it for many weary hours in the night, and after a hard day's work, so anxious was he that his own child should have the necessary quiet, and that the other should not suffer from neglect. It would be endless to repeat similar traits of kindness, which was so universal that Lord Iddesleigh, when suffering from a cold, once made a long speech, chiefly because one of the reporters had incurred a good deal of expense in preparations for telegraphing it to town.

This kindness and gentleness became even prejudicial to Lord Iddesleigh in politics. "The meaning of 'gentle' is equivocal at best," wrote Charles Lamb to Coleridge once, "and almost always means poor-spirited." No charge could be less true of Lord Iddesleigh than the charge of poor-spiritedness. But some men, like the Dandie Dinmonts defended by Dr John Brown, are too full of goodness of heart to enjoy fighting for its own sake, and Lord Iddesleigh was not combative enough for some members of his party. As an example of his calmness in personal danger, we may quote a letter in which he describes to Lady Iddesleigh his sensations during a railway accident: "I hope you got my telegram from Swindon before you heard of the accident. I was afraid it would appear in this morning's paper, and that you would be alarmed. I am really not hurt; but it was a considerable shake, and I am a little stiff and headachy. We ran into a goods train about two and a half miles from Swindon, and our engine crashed into it at almost full speed (the goods train was stationary), and rose like a horse at a fence, falling over on its side into the field. Wonderful to relate, the men on the engine escaped with some bruises and a great shake; they clung to the engine and fell with it. The rest of the train was dragged off the rails, but not off the embankment, and we were all jerked violently forward. A great many of the passengers were cut and bruised, and one was very seriously hurt, having several of his ribs broken, as we believe, and perhaps his thigh also. The guard was a good deal hurt. I was half asleep when the shock came, and was woke up by finding myself flying forward, and hearing a great crash behind me. Happily for the gentleman opposite me I had a soft cap, and as I only grazed his face I did not hurt him much. Major Kirk, who was sitting next me, went straight into his opposite neighbour's face and cut his lip through, but was not hurt himself. The accident happened at 8.15 P.M., and it was 12.15 A.M. before we were got away, and more than 3.30 before we reached London, when I got a bed at the Paddington Hotel and slept till 8, and then made my way to Harley Street and got breakfast. It was a merciful escape; and really when one wandered about among those masses of *débris* covering the line, and saw the engine lying on its side in the field, and people going about tying up their heads and asking for wine and brandy, and all looking scared, one could not but feel how good God had been in averting more mischief. It was happily fine, that is, it did not rain; but it was very dark, and we poked about with lanterns at first, and afterwards lighted great bonfires of the broken carriages. A train was sent from Swindon to take us on board, and we got there pretty well tired, and so much done that I actually swallowed a basin of Swindon soup. It was (to me) the worst part of the accident. There ought to be a row about the affair. The goods train was allowed to leave Wotton Bassett Station 25 minutes after its time, and with an engine too weak to draw the load, and which broke down at the place where we ran into it. My first feeling was, 'Well, here's my accident at last.' I have always felt sure I should meet with one, and now I hope it is over."

This was one of the many accidents of his life, attributable, no doubt, to the evil influence of Saturn in his horoscope!

He was not to be intimidated by mobs: one suspects that he was more at ease with an unfriendly rabble at Birmingham, than with a friendly one at Belfast. He

was present at the Aston Hall disturbances in Birmingham in October 1884.   On his journey, some one at
Cheltenham station prophesied " Rough times at Birmingham."   On arriving, with Lady Iddesleigh, at the hotel
next Aston Park, they learned that a Liberal crowd had
broken down the wall of the park, and was breaking up
the meeting.   Lord Randolph Churchill came in and said
that it was vain to try to speak.   Sir Stafford went into
the hall, however, where Lord Randolph joined him; but
the ladies thought discretion the better part, and attended
another meeting in the hotel.   The windows of the room
where they had been were broken by the Liberal multi-
tude, and presently the ladies were joined by Sir Stafford.
He had found a great uproar in the larger assembly, the
furniture in ruins, and the audience singing " Rule
Britannia."   In this musical exercise he joined, and then
Sir Stafford tried to speak.   The uproar could not be combated—though he thought it was mainly horse-play, and
not very malicious—and his friends hurried him from the
hall.   He only felt nervous about catching his feet in
the wires that protected the flower-beds, as he went
through the garden in the dark.   The crowd was rather
offensive as they drove away; but Colonel Burnaby drew
off its attention by smoking a cigar under a lamp-post.
" His attitude," says Lady Iddesleigh, " standing quietly
smoking and 'chaffing' while the crowd around were
hooting, was calculated to reassure the most timid."
The whole story is more to the credit of Sir Stafford

and his friends than flattering to the chivalry of their opponents.

Such was Lord Iddesleigh in his private life, and in his studies. In a country "tired of squires," he gave one an example of what a squire might be. A man of letters, of affairs, a man of courage and of courtesy, a lover of his own country, and of his own country-side, he was tolerant, candid, no seeker of his own interest, ambitious only in the lines of duty and rectitude. The age for which he was fitted ended ere he died, but he did not live to see the new tumult at its worst. It is pleasant to remember that one of the very latest entries in his last diary mentions a meeting with Mr Gladstone, who was friendly, and gave him some of his books on Homer. It was only in that ancient and imperishable fairy world of the past that the old friendship of these two men could live on, in the old Homeric custom of presenting gifts. In the world of to-day they were divided; but we may say, in the words of Lord Iddesleigh's old fellow-scholar at Balliol—

> "One port, methought, alike they sought,
>   One purpose hold, where'er they fare;
> O bounding breeze, O rushing seas,
>   At last, at last, unite them there!"

One who knew Lord Iddesleigh his whole life long has chosen, as singularly true of him, the words in which Marcus Aurelius the Emperor describes the character of Antoninus :—

Remember his constancy in every act which was conformable to reason, and his evenness in all things, and his piety, and the serenity of his countenance, and his sweetness, and his disregard of empty fame, and his efforts to understand things, and how he would never let anything pass without having first most carefully examined it and clearly understood it ; and how he bore with those who blamed him unjustly, without blaming them in return ; how he did nothing in a hurry, and how he listened not to calumnies; not given to reproach people, nor timid, nor suspicious, nor a sophist ; with how little he was satisfied, such as lodging, bed, dress, food, servants; how laborious and patient; how sparing he was in his diet; his firmness and uniformity in his friendships; how he tolerated freedom of speech in those who opposed his opinions; the pleasure that he had when any man showed him anything better; and how pious he was without superstition.

INDEX.

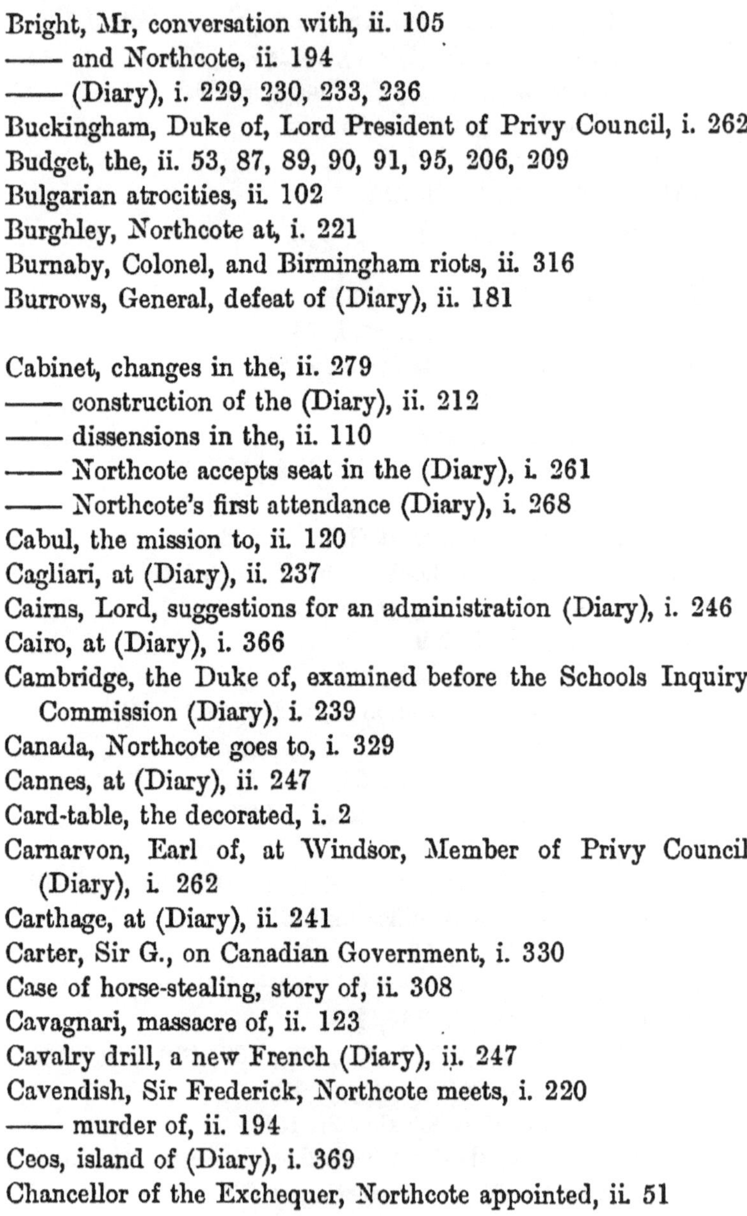

SPEECHES—*continued.*

  International disturbances, ii. 220

  Irish question, the, at Paisley, ii. 224

  Land Act, the, at Larne, ii. 260

  National Debt, the, ii. 68, 69

  Optimism, at Exeter, ii. 188

  Paper Duties, the, i. 165

  Prophecy, a, in Edinburgh, ii. 218, 219

  Reception at Exeter, on his, ii. 215

  Small agricultural holdings, at Lynton, ii. 223

  Suez Canal, the, ii. 82

  Surplus, the, in Liverpool, ii. 63

  Tercentenary, Edinburgh, ii. 269

  Turkey, ii. 118

  His maiden speech, i. 116

  Speeches out of Parliament, ii. 215, 217, 218, 220,
   223, 224, 227

 Queen's, the, i. 209, 233

Sports, Northcote's love of, ii. 305

Squib, a, on the Russian war, i. 114

Sorrento, at (Diary), ii. 239

South African Bill, the, ii. 129, 132

Stamford, Northcote elected for, i. 154, 225

Stanley, Lord, Northcote congratulated on speech by, i. 177

St Margaret's, a sermon at, i. 115

Stories, Devonshire, ii. 308

Story, told by Judge Hoar, ii. 2

—— of an Earl of Kildare, ii. 258

—— of Shanbally Castle, i. 245

—— yeomanry leader, the, i. 80

Strachy, General, and

—— Sir John—Finances and public works of India, i. 276

St Raphael, at (Diary), i. 248

Stucley, Sir George, i. 342

Suez Canal, illuminations on the (Diary), i. 355

—— opening of the (Diary), i. 342, 352

PRINTED BY WILLIAM BLACKWOOD AND SONS.

CATALOGUE

OF

MESSRS BLACKWOOD & SONS' PUBLICATIONS.

PHILOSOPHICAL CLASSICS FOR ENGLISH READERS.

Edited by WILLIAM KNIGHT, LL.D.,
Professor of Moral Philosophy in the University of St Andrews.

In crown 8vo Volumes, with Portraits, price 3s. 6d.

Now ready—

DESCARTES, by Professor Mahaffy, Dublin.—BUTLER, by Rev. W. Lucas Collins, M.A.—BERKELEY, by Professor Campbell Fraser, Edinburgh.—FICHTE, by Professor Adamson, Owens College, Manchester.—KANT, by Professor Wallace, Oxford.—HAMILTON, by Professor Veitch, Glasgow.—HEGEL, by Professor Edward Caird, Glasgow.—LEIBNIZ, by J. Theodore Merz.—VICO, by Professor Flint, Edinburgh.—HOBBES, by Professor Croom Robertson, London.—HUME, by the Editor.—SPINOZA, by the Very Rev. Principal Caird, Glasgow.—BACON: Part I. The Life, by Professor Nichol, Glasgow.—BACON: Part II. Philosophy, by the same Author.—LOCKE, by Professor Campbell Fraser, Edinburgh.

In preparation.
MILL, by the Right Hon. A. J. Balfour.

FOREIGN CLASSICS FOR ENGLISH READERS.
Edited by Mrs OLIPHANT.

In crown 8vo, 2s. 6d.

Contents of the Series.

DANTE, by the Editor.—VOLTAIRE, by Lieut.-General Sir E. B. Hamley, K.C.B.—PASCAL, by Principal Tulloch.—PETRARCH, by Henry Reeve, C.B.—GOETHE, By A. Hayward, Q.C.—MOLIÈRE, by the Editor and F. Tarver, M.A.—MONTAIGNE, by Rev. W. L. Collins, M.A.—RABELAIS, by Walter Besant, M.A.—CALDERON, by E. J. Hasell.—SAINT SIMON, by Clifton W. Collins, M.A.—CERVANTES, by the Editor.—CORNEILLE AND RACINE, by Henry M. Trollope. — MADAME DE SÉVIGNÉ, by Miss Thackeray.—LA FONTAINE, AND OTHER FRENCH FABULISTS, by Rev. W. Lucas Collins, M.A.—SCHILLER, by James Sime, M.A., Author of 'Lessing, his Life and Writings.'—TASSO, by E. J. Hasell.—ROUSSEAU, by Henry Grey Graham.—ALFRED DE MUSSET, by C. F. Oliphant. *Immediately.*

In preparation.
LEOPARDI. By the Editor.

Now COMPLETE.

ANCIENT CLASSICS FOR ENGLISH READERS.
Edited by the Rev. W. LUCAS COLLINS, M.A.

Complete in 28 Vols. crown 8vo, cloth, price 2s. 6d. each. And may also be had in 14 Volumes, strongly and neatly bound, with calf or vellum back, £3, 10s.

Contents of the Series.

HOMER: THE ILIAD, by the Editor.—HOMER: THE ODYSSEY, by the Editor.—HERODOTUS, by George C. Swayne, M.A.—XENOPHON, by Sir Alexander Grant, Bart., LL.D.—EURIPIDES, by W. B. Donne.—ARISTOPHANES, by the Editor.—PLATO, by Clifton W. Collins, M.A.—LUCIAN, by the Editor.—ÆSCHYLUS, by the Right Rev. the Bishop of Colombo.—SOPHOCLES, by Clifton W. Collins, M.A.—HESIOD AND THEOGNIS, by the Rev. J. Davies, M.A.—GREEK ANTHOLOGY, by Lord Neaves.—VIRGIL, by the Editor.—HORACE, by Sir Theodore Martin, K.C.B.—JUVENAL, by Edward Walford, M.A.—PLAUTUS AND TERENCE, by the Editor.—THE COMMENTARIES OF CÆSAR, by Anthony Trollope.—TACITUS, by W. B. Donne.—CICERO, by the Editor.—PLINY'S LETTERS, by the Rev. Alfred Church, M.A., and the Rev. W. J. Brodribb, M.A.—LIVY, by the Editor.—OVID, by the Rev. A. Church, M.A.—CATULLUS, TIBULLUS, AND PROPERTIUS, by the Rev. Jas. Davies, M.A.—DEMOSTHENES, by the Rev. W. J. Brodribb, M.A.—ARISTOTLE, by Sir Alexander Grant, Bart., LL.D.—THUCYDIDES, by the Editor.—LUCRETIUS, by W. H. Mallock, M.A.—PINDAR, by the Rev. F. D. Morice, M.A.

Saturday Review.—"It is difficult to estimate too highly the value of such a series as this in giving 'English readers' an insight, exact as far as it goes, into those olden times which are so remote and yet to many of us so close."

CATALOGUE

OF

MESSRS BLACKWOOD & SONS'

PUBLICATIONS.

ALISON. History of Europe. By Sir ARCHIBALD ALISON, Bart., D.C.L.
1. From the Commencement of the French Revolution to the Battle of Waterloo.
LIBRARY EDITION, 14 vols., with Portraits. Demy 8vo, £10, 10s.
ANOTHER EDITION, in 20 vols. crown 8vo, £6.
PEOPLE'S EDITION, 13 vols. crown 8vo, £2, 11s.
2. Continuation to the Accession of Louis Napoleon.
LIBRARY EDITION, 8 vols. 8vo, £6, 7s. 6d.
PEOPLE'S EDITION, 8 vols. crown 8vo, 34s.
3. Epitome of Alison's History of Europe. Twenty-ninth Thousand, 7s. 6d.
4. Atlas to Alison's History of Europe. By A. Keith Johnston.
LIBRARY EDITION, demy 4to, £3, 3s.
PEOPLE'S EDITION, 31s. 6d.
——— Life of John Duke of Marlborough. With some Account of his Contemporaries, and of the War of the Succession. Third Edition, 2 vols. 8vo. Portraits and Maps, 30s.
——— Essays: Historical, Political, and Miscellaneous. 3 vols. demy 8vo. 45s.

ACTA SANCTORUM HIBERNIÆ; Ex Codice Salmanticensi. Nunc primum integre edita opera CAROLI DE SMEDT et JOSEPHI DE BACKER, e Soc. Jesu, Hagiographorum Bollandianorum; Auctore et Sumptus Largiente JOANNE PATRICIO MARCHIONE BOTHAE. In One handsome 4to Volume, bound in half roxburghe, £2, 2s.; in paper wrapper, 31s. 6d.

AIRD. Poetical Works of Thomas Aird. Fifth Edition, with Memoir of the Author by the Rev. JARDINE WALLACE, and Portrait. Crown 8vo, 7s. 6d.

ALLARDYCE. The City of Sunshine. By ALEXANDER ALLARDYCE. Three vols. post 8vo, £1, 5s. 6d.
——— Memoir of the Honourable George Keith Elphinstone, K.B., Viscount Keith of Stonehaven, Marischal, Admiral of the Red. 8vo, with Portrait, Illustrations, and Maps, 21s.

ALMOND. Sermons by a Lay Head-master. By HELY HUTCHINSON ALMOND, M.A. Oxon., Head-master of Loretto School. Crown 8vo, 5s.

ANCIENT CLASSICS FOR ENGLISH READERS. Edited by Rev. W. LUCAS COLLINS, M.A. Price 2s. 6d. each. *For list of Vols., see page 2.*

AYTOUN. Lays of the Scottish Cavaliers, and other Poems. By W. EDMONDSTOUNE AYTOUN, D.C.L., Professor of Rhetoric and Belles-Lettres in the University of Edinburgh. New Edition. Fcap. 8vo, 3s. 6d.
Another Edition, being the Thirtieth. Fcap. 8vo, cloth extra, 7s. 6d.
Cheap Edition. Fcap. 8vo. Illustrated Cover. Price 1s.

—— An Illustrated Edition of the Lays of the Scottish Cavaliers. From designs by Sir NOEL PATON. Small 4to, in gilt cloth, 21s.

—— Bothwell : a Poem. Third Edition. Fcap., 7s. 6d.

—— Poems and Ballads of Goethe. Translated by Professor AYTOUN and Sir THEODORE MARTIN, K.C.B. Third Edition. Fcap., 6s.

—— Bon Gaultier's Book of Ballads. By the SAME. Fifteenth Edition. With Illustrations by Doyle, Leech, and Crowquill. Fcap. 8vo, 5s.

—— The Ballads of Scotland. Edited by Professor AYTOUN. Fourth Edition. 2 vols. fcap. 8vo, 12s.

—— Memoir of William E. Aytoun, D.C.L. By Sir THEODORE MARTIN, K.C.B. With Portrait. Post 8vo, 12s.

BACH. On Musical Education and Vocal Culture. By ALBERT B. BACH. Fourth Edition. 8vo, 7s. 6d.

—— The Principles of Singing. A Practical Guide for Vocalists and Teachers. With Course of Vocal Exercises. Crown 8vo, 6s.

—— The Art of Singing. With Musical Exercises for Young People. Crown 8vo, 3s.

—— The Art Ballad : Loewe and Schubert. With Music Illustrations. With a Portrait of LOEWE. Second Edition. Small 4to. 6s.

BALLADS AND POEMS. By MEMBERS OF THE GLASGOW BALLAD CLUB. Crown 8vo, 7s. 6d

BANNATYNE. Handbook of Republican Institutions in the United States of America. Based upon Federal and State Laws, and other reliable sources of information. By DUGALD J. BANNATYNE, Scotch Solicitor, New York ; Member of the Faculty of Procurators, Glasgow. Cr. 8vo, 7s. 6d.

BELLAIRS. The Transvaal War, 1880-81. Edited by Lady BELLAIRS. With a Frontispiece and Map. 8vo, 15s.

—— Gossips with Girls and Maidens, Betrothed and Free. New Edition. Crown 8vo, 3s. 6d. Cloth, extra gilt edges, 5s.

BESANT. The Revolt of Man. By WALTER BESANT, M.A. Ninth Edition. Crown 8vo, 3s. 6d.

—— Readings in Rabelais. Crown 8vo, 7s. 6d.

BEVERIDGE. Culross and Tulliallan ; or Perthshire on Forth. Its History and Antiquities. With Elucidations of Scottish Life and Character from the Burgh and Kirk-Session Records of that District. By DAVID BEVERIDGE. 2 vols. 8vo, with Illustrations, 42s.

—— Between the Ochils and the Forth ; or, From Stirling Bridge to Abordour. Crown 8vo, 6s.

BLACK. Heligoland and the Islands of the North Sea. By WILLIAM GEORGE BLACK. Crown 8vo, 4s.

BLACKIE. Lays and Legends of Ancient Greece. By JOHN STUART BLACKIE, Emeritus Professor of Greek in the University of Edinburgh. Second Edition. Fcap. 8vo. 5s.

—— The Wisdom of Goethe. Fcap. 8vo. Cloth, extra gilt, 6s.

—— Scottish Song : Its Wealth, Wisdom, and Social Significance. Crown 8vo. With Music. 7s. 6d.

—— A Song of Heroes. Crown 8vo, 6s.

BLACKWOOD'S MAGAZINE, from Commencement in 1817 to September 1890. Nos. 1 to 899, forming 147 Volumes.

—— Index to Blackwood's Magazine. Vols. 1 to 50. 8vo, 15s.

BLACKWOOD. Tales from Blackwood. Price One Shilling each, in Paper Cover. Sold separately at all Railway Bookstalls. They may also be had bound in cloth, 18s., and in half calf, richly gilt, 30s. Or 12 volumes in 6, roxburghe, 21s., and half red morocco, 28s.

———— Tales from Blackwood. New Series. Complete in Twenty-four Shilling Parts. Handsomely bound in 12 vols., cloth, 30s. In leather back, roxburghe style, 37s. 6d. In half calf, gilt, 52s. 6d. In half morocco, 55s.

———— Tales from Blackwood. Third Series. In Parts. Each price 1s. [*Nos. I. to X. now ready.*

———— Travel, Adventure, and Sport. From 'Blackwood's Magazine.' In Parts. Uniform with 'Tales from Blackwood.' Each price 1s. [*Nos. I. to X. now ready.*

———— Standard Novels. Uniform in size and legibly Printed. Each Novel complete in one volume.

FLORIN SERIES, Illustrated Boards. Or in New Cloth Binding, 2s. 6d.

TOM CRINGLE'S LOG. By Michael Scott.
THE CRUISE OF THE MIDGE. By the Same.
CYRIL THORNTON. By Captain Hamilton.
ANNALS OF THE PARISH. By John Galt.
THE PROVOST, &c. By John Galt.
SIR ANDREW WYLIE. By John Galt.
THE ENTAIL. By John Galt.
MISS MOLLY. By Beatrice May Butt.
REGINALD DALTON. By J. G. Lockhart.

PEN OWEN. By Dean Hook.
ADAM BLAIR. By J. G. Lockhart.
LADY LEE'S WIDOWHOOD. By General Sir E. B. Hamley.
SALEM CHAPEL. By Mrs Oliphant.
THE PERPETUAL CURATE. By Mrs Oliphant.
MISS MARJORIBANKS. By Mrs Oliphant.
JOHN: A Love Story. By Mrs Oliphant.

SHILLING SERIES, Illustrated Cover. Or in New Cloth Binding, 1s. 6d.

THE RECTOR, and THE DOCTOR'S FAMILY. By Mrs Oliphant.
THE LIFE OF MANSIE WAUCH. By D. M. Moir.
PENINSULAR SCENES AND SKETCHES. By F. Hardman.

SIR FRIZZLE PUMPKIN, NIGHTS AT MESS, &c.
THE SUBALTERN.
LIFE IN THE FAR WEST. By G. F. Ruxton.
VALERIUS: A Roman Story. By J. G. Lockhart.

BLACKMORE. The Maid of Sker. By R. D. BLACKMORE, Author of 'Lorna Doone,' &c. New Edition. Crown 8vo, 6s.

BLAIR. History of the Catholic Church of Scotland. From the Introduction of Christianity to the Present Day. By ALPHONS BELLESHEIM, D.D., Canon of Aix-la-Chapelle. Translated, with Notes and Additions, by D. OSWALD HUNTER BLAIR, O.S.B., Monk of Fort Augustus. To be completed in 4 vols. 8vo. Vols. I. and II. 25s. Vol. III. 12s. 6d.

BOSCOBEL TRACTS. Relating to the Escape of Charles the Second after the Battle of Worcester, and his subsequent Adventures. Edited by J. HUGHES, Esq., A.M. A New Edition, with additional Notes and Illustrations, including Communications from the Rev. R. H. BARHAM, Author of the 'Ingoldsby Legends.' 8vo, with Engravings, 16s.

BROUGHAM. Memoirs of the Life and Times of Henry Lord Brougham. Written by HIMSELF. 3 vols. 8vo, £2, 8s. The Volumes are sold separately, price 16s. each.

BROWN. The Forester: A Practical Treatise on the Planting, Rearing, and General Management of Forest-trees. By JAMES BROWN, LL.D., Inspector of and Reporter on Woods and Forests. Fifth Edition, revised and enlarged. Royal 8vo, with Engravings, 36s.

BROWN. The Ethics of George Eliot's Works. By JOHN CROMBIE BROWN. Fourth Edition. Crown 8vo, 2s. 6d.

BROWN. A Manual of Botany, Anatomical and Physiological. For the Use of Students. By ROBERT BROWN, M.A., Ph.D. Crown 8vo, with numerous Illustrations, 12s. 6d.

BRUCE. In Clover and Heather. Poems by WALLACE BRUCE. Crown 8vo, 4s. 6d.
A limited number of Copies on large hand-made paper, 12s. 6d.

BRYDALL. Art in Scotland; its Origin and Progress. By ROBERT BRYDALL, Master of St George's Art School of Glasgow. 8vo, 12s. 6d.

BUCHAN. Introductory Text-Book of Meteorology. By ALEXANDER BUCHAN, M.A., F.R.S.E., Secretary of the Scottish Meteorological Society, &c. Crown 8vo, with 8 Coloured Charts and Engravings, 4s. 6d.

BUCHANAN. The Shirè Highlands (East Central Africa). By JOHN BUCHANAN, Planter at Zomba. Crown 8vo, 5s.

BURBIDGE. Domestic Floriculture, Window Gardening, and Floral Decorations. Being practical directions for the Propagation, Culture, and Arrangement of Plants and Flowers as Domestic Ornaments. By F. W. BURBIDGE. Second Edition. Crown 8vo, with numerous Illustrations, 7s. 6d.

——— Cultivated Plants: Their Propagation and Improvement. Including Natural and Artificial Hybridisation, Raising from Seed, Cuttings, and Layers, Grafting and Budding, as applied to the Families and Genera in Cultivation. Crown 8vo, with numerous Illustrations, 12s. 6d.

BURTON. The History of Scotland : From Agricola's Invasion to the Extinction of the last Jacobite Insurrection. By JOHN HILL BURTON, D.C.L., Historiographer-Royal for Scotland. New and Enlarged Edition. 8 vols., and Index. Crown 8vo, £3, 3s.

——— History of the British Empire during the Reign of Queen Anne. In 3 vols. 8vo. 36s.

——— The Scot Abroad. Third Edition. Crown 8vo, 10s. 6d.

——— The Book-Hunter. New Edition. With Portrait. Crown 8vo, 7s. 6d.

BUTE. The Roman Breviary : Reformed by Order of the Holy Œcumenical Council of Trent; Published by Order of Pope St Pius V.; and Revised by Clement VIII. and Urban VIII.; together with the Offices since granted. Translated out of Latin into English by JOHN, Marquess of Bute, K.T. In 2 vols, crown 8vo. cloth boards, edges uncut. £2, 2s.

——— The Altus of St Columba. With a Prose Paraphrase and Notes. In paper cover, 2s. 6d.

BUTLER. Pompeii : Descriptive and Picturesque. By W. BUTLER. Post 8vo, 5s.

BUTT. Miss Molly. By BEATRICE MAY BUTT. Cheap Edition, 2s.

——— Eugenie. Crown 8vo, 6s. 6d.

——— Elizabeth, and Other Sketches. Crown 8vo, 6s.

——— Novels. New and Uniform Edition. Crown 8vo, each 2s. 6d. Delicia. *Now ready.*

CAIRD. Sermons. By JOHN CAIRD, D.D., Principal of the University of Glasgow. Sixteenth Thousand. Fcap. 8vo, 5s.

——— Religion in Common Life. A Sermon preached in Crathie Church, October 14, 1855, before Her Majesty the Queen and Prince Albert. Published by Her Majesty's Command. Cheap Edition, 3d.

CAMPBELL. Sermons Preached before the Queen at Balmoral. By the Rev. A. A. CAMPBELL, Minister of Crathie. Published by Command of Her Majesty. Crown 8vo, 4s. 6d.

CAMPBELL. Records of Argyll. Legends, Traditions, and Recollections of Argyllshire Highlanders, collected chiefly from the Gaelic. With Notes on the Antiquity of the Dress, Clan Colours or Tartans of the Highlanders. By LORD ARCHIBALD CAMPBELL. Illustrated with Nineteen full-page Etchings. 4to, printed on hand-made paper, £3, 3s.

CANTON. A Lost Epic, and other Poems. By WILLIAM CANTON. Crown 8vo, 5s.

CARR. Margaret Maliphant. A Novel. By Mrs COMYNS CARR, Author of 'La Fortunina,' 'North Italian Folk,' &c. 3 vols. post 8vo, 25s. 6d.

CARRICK. Koumiss ; or, Fermented Mare's Milk : and its Uses in the Treatment and Cure of Pulmonary Consumption, and other Wasting Diseases. With an Appendix on the best Methods of Fermenting Cow's Milk. By GEORGE L. CARRICK, M.D., L.R.C.S.E. and L.R.C.P.E., Physician to the British Embassy, St Petersburg, &c. Crown 8vo, 10s. 6d.

CAUVIN. A Treasury of the English and German Languages. Compiled from the best Authors and Lexicographers in both Languages. By JOSEPH CAUVIN, LL.D. and Ph.D., of the University of Göttingen, &c. Crown 8vo, 7s. 6d.

CAVE-BROWN. Lambeth Palace and its Associations. By J. CAVE-BROWN, M.A., Vicar of Detling, Kent, and for many years Curate of Lambeth Parish Church. With an Introduction by the Archbishop of Canterbury. Second Edition, containing an additional Chapter on Medieval Life in the Old Palaces. 8vo, with Illustrations, 21s.

CHARTERIS. Canonicity; or, Early Testimonies to the Existence and Use of the Books of the New Testament. Based on Kirchhoffer's 'Quellensammlung.' Edited by A. H. CHARTERIS, D.D., Professor of Biblical Criticism in the University of Edinburgh. 8vo, 18s.

CHRISTISON. Life of Sir Robert Christison, Bart., M.D., D.C.L. Oxon., Professor of Medical Jurisprudence in the University of Edinburgh. Edited by his SONS. In two vols. 8vo. Vol. I.—Autobiography. 16s. Vol. II.—Memoirs. 16s.

CHURCH SERVICE SOCIETY. A Book of Common Order : Being Forms of Worship issued by the Church Service Society. Sixth Edition. Crown, 8vo, 6s. Also in 2 vols, crown 8vo, 6s. 6d.

CLELAND. Barbara Allan, the Provost's Daughter. By ROBERT CLELAND, Author of 'Inchbracken,' 'True to a Type,' &c. 2 vols., 17s.

CLOUSTON. Popular Tales and Fictions : their Migrations and Transformations. By W. A. CLOUSTON, Editor of 'Arabian Poetry for English Readers,' 'The Book of Sindibad,' &c. 2 vols. post 8vo, roxburghe binding, 25s.

COBBAN. Master of his Fate. By J. MACLAREN COBBAN, Author of 'The Cure of Souls,' 'Tinted Vapours,' &c. Crown 8vo, 3s. 6d.

COCHRAN. A Handy Text-Book of Military Law. Compiled chiefly to assist Officers preparing for Examination; also for all Officers of the Regular and Auxiliary Forces. Comprising also a Synopsis of part of the Army Act. By Major F. COCHRAN, Hampshire Regiment Garrison Instructor, North British District. Crown 8vo, 7s. 6d.

COLQUHOUN. The Moor and the Loch. Containing Minute Instructions in all Highland Sports, with Wanderings over Crag and Corrie, Flood and Fell. By JOHN COLQUHOUN. Seventh Edition. With Illustrations. 8vo, 21s.

COTTERILL. Suggested Reforms in Public Schools. By C. C. COTTERILL, M.A. Crown 8vo, 3s. 6d.

CRANSTOUN. The Elegies of Albius Tibullus. Translated into English Verse, with Life of the Poet, and Illustrative Notes. By JAMES CRANSTOUN, LL.D., Author of a Translation of 'Catullus.' Crown 8vo, 6s. 6d.

——— The Elegies of Sextus Propertius. Translated into English Verse, with Life of the Poet, and Illustrative Notes. Crown 8vo, 7s. 6d.

CRAWFORD. Saracinesca. By F. MARION CRAWFORD, Author of 'Mr Isaacs,' 'Dr Claudius,' 'Zoroaster,' &c. &c. Fifth Ed. Crown 8vo, 6s.

CRAWFORD. The Doctrine of Holy Scripture respecting the Atonement. By the late THOMAS J. CRAWFORD, D.D., Professor of Divinity in the University of Edinburgh. Fifth Edition. 8vo, 12s.

——— The Fatherhood of God, Considered in its General and Special Aspects, and particularly in relation to the Atonement, with a Review of Recent Speculations on the Subject. By the late THOMAS J. CRAWFORD, D.D., Professor of Divinity in the University of Edinburgh. Third Edition, Revised and Enlarged. 8vo, 9s.

——— The Preaching of the Cross, and other Sermons. 8vo, 7s. 6d.

——— The Mysteries of Christianity. Crown 8vo, 7s. 6d.

CRAWFORD. An Atonement of East London, and other Poems. By HOWARD CRAWFORD, M.A. Crown 8vo, 5s.

CUSHING. The Bull i' th' Thorn. A Romance. By PAUL CUSHING. 3 vols. Crown 8vo, 25s. 6d.

CUSHING.   The Blacksmith of Voe.   Cheap Edition.   Crown 8vo, 3s. 6d.

DAVIES.   Norfolk Broads and Rivers; or, The Waterways, Lagoons, and Decoys of East Anglia.   By G. CHRISTOPHER DAVIES, Author of 'The Swan and her Crew.'   Illustrated with Seven full-page Plates.   New and Cheaper Edition.   Crown 8vo, 6s.

——— Our Home in Aveyron.   Sketches of Peasant Life in Aveyron and the Lot.   By G. CHRISTOPHER DAVIES and Mrs BROUGHALL.   Illustrated with full-page Illustrations.   8vo, 15s.

DAYNE.   In the Name of the Tzar.   A Novel.   By J. BELFORD DAYNE.   Crown 8vo, 6s.

——— Tribute to Satan.   A Novel.   Crown 8vo, 2s. 6d.

DE LA WARR.   An Eastern Cruise in the 'Edeline.'   By the Countess DE LA WARR.   In Illustrated Cover.   2s.

DESCARTES.   The Method, Meditations, and Principles of Philosophy of Descartes.   Translated from the Original French and Latin.   With a New Introductory Essay, Historical and Critical, on the Cartesian Philosophy.   By JOHN VEITCH, LL.D., Professor of Logic and Rhetoric in the University of Glasgow.   A New Edition, being the Ninth.   Price 6s. 6d.

DICKSON.   Gleanings from Japan.   By W. G. DICKSON, Author of 'Japan: Being a Sketch of its History, Government, and Officers of the Empire.'   With Illustrations.   8vo, 16s.

DOGS, OUR DOMESTICATED: Their Treatment in reference to Food, Diseases, Habits, Punishment, Accomplishments.   By 'MAGENTA.'   Crown 8vo, 2s. 6d.

DR HERMIONE.   By the Author of 'Lady Bluebeard,' 'Zit and Xoe.'   Crown 8vo, 6s.

DU CANE.   The Odyssey of Homer, Books I.-XII.   Translated into English Verse.   By Sir CHARLES DU CANE, K.C.M.G.   8vo, 10s. 6d.

DUDGEON.   History of the Edinburgh or Queen's Regiment Light Infantry Militia, now 3rd Battalion The Royal Scots; with an Account of the Origin and Progress of the Militia, and a Brief Sketch of the old Royal Scots.   By Major R. C. DUDGEON, Adjutant 3rd Battalion The Royal Scots.   Post 8vo, with Illustrations, 10s. 6d.

DUNCAN.   Manual of the General Acts of Parliament relating to the Salmon Fisheries of Scotland from 1828 to 1882.   By J. BARKER DUNCAN.   Crown 8vo, 5s.

DUNSMORE.   Manual of the Law of Scotland as to the Relations between Agricultural Tenants and their Landlords, Servants, Merchants, and Bowers.   By W. DUNSMORE.   8vo, 7s. 6d.

DUPRE.   Thoughts on Art, and Autobiographical Memoirs of Giovanni Duprè.   Translated from the Italian by E. M. PERUZZI, with the permission of the Author.   New Edition.   With an Introduction by W. W. STORY.   Crown 8vo, 10s. 6d.

ELIOT.   George Eliot's Life, Related in her Letters and Journals.   Arranged and Edited by her husband, J. W. CROSS.   With Portrait and other Illustrations.   Third Edition.   3 vols. post 8vo, 42s.

——— George Eliot's Life.   (Cabinet Edition.)   With Portrait and other Illustrations.   3 vols. crown 8vo, 15s.

——— George Eliot's Life.   With Portrait and other Illustrations.   New Edition, in one volume.   Crown 8vo, 7s. 6d.

——— Works of George Eliot (Cabinet Edition).   Handsomely printed in a new type, 21 volumes, crown 8vo, price £5, 5s.   The Volumes are also sold separately, price 5s. each, viz.:—

> Romola.   2 vols.—Silas Marner, The Lifted Veil, Brother Jacob.   1 vol.—Adam Bede.   2 vols.—Scenes of Clerical Life.   2 vols.—The Mill on the Floss.   2 vols.—Felix Holt.   2 vols.—Middlemarch.   3 vols.—Daniel Deronda.   3 vols.—The Spanish Gypsy.   1 vol.—Jubal, and other Poems, Old and New.   1 vol.—Theophrastus Such.   1 vol.—Essays.   1 vol.

ELIOT. Novels by GEORGE ELIOT. Cheap Edition. Adam Bede. Illustrated. 3s. 6d., cloth.—The Mill on the Floss. Illustrated. 3s. 6d., cloth.—Scenes of Clerical Life. Illustrated. 3s., cloth.—Silas Marner: the Weaver of Raveloe. Illustrated. 2s. 6d., cloth.—Felix Holt, the Radical. Illustrated. 3s. 6d., cloth.—Romola. With Vignette. 3s. 6d., cloth.

———— Middlemarch. Crown 8vo, 7s. 6d.

———— Daniel Deronda. Crown 8vo, 7s. 6d.

———— Essays. New Edition. Crown 8vo, 5s.

———— Impressions of Theophrastus Such. New Edition. Crown 8vo, 5s.

———— The Spanish Gypsy. New Edition. Crown 8vo, 5s.

———— The Legend of Jubal, and other Poems, Old and New. New Edition. Crown 8vo, 5s.

———— Wise, Witty, and Tender Sayings, in Prose and Verse. Selected from the Works of GEORGE ELIOT. Eighth Edition. Fcap. 8vo, 6s.

———— The George Eliot Birthday Book. Printed on fine paper, with red border, and handsomely bound in cloth, gilt. Fcap. 8vo, cloth, 3s. 6d. And in French morocco or Russia, 5s.

ESSAYS ON SOCIAL SUBJECTS. Originally published in the 'Saturday Review.' A New Edition. First and Second Series. 2 vols. crown 8vo, 6s. each.

EWALD. The Crown and its Advisers; or, Queen, Ministers, Lords and Commons. By ALEXANDER CHARLES EWALD, F.S.A. Crown 8vo, 5s.

FAITHS OF THE WORLD, The. A Concise History of the Great Religious Systems of the World. By various Authors. Being the St Giles' Lectures—Second Series. Crown 8vo, 5s.

FARRER. A Tour in Greece in 1880. By RICHARD RIDLEY FARRER. With Twenty-seven full-page Illustrations by LORD WINDSOR. Royal 8vo, with a Map, 21s.

FERRIER. Philosophical Works of the late James F. Ferrier, B.A. Oxon., Professor of Moral Philosophy and Political Economy, St Andrews. New Edition. Edited by Sir ALEX. GRANT, Bart., D.C.L., and Professor LUSHINGTON. 3 vols. crown 8vo, 34s. 6d.

———— Institutes of Metaphysic. Third Edition. 10s. 6d.

———— Lectures on the Early Greek Philosophy. Third Edition, 10s. 6d.

———— Philosophical Remains, including the Lectures on Early Greek Philosophy. 2 vols., 24s.

FLETCHER. Lectures on the Opening Clauses of the Litany delivered in St Paul's Church, Edinburgh. By JOHN B. FLETCHER, M.A. Crown 8vo, 4s.

FLINT.. The Philosophy of History in Europe. By ROBERT FLINT, D.D., LL.D., Professor of Divinity, University of Edinburgh. 2 vols. 8vo. [New Edition in preparation.

———— Theism. Being the Baird Lecture for 1876. Seventh Edition. Crown 8vo, 7s. 6d.

———— Anti-Theistic Theories. Being the Baird Lecture for 1877. Fourth Edition. Crown 8vo, 10s. 6d.

———— Agnosticism. Being the Croall Lectures for 1887-88.
[In the press.

FORBES. Insulinde: Experiences of a Naturalist's Wife in the Eastern Archipelago. By Mrs H. O. FORBES. Crown 8vo, with a Map. 4s. 6d.

FOREIGN CLASSICS FOR ENGLISH READERS. Edited by Mrs OLIPHANT. Price 2s. 6d. For List of Volumes published, see page 2.

FULLARTON. Merlin: A Dramatic Poem. By RALPH MACLEOD FULLARTON. Crown 8vo, 5s.

GALT.   Annals of the Parish.   By JOHN GALT.   Fcap. 8vo, 2s.
———— The Provost.   Fcap. 8vo, 2s.
———— Sir Andrew Wylie.   Fcap. 8vo, 2s.
———— The Entail ; or, The Laird of Grippy.   Fcap. 8vo, 2s.
GENERAL ASSEMBLY OF THE CHURCH OF SCOTLAND.
———— Prayers for Social and Family Worship.   Prepared by a
Special Committee of the General Assembly of the Church of Scotland.   En-
tirely New Edition, Revised and Enlarged.   Fcap. 8vo, red edges, 2s.
———— Prayers for Family Worship.   A Selection from the com-
plete book.   Fcap. 8vo, red edges, price 1s.
———— Scottish Hymnal, with Appendix Incorporated.   Pub-
lished for Use in Churches by Authority of the General Assembly.   1. Large
type, cloth, red edges, 2s. 6d. ; French morocco, 4s.   2. Bourgeois type, limp
cloth, 1s.; French morocco, 2s.   3. Nonpareil type, cloth, red edges, 6d. ;
French morocco, 1s. 4d.   4. Paper covers, 3d.   5. Sunday - School Edition,
paper covers, 1d.   No. 1, bound with the Psalms and Paraphrases, French
morocco, 8s.   No. 2, bound with the Psalms and Paraphrases, cloth, 2s. ;
French morocco, 3s.
GERARD.   Reata : What's in a Name.   By E. D. GERARD.
New Edition.   Crown 8vo, 6s.
———— Beggar my Neighbour.   New Edition.   Crown 8vo, 6s.
———— The Waters of Hercules.   New Edition.   Crown 8vo, 6s.
GERARD.   The Land beyond the Forest.   Facts, Figures, and
Fancies from Transylvania.   By E. GERARD.   In Two Volumes.   With Maps
and Illustrations.   25s.
GERARD.   Lady Baby.   By DOROTHEA GERARD, Author of
'Orthodox.'   New Edition.   Crown 8vo, 6s.
———— Recha.   Second Edition.   Crown 8vo, 6s.
GERARD.   Stonyhurst Latin Grammar.   By Rev. JOHN GERARD.
Fcap. 8vo, 3s.
GILL.   Free Trade : an Inquiry into the Nature of its Operation.
By RICHARD GILL.   Crown 8vo, 7s. 6d.
———— Free Trade under Protection.   Crown 8vo, 7s. 6d.
GOETHE'S FAUST.   Translated into English Verse by Sir THEO-
DORE MARTIN, K.C.B.   Part I.   Second Edition, post 8vo, 6s.   Ninth Edi-
tion, fcap., 3s. 6d.   Part II.   Second Edition, revised.   Fcap. 8vo, 6s.
GOETHE.   Poems and Ballads of Goethe.   Translated by Professor
AYTOUN and Sir THEODORE MARTIN, K.C.B.   Third Edition, fcap. 8vo, 6s.
GOODALL.   Juxta Crucem.   Studies of the Love that is over us.
By the late Rev. CHARLES GOODALL, B.D., Minister of Barr.   With a Memoir
by Rev. Dr Strong, Glasgow, and Portrait.   Crown 8vo, 6s.
GORDON CUMMING.   At Home in Fiji.   By C. F. GORDON
CUMMING, Author of ' From the Hebrides to the Himalayas.'   Fourth Edition,
post 8vo.   With Illustrations and Map.   7s. 6d.
———— A Lady's Cruise in a French Man-of-War.   New and
Cheaper Edition.   8vo.   With Illustrations and Map.   12s. 6d.
———— Fire-Fountains.   The Kingdom of Hawaii : Its Volcanoes,
and the History of its Missions.   With Map and Illustrations.   2 vols. 8vo, 25s.
———— Wanderings in China.   New and Cheaper Edition.   8vo,
with Illustrations, 10s.
———— Granite Crags : The Yō-semité Region of California.   Il-
lustrated with 8 Engravings.   New and Cheaper Edition.   8vo, 8s. 6d
GRAHAM.   The Life and Work of Syed Ahmed Khan, C.S.I.
By Lieut.-Colonel G. F. I. GRAHAM, B.S.C.   8vo, 14s.
GRANT.   Bush-Life in Queensland.   By A. C. GRANT.   New
Edition.   Crown 8vo, 6s.

GRIFFITHS. Locked Up. By Major ARTHUR GRIFFITHS, Author of 'The Wrong Road,' 'Chronicles of Newgate,' &c. With Illustrations by C. J. STANILAND, R.I. Crown 8vo, 2s. 6d.

HAGGARD. Dodo and I. A Novel. By Captain ANDREW HAGGARD, D.S.O. Second Edition. Crown 8vo, 6s.

HALDANE. Subtropical Cultivations and Climates. A Handy Book for Planters, Colonists, and Settlers. By R. C. HALDANE. Post 8vo, 9s.

HALLETT. A Thousand Miles on an Elephant in the Shan States. By HOLT S. HALLETT, M. Inst. C.E., F.R.G.S., M.R.A.S., Hon. Member Manchester and Tyneside Geographical Societies. 8vo, with Maps and numerous Illustrations, 21s.

HAMERTON. Wenderholme : A Story of Lancashire and Yorkshire Life. By PHILIP GILBERT HAMERTON, Author of 'A Painter's Camp.' A New Edition. Crown 8vo, 6s.

HAMILTON. Lectures on Metaphysics. By Sir WILLIAM HAMILTON, Bart., Professor of Logic and Metaphysics in the University of Edinburgh. Edited by the Rev. H. L. MANSEL, B.D., LL.D., Dean of St Paul's ; and JOHN VEITCH, M.A., LL.D., Professor of Logic and Rhetoric, Glasgow. Seventh Edition. 2 vols. 8vo, 24s.

———— Lectures on Logic. Edited by the SAME. Third Edition. 2 vols., 24s.

———— Discussions on Philosophy and Literature, Education and University Reform. Third Edition, 8vo, 21s.

———— Memoir of Sir William Hamilton, Bart., Professor of Logic and Metaphysics in the University of Edinburgh. By Professor VEITCH, of the University of Glasgow. 8vo, with Portrait, 18s.

———— Sir William Hamilton : The Man and his Philosophy. Two Lectures delivered before the Edinburgh Philosophical Institution, January and February 1883. By the SAME. Crown 8vo, 2s.

HAMLEY. The Operations of War Explained and Illustrated. By General Sir EDWARD BRUCE HAMLEY, K.C.B., K.C.M.G., M.P. Fifth Edition, revised throughout. 4to, with numerous Illustrations, 30s.

———— National Defence ; Articles and Speeches. Post 8vo, 6s.

———— Shakespeare's Funeral, and other Papers. Post 8vo, 7s. 6d.

———— Thomas Carlyle : An Essay. Second Edition. Crown 8vo. 2s. 6d.

———— On Outposts. Second Edition. 8vo, 2s.

———— Wellington's Career ; A Military and Political Summary. Crown 8vo, 2s.

———— Lady Lee's Widowhood. Crown 8vo, 2s. 6d.

———— Our Poor Relations. A Philozoic Essay. With Illustrations, chiefly by Ernest Griset. Crown 8vo, cloth gilt, 3s. 6d.

HAMLEY. Guilty, or Not Guilty? A Tale. By Major-General W. G. HAMLEY, late of the Royal Engineers. New Edition. Crown 8vo, 3s. 6d.

HARRISON. The Scot in Ulster. The Story of the Scottish Settlement in Ulster. By JOHN HARRISON, Author of 'Oure Tounis Colledge.' Crown 8vo, 2s. 6d.

HASELL. Bible Partings. By E. J. HASELL. Crown 8vo, 6s.

———— Short Family Prayers. Cloth, 1s.

HAY. The Works of the Right Rev. Dr George Hay, Bishop of Edinburgh. Edited under the Supervision of the Right Rev. Bishop STRAIN. With Memoir and Portrait of the Author. 5 vols. crown 8vo, bound in extra cloth, £1, 1s. The following Volumes may be had separately—viz.: The Devout Christian Instructed in the Law of Christ from the Written Word. 2 vols., 8s.—The Pious Christian Instructed in the Nature and Practice of the Principal Exercises of Piety. 1 vol., 3s.

HEATLEY. The Horse-Owner's Safeguard. A Handy Medical Guide for every Man who owns a Horse. By G. S. HEATLEY, M.R.C.V.S. Crown 8vo, 5s.

———— The Stock-Owner's Guide. A Handy Medical Treatise for every Man who owns an Ox or a Cow. Crown 8vo, 4s. 6d.

HEDDERWICK. Lays of Middle Age ; and other Poems. By JAMES HEDDERWICK, LL.D. Price 3s. 6d.

HEMANS. The Poetical Works of Mrs Hemans. Copyright Editions.—Royal 8vo, 5s.—The Same, with Engravings, cloth, gilt edges, 7s. 6d.—Six Vols. in Three, fcap., 12s. 6d.
SELECT POEMS OF MRS HEMANS. Fcap., cloth, gilt edges, 3s.

HOME PRAYERS. By Ministers of the Church of Scotland and Members of the Church Service Society. Second Edition. Fcap. 8vo, 3s.

HOMER. The Odyssey. Translated into English Verse in the Spenserian Stanza. By PHILIP STANHOPE WORSLEY. Third Edition, 2 vols. fcap., 12s.

———— The Iliad. Translated by P. S. WORSLEY and Professor CONINGTON. 2 vols. crown 8vo, 21s.

HUTCHINSON. Hints on the Game of Golf. By HORACE G. HUTCHINSON. Fifth Edition. Fcap. 8vo, cloth, 1s. 6d.

IDDESLEIGH. Lectures and Essays. By the late EARL OF IDDESLEIGH, G.C.B., D.C.L., &c. 8vo, 16s.

———— Life, Letters, and Diaries of Sir Stafford Northcote, First Earl of Iddesleigh. By ANDREW LANG. With Three Portraits and a View of Pynes. 2 vols. Post 8vo, 31s. 6d.

INDEX GEOGRAPHICUS : Being a List, alphabetically arranged, of the Principal Places on the Globe, with the Countries and Subdivisions of the Countries in which they are situated, and their Latitudes and Longitudes. Imperial 8vo, pp. 676, 21s.

JAMIESON. Discussions on the Atonement : Is it Vicarious ? By the Rev. GEORGE JAMIESON, A.M., B.D., D.D., Author of 'Profound Problems in Philosophy and Theology.' 8vo, 16s.

JEAN JAMBON. Our Trip to Blunderland ; or, Grand Excursion to Blundertown and Back. By JEAN JAMBON. With Sixty Illustrations designed by CHARLES DOYLE, engraved by DALZIEL. Fourth Thousand. Cloth, gilt edges, 6s. 6d. Cheap Edition, cloth, 3s. 6d. Boards, 2s. 6d.

JENNINGS. Mr Gladstone : A Study. By LOUIS J. JENNINGS, M.P., Author of 'Republican Government in the United States,' 'The Croker Memoirs,' &c. Popular Edition. Crown 8vo, 1s.

JERNINGHAM. Reminiscences of an Attaché. By HUBERT E. H. JERNINGHAM. Second Edition. Crown 8vo, 5s.

———— Diane de Breteuille. A Love Story. Crown 8vo, 2s. 6d.

JOHNSTON. The Chemistry of Common Life. By Professor J. F. W. JOHNSTON. New Edition, Revised, and brought down to date. By ARTHUR HERBERT CHURCH, M.A. Oxon.; Author of 'Food: Its Sources, Constituents, and Uses,' &c., &c. Illustrated with Maps and 102 Engravings on Wood. Complete in one volume, crown 8vo, 7s. 6d.

———— Elements of Agricultural Chemistry and Geology. Revised, and brought down to date. By Sir CHARLES A. CAMERON, M.D., F.R.C.S.I., &c. Fifteenth Edition. Fcap. 8vo, 6s. 6d.

———— Catechism of Agricultural Chemistry and Geology. New Edition, revised and enlarged, by Sir C. A. CAMERON. Eighty-sixth Thousand, with numerous Illustrations, 1s.

JOHNSTON. Patrick Hamilton : a Tragedy of the Reformation in Scotland, 1528. By T. P. JOHNSTON. Crown 8vo, with Two Etchings. 5s.

KER. Short Studies on St Paul's Letter to the Philippians. By Rev. WILLIAM LEE KER, Minister of Kilwinning. Crown 8vo, 5s.

KING. The Metamorphoses of Ovid. Translated in English Blank Verse. By HENRY KING, M.A., Fellow of Wadham College, Oxford, and of the Inner Temple, Barrister-at-Law. Crown 8vo 10s. 6d.

KINGLAKE. History of the Invasion of the Crimea. By A. W. KINGLAKE. Cabinet Edition, revised. Illustrated with Maps and Plans. Complete in 9 Vols., crown 8vo, at 6s. each. The Vols. respectively contain: I. THE ORIGIN OF THE WAR. II. RUSSIA MET AND INVADED. III. THE BATTLE OF THE ALMA. IV. SEBASTOPOL AT BAY. V. THE BATTLE OF BALACLAVA. VI. THE BATTLE OF INKERMAN. VII. WINTER TROUBLES. VIII. and IX. FROM THE MORROW OF INKERMAN TO THE DEATH OF LORD RAGLAN. With an Index to the Complete Work.

———— History of the Invasion of the Crimea. Demy 8vo. Vol. VI. Winter Troubles. With a Map, 16s. Vols. VII. and VIII. From the Morrow of Inkerman to the Death of Lord Raglan. With an Index to the Whole Work. With Maps and Plans. 28s.

———— Eothen. A New Edition, uniform with the Cabinet Edition of the 'History of the Invasion of the Crimea,' price 6s.

KNOLLYS. The Elements of Field-Artillery. Designed for the Use of Infantry and Cavalry Officers. By HENRY KNOLLYS, Captain Royal Artillery; Author of 'From Sedan to Saarbrück,' Editor of 'Incidents in the Sepoy War,' &c. With Engravings. Crown 8vo, 7s. 6d.

LAMINGTON. In the Days of the Dandies. By the late Lord LAMINGTON. Crown 8vo. Illustrated cover, 1s.; cloth, 1s. 6d.

LAWLESS. Hurrish: a Study. By the Hon. EMILY LAWLESS, Author of 'A Chelsea Householder,' &c. Fifth Edition, crown 8vo, 6s.

LAWSON. Spain of To-day: A Descriptive, Industrial, and Financial Survey of the Peninsula, with a full account of the Rio Tinto Mines. By W. R. LAWSON. Crown 8vo, 3s 6d.

LEES. A Handbook of Sheriff Court Styles. By J. M. LEES, M.A., LL.B., Advocate, Sheriff-Substitute of Lanarkshire. New Ed., 8vo, 21s.

———— A Handbook of the Sheriff and Justice of Peace Small Debt Courts. 8vo, 7s. 6d.

LETTERS FROM THE HIGHLANDS. Reprinted from 'The Times.' Fcap. 8vo, 4s. 6d.

LIGHTFOOT. Studies in Philosophy. By the Rev. J. LIGHTFOOT, M.A., D.Sc., Vicar of Cross Stone, Todmorden. Crown 8vo, 4s. 6d.

LITTLE HAND AND MUCKLE GOLD. A Study of To-day. In 3 vols. post 8vo, 25s. 6d.

LOCKHART. Doubles and Quits. By LAURENCE W. M. LOCKHART. New Edition. Crown 8vo, 3s. 6d.

———— Fair to See: a Novel. New Edition. Crown 8vo, 3s. 6d.

———— Mine is Thine: a Novel. New Edition. Crown 8vo, 3s. 6d.

LORIMER. The Institutes of Law: A Treatise of the Principles of Jurisprudence as determined by Nature. By the late JAMES LORIMER, Professor of Public Law and of the Law of Nature and Nations in the University of Edinburgh. New Edition, revised and much enlarged. 8vo, 18s.

———— The Institutes of the Law of Nations. A Treatise of the Jural Relation of Separate Political Communities. In 2 vols. 8vo. Volume I., price 16s. Volume II., price 20s.

M'COMBIE. Cattle and Cattle-Breeders. By WILLIAM M'COMBIE, Tillyfour. New Edition, enlarged, with Memoir of the Author. By JAMES MACDONALD, of the 'Farming World.' Crown 8vo, 3s. 6d.

MACRAE. A Handbook of Deer-Stalking. By ALEXANDER MACRAE, late Forester to Lord Henry Bentinck. With Introduction by HORATIO ROSS, Esq. Fcap. 8vo, with two Photographs from Life. 3s. 6d.

M'CRIE. Works of the Rev. Thomas M'Crie, D.D. Uniform Edition. Four vols. crown 8vo, 24s.

M'CRIE. Life of John Knox. Containing Illustrations of the History of the Reformation in Scotland. Crown 8vo, 6s. Another Edition, 3s. 6d.

———— Life of Andrew Melville. Containing Illustrations of the Ecclesiastical and Literary History of Scotland in the Sixteenth and Seventeenth Centuries. Crown 8vo, 6s.

———— History of the Progress and Suppression of the Reformation in Italy in the Sixteenth Century. Crown 8vo, 4s.

———— History of the Progress and Suppression of the Reformation in Spain in the Sixteenth Century. Crown 8vo, 3s. 6d.

———— Lectures on the Book of Esther. Fcap. 8vo, 5s.

MACDONALD. A Manual of the Criminal Law (Scotland) Procedure Act, 1887. By NORMAN DORAN MACDONALD. Revised by the LORD JUSTICE-CLERK. 8vo, cloth. 10s. 6d.

MACGREGOR. Life and Opinions of Major-General Sir Charles MacGregor, K.C.B., C.S.I., C.I.E., Quartermaster-General of India. From his Letters and Diaries. Edited by LADY MACGREGOR. With Portraits and Maps to illustrate Campaigns in which he was engaged. 2 vols. 8vo, 35s.

M'INTOSH. The Book of the Garden. By CHARLES M'INTOSH, formerly Curator of the Royal Gardens of his Majesty the King of the Belgians, and lately of those of his Grace the Duke of Buccleuch, K.G., at Dalkeith Palace. 2 vols. royal 8vo, with 1350 Engravings. £4, 7s. 6d. Vol. I. On the Formation of Gardens and Construction of Garden Edifices. £2, 10s. Vol. II. Practical Gardening. £1, 17s. 6d.

MACINTYRE. Hindu-Koh : Wanderings and Wild Sports on and beyond the Himalayas. By Major-General DONALD MACINTYRE, V.C., late Prince of Wales' Own Goorkhas, F.R.G.S. *Dedicated to H.R.H. The Prince of Wales.* 8vo, with numerous Illustrations, 21s.

MACKAY. A Sketch of the History of Fife and Kinross. A Study of Scottish History and Character. By Æ. J. G. MACKAY, Sheriff of these Counties. Crown 8vo, 6s.

MACKAY. A Manual of Modern Geography ; Mathematical, Physical, and Political. By the Rev. ALEXANDER MACKAY, LL.D., F.R.G.S. 11th Thousand, revised to the present time. Crown 8vo, pp. 688. 7s. 6d.

———— Elements of Modern Geography. 53d Thousand, revised to the present time. Crown 8vo, pp. 300, 3s.

———— The Intermediate Geography. Intended as an Intermediate Book between the Author's 'Outlines of Geography' and 'Elements of Geography.' Fifteenth Edition, revised. Crown 8vo, pp. 238, 2s.

———— Outlines of Modern Geography. 185th Thousand, revised to the present time. 18mo, pp. 118, 1s.

———— First Steps in Geography. 105th Thousand. 18mo, pp. 56. Sewed, 4d. ; cloth, 6d.

———— Elements of Physiography and Physical Geography. With Express Reference to the Instructions issued by the Science and Art Department. 30th Thousand, revised. Crown 8vo, 1s. 6d.

———— Facts and Dates ; or, the Leading Events in Sacred and Profane History, and the Principal Facts in the various Physical Sciences. The Memory being aided throughout by a Simple and Natural Method. For Schools and Private Reference. New Edition. Crown 8vo, 3s. 6d.

MACKAY. An Old Scots Brigade. Being the History of Mackay's Regiment, now incorporated with the Royal Scots. With an Appendix containing many Original Documents connected with the History of the Regiment. By JOHN MACKAY (late) OF HERRIESDALE. Crown 8vo, 5s.

MACKENZIE. Studies in Roman Law. With Comparative Views of the Laws of France, England, and Scotland. By LORD MACKENZIE, one of the Judges of the Court of Session in Scotland. Sixth Edition, Edited by JOHN KIRKPATRICK, Esq., M.A., LL.B., Advocate, Professor of History in the University of Edinburgh. 8vo, 12s.

M'PHERSON. Summer Sundays in a Strathmore Parish. By J. GORDON M'PHERSON, Ph.D., F.R.S.E., Minister of Ruthven. Crown 8vo, 5s.

MAIN. Three Hundred English Sonnets. Chosen and Edited by DAVID M. MAIN. Fcap. 8vo, 6s.

MAIR. A Digest of Laws and Decisions, Ecclesiastical and Civil, relating to the Constitution, Practice, and Affairs of the Church of Scotland. With Notes and Forms of Procedure. By the Rev. WILLIAM MAIR, D.D., Minister of the Parish of Earlston. Crown 8vo. With Supplements, 8s.

MARMORNE. The Story is told by ADOLPHUS SEGRAVE, the youngest of three Brothers. Third Edition. Crown 8vo, 6s.

MARSHALL. French Home Life. By FREDERIC MARSHALL. Second Edition. 5s.

―――― Claire Brandon. A Novel. 3 vols. crown 8vo, 25s. 6d.

MARSHMAN. History of India. From the Earliest Period to the Close of the India Company's Government; with an Epitome of Subsequent Events. By JOHN CLARK MARSHMAN, C.S.I. Abridged from the Author's larger work. Second Edition, revised. Crown 8vo, with Map, 6s. 6d.

MARTIN. Goethe's Faust. Part I. Translated by Sir THEODORE MARTIN, K.C.B. Second Ed., crown 8vo, 6s. Ninth Ed., fcap. 8vo, 3s. 6d.

―――― Goethe's Faust. Part II. Translated into English Verse. Second Edition, revised. Fcap. 8vo, 6s.

―――― The Works of Horace. Translated into English Verse, with Life and Notes. 2 vols. New Edition, crown 8vo, 21s.

―――― Poems and Ballads of Heinrich Heine. Done into English Verse. Second Edition. Printed on *papier vergé*, crown 8vo, 8s.

―――― The Song of the Bell, and other Translations from Schiller, Goethe, Uhland, and Others. Crown 8vo, 7s. 6d.

―――― Catullus. With Life and Notes. Second Ed., post 8vo, 7s. 6d.

―――― Aladdin : A Dramatic Poem. By ADAM OEHLENSCHLAEGER. Fcap. 8vo, 5s.

―――― Correggio : A Tragedy. By OEHLENSCHLAEGER. With Notes. Fcap. 8vo, 3s.

―――― King Rene's Daughter : A Danish Lyrical Drama. By HENRIK HERTZ. Second Edition, fcap., 2s. 6d.

MARTIN. On some of Shakespeare's Female Characters. In a Series of Letters. By HELENA FAUCIT, LADY MARTIN. Dedicated by permission to Her Most Gracious Majesty the Queen. Third Edition. 8vo, with Portrait, 7s. 6d.

MATHESON. Can the Old Faith Live with the New? or the Problem of Evolution and Revelation. By the Rev. GEORGE MATHESON, D.D. Third Edition. Crown 8vo, 7s. 6d.

―――― The Psalmist and the Scientist; or, Modern Value of the Religious Sentiment. Crown 8vo, 7s. 6d.

―――― Sacred Songs. Crown 8vo, 4s.

MAURICE. The Balance of Military Power in Europe. An Examination of the War Resources of Great Britain and the Continental States. By Colonel MAURICE, R.A., Professor of Military Art and History at the Royal Staff College. Crown 8vo, with a Map. 6s

MEREDYTH. The Brief for the Government, 1886-90. A Handbook for Conservative and Unionist Writers, Speakers, &c. By W. H. MEREDYTH. Crown 8vo, 1s. 6d.

MICHEL. A Critical Inquiry into the Scottish Language. With the view of Illustrating the Rise and Progress of Civilisation in Scotland. By FRANCISQUE-MICHEL, F.S.A. Lond. and Scot., Correspondant de l'Institut de France, &c. 4to, printed on hand-made paper. and bound in Roxburghe, 66s.

MICHIE. The Larch : Being a Practical Treatise on its Culture and General Management. By CHRISTOPHER Y. MICHIE, Forester, Cullen House. Crown 8vo, with Illustrations. New and Cheaper Edition, enlarged, 5s.

―――― The Practice of Forestry. Cr. 8vo, with Illustrations. 6s.

MIDDLETON. The Story of Alastair Bhan Comyn ; or, The Tragedy of Dunphail. A Tale of Tradition and Romance. By the Lady MIDDLETON. Square 8vo, 10s. Cheaper Edition, 5s.

MILNE. The Problem of the Churchless and Poor in our Large Towns. With special reference to the Home Mission Work of the Church of Scotland. By the Rev. ROBT. MILNE, M.A., D.D., Ardler. Crown 8vo, 3s. 6d.

MILNE-HOME. Mamma's Black Nurse Stories. West Indian Folk-lore. By MARY PAMELA MILNE-HOME. With six full-page tinted Illustrations. Small 4to, 5s.

MINTO. A Manual of English Prose Literature, Biographical and Critical : designed mainly to show Characteristics of Style. By W. MINTO, M.A., Professor of Logic in the University of Aberdeen. Third Edition, revised. Crown 8vo, 7s. 6d.

———— Characteristics of English Poets, from Chaucer to Shirley. New Edition, revised. Crown 8vo, 7s. 6d.

MOIR. Life of Mansie Wauch, Tailor in Dalkeith. With 8 Illustrations on Steel, by the late GEORGE CRUIKSHANK. Crown 8vo, 3s. 6d. Another Edition, fcap. 8vo, 1s. 6d.

MOMERIE. Defects of Modern Christianity, and other Sermons. By ALFRED WILLIAMS MOMERIE, M.A., D.Sc., LL.D., Professor of Logic and Metaphysics in King's College, London. Fourth Edition. Crown 8vo, 5s.

———— The Basis of Religion. Being an Examination of Natural Religion. Third Edition. Crown 8vo, 2s. 6d.

———— The Origin of Evil, and other Sermons. Sixth Edition, enlarged. Crown 8vo, 5s.

———— Personality. The Beginning and End of Metaphysics, and a Necessary Assumption in all Positive Philosophy. Fourth Ed. Cr. 8vo, 3s.

———— Agnosticism. Second Edition, Revised. Crown 8vo, 5s.

———— Preaching and Hearing ; and other Sermons. Third Edition. Crown 8vo, 5s.

———— Belief in God. Second Edition. Crown 8vo, 3s.

———— Inspiration ; and other Sermons. Second Edition. Crown 8vo, 5s.

———— Church and Creed. Second Edition. Crown 8vo, 4s. 6d.

MONTAGUE. Campaigning in South Africa. Reminiscences of an Officer in 1879. By Captain W. E. MONTAGUE, 94th Regiment, Author of 'Claude Meadowleigh,' &c. 8vo, 10s. 6d.

MONTALEMBERT. Memoir of Count de Montalembert. A Chapter of Recent French History. By Mrs OLIPHANT, Author of the 'Life of Edward Irving,' &c. 2 vols. crown 8vo, £1, 4s.

MORISON. Sordello. An Outline Analysis of Mr Browning's Poem. By JEANIE MORISON, Author of 'The Purpose of the Ages,' 'Ane Booke of Ballades,' &c. Crown 8vo, 3s.

MUNRO. On Valuation of Property. By WILLIAM MUNRO, M.A., Her Majesty's Assessor of Railways and Canals for Scotland. Second Edition. Revised and enlarged. 8vo, 3s. 6d.

MURDOCH. Manual of the Law of Insolvency and Bankruptcy : Comprehending a Summary of the Law of Insolvency, Notour Bankruptcy, Composition-contracts, Trust-deeds, Cessios, and Sequestrations ; and the Winding-up of Joint-Stock Companies in Scotland ; with Annotations on the various Insolvency and Bankruptcy Statutes ; and with Forms of Procedure applicable to these Subjects. By JAMES MURDOCH, Member of the Faculty of Procurators in Glasgow. Fifth Edition, Revised and Enlarged, 8vo, £1, 10s.

MY TRIVIAL LIFE AND MISFORTUNE : A Gossip with no Plot in Particular. By A PLAIN WOMAN. New Edition, crown 8vo, 6s.

By the SAME AUTHOR.

POOR NELLIE. New and Cheaper Edition. Crown 8vo, 6s.

NAPIER. The Construction of the Wonderful Canon of Logarithms (Mirifici Logarithmorum Canonis Constructio). By JOHN NAPIER of Merchiston. Translated for the first time, with Notes, and a Catalogue of Napier's Works, by WILLIAM RAE MACDONALD. Small 4to, 15s. *A few large paper copies may be had, printed on Whatman paper, price 30s.*

NEAVES. Songs and Verses, Social and Scientific. By an Old Contributor to 'Maga.' By the Hon. Lord NEAVES. Fifth Ed., fcap. 8vo, 4s.

———— The Greek Anthology. Being Vol. XX. of 'Ancient Classics for English Readers.' Crown 8vo, 2s. 6d.

NICHOLSON. A Manual of Zoology, for the Use of Students. With a General Introduction on the Principles of Zoology. By HENRY ALLEYNE NICHOLSON, M.D., D.Sc., F.L.S., F.G.S., Regius Professor of Natural History in the University of Aberdeen. Seventh Edition, rewritten and enlarged. Post 8vo, pp. 956, with 555 Engravings on Wood, 18s.

———— Text-Book of Zoology, for the Use of Schools. Fourth Edition, enlarged. Crown 8vo, with 188 Engravings on Wood, 7s. 6d.

———— Introductory Text-Book of Zoology, for the Use of Junior Classes. Sixth Edition, revised and enlarged, with 166 Engravings, 3s.

———— Outlines of Natural History, for Beginners ; being Descriptions of a Progressive Series of Zoological Types. Third Edition, with Engravings, 1s. 6d.

———— A Manual of Palæontology, for the Use of Students. With a General Introduction on the Principles of Palæontology. By Professor H. ALLEYNE NICHOLSON and RICHARD LYDEKKER, B.A. Third Edition. Rewritten and greatly enlarged. 2 vols. 8vo, with Engravings, £3, 3s.

———— The Ancient Life-History of the Earth. An Outline of the Principles and Leading Facts of Palæontological Science. Crown 8vo, with 276 Engravings, 10s. 6d.

———— On the "Tabulate Corals" of the Palæozoic Period, with Critical Descriptions of Illustrative Species. Illustrated with 15 Lithograph Plates and numerous Engravings. Super-royal 8vo, 21s.

———— Synopsis of the Classification of the Animal Kingdom. 8vo, with 106 Illustrations, 6s.

———— On the Structure and Affinities of the Genus Monticulipora and its Sub-Genera, with Critical Descriptions of Illustrative Species. Illustrated with numerous Engravings on wood and lithographed Plates. Super-royal 8vo, 18s.

NICHOLSON. Communion with Heaven, and other Sermons. By the late MAXWELL NICHOLSON, D.D., Minister of St Stephen's, Edinburgh. Crown 8vo, 5s. 6d.

———— Rest in Jesus. Sixth Edition. Fcap. 8vo, 4s. 6d.

NICHOLSON. A Treatise on Money, and Essays on Present Monetary Problems. By JOSEPH SHIELD NICHOLSON, M.A., D.Sc., Professor of Commercial and Political Economy and Mercantile Law in the University of Edinburgh. 8vo, 10s. 6d.

———— Thoth. A Romance. Third Edition. Crown 8vo, 4s. 6d.

———— A Dreamer of Dreams. A Modern Romance. Second Edition. Crown 8vo, 6s.

NICOLSON AND MURE. A Handbook to the Local Government (Scotland) Act, 1889. With Introduction, Explanatory Notes, and Index. By J. BADENACH NICOLSON, Advocate, Counsel to the Scotch Education Department, and W. J. MURE, Advocate, Legal Secretary to the Lord Advocate for Scotland. Ninth Reprint. 8vo, 5s.

OLIPHANT. Masollam : a Problem of the Period. A Novel. By LAURENCE OLIPHANT. 3 vols. post 8vo, 25s. 6d.

———— Scientific Religion ; or, Higher Possibilities of Life and Practice through the Operation of Natural Forces. Second Edition. 8vo, 16s.

OLIPHANT. Altiora Peto. By LAURENCE OLIPHANT. New and Cheaper Edition. Crown 8vo, boards, 2s. 6d.; cloth, 3s. 6d. Illustrated Edition. Crown 8vo, cloth, 6s.

——— Piccadilly: A Fragment of Contemporary Biography. With Eight Illustrations by Richard Doyle. Eighth Edition, 4s. 6d. Cheap Edition, in paper cover, 2s. 6d.

——— Traits and Travesties; Social and Political. Post 8vo, 10s. 6d.

——— The Land of Gilead. With Excursions in the Lebanon. With Illustrations and Maps. Demy 8vo, 21s.

——— Haifa: Life in Modern Palestine. 2d Edition. 8vo, 7s. 6d.

——— Episodes in a Life of Adventure; or, Moss from a Rolling Stone. Fifth Edition. Post 8vo, 6s.

——— Fashionable Philosophy, and other Sketches. 1s.

OLIPHANT. Katie Stewart. By Mrs Oliphant. 2s. 6d.

——— The Duke's Daughter, and The Fugitives. A Novel. 3 vols. crown 8vo, 25s. 6d.

——— Two Stories of the Seen and the Unseen. The Open Door —Old Lady Mary. Paper Covers, 1s.

——— Sons and Daughters. Crown 8vo, 3s. 6d.

OSBORN. Narratives of Voyage and Adventure. By Admiral SHERARD OSBORN, C.B. 3 vols. crown 8vo, 12s.

OSSIAN. The Poems of Ossian in the Original Gaelic. With a Literal Translation into English, and a Dissertation on the Authenticity of the Poems. By the Rev. ARCHIBALD CLERK. 2 vols. imperial 8vo, £1, 11s. 6d.

OSWALD. By Fell and Fjord; or, Scenes and Studies in Iceland. By E. J. OSWALD. Post 8vo, with Illustrations. 7s. 6d.

PAGE. Introductory Text-Book of Geology. By DAVID PAGE, LL.D., Professor of Geology in the Durham University of Physical Science, Newcastle, and Professor LAPWORTH of Mason Science College, Birmingham. With Engravings and Glossarial Index. Twelfth Edition. Revised and Enlarged. 3s. 6d.

——— Advanced Text-Book of Geology, Descriptive and Industrial. With Engravings, and Glossary of Scientific Terms. Sixth Edition, revised and enlarged, 7s. 6d.

——— Introductory Text-Book of Physical Geography. With Sketch-Maps and Illustrations. Edited by CHARLES LAPWORTH, LL.D., F.G.S., &c., Professor of Geology and Mineralogy in the Mason Science College, Birmingham. 12th Edition. 2s. 6d.

——— Advanced Text-Book of Physical Geography. Third Edition, Revised and Enlarged by Prof. LAPWORTH. With Engravings. 5s.

PATON. Spindrift. By Sir J. NOEL PATON. Fcap., cloth, 5s.

——— Poems by a Painter. Fcap., cloth, 5s.

PATON. Body and Soul. A Romance in Transcendental Pathology. By FREDERICK NOEL PATON. Third Edition. Crown 8vo, 1s.

PATTERSON. Essays in History and Art. By R. HOGARTH PATTERSON. 8vo, 12s.

——— The New Golden Age, and Influence of the Precious Metals upon the World. 2 vols. 8vo, 31s. 6d.

PAUL. History of the Royal Company of Archers, the Queen's Body-Guard for Scotland. By JAMES BALFOUR PAUL, Advocate of the Scottish Bar. Crown 4to, with Portraits and other Illustrations. £2, 2s.

PEILE. Lawn Tennis as a Game of Skill. With latest revised Laws as played by the Best Clubs. By Captain S. C. F. PEILE, B.S.C. Fifth Edition, fcap. cloth, 1s. 6d.

PETTIGREW. The Handy Book of Bees, and their Profitable
Management. By A. PETTIGREW. Fifth Edition, Enlarged, with Engravings. Crown 8vo, 3s. 6d.

PHILIP. The Function of Labour in the Production of Wealth.
By ALEXANDER PHILIP, LL.B., Edinburgh. Crown 8vo, 3s. 6d.

PHILOSOPHICAL CLASSICS FOR ENGLISH READERS.
Companion Series to Ancient and Foreign Classics for English Readers.
Edited by WILLIAM KNIGHT, LL.D., Professor of Moral Philosophy, Uni-
versity of St Andrews. In crown 8vo volumes, with portraits, price 3s. 6d.
[For list of Volumes published, see page 2.

POLLOK. The Course of Time : A Poem. By ROBERT POLLOK,
A.M. Small fcap. 8vo, cloth gilt, 2s. 6d. Cottage Edition, 32mo, 8d. The
Same, cloth, gilt edges, 1s. 6d. Another Edition, with Illustrations by Birket
Foster and others, fcap., cloth, 3s. 6d., or with edges gilt, 4s.

PORT ROYAL LOGIC. Translated from the French ; with Introduction, Notes, and Appendix. By THOMAS SPENCER BAYNES, LL.D., Professor in the University of St Andrews. Tenth Edition, 12mo, 4s.

POTTS AND DARNELL. Aditus Faciliores : An easy Latin Construing Book, with Complete Vocabulary. By the late A. W. POTTS, M.A.,
LL.D., and the Rev. C. DARNELL, M.A., Head-Master of Cargilfield Prepara-
tory School, Edinburgh. Tenth Edition, fcap. 8vo, 3s. 6d.

——— Aditus Faciliores Graeci. An easy Greek Construing Book,
with Complete Vocabulary. Fourth Edition, fcap. 8vo, 3s.

PRINGLE. The Live-Stock of the Farm. By ROBERT O. PRINGLE.
Third Edition. Revised and Edited by JAMES MACDONALD. Cr. 8vo, 7s. 6d.

PUBLIC GENERAL STATUTES AFFECTING SCOTLAND
from 1707 to 1847, with Chronological Table and Index. 3 vols. large 8vo, £3, 3s.

PUBLIC GENERAL STATUTES AFFECTING SCOTLAND,
COLLECTION OF. Published Annually with General Index.

RADICAL CURE FOR IRELAND, The. A Letter to the People
of England and Scotland concerning a new Plantation. With 2 Maps. 8vo, 7s. 6d.

RAMSAY. Rough Recollections of Military Service and Society.
By Lieut.-Col. BALCARRES D. WARDLAW RAMSAY. Two vols. post 8vo, 21s.

RAMSAY. Scotland and Scotsmen in the Eighteenth Century.
Edited from the MSS. of JOHN RAMSAY, Esq. of Ochtertyre, by ALEXANDER
ALLARDYCE, Author of 'Memoir of Admiral Lord Keith, K.B.,' &c. 2 vols.
8vo, 31s. 6d.

RANKIN. A Handbook of the Church of Scotland. By JAMES
RANKIN, D.D., Minister of Muthill; Author of 'Character Studies in the
Old Testament,' &c. An entirely New and much Enlarged Edition. Crown
8vo, with 2 Maps, 7s. 6d.

RANKINE. A Treatise on the Rights and Burdens incident to
the Ownership of Lands and other Heritages in Scotland. By JOHN RANKINE,
M.A., Advocate, Professor of Scots Law in the University of Edinburgh.
8vo. *[New Edition in preparation.*

RECORDS OF THE TERCENTENARY FESTIVAL OF THE
UNIVERSITY OF EDINBURGH. Celebrated in April 1884. Published
under the Sanction of the Senatus Academicus. Large 4to, £2, 12s. 6d.

RICE. Reminiscences of Abraham Lincoln. By Distinguished
Men of his Time. Collected and Edited by ALLEN THORNDIKE RICE, Editor
of the 'North American Review.' Large 8vo, with Portraits, 21s.

ROBERTSON. Orellana, and other Poems. By J. LOGIE ROBERT-
SON, M.A. Fcap. 8vo. Printed on hand-made paper. 6s.

ROBERTSON. Our Holiday Among the Hills. By JAMES and
JANET LOGIE ROBERTSON. Fcap. 8vo, 3s. 6d.

ROSCOE. Rambles with a Fishing-rod. By E. S. ROSCOE. Crown
8vo, 4s. 6d.

ROSS. Old Scottish Regimental Colours. By ANDREW ROSS,
S.S.C., Hon. Secretary Old Scottish Regimental Colours Committee. Dedicated by Special Permission to Her Majesty the Queen. Folio. £2, 12s. 6d.

RUSSELL. The Haigs of Bemersyde. A Family History. By JOHN RUSSELL. Large 8vo, with Illustrations. 21s.

RUSSELL. Fragments from Many Tables. Being the Recollections of some Wise and Witty Men and Women. By GEO. RUSSELL. Cr. 8vo, 4s. 6d.

RUSSELL. Essays on Sacred Subjects for General Readers. By the Rev. WILLIAM RUSSELL, M.A. 8vo, 10s. 6d.

RUTLAND. Notes of an Irish Tour in 1846. By the DUKE OF RUTLAND, G.C.B. (Lord JOHN MANNERS). New Edition. Crown 8vo, 2s. 6d.

——— Correspondence between the Right Honble. William Pitt and Charles Duke of Rutland, Lord Lieutenant of Ireland, 1781-1787. With Introductory Note by John Duke of Rutland. 8vo, 7s. 6d.

RUTLAND. Gems of German Poetry. Translated by the DUCHESS OF RUTLAND (Lady JOHN MANNERS). *[New Edition in preparation.*

——— Impressions of Bad-Homburg. Comprising a Short Account of the Women's Associations of Germany under the Red Cross. Crown 8vo, 1s. 6d.

——— Some Personal Recollections of the Later Years of the Earl of Beaconsfield, K.G. Sixth Edition, 6d.

——— Employment of Women in the Public Service. 6d.

——— Some of the Advantages of Easily Accessible Reading and Recreation Rooms, and Free Libraries. With Remarks on Starting and Maintaining Them. Second Edition, crown 8vo, 1s.

——— A Sequel to Rich Men's Dwellings, and other Occasional Papers. Crown 8vo, 2s. 6d.

——— Encouraging Experiences of Reading and Recreation Rooms, Aims of Guilds, Nottingham Social Guild, Existing Institutions, &c., &c. Crown 8vo, 1s.

SCHILLER. Wallenstein. A Dramatic Poem. By FREDERICK VON SCHILLER. Translated by C. G. A. LOCKHART. Fcap. 8vo, 7s. 6d.

SCOTCH LOCH FISHING. By "Black Palmer." Crown 8vo, interleaved with blank pages, 4s.

SCOUGAL. Scenes from a Silent World; or, Prisons and their Inmates. By FRANCIS SCOUGAL. Crown 8vo, 6s.

SELLAR. Manual of the Education Acts for Scotland. By the late ALEXANDER CRAIG SELLAR, M.P. Eighth Edition. Revised and in great part rewritten by J. EDWARD GRAHAM, B.A. Oxon., Advocate. With Rules for the conduct of Elections, with Notes and Cases. With a Supplement, being the Acts of 1889 in so far as affecting the Education Acts. 8vo, 12s. 6d.

[SUPPLEMENT TO SELLAR'S MANUAL OF THE EDUCATION ACTS FOR SCOTLAND. 8vo, 2s.]

SETH. Scottish Philosophy. A Comparison of the Scottish and German Answers to Hume. Balfour Philosophical Lectures, University of Edinburgh. By ANDREW SETH, M.A., Professor of Logic, Rhetoric, and Metaphysics in St Andrews University. Second Edition. Crown 8vo, 5s.

——— Hegelianism and Personality. Balfour Philosophical Lectures. Second Series. Crown 8vo, 5s.

SHADWELL. The Life of Colin Campbell, Lord Clyde. Illustrated by Extracts from his Diary and Correspondence. By Lieutenant-General SHADWELL, C.B. 2 vols. 8vo. With Portrait, Maps, and Plans. 36s.

SHAND. Half a Century; or, Changes in Men and Manners. By ALEX. INNES SHAND, Author of 'Against Time,' &c. Second Ed., 8vo, 12s. 6d.

——— Letters from the West of Ireland. Reprinted from the 'Times.' Crown 8vo, 5s.

SHARPE. Letters from and to Charles Kirkpatrick Sharpe. Edited by ALEXANDER ALLARDYCE, Author of 'Memoir of Admiral Lord Keith, K.B.,' &c. With a Memoir by the Rev. W. K. R. BEDFORD. In two vols. 8vo. Illustrated with Etchings and other Engravings. £2, 12s. 6d.

SIM. Margaret Sim's Cookery. With an Introduction by L. B. WALFORD, Author of 'Mr Smith: A Part of His Life,' &c. Crown 8vo, 5s.

SKELTON. Maitland of Lethington ; and the Scotland of Mary Stuart. A History. By JOHN SKELTON, C.B., LL.D., Author of 'The Essays of Shirley.' Demy 8vo. 2 vols., 28s.

—— The Handbook of Public Health. A Complete Edition of the Public Health and other Sanitary Acts relating to Scotland. Annotated, and with the Rules, Instructions, and Decisions of the Board of Supervision brought up to date with relative forms. 8vo, 7s. 6d.

—— The Local Government (Scotland) Act in Relation to Public Health. A Handy Guide for County and District Councillors, Medical Officers, Sanitary Inspectors, and Members of Parochial Boards. Second Edition. With a new Preface on appointment of Sanitary Officers. Crown 8vo, 2s.

SMITH. Thorndale ; or, The Conflict of Opinions. By WILLIAM SMITH, Author of 'A Discourse on Ethics,' &c. New Edition. Cr. 8vo, 10s. 6d.

—— Gravenhurst ; or, Thoughts on Good and Evil. Second Edition, with Memoir of the Author. Crown 8vo, 8s.

—— The Story of William and Lucy Smith. Edited by GEORGE MERRIAM. Large post 8vo, 12s. 6d.

SMITH. Memoir of the Families of M'Combie and Thoms, originally M'Intosh and M'Thomas. Compiled from History and Tradition. By WILLIAM M'COMBIE SMITH. With Illustrations. 8vo, 7s. 6d.

SMITH. Greek Testament Lessons for Colleges, Schools, and Private Students, consisting chiefly of the Sermon on the Mount and the Parables of our Lord. With Notes and Essays. By the Rev. J. HUNTER SMITH, M.A., King Edward's School, Birmingham. Crown 8vo, 6s.

SMITH. Writings by the Way. By JOHN CAMPBELL SMITH, M.A., Sheriff-Substitute. Crown 8vo, 9s.

SMITH. The Secretary for Scotland. Being a Statement of the Powers and Duties of the new Scottish Office. With a Short Historical Introduction and numerous references to important Administrative Documents. By W. C. SMITH, LL.B., Advocate. 8vo, 6s.

SORLEY. The Ethics of Naturalism. Being the Shaw Fellowship Lectures, 1884. By W. R. SORLEY, M.A., Fellow of Trinity College, Cambridge, Professor of Logic and Philosophy in University College of South Wales. Crown 8vo, 6s.

SPEEDY. Sport in the Highlands and Lowlands of Scotland with Rod and Gun. By TOM SPEEDY. Second Edition, Revised and Enlarged. With Illustrations by Lieut.-Gen. Hope Crealocke, C.B., C.M.G., and others. 8vo, 15s.

SPROTT. The Worship and Offices of the Church of Scotland. By GEORGE W. SPROTT, D.D., Minister of North Berwick. Crown 8vo, 6s.

STAFFORD. How I Spent my Twentieth Year. Being a Record of a Tour Round the World, 1886-87. By the MARCHIONESS OF STAFFORD. With Illustrations. Third Edition, crown 8vo, 8s. 6d.

STARFORTH. Villa Residences and Farm Architecture : A Series of Designs. By JOHN STARFORTH, Architect. 102 Engravings. Second Edition, medium 4to, £2, 17s. 6d.

STATISTICAL ACCOUNT OF SCOTLAND. Complete, with Index, 15 vols. 8vo, £16, 16s.
Each County sold separately, with Title, Index, and Map, neatly bound in cloth, forming a very valuable Manual to the Landowner, the Tenant, the Manufacturer, the Naturalist, the Tourist, &c

In course of publication.

STEPHENS' BOOK OF THE FARM ; detailing the Labours of the Farmer, Farm-Steward, Ploughman, Shepherd, Hedger, Farm-Labourer, Field-Worker, and Cattleman. Illustrated with numerous Portraits of Animals and Engravings of Implements. Fourth Edition. Revised, and in great part rewritten by JAMES MACDONALD, of the 'Farming World,' &c., &c. Assisted by many of the leading agricultural authorities of the day. To be completed in Six Divisional Volumes.
[Divisions I. to V., price 10s. 6d. each, now ready.

STEPHENS. The Book of Farm Buildings; their Arrangement and Construction. By HENRY STEPHENS, F.R.S.E., and ROBERT SCOTT BURN. Illustrated with 1045 Plates and Engravings. Large 8vo. £1, 11s. 6d.

———— The Book of Farm Implements and Machines. By J. SLIGHT and R. SCOTT BURN, Engineers. Edited by HENRY STEPHENS. Large 8vo, £2, 2s.

STEVENSON. British Fungi. (Hymenomycetes.) By Rev. JOHN STEVENSON, Author of 'Mycologia Scotia,' Hon. Sec. Cryptogamic Society of Scotland. 2 vols. post 8vo, with Illustrations, price 12s. 6d. each. Vol. I. AGARICUS—BOLBITIUS. Vol. II. CORTINARIUS—DACRYMYCES.

STEWART. Advice to Purchasers of Horses. By JOHN STEWART, V.S. New Edition. 2s. 6d.

———— Stable Economy. A Treatise on the Management of Horses in relation to Stabling, Grooming, Feeding, Watering, and Working. Seventh Edition, fcap. 8vo, 6s. 6d.

STODDART. Angling Songs. By THOMAS TOD STODDART. New Edition, with a Memoir by ANNA M. STODDART. Crown 8vo, 7s. 6d.

STORMONTH. Etymological and Pronouncing Dictionary of the English Language. Including a very Copious Selection of Scientific Terms. For Use in Schools and Colleges, and as a Book of General Reference. By the Rev. JAMES STORMONTH. The Pronunciation carefully Revised by the Rev. P. H. PHELP, M.A. Cantab. Tenth Edition, Revised throughout. Crown 8vo, pp. 800. 7s. 6d.

———— Dictionary of the English Language, Pronouncing, Etymological, and Explanatory. Revised by the Rev. P. H. PHELP. Library Edition. Imperial 8vo, handsomely bound in half morocco, 31s. 6d.

———— The School Etymological Dictionary and Word-Book. Fourth Edition. Fcap. 8vo, pp. 254. 2s.

STORY. Nero; A Historical Play. By W. W. STORY, Author of 'Roba di Roma.' Fcap. 8vo, 6s.

———— Vallombrosa. Post 8vo, 5s.

———— Poems. 2 vols. fcap., 7s. 6d.

———— Fiammetta. A Summer Idyl. Crown 8vo, 7s. 6d.

———— Conversations in a Studio. 2 vols. crown 8vo, 12s. 6d.

STRICKLAND. Life of Agnes Strickland. By her SISTER. Post 8vo, with Portrait engraved on Steel, 12s. 6d.

STURGIS. John-a-Dreams. A Tale. By JULIAN STURGIS. New Edition, crown 8vo, 3s. 6d.

———— Little Comedies, Old and New. Crown 8vo, 7s. 6d.

SUTHERLAND. Handbook of Hardy Herbaceous and Alpine Flowers, for general Garden Decoration. Containing Descriptions of upwards of 1000 Species of Ornamental Hardy Perennial and Alpine Plants; along with Concise and Plain Instructions for their Propagation and Culture. By WILLIAM SUTHERLAND, Landscape Gardener; formerly Manager of the Herbaceous Department at Kew. Crown 8vo, 7s. 6d.

TAYLOR. The Story of My Life. By the late Colonel MEADOWS TAYLOR, Author of 'The Confessions of a Thug,' &c. &c. Edited by his Daughter. New and cheaper Edition, being the Fourth. Crown 8vo, 6s.

THOLUCK. Hours of Christian Devotion. Translated from the German of A. Tholuck, D.D., Professor of Theology in the University of Halle. By the Rev. ROBERT MENZIES, D.D. With a Preface written for this Translation by the Author. Second Edition, crown 8vo, 7s. 6d.

THOMSON. Handy Book of the Flower-Garden: being Practical Directions for the Propagation, Culture, and Arrangement of Plants in Flower-Gardens all the year round. With Engraved Plans. By DAVID THOMSON, Gardener to his Grace the Duke of Buccleuch, K.T., at Drumlanrig. Fourth and Cheaper Edition, crown 8vo, 5s.

THOMSON. The Handy Book of Fruit-Culture under Glass: being a series of Elaborate Practical Treatises on the Cultivation and Forcing of Pines, Vines, Peaches, Figs, Melons, Strawberries, and Cucumbers. With Engravings of Hothouses, &c., most suitable for the Cultivation and Forcing of these Fruits. By DAVID THOMSON, Gardener to his Grace the Duke of Buccleuch, K.T., at Drumlanrig. Second Ed. Cr. 8vo, with Engravings, 7s. 6d.

THOMSON A Practical Treatise on the Cultivation of the Grape Vine. By WILLIAM THOMSON, Tweed Vineyards. Tenth Edition, 8vo, 5s.

THOMSON. Cookery for the Sick and Convalescent. With Directions for the Preparation of Poultices, Fomentations, &c. By BARBARA THOMSON. Fcap. 8vo, 1s. 6d.

THORNTON. Opposites. A Series of Essays on the Unpopular Sides of Popular Questions. By LEWIS THORNTON. 8vo, 12s. 6d.

TOM CRINGLE'S LOG. A New Edition, with Illustrations. Crown 8vo, cloth gilt, 5s. Cheap Edition, 2s.

TRANSACTIONS OF THE HIGHLAND AND AGRICULTURAL SOCIETY OF SCOTLAND. Published annually, price 5s.

TULLOCH. Rational Theology and Christian Philosophy in England in the Seventeenth Century. By JOHN TULLOCH, D.D., Principal of St Mary's College in the University of St Andrews; and one of her Majesty's Chaplains in Ordinary in Scotland. Second Edition. 2 vols. 8vo, 16s.

—————— Modern Theories in Philosophy and Religion. 8vo, 15s.

—————— Luther, and other Leaders of the Reformation. Third Edition, enlarged. Crown 8vo, 3s. 6d.

—————— Memoir of Principal Tulloch, D.D., LL.D. By Mrs OLIPHANT, Author of 'Life of Edward Irving.' Third and Cheaper Edition. 8vo, with Portrait. 7s. 6d.

VEITCH. Institutes of Logic. By JOHN VEITCH, LL.D., Professor of Logic and Rhetoric in the University of Glasgow. Post 8vo, 12s. 6d.

—————— The Feeling for Nature in Scottish Poetry. From the Earliest Times to the Present Day. 2 vols. fcap. 8vo, in roxburghe binding. 15s.

—————— Merlin and Other Poems. Fcap. 8vo. 4s. 6d.

—————— Knowing and Being. Essays in Philosophy. First Series. Crown 8vo, 5s.

VIRGIL. The Æneid of Virgil. Translated in English Blank Verse by G. K. RICKARDS, M.A., and Lord RAVENSWORTH. 2 vols. fcap. 8vo, 10s.

WALFORD. A Stiff-Necked Generation. By L. B. WALFORD, Author of 'Mr Smith,' &c. Cheap Edition. Crown 8vo, 6s.

—————— Four Biographies from 'Blackwood': Jane Taylor, Hannah More, Elizabeth Fry, Mary Somerville. Crown 8vo, 5s.

WARREN'S (SAMUEL) WORKS :—

Diary of a Late Physician. Cloth, 2s. 6d.; boards, 2s.

Ten Thousand A-Year. Cloth, 3s. 6d.; boards, 2s. 6d.

Now and Then. The Lily and the Bee. Intellectual and Moral Development of the Present Age. 4s. 6d.

Essays : Critical, Imaginative, and Juridical. 5s.

WARREN. The Five Books of the Psalms. With Marginal Notes. By Rev. SAMUEL L. WARREN, Rector of Esher, Surrey; late Fellow, Dean, and Divinity Lecturer, Wadham College, Oxford. Crown 8vo, 5s.

WEBSTER. The Angler and the Loop-Rod. By DAVID WEBSTER. Crown 8vo, with Illustrations, 7s. 6d.

WELLINGTON. Wellington Prize Essays on "the System of Field Manœuvres best adapted for enabling our Troops to meet a Continental Army." Edited by Lieut.-General Sir EDWARD BRUCE HAMLEY, K.C.B. 8vo, 12s. 6d.

WENLEY. Socrates and Christ : A Study in the Philosophy of Religion. By R. M. WENLEY, M.A., Lecturer on Mental and Moral Philosophy in Queen Margaret College, Glasgow; Examiner in Philosophy in the University of Glasgow. Crown 8vo, 6s.

WERNER. A Visit to Stanley's Rear-Guard at Major Barttelot's Camp on the Aruhwimi. With an Account of River-Life on the Congo. By J. R. WERNER, F.R.G.S., Engineer, late in the Service of the Etat Independant du Congo. With Maps, Portraits, and other Illustrations. 8vo. 16s.

WESTMINSTER ASSEMBLY. Minutes of the Westminster Assembly, while engaged in preparing their Directory for Church Government, Confession of Faith, and Catechisms (November 1644 to March 1649). Edited by the Rev. Professor ALEX. T. MITCHELL, of St Andrews, and the Rev. JOHN STRUTHERS, LL.D. With a Historical and Critical Introduction by Professor Mitchell. 8vo, 15s.

WHITE. The Eighteen Christian Centuries. By the Rev. JAMES WHITE. Seventh Edition, post 8vo, with Index, 6s.

—— History of France, from the Earliest Times. Sixth Thousand, post 8vo, with Index, 6s.

WHITE. Archæological Sketches in Scotland—Kintyre and Knapdale. By Colonel T. P. WHITE, R.E., of the Ordnance Survey. With numerous Illustrations. 2 vols. folio, £4, 4s. Vol. I., Kintyre, sold separately, £2, 2s.

—— The Ordnance Survey of the United Kingdom. A Popular Account. Crown 8vo, 5s.

WILLIAMSON. Poems of Nature and Life. By DAVID R. WILLIAMSON, Minister of Kirkmaiden. Fcap. 8vo, 3s.

WILLS AND GREENE. Drawing-room Dramas for Children. By W. G. WILLS and the Hon. Mrs GREENE. Crown 8vo, 6s.

WILSON. Works of Professor Wilson. Edited by his Son-in-Law Professor FERRIER. 12 vols. crown 8vo, £2, 8s.

—— Christopher in his Sporting-Jacket. 2 vols., 8s.

—— Isle of Palms, City of the Plague, and other Poems. 4s.

—— Lights and Shadows of Scottish Life, and other Tales. 4s.

—— Essays, Critical and Imaginative. 4 vols., 16s.

—— The Noctes Ambrosianæ. 4 vols., 16s.

—— Homer and his Translators, and the Greek Drama. Crown 8vo, 4s.

WINGATE. Lily Neil. A Poem. By DAVID WINGATE. Crown 8vo, 4s. 6d.

WORDSWORTH. The Historical Plays of Shakspeare. With Introductions and Notes. By CHARLES WORDSWORTH, D.C.L., Bishop of S. Andrews. 3 vols. post 8vo, each price 7s. 6d.

WORSLEY. Poems and Translations. By PHILIP STANHOPE WORSLEY, M.A. Edited by EDWARD WORSLEY. Second Edition, enlarged. Fcap. 8vo, 6s.

YATE. England and Russia Face to Face in Asia. A Record of Travel with the Afghan Boundary Commission. By Captain A. C. YATE, Bombay Staff Corps. 8vo, with Maps and Illustrations, 21s.

YATE. Northern Afghanistan; or, Letters from the Afghan Boundary Commission. By Major C. E. YATE, C.S.I., C.M.G. Bombay Staff Corps, F.R.G.S. 8vo, with Maps. 18s.

YOUNG. A Story of Active Service in Foreign Lands. Compiled from letters sent home from South Africa, India, and China, 1856-1882. By Surgeon-General A. GRAHAM YOUNG, Author of 'Crimean Cracks.' Crown 8vo, Illustrated, 7s. 6d.

YULE. Fortification: for the Use of Officers in the Army, and Readers of Military History. By Col. YULE, Bengal Engineers. 8vo, with numerous Illustrations, 10s. 6d.